PROMETHEUS' GIFT

JOHN SANGSTER

authorHOUSE®

AuthorHouse™
1663 Liberty Drive
Bloomington, IN 47403
www.authorhouse.com
Phone: 833-262-8899

Published by AuthorHouse 06/18/2021

ISBN: 978-1-6655-2822-1 (sc)
ISBN: 978-1-6655-2820-7 (hc)
ISBN: 978-1-6655-2821-4 (e)

Library of Congress Control Number: 2021911670

Print information available on the last page.

Chapter 1

It was like an episode of Star Wars. The atmosphere was super hot, deadly, and so thick visibility was less than three feet. Through the thick, swirling, and pulsating mists, flashes of light, like from a light saber, were dancing around and getting lost in the thick atmosphere. Sounds of heavy breathing and muffled voices, like that coming from the mask of Darth Vader, could be heard. The noise was a cacophony of crackling, snapping, and sounds of things crashing and breaking. Brief openings in the swirling mists would allow furtive glimpses of five figures moving through this mess. Each of these creatures had a strange hump on the back, a light at the top that moved when the creature's head moved, and, except for a strange protrusion where a human's mouth should be, a featureless face. The creatures' skin had a few reflective bands, making them a little bit easier to see in the swirling mess. And the heads of four of these creatures were a yellow color while the fifth one had a white colored head. The creatures were emanating sounds as though they were talking to each other, but the sounds were more noise than words. Sometimes the creatures acted like bipeds, walking on two legs, but most of the time they were on all four appendages. Two of the creatures were each holding a device that looked to be spraying something while two others were dragging a long tail attached to each of the spraying devices. This could have been a movie scene being filmed at the Elstree Studios in England by Lucasfilms, but it wasn't. This was real.

The location was a house in Prairie City, a small community of about five thousand residents. The atmosphere was charged with thick, heavy smoke heated to nearly a thousand degrees. The lighting was supplied by a mix of the flames, the flashing red lights and scene lights from the fire engines, and helmet mounted flashlights on the firefighters. It was in the middle of the night, so the noise and lights broke the normally peaceful setting of the community. The creatures moving around inside the dangerous atmosphere were assistant fire chief Bill and his four volunteer firefighters, all in full protective gear. The enemy they were busy attacking was a house fire, a voracious house fire that wanted to gobble everything in its path.

While leading the interior attack, Bill was thinking back to when he first became a volunteer firefighter. He'd been used to going toe to toe with wildland fires for a few years, but upon signing up as a volunteer, Bill had to learn how to fight all types of fires, not just wildland ones. Bill remembered the first time he was outfitted in full protective gear and went inside a burning house. He was wearing a heavy pair of pants and a coat, called turnouts or bunker gear, similar to what he was wearing now. Both the pants and the coat consisted of two pieces, an outer protective shell of a fire resistant and puncture resistant material, and an inner shell that acted like a thermal barrier to keep some of the fire's heat from damaging the human body. A hood over his head, with a cutout for the face, provided some heat protection to the neck and head area. A special helmet, like a backwards baseball cap, was worn over the hood to protect the head and neck from some of the falling debris associated with a fire. Heavy rubber boots protected his feet, while special fire and puncture resistant gloves protected his hands.

Strapped to his back was the self contained breathing apparatus, or SCBA. The SCBA consisted of a backpack, holding a cylinder of air, with a face mask to place over the entire face, and a visible gauge to show the wearer how much air is left in the tank. When the tank's air supply is down to about eight minutes of breathing time left, a warning bell or buzzer goes off signifying that the wearer had better leave the building now. Generally, for a firefighter in good shape, a standard SCBA air tank could provide nearly thirty minutes of air. When working in extreme heat, digging or pulling, or when in not top physical condition, the air tank would be drained much faster. Bill remembered his first time following a seasoned firefighter into a burning building, the fear of crawling into the mouth of that fire breathing dragon. He felt like an armored knight trying to fight an angry dragon with a voracious appetite and a deadly breath of fire. Well, that was over twenty years ago, and every time Bill had to don the SCBA and go into a burning structure, he still felt like he was battling a powerful dragon. It was brute force against cunning, and hopefully his cunning would win.

Bill's interior attack crew had done a good job racing through much of the house, combining the search for people with a quick fire knockdown. The four volunteer firefighters making up the attack crew were working as two teams, each team consisting of a person operating the nozzle at the end of the hose and the other person behind the nozzleman helping with pulling and guiding the hose. The heat, the tension of trying to get to the fire before the fire gets to you, and the pulling and dragging the nearly 200 lbs. of fire hose around door ways and numerous obstacles start to fatigue the interior firefighters. But they know they must go on. Their job was not finished, the dragon still lived.

Having pushed the fire back down the hall toward the rear of the house, one of the hose teams was getting positioned to enter the last bedroom. Kneeling at the threshold of the doorway into the bedroom, the nozzleman aimed the nozzle upward toward where the ceiling should be. With the heavy smoke rolling throughout the room, the nozzleman could not see the ceiling, nor any part of the room. The firefighters had to rely on their experience and hope the swirling mass of smoke would thin out enough to see. Pointing the nozzle upward, the nozzleman gave a few quick squirts of water by opening the nozzle for a second or two then closing the nozzle. This was called penciling, and the object was to both test the ceiling and slightly cool the extremely hot air at the ceiling. If the ceiling were weakened by the fire, then hitting it with a straight stream of water would cause some of the ceiling to come crashing down. So it was better to have that happen before the firefighters got into the room. Temperatures at the ceiling could easily be over 1000 degrees, and could lead to a flash over in which everything in the room, firefighters included, would burn explosively. Too much water shot to the ceiling could force the heat and heavy smoke to drop down to the floor, where the firefighters were trying to keep out of such conditions. So a few short bursts of water to the ceiling could be just enough to break the temperature chain reaction, and make entry into the fiery room slightly safer.

Finished with the penciling, the nozzleman started crawling into the fiery, smoky room. Aiming the nozzle at anything that glowed red, the nozzleman quickly knocked the fire down. With the quick fire knockdown in the room, it was time to do a search. The room was a claustrophobic mess. With zero visibility, caused by a combination of dense smoke and steam, disorientation was something that could hit the unprepared. Using the doorway as the base, the nozzleman kept one hand touching the wall and worked along the wall to the right. The hoseman, keeping touch with the nozzleman, used the thermal imaging camera he was carrying to sweep the room.

The thermal camera is a small hand held device that displays on a screen the temperature of the object the device is pointing at. The image of the object the device is pointing at shows up in the screen as variations of blacks, grays and whites. Hot objects would show up as white, and the brighter the white the hotter the temperature of the object. By pushing a button on the camera, the display could be changed to a color display where shades of yellow, orange and red signify temperatures. During the initial search for fire or victims, the white/black screen is the preferred choice, and when doing mopup or clean up work on a knocked down fire, the color screen is preferred.

Moving to make sure they cover the entire bedroom quickly, both firefighters crawled along the floor, one using the wall and the other using the fellow firefighter's boot as a guide, just like they'd done in the other rooms. The thermal camera showed an image of something slightly brighter white then the surrounding stuff on the floor of the room near what looked like a bed. One of the firefighters, while reaching out to touch this object, felt his gloved fingers touch a surface that gave a little, unlike the furniture he had been bumping into. Getting closer and yelling at his partner to shine his light on the object too, they quickly determined this was not a piece of charred furniture. Both firefighters quickly finished their room search, pulled the hose out of the room and found Bill in the hallway. One of the firefighters yelled through his face mask, "Bill, found something over here you'd better see. We think it's a body."

Chapter 2

It was less than an hour ago that Bill was enjoying a sound sleep when the fire department hand held radio and pager standing on his night stand went beep, beep, beep, beep. "Prairie Fire, respond to a structure fire at 17 Canola Street," announced the Dispatcher. Jumping up like cold water was tossed on him, Bill quickly put on his socks, his pants over the top of his pajamas, stepped into his slippers and raced out the bedroom door. Bill was single, his wife had left him many years ago, so there was no sleepy 'be careful dear' following him out the door like some of the other volunteers had. Reaching the outside door of his house, Bill heard the radio blare a second time with the warning beeps. The Dispatcher repeated the message, "Prairie Fire, respond to a structure fire at 17 Canola St., 0128."

Bill radioed the Dispatcher that 672, his fire department call sign, was responding. Looking across town Bill could see in the night sky an orange red glow. Damn it, it's a real fire, not a chimney fire or smoke call. He was just about to the fire station when the Dispatcher announced, "Prairie Fire, the neighbor says he thinks the people are still in the house." Bill was hoping the neighbor was wrong, but if not, this could be a very bad night.

Bill arrived to the fire station right behind a couple of younger and faster volunteer firefighters. While Bill and the second volunteer were jumping into their turnouts, the first volunteer was starting the attack engine. With all three on board, the attack engine headed out the station door, siren quiet in the middle of the night but lights flashing. Having three seated on the bench seat of the attack engine felt like being in a sardine can, but thank goodness all of the volunteers were on friendly terms. The middle firefighter in the cab grabbed the radio's microphone and called in to Dispatch reporting that Engine 1 was responding, three on board. The three were still trying to wake up. This business of being rudely awakened at some ungodly hour in the middle of the night by that damn little radio left them all still shaky, groggy and a bit cranky.

The attack engine was barely a block from the fire station when the city police officer announced over the radio that she was 10 23, on scene, that there's lots of flame and smoke, and was unable to verify if the people got out. Damn. All the volunteers were awake now, realizing that they may have more than just a fire to deal with.

As they got closer to the fire, the worse it looked. Pulling up to the burning house, Bill ran over to Chief Frank, who had arrived a minute earlier, responding directly from his residence. In the meantime, the driver jumped into his turnout gear and both volunteers donned their SCBAs. Engine 2 arrived with five volunteers and was guided to the nearest fire hydrant. This fire was going to take a lot of water. George, the second assistant chief, came running over from jumping off engine 2, and joined the discussion between Frank and Bill. "Bill, take two teams and advance two attack lines into the front door. George, you send two geared up interior guys to Bill, get three geared and on the roof for ventilation, and get four more geared up as backup."

Engine 3 arrived on scene with three firefighters on board, and they hooked into another fire hydrant. Bev, the police officer, came over and asked Frank what he would like her to do. "Bev, if you could get one of your fellow officers or a Deputy to help block traffic for now, it would be appreciated. Also, if you could keep your eyes open for anyone looking kind of suspicious. Maybe even photograph the people looking on, if you could."

Even though it was in the middle of the night, many locals have police scanners and had heard about the fire and where it was. Some of these concerned citizens just wanted to see what was going on instead of waiting to see or hear about it on the news. Some of the by standers' faces may show up in a photograph with all the flashing lights providing some lighting.

With a few volunteers having arrived in their own vehicles to the fire, there were seventeen firefighters now on scene. Bill had his four firefighters, two to an attack line, ready to go with both attack lines charged off engine 2. Flames were roaring out the back and rear sides, but the front was showing signs of less fire, so that was to be their entry point. The object was to push the fire back onto itself, toward the rear of the house, knocking the fire down in all the rooms and searching for victims. With the flames roaring out some of the windows, there was no fear of an explosive backdraft situation upon breaching the front door. And, unfortunately, with the heavy amount of flame and smoke roaring out the house the chances of a rescue were extremely slight to zero. If there were people inside it looked more like this was going to be a recovery operation. Yep, the night just went to hell.

Ladders were set up quickly, and the lead roof man started up the chain saw, making sure it was running before heading up the ladder. Turning off the saw, the lead roof man climbed up the ladder and moved out of the way for the second roof man. A roof ladder was manhandled up the ladder and laid on the roof. After opening the hooks on the upper end of the roof ladder, it was positioned near the spot where the roof team wanted to cut a vent hole. With the hooks in place over the ridge of the roof, the lead roof man climbed up the roof ladder with the chain saw until he reached the spot to start cutting into the roof. The second roof man, carrying an axe, moved in behind the lead roof man, ready to help with the vent hole. The third member of the team, carrying a pike pole for poking and pulling pieces of the ceiling, stayed at the bottom of the roof ladder ready to lend a hand. Even though the fire had already vented itself out a few windows, a vertical ventilation to remove the tremendous build up of hot gases and black smoke would be a help to the interior firefighters. So the roof team made about a three foot by three foot opening in the roof, then carefully poked through the plaster board ceiling. As soon as the hole was made, out rushed flame and smoke, like a volcano belching out its stored gases.

Coordination is a key to an effective firefight, and in this case, as soon as the vent hole was made, the interior attack teams started through the door. Everyone was on their knees crawling into the front room, trying to stay low out of the intense heat and heavy smoke. The nozzleman of team one angled off to the right, staying close to the wall while the nozzleman on team two went to the left. Alternating the nozzle settings between straight stream and fog patterns, the nozzleman had a stressful task of trying to knock down the fire and keeping his team safe from the ravenous flames that can play hide and seek in the thick black smoke. The straight stream was great for hitting fire from a distance with a lot of water quickly, while the fog pattern was best for putting a lot of fine water droplets in the air, causing the heat to turn the water droplets into steam. If you remember your high school chemistry, it takes about 800 to 900 btus of energy (heat) to convert one pound of water (1/8 gallon) to steam. If the nozzle is cranking out 150 to 200 gallons of water per minute, a lot of btus are being taken away from the ravenous fire. Plus steam will expand, pushing oxygen out to make room for the steam. Therefore, the trick is to put enough water onto the fire to rob it of both heat energy as well as oxygen.

Crawling deeper into the burning house, the firefighters' breathing rate in the air masks could be heard getting faster and deeper. The heavy turnouts, the high heat, the claustrophobic conditions, the exertions of dragging the fire hose through a maze of doors and furniture, and the specter of finding a body, all added to the flow of adrenaline. And the adrenaline needed oxygen, lots of it. Ok dragon, we are here to put you down. The fight was on.

Chapter 3

Bill followed both firefighters into the bedroom to see what they had found. Carefully removing some debris from the pile on the floor, Bill and his fellow firefighters realized what they had hoped to not find was there in front of them. With all three headlamps illuminating the object in question, it was identifiably a badly burnt body. Damn it. After telling his crew to keep knocking down the fire but do not touch anything unless absolutely necessary, Bill walked out to find the fire chief. Removing his air mask so he could talk normally, he said to the chief, "Frank, we found a body in the bedroom at sides C and D."

As Bill was briefing Frank about the found body, an alarm starting dinging in the house. The alarm was distinctive and signaled that a firefighter's air tank was dangerously low on air. This triggered an egress of the firefighter teamed up with the one whose air was getting low. As the attack team crawled out following the hose they had advanced, a couple of firefighters standing by outside the structure were waiting with spare air tanks in hand. Both firefighters crawled out of the house and walked a short distance to the waiting air tanks. They bent over, opened their face masks so they could breathe the outside air and waited.

The SCBA system consisted of a tank of compressed air strapped to a backpack frame, with a regulator and hoses to control and provide air to the firefighter wearing the SCBA. The firefighter with the spare air tank quickly shut off the air supply, unscrewed the air hose from the nearly empty tank and released the strap holding the air tank on the backpack frame. Sliding the air tank out of the frame, and sliding the full air tank into the frame, the firefighter tightened the clamp, screwed the air hose to the tank, and opened the air flow. The bent over firefighter had his face mask back on and sealed, and after feeling the slap on the back, was standing up straight and waiting for his partner to finish the same ritual. In less than five minutes, the attack crew was back inside working the nozzle while the second team had to leave and get their air tanks replaced the same way. This wasn't quite as fascinating to watch as the Indy car racing pit crews, but it got the job done.

Bill spoke to Frank, "My guys have been warned to do as little damage as possible, to knock down the fire but not to overhaul yet." Frank told Bill that sounded good, and to let him know as soon as it was clear enough to safely enter the room where the body was found. He reminded Bill that there had been two people living in the house, and their name was Symsin.

"Bill, as soon as you can, have your crews do another search, just in case the quick search missed a second body. What's the status on the rest of the rooms?"

Bill responded, "We have the kitchen to finish yet. Both crews are just starting their second tanks of air." Both knew that once the attack teams had finished their second tank of air, they were to take a breather while a fresh team takes over inside.

The chief said, "Sounds good, and while you are doing that I will go talk to the police."

Frank found Bev, the on duty police officer. "Bev, my guys just found a body in the bedroom on the north side. They haven't found the second person yet. We should be able to go inside in about 20 minutes."

"Okay, Frank," said Bev. "I'll phone my boss and let him know. I still have my camera with me so let me know when you want to go in."

Frank then called Dispatch by cell phone and said he needed a fire investigator as soon as possible, explaining they had a fatality situation. He would also need the coroner or a deputy to officially pronounce the body a code black, meaning deceased.

Officer Bev, a gorgeous red head of 5 feet 7 inches, captivated everyone with her piercing green eyes. She looked younger than her thirty two years of age, but as soon as she would start talking people realized she was much more than just a gorgeous, athletic body. She had had many male admirers, thanks to her super model looks. However, many of the admirers felt intimidated by her intelligence, while others felt intimidated by her job as a cop. So she dedicated herself to her job, and left the fast and fun times to others. Her dad and one brother had been police officers. So Bev, who could have been strutting down the fashion ramp in Paris, making big money wearing clothes that few women could wear or afford, followed their footsteps and joined the police force instead.

She had spent her early years as a police officer, working in a larger city with much more and varied crime. It was brutal work, and not all of it caused by the criminals. Her male co workers were often worse than the criminals she was arresting. With her fabulous looks, she was in demand, by both bachelors and married officers. Her fellow workers thought of her as a sex machine, not giving her the respect for her intelligence and hard work. She even went to the Board regarding the sexual harassment, but the all male Board claimed she caused her own problems by her dress and manners. She was incensed, being called the cause of her problems. To add insult to injury, after the meeting, one of the Board members had the gall to ask her to go home with him. After she blew up and called him every dirty word she could think of, she stormed out of the room, and started thinking of a different career.

Bev found herself stuck behind a desk, shuffling papers, since her patrol and beat job had been taken away from her. While checking an internet site listing law enforcement jobs available, she saw a small listing for a police officer. The short and smallness of the listing intrigued her. Most of the other listings were huge and boastful, sounding suspiciously no different than her current situation. She looked up Prairie City, and found it on a map. The first thing she noticed is the size of the dot. Looking at the map legend, she found where the dot size represented a population less than 10,000. Next, she noticed a few smaller dots scattered around Prairie City, but the closet looked like about 16 to 20 miles. Bev pictured an area of few people, which sure sounded a hell of a lot better than where she was at. The more she thought about it, the more she wanted to check it out. "What the heck, I have some vacation time coming and I really, really need to get away from this place." So she packed for a short trip, and drove to Prairie City.

Arriving in Prairie City after a few days' drive, she immediately fell in love with the area. It's beauty of prairie and forest coming together formed a tranquil picture. It took only a stop at the diner to have her fall in love with the friendly atmosphere. She met with the police chief, who immediately impressed her as being more interested in her abilities as a law enforcement professional than her physical assets. Bev had the foresight to have brought her own file of employment history and a ledger of her work in law enforcement. The police chief seemed impressed with Bev's attention to detail, and asked what her plans were for the next couple of days. Bev said she was taking some vacation time to come here, and she could stay a couple of days before needing to return. Walt, the chief, told her if she could stay he would see if he could make it worth her while. "I need to review your records, talk to a few people, and meet with the mayor and town council. I should be able to meet with the council tomorrow evening. After that I expect to be letting you know the next morning about the police officer's job."

After a moment to let the plan settle with Bev, Walt suggested she ride with him. "Unless you've got something to do, or someplace to see, how about you ride with me and I will show you our community. And if it works out, I can have the Sheriff show you around the County tomorrow."

Bev was excited, and expressed her gratitude. She realized this did not necessarily mean she had the job, but she felt like she could easily be a part of this community. It would be great if she could be accepted for her aptitude and not her attributes.

Bev enjoyed both the drive around the community with Walt, and the drive around a part of the County with the Sheriff. Even the Sheriff treated her with respect, especially after Walt had filled him in on her qualifications. The Sheriff commented that if Walt thought she could handle the job, certainly he would have no problems. By the end of that second day in Prairie City, Bev was riding on a high that she hoped would not come crashing down. Of course, just thinking of returning to her current situation was like dousing the fire of hope, but Bev held on to a flicker of hope that this would be her community very soon.

Late that evening, Bev was surprised to hear the motel room phone ring and awaken her. "Bev, this is Chief Walt. Sorry to call at such a late hour but I didn't want you to wait until morning. How soon can you start?"

"Chief, I hope you are not teasing me! If this is for real, I wish I could start tomorrow, but I had better follow the proper procedures. I really have the job?"

Walt laughed and assured her the Council and mayor agreed with Walt that Bev's credentials were top notch and gave him the okay to move forward on hiring Bev. "I sure appreciate this Chief, and I appreciate the Council in accepting my credentials. I can't wait to get started. I will call my boss first thing tomorrow morning, and drive back to home. I will keep you up to date as to when I can officially leave. By the way, do you have someone who can help me find a place to live?"

That was four years ago, and Bev has never looked back. This was her town, these were her people, and she was their police officer. During this time she had only a few instances of idiotic young males high on hormones and beer wanting to find out what she looked like under her uniform. A far cry from the daily abuse she dealt with prior to moving to Prairie City. And the crime was so much less. For the first time she felt like her choice of profession was correct for her. Even though she did not date much in the big city, she did miss the bigger selection of places to have fun at and people to have fun with. Bev had made a few good friends, like Dora at the café, and Bill at the fire department, but friends her age and single were seriously lacking. She was lonely, but as before, she put herself into her work. Even with being lonely, Prairie City was still much better than her previous abode. Tonight, however, she had to admit that this fire situation had the look and feel of something she had thought she left behind in the big city a few years ago.

Chapter 4

George, the second assistant fire chief, was in charge of the exterior operations on this fire. The roof crew had finished their job and was on the ground waiting to assist with the mop up. He had seven volunteer firefighters working the various tasks necessary to support the interior attack as well as handle any fire on the outside of the structure. Stan, a volunteer training to be an assistant chief, was doing a outside recon for the chief when he found a couple of empty plastic milk jugs near the back door. Looking around, Stan felt like something just wasn't right, since there was no other trash, nothing scattered about. So he called George by radio, asking George to meet him at the backdoor, side C. In a couple of minutes George caught up with Stan at the back door, and Stan pointed out the plastic jugs. "George, something doesn't feel right."

As George looked around, he got the same feeling. "Stan, good eyes. Stay here and protect this area while I go talk to Frank. I don't want any more footprints near here in case those jugs were used in starting this fire."

George caught up with Frank in front of the structure. Bev was there also, so George was able to tell both of them what was found at the back door. "George, as long as you have Stan protecting that area, Bev and I will go inside first and check out the body and surroundings. My suspicions of arson are getting stronger by the minute. Sound good to you, Bev?" Bev said it was fine with her, and that her boss, the police chief, was on his way.

The fire was knocked down, and the interior guys were going through each room again, trying to find the second body, while making sure no fire was still playing hide and seek. Unfortunately they couldn't do a complete overhaul because this fire definitely needed to be investigated. Anything done to the building prior to the investigation could easily ruin the results of the investigation. Walt, the police chief, arrived just as Bill gave the all clear to Frank that the air in the room was breathable. Walt, Frank and Bev carefully walked into the structure, with Bill in the lead. In the light of a couple of battle lanterns, which were powerful hand held rechargeable lights, Frank was watching for tell tale signs left by the fire, while Bill was pointing out a few things he had noticed.

Frank, the only one on the Department with more fire fighting experience then Bill, was starting to feel his sixty nine and a half years. He had been threatening to retire and leave the Department in Bill's hands, but his wife Dora had brought him back to reality by asking him what would he then do? Dora and Frank had been married for forty six years, surviving through raising three children and the numerous up and downs of life. Dora worked as a waitress, with the work keeping her trim and active. Frank was starting to show signs of a less active life style, and his age was starting to show as well. He teased about his bald head, calling it a solar panel for a sex machine. Dora would just pat his head, laugh and say, "Just keep telling yourself that, darling." Frank smiled as he remembered, but then was brought back to reality, a reality of death and destruction.

Carefully walking over and around debris left by the fire's wake, Bill, Frank, Walt and Bev arrived in the bedroom and started looking around the room. The body was on the floor, between the bed and the closet. Looking around, all four had a similar feeling that this was not an accidental fire. The amount of fire and damage was way more than what would have been found in a normal accidental fire. While Bev was taking pictures, Frank said to Bill, "remind the guys to be careful and not disturb anymore of the structure than necessary."

Frank, Walt and Bev went outside to the back door to look at what Stan had found. Noting down in his pocket notebook the location and arrangement of the plastic jugs, Walt asked Bev to get the Police Line Do Not Cross barrier tape out of his car. Walt agreed that this strengthened their notion of arson, and was glad Frank had called for an investigator. Frank told Walt he had requested the coroner or a deputy to officially determine that the body was indeed dead. "We can't remove the body yet until the investigator has a chance to look it over, but at least the coroner can carefully do a quick check and make the ruling while we are waiting for the investigator."

Walt, Bev, and Frank walked to the front of the building where they met with George and Bill. Seeing this street meeting of police and fire 'heavies', Nick, the local news reporter, moved from his picture taking vantage point to get closer to the meeting. Nick sensed a story in that meeting, and was trying to eavesdrop. Pictures of the awesome flames and firefighters working their butts off were fine, but he wanted a story to go with those pictures. He sensed the stirrings of a story, his reporter's instinct tingling. Seeing that Nick was close by, Frank and Walt agreed to discuss this incident later in Walt's office where it would be more secure. Frank asked Bill and George to make sure all the volunteers knew to keep their mouths shut, to tell no one about this incident, especially Nick. By this time most of the volunteers had been made aware of the body being found so it was especially crucial to tell everyone to zip their lips.

Frank's cell phone buzzed, and it was the Dispatcher relaying that the State Police will have an officer there in about 45 minutes, and the Fire Investigator will be there in about four hours. After Frank told Walt about the etas (estimated time of arrival) for the State Police and investigator, Frank, Bill, and George went around the building and into each room, taking a look at the destruction and burn patterns. A couple of the volunteers were still checking the rooms using a thermal imaging camera. These thermal imaging cameras were handy in looking for hot spots. During the initial attack, these same cameras were used to pin point the hottest areas as well as to look through the thick smoke trying to find a hidden body. When the thermal imaging camera's screen designated an area hotter than the adjacent area, the volunteers went to work trying to get water onto the hot spot. Normally the hot spot would be dug or chopped out, making sure it was completely extinguished. But in trying to keep the fire suppression damage as little as possible, the firefighters had to limit themselves to squirting water. No second body was found during this more intense search.

While the chiefs were doing the walk through, Walt had steered Nick away from the immediate action, providing as much information as he safely could. He figured that providing a little bit is better than clamming up completely. Of course, it is a gamble whether a reporter senses a snow job and wants more or whether he or she will do the story with what was available. By this time the smoke and flames were long gone. Since the picture taking was long ago finished and Nick had as much as he can get out of Walt for now, Nick left to head back to the News office to ready the story for the internet and the paper. The chiefs had just completed their walk through, and Frank had one of the volunteers help Bev run out the barrier tape around the entire property to secure it. The hard work for the firefighters was done. Now it was up to the eyes of experience and the knowledge of science to find out what this fire was all about.

Chapter 5

Back at the newspaper office, Nick remembered doing a story on the new Police Chief some twelve years ago. By the trim figure he presented in his uniform, Walt was a fitness nut. He was then and he still is now, thought Nick, seeing him running on the back roads or working on a gym treadmill. Walt had migrated like many other officers from the hard crime areas of California, getting more than a life time of police work in a just a few short years. The job of Chief of Police for Prairie City was advertised minimally, but it didn't take long for the job notice to make its way out of State. Walt was looking for an out, wanting to get away from the senseless and tragic lifestyle he was supposed to be doing something about. He was sick and tired of laws that instead of protecting the innocent, protected the guilty. Of politicians thinking they were gods and hence not subject to the laws. And of vociferous movie stars out of touch with reality, yet so full of themselves thinking they had all the answers. When Walt saw the job notice and saw where Prairie City was, there was no question about should he apply. Biting nails and trying to be patient awaiting word of the job, Walt finally received a call letting him know he was one of three contenders, and he needed to visit Prairie City for an interview. When he arrived in Prairie City, he fell in love with the community immediately. Of course it didn't take much to be a far cry better than where he came from. He was hired, moved, and started working as the new Police Chief. He could actually enjoy being a cop, a guardian, and a friend in uniform. Crime in Prairie City was nothing like where he had been. But something about this fire told him things had now changed.

Walt released Bev to continue her patrolling and he stayed with Frank to await the State Police. The Sheriff of Twin Rivers County, of which Prairie City was the County Seat, arrived and checked in with Walt and Frank to see what his Department could do to help. There wasn't too much information for Walt to pass along, but he brought the Sheriff up to speed. There had been a couple living in this house, a man and woman, in their 60s, and their name was Symsin. One body was found and was badly burned and needed to be identified. The couple's pickup was missing. Walt needed to find a photograph of the Symsins, the couple living in the house, so he can get their pictures out to fellow law enforcement people. And Walt needed a description of the vehicle that the couple owned, since it was missing as well. The Sheriff said he would work on locating the pickup, once he looked up the records for a description. At least that would be one less thing on Walt's plate.

While most of the volunteers were draining and loading the fire hoses back onto the engines, Frank asked Bill to grab a couple of volunteers and carefully go through the house looking for any photograph of the Symsins. Concentrating on the living room, hallway, and bedroom where the body was discovered, one of the volunteers did find a useable photograph in one of the dresser drawers where the heat and fire had not seriously affected the contents of the drawer. Walt was handed the photograph, so he headed back to his office to start notifying adjacent agencies of the missing person situation.

The volunteers had been on this fire for about three hours, and there was no sense in holding all of the volunteers at the scene waiting for the investigator. So Frank discharged the others to return to the station, get everything ready for the next fire, and then go home. Frank kept Bill and the attack engine crew on scene in case of a flare up of the fire, and told George to talk with the volunteers back at the station, reminding them of the sealed lips orders.

Since this looked like a deadly arson fire, it was going to be critical to maintain control of the scene and the chain of custody. Therefore, until the investigator released the scene, the police department or fire department was to have an officer on scene at all times. The Sheriff offered the services of his deputies to assist with maintaining control of the scene, but it made sense for the fire department to maintain control of the structure while waiting for the investigator. So Bill, Frank and the two volunteers with engine 1 stayed on scene, and spent the time talking about the fire. Then when bored with that subject, they hit on a few typically small town USA rumors and stories. But the normal joking and ribbing after a difficult fire fight was not there. It was a more somber wait.

During this lull, Frank had told the assistant chiefs that he will put in a request for a stress management team to assist with the after action stress of a fatal fire. Sometimes the stress of a deadly fire can affect a person in strange, unrecognized ways. And it may take days or weeks before the symptoms of stress related behavior are apparent. Some will silently deal with the tragedy on their own, some will be 'macho man' and refuse to let the events phase them, and others will quietly welcome assistance from others trained in the recognition and abatement of stress induced behavior. Frank did not want any of his volunteers to be unduly burdened by what had just happened, nor did he want any of this tragedy to badly affect his volunteers' families. During a few of the training sessions over the years, they had talked about hoping there would never be a time when such a team would be needed. Bill summed up everyone's thoughts by stating out loud, "Things were just fine. We sure didn't need this shit."

At the Station, it was a more somber atmosphere then normal after a fire; it was unusually quiet. Not even the couple of jokesters trying to liven up their fellow firefighters. Wet, filthy, and very smelly turnout gear that was worn by the firefighters was hung up to dry. Before the fire the turnout gear had been a light brown color, but was now smeared black and gray with the filthy residue and stench of the fire fight. Soaking wet leather and Kevlar gloves were laid out to dry, as well as the Nomex hoods used to protect the firefighter's face and neck. Engines were refilled with water and foam. Airmasks were taken apart, the face pieces washed and dried, and the air tanks refilled. While everyone was working on their fire equipment, George found Francis helping with refilling the air bottles, and asked if he would follow him upstairs to the training room for a couple of minutes. When they both got upstairs, George asked Francis if he was okay with the situation, if he needed someone to counsel him. Francis said he should be okay, so George then asked Francis if he would be willing to provide counseling to any of the fellow firefighters. Francis said he would make himself available, at any time. Francis, a Catholic priest, had been through numerous tragic death situations in the past, mostly when he served in the military. So he was somewhat more used to handling death and counseling people. He felt in this situation he especially wanted to help, since these fellow firefighters were his very close friends.

Francis, or Father Francis to his parishioners, had been on the other side of counseling before. He had been in the Gulf War, part of the 'shock and awe' that struck back at Iraq. At the Battle of Khafji, he survived a missile attack, a 'friendly fire' mistake that killed a bunch of his fellow Marines. He had desperately needed someone to talk to, someone to absorb his anger and frustration and loss. Ever since that terrible tragedy, Francis worked to see that he could provide a level of counseling that he didn't have. That was quite a few years ago, and after his military tour of duty ended, he spent a couple of years flailing and trying to figure out what he needed to be doing with his life. Finally one morning over a cup of coffee, reading some bleak news and realizing his life at this stage was also bleak, he was hit by a thought, like a light bulb just turned on. Francis thought long and hard about this idea that had invaded his doldrums, and finally decided to follow his idea. He studied and after a few years became a priest. As soon as he started working in his first parish, and was able to counsel his parishioners and guide them in spiritual as well as some human needs, he had realized he was where he wanted to be, where he felt he needed to be.

Francis was a forty six year old of Latino decent. Having worked in the fields with his parents and the experiences he faced in the military, Francis felt he could fit in and empathize with the people of Prairie City. So it was no surprise to see him participating in stress management groups, trying to be there to listen, to make sure others would not be denied counseling services.

Francis loved to play basketball. While growing up he played hoops with his fellow field hands as much as he could when time and weather allowed. With the experience in rough and tumble basketball on some crude courts, he became a fairly successful guard during his high school days. His parents made sure he went to school, wanting to see their child make something of himself and do better than a field worker. So Francis went on to college and continued to play basketball while working and studying. His short stature was offset by his tremendous speed on the court, something that caught the eyes of big league recruiters. However, something kept turning Francis from committing to a future in basketball stardom, and like many others, Francis enlisted and became a Marine after getting his degree.

Even at his current age, he could still put up a good challenge on the basketball court. So it was often that Fr. Francis would be out on the play ground shooting hoops with high school students and helping them with their game. He did what he could to be available to the people of his community. His life was dedicated to others, and not just spiritually. That was one of the reasons he became a volunteer fire fighter, seeing a need to be available to the entire community, not just the members of his Church. It took a long and hard fought battle of words with the Bishop of the Diocese, but Fr. Francis did become a volunteer fire fighter, increasing his joy at assisting more people.

George had everyone stop what they were doing and reminded them of the keep your mouth shut orders, and told them that there will be a voluntary stress management team review as soon as the chief hears back from the team leader. In the meantime, if anyone was having a problem with tonight's fire and needed immediate assistance in dealing with the tragedy, let him know as soon as everyone was finished with getting the trucks ready for the next fire call. George went to the office and started working on the paperwork while Stan made sure all was going smoothly with the replenishment. Some of the volunteers had gotten into the refrigerator in the back room and popped open some soda pop, trying to get some sugar and caffeine into their system. A couple of the volunteers stepped outside to light up a cigarette, not even getting the normal razz by their buddies as to the need to inhale more smoke after inhaling smoke. Yep, this had not been a normal fire.

Back at the scene, the State Police officer, a Sergeant Liz, arrived and both Bev and Walt pulled up to join in. After a brief overview, Sergeant Liz was given a tour of the incident. Liz was there as more of a formality, in a way, to make sure that the 'small town' police and fire department were handling the situation okay. Since Liz had been experienced in assisting in the investigation of a few deadly fires, she would be a good resource and promptly showed her knowledge by asking serious questions regarding the situation from the first arrival to the current time.

Sergeant Liz's small Asian frame, youthful looks and soft almond eyes fooled everyone into assuming she was a soft spoken push over. For those who thought Liz was a demure pushover, those almond eyes and the command in her voice would zero in on the unsuspecting, and it was a terrible thing to watch. Those caught with their defenses down were lucky to walk away with only bruises to their esteem. The forty something Sergeant Liz was no statistic to simply meet a federal mandate for equal opportunity. She earned her title, with dignity and distinction. She was born to a hard working Japanese American farming couple. By the time she was four, she was doing chores around the farm. When she became a young teenager, and could reach the pedals on the tractor, she was tilling the fields. While her grandparents were still alive, they would teach Liz to speak some words in their native Japanese tongue. Her parents were of the mind that since they lived in America, and were citizens, they should speak 'American'.

After graduating with honors from high school, Liz went on to college, where she acquired an interest in law enforcement. She worked part time as a security guard at one of the malls, and after getting her degree, worked full time as a security guard, until a better job came up. Watching the job listings, she saw an opening being advertised for the State Police. This interested her, so she applied and waited. Liz was pleasantly surprised to be called in for an interview, and even more surprised when she was told she had the job.

Liz applied herself to the boot camp, and became a leader in her squad of cadets. As in all things she did, Liz was out to do her best, and it showed at graduation, when she was assigned a patrol while her fellow cadets had to wait for an opening. Liz moved up the ladder through her diligence and work ethics, and it wasn't long before she made Sergeant, a coveted position. And it was this Sergeant Liz who was looking over the scene of this tragic fire, trying to help solve a puzzle. Liz was concerned over the numerous boot prints outside, but realized that was not to be helped. As was some of the damage inside during the rush to get the fire knocked down. While Liz was filling out her forms and double checking with Bev and Frank, Bill noticed the disappearing black of the early morning sky. The Supreme artist was busy painting the eastern sky with dawn colors. It's going to be a long, long day he thought to himself.

Chapter 6

The arsonist had watched the fire from a distance, careful to avoid the searching eyes of the lady police officer. Even though it was dark, and the arsonist was a distance from the fire, this was not a time to be careless. Not a rookie to this type of operation, the arsonist had an impressive and growing resume of burn jobs.

Having been in this area for a week, scoping out the city, police force, businesses, and of course the primary reason for being here, the old couple, the arsonist jumped at a chance to get this job finished. Preferring the largeness of the big city, where one could easily get lost in the crowds, it was time to get out of here, where a new comer stood out like a sore thumb. While watching the firefighters hard at work, the arsonist was hit with a strange sensation, a feeling of something barely familiar, briefly shook the fire setter from toes to head. The arsonist was not at ease with this new, strange feeling. The arsonist had never been to this place before, yet there was a hint of familiarity to this strange feeling. But now was not the time to dwell on it, so the feeling got shoved to the back of the arsonist's mind.

The arsonist was not alone. A 'family' hitman was sent to assist with the job. Through gifts of money to the right people in the right places, the arsonist's employer had finally located the old couple hidden by the Witness Security Program. It was time the 'family' took care of the rat, and sent the arsonist and hitman to deal with the problem. The 'family' had been damaged by testimony provided by Roger Symsin, one of their oldest hitmen.

Edwardo had been his given name, and he had followed in his father's footsteps to become a hitman for the 'family'. Edwardo had been caught on a sting, and realizing his options, went for the chance of living, and with his wife, came into the Witness Security Program. Adamo, the head of the 'family', had not taken kindly to the switch of allegiance, and vowed to get revenge. It was a long and expensive search, but the money finally paid off and the right people talked. Edwardo, or now called Roger, had been found, and now the price for infidelity was to be paid. The instructions to the arsonist were simple; "Just take care of the problem. You've been paid good money, your reputation is good, and we expect a satisfactory conclusion." So, after arriving to the area and checking things out quickly, the arsonist settled in and started watching the couple and planning the operation.

The hitman, Elmo, wanted the hit to be a bloody mess. Not surprising, for Elmo had that kind of reputation, and the young arsonist despised having to work with him. Elmo had been with the 'family' for a number of years longer than the arsonist. Elmo's father had worked for the 'family', so it was natural for Elmo to have a job with the 'family'. It was also natural that Elmo take up his father's penchant for excessive force, enjoying the pain and suffering he could bring on someone else. When it came to a special job requiring no finesse, just brute force, Elmo was the one. His grandmother used to tell him Elmo meant protection. It seemed a good fit and Elmo took it very seriously, considering nearly anything a threat to the 'Domo'. After much arguing over the manner of the hit, a détente had been worked out and a plan agreed upon between the arsonist and the over eager Elmo. The arsonist didn't like it but it was the best of the worst, and so the two started working on their agreed upon tasks.

After scoping out the community, Elmo found a cold storage locker for rent. A popular pastime, hunting was big in this area and the cold storage locker came in handy for temporary storage of successfully hunted game. Having paid cash and provided fictitious credentials, Elmo rented a locker and made sure the access to the facility was not being monitored. In the meantime the arsonist was gathering up the necessary supplies for the incendiary part of the plan. Fortunately this community had not caught up to the rest of the world yet—heck, people still left their keys in the vehicles and didn't lock their home doors. The local people even greeted each other on the street or in the store. Well, it made the job easier on the one hand but the friendliness made the arsonist uneasy at the same time.

Nicknamed "the Burner", the arsonist had earned a reputation amongst the high class mobsters of today, and was earning a reputation among the law enforcement agencies as well. Typical of many arsonists, the type of accelerant used, or the type of timer used, or something left at the scene were 'calling cards', hints as to who the arsonist was. Part of it was a game, like catch me if you can. So far the Burner was very good, using a special mix of fuel to start the fires and taunt the investigators, but remained allusive.

The Burner had watched the Prairie City fire and police departments, studying their responses to the day to day operations in and out of town. After a week of this the Burner got a feel for the community as best as possible in such a short time, and decided when to activate the plan. On the chosen night, just past midnight, the arsonist and hitman went to the couple's home and entered the unlocked back door. As expected, the couple were in bed, sound asleep. While the Burner was getting the house ready to burn, Elmo approached the bed, holding a metal pipe that he had brought along. Figuring the woman was the lighter sleeper, the gleeful hitman brought the pipe down hard on her head. The man was starting to wake up, like he had heard something, but the hitman was fast and ready, and brought the pipe down hard on his head too.

Both the man and woman were knocked out, but still breathing. Elmo took out the hunting knife that he always carried, and without pause, fatally stabbed the woman, then rolled her off unto the floor between the bed and closet. There was no remorse on the part of the hitman, it was just business, a business he took pleasure in. The young arsonist didn't like the killing, but orders were orders. Trussing up the old man, the hitman dragged him out to the man's pickup truck, dumping him in the back.

It was the Burner's turn now. The arsonist had brought a couple of plastic jugs of gasoline mixed with the M4 thickener. The M4 mix was the trademark of the Burner, and just another 'catch me if you can' taunt. "Heck, this place is 'poedunkville', and if they can't catch me in Jersey, they sure won't out here."

After spreading gas over the dead woman to make it harder to identify her, the Burner spread the remaining gas in the bedroom, hallway, kitchen and the back door porch area. Stopping briefly to inhale the smell of the fuel mix, the Burner let out a sigh of pleasure. Next, the pyromaniac set a crude timer, just a book of matches, down at the end of the laid gas trail, lit one of the matches, and hopped into the pickup truck and drove off to follow Elmo, who was driving Roger's pickup truck.

Finding a deserted place to pull over, the hitman grabbed a syringe of meth and hopped into the back of the pickup where the old man had been dumped and covered. After administering enough meth to kill the old man, the evidence was sealed in a bag to be used later. Carefully driving over to the rented cold storage unit, making sure no one was around, Elmo and the Burner dragged the old man into the cold storage unit. With the old man safely tucked away in the freezer and the guy's pickup truck well hidden, it was time to meander over to the fire and watch the fun. Finding a place out of the way from which the fire could be seen, the pyromaniac grabbed a pair of binoculars and sat on the tailgate of the rented pickup truck, enjoying the view. "Damn I do good work."

It didn't take too long for the Burner to recognize the firefighters had worked their butts off, and knocked the fire down. There was nothing left to enjoy, so the arsonist took off and went back to the rented room after dropping off Elmo at his rented car. Getting ready for bed, the Burner thought about the weird sensation that hit while watching the firefighters tackle the fire. Realizing that dwelling on the strange feeling was getting the arsonist nowhere, the Burner thought about the next and final step in the plan. The Burner felt giddy since this next step would be something the arsonist has not done yet, stepping into a new territory as it were.

Chapter 7

George, having finished the initial paperwork and seeing that the last firefighter was headed home, locked the Station and returned to the burnt house to catch up with Frank and Bill. After being introduced, Sergeant Liz asked George a few questions regarding the situation on the outside of the building during the initial fire attack. Since the investigator was still a couple of hours away, Frank called the café where his wife Dora worked, and asked if she had time to put together some breakfasts that he would pickup when ready.

Dora, a very outgoing woman, was pretty much the life of the café. She liked to change her hair color fairly often, and some people came to the café for a coffee and cinnamon roll just to see what color hair Dora was sporting for the day. She had been a waitress there for many years, having started to work there while in high school. It was during high school that she had been swept off her feet by a young basketball player named Frank. After graduation, with promises sealed by kisses and hugs, Frank went into the Air Force and fulfilled his tour of duty. Finished with his Air Force tour of duty, Frank hurried home, and keeping their promise to each other, Dora and Frank were married. Frank took over the work on his parent's farm and Dora continued at the café, until she became pregnant with their first of two children. For awhile, Dora stayed home to help raise their two children. Once the children were old enough to do the chores and help Frank with the farm, Dora went back to work at the café to help earn money to live on. Nearly everyone who came to the café was called darling or honey. Very few customers were affronted by the term of affection, and very few customers were denied that term. You had to be a rotten scoundrel to not be called darling or honey by Dora. Dora loved her man, missed her children who couldn't wait to get to a big city, and loved her community. And her man loved her, and most of the community loved her back.

It was during this period of let down, when the rigors of the fire fight are behind, and it becomes a waiting game, that fatigue catches up. Frank had picked up a box of breakfasts and a couple of thermoses of coffee from Dora and delivered the welcomed food and drink to the volunteers and police still on scene. Hot coffee and a warm breakfast was just the ticket, somewhat rejuvenating. While finishing with the welcomed breakfast, the arson inspector arrived. Liz knew Amrit, the inspector, quite well, having worked on numerous cases together. Frank had met him once, but Bev, George and Bill had not met Amrit before. After the introductions, the group provided Amrit with a quick overview of the situation while Amrit was getting into his turnout gear.

Amrit was born Amrit Jai, fifty three years ago, in India. His parents decided to immigrate to the United States when Amrit was only three years old, and together with a couple of relatives, purchased a small town motel. In a matter of a couple of years the family owned three motels in two nearby communities, the result of hard work and sacrifices. During this period, Amrit, thanks to his parent's instilled work ethic, was a studious teenager not found often at the social events common among his fellow teenagers. He graduated from high school as the valedictorian, and moved onto a Bachelors and a Masters in Chemical Engineering. During his sojourn as a college student, he joined the local Fire Department in the student firefighter program. Through this special program, Amrit received a free room in the fire station, and a stipend that helped pay for food and books. He and a couple other student firefighters were responsible to get the fire engines fired up and ready to roll to a fire call, as well as assist in the fire fight. His fire training would prove to be valuable later on. He was working for a large city crime lab when he heard of an arson investigation job in a rural state. Sick of the big city life, and overabundance of crime, and especially worried over his family's safety, Amrit went for the job. It turned out to be a win win situation, with the State happy to get a person of Amrit's background, and Amrit happy to be moving his family to a less stressful environment. It took a while, but his family had grown to love the area, and especially the lower crime rate. And Amrit's reputation as an exceptional investigator continued to grow.

Amrit needed to get a quick assessment of the exterior of the structure, then move inside and look over the damage. Grabbing his notepad, Amrit walked around the outside of the building, making quick notes and notations for further assessment. Then he did the same to the inside of the structure, with Frank going inside with Amrit for safety reasons. While memories were still fresh, Amrit wanted to interview the volunteers regarding the circumstances surrounding the response to this fire. Also, he needed to interview any witnesses still in the area, and review any statements taken by Bev earlier while the initial fire attack was on going. But recognizing the need to get the body taken care of, Amrit grabbed his investigation kit out of the car and went back inside with Frank. The interviews will have to wait.

The body, barely recognizable as once being a human, still needed to be treated with dignity and given proper respect. Not wanting to move the body just yet, Amrit carefully looked over the body, noting the position of the body and its orientation. Amrit took a series of pictures of the body and the surrounding area. Measurements were taken in order to properly place the body in the room with the location of furniture items, the window and door, and the closet. He scraped up some samples of the debris on the floor surrounding the body, placing them in sealable jars. Then he traced an outline of the body on the floor, since once the body was removed, it could not be placed back. He started checking the body for any clothing that could be recognized as such, and any burn patterns on the body. Just like checking the structure for burn patterns can point to indicators of fire behavior and probable starting point, burn patterns on a body can indicate fire behavior in a more localized area. While closely examining the body, Amrit was also looking for any signs of injury that may not have been caused by the fire. He knew, however, that as badly burned as this body was, finding any signs of injury that happened before the fire was going to be up to the medical examiner. Amrit was anxious to roll the body over, hoping there may be some evidence underneath the body that was protected from being burned. But patience and being methodical are the keys to getting the job done not only right, but also strong enough to stand up in a court battle.

Amrit made a list of the important tests and examinations he wanted the medical examiner to do. The medical examiner will do the autopsy, and will hopefully be able to establish the identity of the victim, cause and manner of death, and the time of death. He knew the medical examiner would follow standard procedures, but Amrit still referenced the need for blood tests for carbon monoxide, blood alcohol and drugs, stomach contents, condition of airways, internal body temperature, xrays of the body, assessment of the type and extent of the burns and how the burns were acquired. In addition, Amrit wanted testing done to see if there was any evidence of ignitable liquid and to evaluate the burn patterns in more detail than he was able to do at the scene. After Amrit had Walt review and approve the notes and map work, and run through the digital photographs, the body was ready for removal.

The mortician, who also happened to be the coroner, had been patiently waiting outside in his vehicle. Upon being notified he can finally remove the body, he grabbed some clean, white sheets from his vehicle, and a body bag. With the help of Bill and one other volunteer firefighter who agreed to assist, the coroner draped a sheet over the body, getting a second one ready, and making sure the body bag was close by. Being extra careful, the coroner had the volunteers help him move the body ever so slightly, turning it over so another sheet could protect the other side of the body. While slowly and carefully turning over the body, Amrit was watching, photographing, and checking for any evidence that he could remove and protect. The coroner draped the second sheet over the victim, then instructed the volunteers on the next tricky part, getting the body into the body bag. With Amrit's help, they were able to carefully lift and place the body on top of the open body bag, which was then closed and sealed. Placing the bag on a stretcher, the volunteers were able to help the coroner carry the stretcher out to the waiting vehicle. Before the coroner drove off, Amrit asked the coroner if he could tell if the body was male or female. The coroner was not one hundred percent sure, but was fairly certain the victim was a female, the same conclusion that Amrit arrived at.

Once the body was removed, and the immediate area of where the body was had been assessed, Amrit moved to the exterior. Starting from the least damaged area, he looked for things such as holes in the building caused by the fire or the firefighters. He looked at the windows and doors, to see what kind of damage and what the smoke stains on the windows and openings around the windows and doors looked like. He worked his way to the most heavily damaged area of the exterior, the back of the house, where the plastic jugs were laying. Having taken pictures and documented what he saw through notes and a map, he moved to the inside of the house and started from the least damaged area. He noted the appearance of light bulbs, if they had a bulge and what direction the bulge was pointing. As he got closer to the heavier damage, he noted the charring, and watched for V and U patterns of black left on the walls. Taking plenty of pictures, and drawing a map of each room, he methodically aimed for the back of the house, toward the back door.

Studying the various V and U burn patterns on the walls, and measuring some of the char depth, he narrowed down the path of the fire to three points at the back of the house inside. At these points he noticed some patterns that were inconsistent with the rest of the burnt areas surrounding these three points. Amoeba like patterns of burnt surfaces could be seen, both on the carpets in two of the points and on the linoleum at the third location. In his experience he knew these points were arson starts, but he needed the data to prove it, and that was the tough part. Amrit had seen enough to want to talk with Walt and get a warrant to continue the search, specifically to identify the what, how, and why. Even though the Fire Department had the legal authority to enter a property to extinguish a fire, and an obligation to determine origin and cause, an investigation going beyond a "reasonable period of time," and involving a possible criminal activity would require a warrant. And Amrit was a stickler for following procedure to a "T". Too many times an arson case was thrown out of the courtroom for lack of scientific procedure, and for lack of proper legal procedure in the beginning stages of the investigation. Just following the guidelines of NFPA (National Fire Protection Association) Guides 921 and 1033 wasn't enough anymore when it came to a court battle.

The local judge was still at home, but agreed to meet with Amrit and Walt once he heard the reason for the call. After hearing the reason for needing a search warrant, the judge had no problem issuing the warrant. Although there was no one to serve the warrant to, since the owners were missing, Amrit wanted to make sure the legal status of his continuing investigation was covered.

Amrit and Walt talked about the need to set up a command structure for handling the investigation of this fire. Similar to a working fire, someone needed to be in charge, especially because there were numerous pieces of this fire that different agencies were going to work on. It was agreed that Walt would act as Incident Commander, and he would tie the various agencies together. The Fire Department would assist Amrit, the Police would work on the missing persons with the help of the Sheriff's Department, and the State Police would work on positively identifying the body and providing the lab to test the evidence. The State Police also had a hand in the search for the missing persons, contacting other agencies in the State with a description of the couple and the missing vehicle. Amrit asked Liz to monitor the medical examination schedule, getting a firm time and date when the body was to be examined. He needed to be there during the examination. Not something he wanted to do, but since this was his investigation, he was going to follow procedure.

Walt was asked to assist Amrit in carrying out the interviews, and the Sheriff mentioned that if they needed help to let him know and he could work some time into his schedule. With the first meeting of the team finished, Liz went to her State Police cruiser and called her boss to bring him up to date on the situation. Walt suggested Bev go home and get a couple hours of rest. Amrit asked if the Fire Department could stay on for about another hour or so while he finished investigating the structure. He told Frank that once he was done with the investigation of the structure, and Frank felt there was no danger of a rekindle, the Fire Department could be released. That was fine with Frank.

Amrit grabbed some evidence containers from his car and started working on the points of origin. Where there was carpet at the points of origin, he cut a piece from inside the burn mark and one from outside the burn mark. He did the same with the linoleum. Then he took some char from the walls, after measuring the depth and placing a note on the map where ever he took a sample. He carried larger containers for securing the plastic jugs found in the backyard, and properly marked the containers and the map location. Having gathered what he could for now, he arranged to personally take the items to a small rented storage facility, with Walt signing as a witness to the operation of securing the listed items. He needed to get some of the samples to the testing lab, as soon as arrangements could be made through the State Police. He would be talking to Sergeant Liz for help with this aspect of the investigation as well.

Amrit finished his investigation of the structure, and Frank, along with Bill and the two volunteers, went through the structure one last time checking for hot spots and smokes. Finding none, Frank asked Walt if he could provide one of his police officers to monitor the scene until Amrit released the scene. Frank released Bill and engine 1 back to the station, and on to home to rest, while he waited for the officer. Once the police officer was given his assignment, Frank was free to leave and go home to get some rest.

Chapter 8

Bill finally arrived home after hours away on the fire, and drug himself toward a welcomed hot shower. While starting the shower, Bill remembered the strange sensation he had as they were just starting to mop up the fire earlier this morning. He felt something like a very low grade electrical charge course through his body, ever so briefly. He hadn't remembered ever feeling like that before. At the time, he was too busy to really think about that weird feeling. But now that he was starting to relax a little in the welcomed caress of the shower, Bill thought about that strange sensation. However, he could not think of anything like it happening before, nor could he think of anything that would have triggered something like that feeling. Bill just could not come up with an answer, so he just filed the strange sensation away for future reference. He concentrated on trying to scrub away the grime of the fire fight and the smell of death.

Maybe it was the tiredness, but the shower brought back memories of Bill's surfing days as a teenager in southern California, standing in the shower washing the salt water off after a fun time at the beach. Back then his hair was longer and more blond, thanks to hours spent sitting on an old iron board waiting for a big enough wave to ride. Bill couldn't afford his own surfboard, and he was not good enough to handle the new 6 and 8 foot sleek surfboards that his friends were using. So he would borrow the huge 12 foot long 'iron' board belonging to the lifeguard, and ride the bigger waves with it. Bill worked as a cook and dishwasher in a fast food joint. His shift didn't start until 3pm, so he could surf the morning hours when the beach wasn't too busy. Bill would sit on the board, alternately watching the waves and watching the beach. When the roll of a big wave would show, Bill would turn and paddle the board into position, trying to get into that sweet spot just on top of the wave crest where the wave was starting to roll toward itself. The power of the wave was in this roll. If the speed of the board was just right, and the wave was still building, and you could get up from the prone paddling position to a standing position quickly, you were in for a sweet ride. Ah, the remembered exhilaration of piloting the heavy board just slightly ahead of the wave's curl as the wave pushed toward the beach. Bill's hazel eyes could remember visions of blonde haired bikinied beach babes lying on their colorful towels tanning under the sun's rays. How he had envied the sun caressing the skin of those beautifully tanned girls. Damn, those were some terrific days, Bill thought to himself, shaking away the day dream while shaking off the water from the shower.

After toweling off, Bill padded over to the kitchen and started himself a cup of coffee. While the coffee was brewing and filling the kitchen with the aroma of fresh coffee, Bill roamed the refrigerator. Being a bachelor for many years, one never knew what was going to be found in the refrigerator, or what color it may be. Giving up on the contents of the refrigerator, and remembering he had had a breakfast a while ago, Bill sat down to enjoy some coffee. Bill was thinking about the fire, and the charred body they had found and had to deal with. In his over thirty years of firefighting, there had been a few deadly fires in the past, but nothing as gruesome as this one.

Bill was thinking about the double homicide and arson fire in a home here in town a number of years ago. Not too far from his house, as a matter of fact. Bill remembered he was working on the laundry when the page went out for a structure fire, at an address only two doors down from his. Running to the house he found a neighbor trying to kick in the door, saying that he thought the man and his wife were still inside. Where the neighbor had already broken out the window in the door, dark black smoke was billowing out. Afraid the neighbor would cause a back draft and get badly burned by the fire if he kicked open the door, Bill yelled to the neighbor to get away from the door, right now. Thankfully the neighbor did what he was told, moving quickly out of the way. By then the fire chief had arrived and then the fire engines started arriving.

Bill ran to the engine that had just arrived at the alley side of the burning house, and quickly dressed into his turnouts. He briefly had trouble with his airmask, which meant he lagged behind the first team going into the burning structure. Fixing the airmask problem, he grabbed a second hose line and jumped in behind the first team. He worked to extinguish the fire burning in the library, then started opening windows to get the hot gases and smoke out of the house. The first team stumbled upon the bodies, while Bill and a couple of volunteers finished with the search of the rest of the house. Bill helped drag both bodies out of the bedroom and into the living room where they could be checked and legally pronounced dead. It was discovered they had been stabbed. The perpetrator had set fires throughout the house in an attempt to destroy the evidence. Bill and a few of the interior firefighters had found rolled up newspaper strung along the floor, and realized this was the killer's method of getting the fires to spread. Most of the set fires burned themselves out, with only the fire set in the library extending and filling the house with thick black smoke. The bodies were not burned, unlike this morning's tragedy. Years later this homicide had still not been solved.

Or there was the semi truck a few years ago, where Bill and another volunteer were trying to put out the fiery cab of a semi truck that had careened off the highway and down a steep hillside of boulders and trees. Bill remembered his fellow volunteer telling him that the object leaning out of the broken windshield with flames roaring all around it looked like the head and part of an upper torso of a body. With both powerful headlamps shining on the suspicious object, Bill and the other volunteer confirmed it was, unfortunately, a body. Bill remembered the semi truck and trailer, precariously balanced on top of a rock slide, was moving a little while he and his fellow firefighter tackled the flames shooting out of both the cab and trailer. The fire was finally extinguished, but the body remained in the burned out cab until the truck and trailer were secured by a crane and tow truck. Yep, you don't easily forget those situations of tragedy.

This morning's fire was the stuff you would maybe expect in the big city, but not here in rural small town USA. An accidental deadly fire is one thing, but a purposely set deadly fire is a whole different situation.

While drinking his coffee, Bill was talking to himself, something he did a lot of since he had no one to share his home with. After about two years of marriage and no child, Bill's wife Armida had had enough of Bill's being gone so much, working on fires around the western United States.

Bill longingly remembered how he and Armida met, many years ago. It was on a large wildfire in eastern Montana. Armida was working in the mobile kitchen for a catering service supplying the firefighters with cooked meals. Bill and his fellow crew members had been working on a remote section of the fireline, spending a couple of nights out in a spike camp close to the fireline. The Incident Command team decided to move Bill's crew to a different section of the fire, which was closer to the main camp. So that first evening at the main camp, Bill was standing in line waiting to be served with dinner after a long day on the fire line. He stunk, was tired and filthy, but so was the rest of his crew, and most everyone else coming in off the fire line. Imagine taking a chunk of charcoal and streaking your face and clothes with it. This is what Bill and most of the firefighters coming off the line looked like. And stink, well, Bill was ripe with days of not showering. So the change of venue to the main camp was hopefully going to get Bill and his fellow firefighters a chance for good food and a shower.

A beautiful young blonde woman was spooning mashed potatoes onto the meal trays as the firefighters walked by the open window of the serving trailer. Bill looked up into the young woman's green eyes and felt like a deer caught in the headlights. From the interior lighting of the serving trailer, Bill could see a beautiful olive toned face framed by gorgeous blonde hair. After a bit, Bill's squad boss finally poked him in the back with his dinner tray and said jokingly, "Come on lover boy, move the damn line. We're starving here!"

Later that same evening, while Bill was finishing his welcomed dinner and nearly falling asleep into his plate, the same beautiful woman walked by bussing the tables. She asked Bill if there was anything else he needed. He had trouble finding his voice, but finally said no. He thanked her, and told her his name was Bill. She said it was nice to meet him, and said her name was Armida. As he was leaving the mess tent, he told Armida it was very nice to have met her, and to have a good night. The next evening was a repeat of that first evening, except Bill asked if Armida could join him for a short time at the table.

For the next couple of days, Bill looked forward to their short visits in the mess tent. Unfortunately for Bill, the fire was contained and the need for Bill's hot shot crew was elsewhere. Bill found Armida and explained that his crew was being demobbed and heading to another fire. They were both disappointed, but they exchanged contact information in hopes this short term friendship would grow. During the trip to the next fire, Bill took a bunch of good natured ribbing from his fellow crew members. He just smiled, knowing his buddies were jealous that he found such a gorgeous young woman in the middle of nowhere. When Bill got home from another fire assignment, he found a letter from Armida, and their love grew. Curious as to the name Armida, Bill researched the internet and found that Armida meant Enchantress. Bill thought the name sure fit, for Armida was definitely enchanting to be with. So Bill started calling Armida his Enchantress.

After the fire season had ended for most of the country, both Armida and Bill had more free time to get together. They spent the winter together as much as possible, and Bill learned that Armida had run away from her family. Armida told Bill her family was a mess. Her mother died before Armida had turned two years old, and she and her older brother were raised by a mean and uncaring step mom. Her father was so immersed in his business that he never had time for the children. As she grew older, she started getting suspicious that her family was involved in things that she considered to be very wrong. She and her brother, Marino, spent a lot of time talking, and they both felt the same way. Armida and her brother were very close, especially since their father and step mother treated them like they were a burden. As the two grew into their early teens, they thought about their mother's death and the unanswered questions. No one seemed willing to talk about how their mother had died. As often happens, the lack of any information can lead to wild notions in trying to fill in the blanks. The siblings were left to guess on how their mother died, and the way the subject was immediately changed whenever Armida or Marino brought it up left them to think the worst; that someone killed her.

Their father had quickly remarried after their mom's death, and his high maintenance, trophy wife wanted nothing to do with Armida or Marino, especially since they were not her children. So Armida and her brother grew close, and pretty much raised themselves. Their father desperately wanted Marino to become involved in the family business, but Marino wanted nothing to do with it, sharing Armida's suspicions that the family business was dirty.

Armida was growing into a gorgeous teenager, a couple of years from becoming an adult. One day, Armida was told by her stepmother to serve the old man that kept coming to visit every Sunday afternoon. Her step mother told her to make sure he was comfortable, and had plenty to eat and drink and to give him whatever he wanted. When Armida told her stepmother that she didn't like being fondled, or to have the old man's boney, age spotted hands freely roam her body, the stepmother told Armida she could not refuse the old man. Armida discovered that her father and stepmother had plans for her marrying into another 'family' to tie the families' operations together. The old man was the future husband for her. Armida made it clear she would die before that would happen. Of course, that only earned her a hard slap from her stepmother and a stern warning from her father. After all, she was his daughter, living in his house, and his to command.

Marino had his own problems as well. Once their father found out that Armida's brother was gay, the brother was disowned and their father sent him away to finish life somewhere else. Marino was old enough to be on his own, but he hated to leave Armida alone in that house. He could also feel that Father and Step Mother had plans for Armida that were not in Armida's best interest. But Marino was kicked out and had to make do. He found a place that he and his partner could live in, and secretly got word to Armida that she was welcome anytime.

Bill was an avid listener, but he had to reign in his emotions of hate at what his beloved Armida had to go through. With Bill's arms around her, holding her tight to him, Armida found the courage to continue telling her story. Her life was going downhill, made miserable by her family situation. She had lived in her dad's huge house, with a stepmother that had no interest in her, her brother kicked out, and she was being groomed for a wedding of convenience to an old guy more than three times her age. She was living under the pal of a family she thought dirty, corrupt, lawless, and many other terms she could conjure up for something she hated. She got into serious trouble, trying to make sense of her life, and ended up trying drugs, alcohol, and sex to see if she could find a happy place where she felt she belonged. After calling in some markers with the local police, and getting them to look the other way regarding Armida's exploits, Armida's father sent her away to a rehab center. When she had finished her stay at the center, she headed not to her father's house, but to be with her brother Marino.

Armida moved in with her brother and his partner, and started working a job as a waitress in a swanky club in New York where Marino worked. The money was very good, but the living arrangements were less than desirable, having to share an apartment with her brother and his lover. And the climate at the club was threatening to bring her back into her drug, drunk, and sex days. She was proud that she, with help, had managed to disassociate herself from the downhill run her life was going, giving up the drugs and drinking and being much more careful with the sex. She didn't need or want that dark segment of her life back.

Needing to get out on her own, Armida watched the want ads, hoping to find an interesting job somewhere other than where she was. Although an ad for a server and kitchen help did not interest her, she happened to see the catering company requiring the employee was based in New Mexico, and the job required extensive traveling. New Mexico was a long ways from New Jersey, and she wanted to get far away from her father and his affairs. After a phone call to the Human Resources division, she was left intrigued with what she learned. Armida anxiously applied on line, and after a week had gone by, called the company to check on the status of the application. The lady in charge of hiring was out, so Armida had to wait for the weekend to go by. Finally, Monday afternoon the phone call Armida was hoping for happened, and Armida was offered the job.

Her brother hated to see her go, especially so far away, but he understood her need to move on, and get far away from their family. He helped her get a car and pack up for the long drive. He even took time off work to go with her, sharing the driving time and enjoying the time together. The long drive was fun, as Armida remembered it. They talked a lot, about their family, about their mother and how they missed her, although they could hardly remember the brief moments they had shared with her before s was gone. They arrived in Albuquerque, found the company offices, ar found a decent apartment for Armida. Her brother helped her unpack and after making sure she was fine, Armida's brother flew back to his lif in New York. Armida started her adventure, which three years later lead her to bump in to Bill.

The winter of learning about each other gradually metamorphosed into a gorgeous spring, with greens and brilliant colors replacing drab grays and whites. It was quick, but Bill proposed and Armida accepted, each wanting to spend their lives together. They ended up getting married as the spring flowers were blooming. Bill could remember how gorgeous Armida looked in her wedding gown. It was a time of tremendous joy. It was a time when the two love birds felt the world was theirs for the taking.

A couple of years later, after coming home from a two week tour of duty on a remote fire in Colorado, Bill found Armida and all her stuff gone. On the kitchen table were divorce papers, all filled in and ready for his signature. A letter was left with the divorce papers threatening Bill if he should try to contact Armida in any way. There was nothing from Armida, nothing at all. The papers were all courtesy of some law firm back east, one of those with a bunch of last names for a company name. He did not expect Armida to run to her father's house, so he called her brother Marino to see if he knew where she went. Marino did not know anything about the situation, and became as worried as Bill. Marino warned Bill not to call his father's house, that he would see what he could find out. Out of frustration, Bill called Armida's family house anyway, and found out why Marino warned him not to call. His call to Armida's family was answered by a secretary, who after finding out it was Bill calling, switched the call to someone named Elmo. Elmo, Bill remembered from one of Armida's stories, was the head 'family' hitman, and mean as a snake. Elmo emphatically told Bill he had made a big mistake in calling, and he will suffer the consequences of not abiding by the lawyer's letter. Bill slammed the phone down, and when he stopped shaking from anger and fear, wondered how Elmo knew about the lawyer's letter. A few days later, Bill was visited in the morning by a vicious looking man, introducing himself as Elmo. Elmo told Bill this was his lucky day. "I was going to kill you, but I was told not to, this time. But you had better hope there is not going to be a next time, or you will be on the wrong side of the grass."

Bill was told he will discontinue all efforts to find Armida, and forget he ever knew her. "Bill, if not, I will be back and before you leave this world, you will wish you had never been born. Capisce? Now sign the goddamn papers."

Of Armida's family, Bill only met her brother, who was gracious enough to come to the wedding and give the gorgeous bride away. Bill had liked Armida's brother right off, and Marino being there for the wedding gave Armida a boost. Bill had contacted Marino to tell him of the scary visitor, and more importantly to ask if him if he heard anything of Armida. Marino felt sorry for Bill and was worried over Armida, but warned Bill there was nothing they could do. The 'family' is dangerous to go up against, he told Bill. It seemed everything was designed to keep Bill from finding Armida. Even Marino disappeared, his phone number disconnected. After awhile, Bill reluctantly gave up on trying to find Armida. Years later it still hurt, and it still affected his few relationships with other women. So he was still single, and right now wishing he had Armida in front of him. Not only would the site of her breath taking beauty bring happiness, more importantly, she had been a ready and willing listener that wasn't afraid to say what she thought. It was times like this when being alone was very lonely.

Chapter 9

With the evidence locked up and an idea of the origin and cause, Amrit needed to get on with the interviews to see if his theory about the cause and origin of the fire was supported. Thanks to Bev's preliminary work during the fire, Amrit had pictures and a partial list of names of the people watching the fire from the sidelines. Sitting down with Bev and Walt, Amrit got addresses to go with the names, and both Bev and Amrit headed out to start the interviews, while Walt worked on the missing person aspect. The first interviewee, one of the neighbors, invited Bev and Amrit into his home. Amrit, having told his plan to Bev before they arrived, explained the interview procedure and then read the Miranda rights to the interviewee. After hearing the Miranda rights, the neighbor got scared and defensive, but both Bev and Amrit calmed him down by explaining again what the interview was for and that the reading of the Miranda rights was a requirement in a criminal situation, and that he was not considered a suspect. Having calmed the neighbor, the interview proceeded with Bev operating the tape recorder and Amrit asking the questions.

The neighbor said he was unaware there was a fire next door until he heard shouting, waking him up to see flashing red lights against his walls. By the time he dressed and ran out to see what was going on, the fire attack was already in operation. His estimate of the time was pretty close to what the Fire Department report showed. Amrit asked the neighbor if he had been in the Symsin's house before, and the neighbor said he had visited numerous times with Roger, the man of the house next door. The lady of the house was named Jill, and they talked for short periods of time. Amrit wanted to know about the arrangement of appliances and furniture, especially in the back of the house. The neighbor had been in the kitchen only twice, but remembered a couple of things. Otherwise he had been in the living room the rest of the visits. What he mentioned as to items in the living room and their general location seemed to coincide with what Amrit had mapped out. From the answers to a few questions, Amrit was able to see that Roger and Jill were somewhat quiet, not socially active, but did have a few not so close friends. After thanking the neighbor, Amrit and Bev moved on.

The next interview started the same way, but the couple calmed down after the interview reason was presented a second time. This couple lived across the back alley from the burnt house, and the man said he was awakened by a strange noise, like a door being slammed. He quickly checked his house, and not finding anything amiss, he happened to glance out the window toward the backyard, toward Roger's house. He could see a reddish glow, dancing, at the back door. As he was trying to focus his sleepy eyes, there was a flash and the reddish glow grew quickly. He heard a whoosh sound shortly after. After yelling for his wife to call 911 to report the neighbor's house on fire, he quickly ran to the back door of the neighbor's house but couldn't get close due to the heat. He said he ran around the side to the front door and beat on the door, but there was no answer. Afraid to try and break down the door, he was getting ready to find a window to break when Bev arrived in her police car. When asked if he remembered what the inside looked like, he couldn't help because he had only been inside one time, and that was a while ago.

Amrit was getting tired, like everyone else that had been awakened at some god awful time early in the morning. He didn't think he could make the four and a half hour drive back to his office, so he spent the night in a motel room. He appreciated Frank's offer of sitting in on the stress management session that evening at the fire station, but Amrit had had enough experience in these matters that he could handle the stress. Going over the list of things accomplished and yet to do, Amrit fell asleep. He would be heading back to his office early in the morning after a night's sleep.

Chapter 10

The next morning, a few of the volunteers, including Bill, made it out of bed but with many muscles and joints rebelling against the decision to move. Amrit, after checking in with Walt and gathering some of the evidence he had collected the day before, started on the hours long drive back to his office. The day was a start into getting back to normal, whatever normal meant.

Frank called a special meeting of the volunteers that evening, a day after the tragic fire. As the volunteers gathered in the meeting room of the fire station, Frank announced the reason for this special meeting. "Guys, yesterday's fire was one of those situations I was hoping we would never have to deal with. We are here to talk about yesterday's tragic fire. Before we start, there are a couple of things. First, remember that what is said here stays here. Second, I called in the County's stress management team and they will be listening in. Their job is to help us deal with what might be eating away inside of us. Tonight we are going to discuss what happened, just like we do on most fires. However, when it comes to dealing with the discussion surrounding the body, the stress team may want to ask a few questions, but they are here mainly to listen. After we finish our meeting, anyone who wishes to speak with the team or any member of the team are more than welcome, and you can use my office, or set up an appointment with the team later on. This team has been put together by the County to help first responders deal with tragic events.

"Instead of all of us being joe macho and holding everything inside, we have an opportunity to talk out what we may be feeling, and have some guidance in dealing with the stress caused by this tragic event. If I hear anyone making fun of this situation, especially if I hear of someone teasing another over this stress stuff, you will feel my wrath. Just because someone may want to take advantage of the services offered for free by this team, that doesn't mean that person is a weakling. As a matter of fact, that person is probably better off than those of us who think we are superman and impervious to the stress of a tragic death. So think about it. Let me introduce the stress management team working with us tonight."

With the introductions finished, Frank started with a typical after action discussion, with Bill drawing stuff on the white board, diagramming the scene as the first units arrived. The discussion moved along, driven by various input from the volunteers that had been on the scene. Through this discussion, each volunteer present got a better idea of the whole picture of the fire, rather than just the piece of the fire they may have participated in. And it was good for the few volunteers that hadn't been able to make it to the fire. The stress team listened in, getting an idea of the scene from the people who were thrown into it. The team consisted of a minister, a fire chief, an advanced EMT, a doctor, an emergency room nurse, a military veteran with the local National Guard, and a County Sheriff. These people, not necessarily from the same community, deal with death often and could better relate with the stress of a tragic event. So they were listening to the actions of the volunteers, jotting down notes regarding things each of the team members might want to interject when their turn came.

Other than a couple of snide comments that got the finger pointing and angry stare of Frank, the after action discussion went smoothly and the overall atmosphere was on the somber side. Stress team members asked a couple of questions just for clarification. The discussion on the fire wound down, and a few of the volunteers were talking about other topics in their own little groups, so Frank figured it was time to call the meeting finished. The leader of the stress team reiterated their role, their availability to sit down with any of the volunteers to assist in dealing with the situation and help them move on past it.

The team members made a couple of suggestions on how to deal with the tragedy as the volunteers play it back in their minds. The team leader knew Francis, since Francis had been part of the team in a few stress situations in the past. "If you would rather meet with Francis instead of one of us, that's fine. Francis is a member of our team, and I understand your chiefs have already talked with Francis, who is willing to assist. We are here to help, so put us to work!"

With that, the team leader handed out business cards with the contact information, making it easier for anyone to contact the team on their own and in private. Gathering around the refrigerator, the volunteers grabbed up beer or pop, and started in on local gossip, jokes, and the standard bantering that goes on after each training session. Back to normal, well not quite. The atmosphere of calm felt forced. One could still feel an uneasiness in the air, like innocence lost, something that once given up was never to be again.

Chapter 11

Having laid low and moved about the forest outside Prairie City for three days after the house fire, the arsonist decided it was time to put into effect the rest of the plan, then get out of this area and get back to big city civilization. Soon, the US Marshall's office would find out what happened to the couple under protection of the Department of Justice, and all hell would break loose. The Burner wanted to be gone before that happened.

While Elmo stayed in his motel room, the Burner had spent time driving around the forest outside of town, looking for the perfect spot to set up the finale. In an attempt to self improve the skills at fire setting, the arsonist had been reading numerous books on arson fires, some true and some fictional. Some of the read materials included brief discussions of arson fires in the wildlands, stimulating the Burner's interest. With the knowledge gained from numerous set fires in the urban environment, the Burner tried to visualize getting a fire going in the wildland environment. This was new territory for the Burner. Based on some of the descriptions of fuel arrangement and types that the arsonist had read about, it took awhile, but the Burner finally found a spot that contained the necessary ingredients for a hopefully successful fire. So the Burner had the location, now to put the plan to work.

The plan was somewhat tricky. They had to get the body of the now dead Roger into his pickup. Then drive the pickup to the forest site, with the Burner following in the rented vehicle. While Elmo was getting Roger dumped into the seat of the pickup, the Burner would set up the fire. Then both would get back to the rented vehicle, and head to where Elmo left his rented vehicle. All this without being seen or stumbled upon. Thank goodness the Burner loved a challenge.

The Burner waited until night, then helped the hitman load Roger into the pickup. The arsonist lead Elmo, who was driving Roger's pickup, to the site where this final part of the overall plan was to take place. Driving to the forest location, the Burner was careful to keep a sharp lookout for any vehicles, especially a sheriff's pickup on patrol. At this early morning hour, chances are there was no one out driving around, but it paid to be cautious. The arsonist's luck was still holding, arriving to the forest clearing without incident. It was about 3:30 in the morning when most things human were very quiet. Having read that after 3:00 in the afternoon is when the wildland fuels are their driest and more ready to burn, the Burner fixed up a timer, a more elaborate system then the simple book of matches used at the old couple's house. Wanting this event to happen around twelve hours from now, the Burner adjusted the crafted timer accordingly.

Wanting to make sure that once the pickup caught fire, the fire would transition into the forest, the arsonist piled up plenty of fuel that was found lying around. The Burner then splashed the M4 fuel mix liberally around. The young arsonist had seen in the day light a series of trees with ladder fuels, branches that hung clear down to the ground. These ladder fuels would help the fire move up to the tree tops, helping the created fire grow quickly. So the Burner piled debris against a few nearby ladder trees and made sure there was an unbroken line of burnable material from the pickup to the ladder trees. A true pyromaniac, the Burner wanted a big fire, the bigger the better, one that would take awhile to put out. And for the very first attempt at a wildland fire, the arsonist wanted it to be spectacular. Too bad the Burner wouldn't be around to see the handy work, but another job was waiting back in the big city. Once the interior of the pickup cab had been splashed with the signature fuel mix, the Burner was satisfied all was ready. The Burner and Elmo headed back to Prairie City, where Elmo got into his hidden rental vehicle and left town. Before leaving town, the Burner figured it was time to get a quick breakfast after a hard night's work, then head back east.

Chapter 12

The café was nearly empty at this early hour of the morning, which was the Burner's preference. An older waitress, a motherly type with a name tag that said Dora, took the arsonist's order, and brought a cup of hot coffee. The Burner was impressed with how Dora handled the job, making every movement an efficient and waste free art of serving. Most of the places the arsonist had patronized back home were staffed by servers who did not know the meaning of serve. While waiting for the breakfast, the Burner glanced through the small table paper that listed local businesses and various public facilities, such as churches. The Burner noticed a listing for a Catholic Church, a St. Michael's. Checking the schedule once again, the Burner figured there was enough time to go to confession and get rid of the stain of sin before flying back east. Should make the trip home more enjoyable, thought the arsonist. The waitress brought the heaping plate of breakfast, and the famished Burner dug in with relish. The Burner had never had a country breakfast before. Wow, breakfast was huge. Damn, the meals in the big city were a heck of a lot smaller and a heck of a lot more money. After a few bites the arsonist also added that the meal was so much better tasting than that stuff in the big city. Maybe life in the smaller cities wasn't all bad after all.

Francis was holding an early morning confession in St. Michael's Catholic Church, trying to accommodate as many practicing Catholics as possible by varying the hours of the confessional. Abiding by the old style practice of confession, Fr. Francis was seated in the middle of a

51

three partitioned room, along one side of the inside of the Church. Two members of the Church could be kneeling on either side of Fr. Francis, each waiting in their little room, separated from the priest by a partition with a sliding window. This window between the penitent and the priest was specially screened, so when the window was open, neither the priest nor the penitent could be seen, just heard. This was to protect the anonymity of the penitent. The Church took confession very seriously, providing a system by which the penitent could securely bare his or her soul to God through the medium of the priest. The priest, or confessor, was bound by a Church decree of absolute secrecy, set back in 1682 by Church doctrine. The confessor cannot be compelled by law to divulge the contents of a confession, since the sacrament of penance is considered a sacred bond of trust. The Burner did not like the new style of confessional, where the priest and penitent sat face to face in a comfortable room, discussing the sinful nature of the penitent. So the young arsonist was hoping this church still practiced the old style confession.

Watching from the rental pickup, the arsonist kept on eye on St. Michael's Catholic Church, waiting to make sure no one was going into the church. The Burner had a little time before leaving for the airport, so might as well do the religious thing and be done with it. "The sooner the priest hears my confession, the sooner I get pardoned for my sins."

To the Burner, it was important to be pardoned, and felt the next job could not happen until being pardoned by God, through the intercession of the priest. So far the carefully laid out plans had worked like a charm, so the pyromaniac was going to confess and get the heck out of town, back to the big city life. The Burner ambled into the church, and swept the inside with trained eyes. No one was in the pews, and the confessional light above the priest's door was on, meaning he was still inside. Neither light above the doors on either side of the confessor's door was lit, meaning the confessionals were empty. So the arsonist walked over to the door on the left, closest to the doors at the back of the Church. Upon entering the confessional, the Burner knelt down and after hearing the window slide open, promptly recited the starting prayer of penance, one that the Burner had recited thousands of times over a lifetime as a Catholic. It was something left over from years of attending parochial schools and being forced to go to Sunday mass with the step mother. The Burner still followed the practice whenever possible. It was at the very least a cleansing of the soul.

"Bless me Father for I have sinned. My last confession was two months ago." And with a blessing and a welcoming prayer from Fr. Francis, the Burner unburdened the soul, at least part of it. The arsonist was sorry for using the Lord's name in vain, for continuing to have lewd thoughts, and for helping in the killing of two people recently. With that last statement, there was a period of silence from both the pyromaniac and Fr. Francis. Finally, Fr. Francis broke the abnormally long silence. "My child, you have asked God for forgiveness of your sins. Are you truly repentant?" "Yes, Father, I am. Even though I didn't kill them, I didn't stop the person who did."

"My child, I am sure God would want you to go to the authorities and explain your part in this tragic situation. And I am sure He would want you to promise to stay away from those who would kill, and to abide by any decision the authorities would make regarding your confession to them of this terrible tragedy. I am just an instrument of God, and your true penance needs to be between God and you. As an instrument of God, I would suggest you say three Rosaries, as a beginning to many prayers asking God to not only forgive but to guide you away from the path you are on. If you are in need of a Rosary, you will find some at the back of the Church, along with a booklet on the Mysteries and how to use the Rosary."

"Thank you Father, I have my own Rosary."

"Very good. Now I want you to pray the Our Father while I bless you."

After the prayers, Fr. Francis once again asked that this penitent on the other side of the window go to the authorities. "My child, go in peace now to serve the Lord."

"Thank you Father." As the Burner walked out of the confessional, feeling lightened by unburdening a part of the soul, the trained eyes scanned the inside of the Church once again, making sure no one was looking. In a hurry to leave, the arsonist promised to recite the Rosaries later. Driving away from the Church, the Burner checked the time, wanting very much to get out of this backwoods place. The Burner was anxious to get to a meeting with the benefactor, regarding a next assignment. It was very dangerous to get the employer upset.

Chapter 13

It had been just four days since the fatal house fire, and Bill was out checking on the underground sprinkler system on this hot and dry summer afternoon. The small par three golf course, where he was the superintendent of the greens, was looking a little on the dry side. It was a struggle trying to keep the fairways looking nice and green. Not only was the summer dryness a factor, but some of the Arnold Palmer wannabes felt it was beneath their dignity to stoop to repair their divots, leaving browning holes in the fairway. This meant Bill had to spend time trying to fix pieces of the fairway that looked like small land mines had gone off.

Bill was in his favorite recurring day dream, getting to the part where he was just getting ready to undo the tie on the teeny tiny bikini practically painted onto a well endowed blonde beach beauty, kissed by the sun to a nice light bronze. Beep, beep, beep, beep and his beach babe day dream was instantly shattered. "Prairie Fire, respond to approximately milepost 9 on Lookout Road for a possible wildland fire."

As Bill sprinted to his pickup, the page was repeated. As soon as the Dispatcher finished the second page, Bill used his pager/radio to notify the Dispatcher that he was responding. With emergency flashers turned on, he drove his pickup truck quickly to the fire station. Frank was out of town on a delivery, so Bill was to be in charge of the Prairie Fire resources. It was about 4:30 in the afternoon, a time when wildfires get a good start and can move rapidly until dark.

Arriving at the station, there was just one other volunteer so far, and

54

she had rural engine 1 warming up. As two other volunteers ran into the station, Bill yelled for one of them to hop in with him. Bill told the other volunteer to warm up rural engine 2 and as soon as two more volunteers show up, head to the fire. As Sue, sitting behind the steering wheel of engine 1, flips the siren and heads out of the station, Bill calls George on the radio and asks him to stay in town in case there is a fire in town. Bill radioed Dispatch that engine 1 is responding with three on board as the engine was heading down main street going toward the fire.

As engine 1 was approaching the edge of town, Bill could see smoke lifting into the sky from about where the location was given. "Dispatch, this is 672."

"Go ahead 672."

"Dispatch, has the Forest Service been notified of this fire?"

"672, the Multiagency Dispatch has been notified."

"Dispatch, this is 672. I copy. Thanks, and 672 is switching to tac 1 frequency."

"672, Dispatch copies. 1635."

Switching to the tac 1 frequency, Bill contacted the Multiagency Dispatch Center to let them know he was responding. This fire was outside of the District, so this was a mutual aid response. Bill didn't want to assume that communications were working as they should, since there had been a few instances in the past where the communication between both Dispatch offices broke down. Bill was remembering the old saying: 'assume' stands for making an *ass* out of *you* and *me*. As Bill watched the developing smoke column coming from the location they were headed to, he thought this is not good, this fire looks like it wants to move.

About eight minutes after leaving the station, engine 1 was entering the forest, leaving the flat terrain of the prairie for the more rugged terrain of the forest. "672, this is Agency Dispatch."

"Agency Dispatch, this is Prairie 672 with engine 1."

"672, this is Agency Dispatch. We have helicopter Alpha Tango 49 Romeo in bound with an eta of 10, and IDL engine 5467 with an eta of 18 minutes. Forest Service engines 331 and 534 have etas of approximately 20."

"Agency Dispatch, this is 672. Copy that. I will be on scene in about 3 minutes and will give you an update."

"Agency Dispatch copies you will be on scene in 3. KOD837."

Rounding a bend in the gravel road, all three firefighters on board engine 1 spotted the dark smoke and some orange flames up ahead. Getting as close as they dare, Bill radioed the Sheriff Dispatcher that engine 1 was on scene. After confirmation from the Dispatcher, Bill radioed Agency Dispatch. "Agency Dispatch, this is 672."

"672, this is Agency Dispatch, go ahead."

"Agency Dispatch, we have a fire burning both sides of Lookout Road. Winds are light, out of the southwest. A few individual trees are torching, but the fire is still on the ground at this time. I will attempt to scout and report back."

"Prairie 672, copied fire is on the ground, winds light and out of the southwest, some tree torching, and you will try to scout the fire."

"Agency Dispatch, 10-4, 672 clear."

The billowing smoke and ash nearly obscured the road, so Bill had Sue hold engine 1 at their location on the east flank of the fire. Bill told Sue and the other volunteer to run out an attack line, and to be heads up. There was a threat of spot fires, as well as the fire below the road making another run. He didn't want them going below the road more than fifty feet, and he made sure both had on their wildland gear. Each had dressed into fire resistant pants and shirt, finishing off with boots, hard hat, gloves, and a fire shelter. Dressed in his wildland gear as well, Bill took off walking the road through the swirling smoke and ash. Sue made sure the pump was running, and her fellow volunteer was in control of the nozzle. She not only ran the pump, but was also set up as a lookout, ready to yell if the fire hooked under the volunteer working the nozzle. Through their annual wildland training, the volunteers recognized some of the age old ten standard fire fighting orders and the eighteen watch out situations. The ninth Watch Out was building line downhill with the fire below you. And Firefighting Order number five, post a lookout when there is danger. Bill wanted to make sure he and his crew made it home when the fire was out. Each of the firefighting orders and watch out situations were made because someone did not make it home.

Bill wanted to check the road to see if it was driveable, as well as find out if he could see any better from the other side of the fire. Since he would only have five volunteers beside himself, he would be limited in what could be done initially. Unfortunately, this fire was not like fighting a grass fire, where you could do a sneak attack, driving the engine into the burned area and attack the flames from inside. This fire in the forest required an assault from outside of the fire, which was hard on the resources. You couldn't sneak up on it from inside.

The walk through the thick smoke seemed like it took forever until he broke into fresh air and blue sky at the west side of the fire. After sucking in some fresh air, Bill heard engine 2 radio that they had just arrived. Bill told them to carefully head through the smoke and ash and meet him on the other side of the fire. Monitoring the tac 1 radio frequency, Bill heard the helicopter calling him. "Alpha Tango 49 Romeo, this is 672, go ahead."

"672, this is Alpha Tango 49 Romeo. We are scouting your fire. Looks like it is about 7 acres, threatening to move into a thicker stand of trees to the northeast. I have two air tankers in bound in 6 minutes. What are your plans?"

"Alpha Tango 49 Romeo, this is 672. I have engine 1 protecting the road on the east side while engine 2 is just starting a direct attack on the west flank below the road. You have a better view of the fire than I do. What do you recommend?"

"672, Alpha Tango 49 Romeo copied. I suggest the air tankers start hitting the head then work the flanks."

"Alpha Tango 49 Romeo, 672 copies. Sounds good to me."

"672, Alpha Tango 49 Romeo copies. We will start hitting the head as soon as the tankers get here. Be aware there is something producing a very dark black smoke column coming from the middle of the fire, southeast of your location. I am unable to identify what is burning, but I will continue to check on it as best I can."

"Alpha Tango 49 Romeo, 672 copied. I'll work my way to that area as soon as I can and check it out."

"672, Alpha Tango 49 Romeo copied. Just flying over the east flank and I can see engine 5467 is almost to your engine 1."

Bill acknowledged the transmission from the helicopter, and radioed engine 5467 to stage alongside engine 1 and wait for him. Making sure engine 2 was progressing along the west flank, Bill walked back to engine 1 to meet with engine 5467.

The engine foreman on 5467 was rated as a type 3 incident commander, a higher designation then that of Bill's. Under the auspices of the National

Wildfire Coordinating Group (NWCG), resources utilized in fighting wildfires are designated a type number. This type number signifies the capabilities of the resource. The lower the number the more capability the resource has. And the type number is not just easily handed out. Personnel have to go through training and testing as well as on-the-fire evaluation before being given the type designation printed on a wallet card. In the old days this card was called a red card, and it was actually red. Back when Bill first started fighting wildfires, he was given a red card listing the qualifications he had trained and been approved for.

Now a days the card is no longer red and is referred to as the quals card. Equipment had to go through inspections and meet certain minimum standards before being assigned a type designation as well. This effort was part of the Incident Command System, which was developed to better streamline the overwhelming logistical and tactical efforts in fighting a wildfire. For the IC, the incident commander, the ordering of resources becomes a little easier through this system. For example, if a wildfire is threatening structures, the IC may want to order type 1 and type 2 engines, which are the engines you would find in the cities fighting structure fires. Or the IC could order type 3 and type 4 engines which are wildland engines that can switch between structure protection and wildfire work. The entire command structure is given a designation as well. A type 1 Incident Team is the one called in to manage the most challenging fire, while a type 4 or 5 Incident Team is usually found on small, simple fires. In many cases, the type 4 or 5 Incident Commander is an Engine Boss or Fire Chief, and probably is the entire command structure.

So after the quick briefing presented by Bill, Bill turned over command of the fire to the engine foreman, a young man named Swartz. Swartz turned over the job of engine foreman to his assistant, then radioed to Interagency Dispatch that he was taking over the command of the fire. After Dispatch acknowledged the change in command, Swartz radioed Alpha Tango 49 Romeo and asked if he could meet, and get an aerial view of the fire. Alpha Tango 49 Romeo was talking with the two single engine air tankers (SEATs), both having just entered the airspace of the fire. The spotter on board the helicopter contacted Swartz, advising him that the SEATs are over head and he was recommending two drops on the north flank, at the head of the fire. Swartz thought that was a good idea, and to let him know when they could pick him up. Engine 5467 was assigned to assist engine 1 at this time, working the lower east flank and protecting the road. Forest Service engines 331 and 534 had just arrived and the IC had them work from the road at engine 1's location and head uphill toward the head of the fire.

As soon as the SEATs finished their retardant drops, the helicopter was able to rendezvous with Swartz, finding a workable landing spot not far from the west side of the fire. While observing the fire from above, the IC was able to get a better perspective and estimate the fire had grown to about twelve acres. He radioed Interagency Dispatch, providing them with an update on status, and then a request for more resources. He wanted three more type 6 engines and a type 2 hand crew, which consists of twenty trained firefighters versed in hacking out fireline. If the fire moves into the thick timber, they may need a type 1 crew, which consists of twenty, more highly trained firefighters that are normally placed into the worst fire situations. He also asked for a type 2 helicopter for water drops, and that the SEAT retardant drops continue. The helicopter he was riding in at the moment will convert to water dropping mode as soon as the recon is finished and the helitack crew hooks up the water bucket to the underside of the helicopter. Dispatch acknowledged the request, and told Swartz that another Department of Lands engine, number 6813, and Forest Service engine 531, have an eta of 15 minutes, and that a brush crew of six firefighters is on the way to augment the engine crews, eta of 20 minutes. The type 2 hand crew was still over an hour away.

After the recon flight, while heading back to the helibase at the airport, the pilot was looking for a water source that would be accessible by helicopter. Having found a fairly good sized pond in an open field just a few air miles from the fire, the pilot radioed Interagency Dispatch, gave the Dispatcher the location, and asked if they could get the landowner's permission to use the pond. While the helicopter was landing at the air center to hook up the water bucket, the MultiAgency Dispatch office, buzzing with activity, found in the preplan folder of this area done a few years ago that the landowner had signed a blanket permission to use the pond as necessary. Having radioed back the ok to use, the helicopter took off and headed to the pond. In the meantime, an air attack plane joined in the battle, flying into the airspace over the fire just as the two SEATS were arriving for their second drop. Air attack contacted the IC to let him know they were over head, and ask what they can do for him. The IC explained his concern for the northeast section, and to concentrate air resources in that area for now. With marching orders received, air attack took over the guiding of the SEATs, and helicopter Alpha Tango 49 Romeo began dropping water, trying to slow the fire growth.

Engines 6813 and 531 arrived on scene, and the IC promptly moved them to join engine 2 on the cooler west side. The plan was to have both engine crews work the up hill side of the road and flank around to the head of the fire. This was to be a pinching attack, where engines 331 and 534 on the east side, and engines 6813 and 531 on the west side were tied into the road and working north building a quick hand line. Engines 1 and 5467 continued to work the east flank below the road while engine 2 worked the cooler west flank below the road.

Chapter 14

Bill and Swartz were discussing the strategy and efforts of the attack when Forest Service engine 412 arrived. Remembering the black smoke concern earlier, and now that the area of that black smoke was cooler, Swartz had engine 412 take over for engine 1, and engine 1 was to head to that location, taking the old logging road as best they can. In the meantime, Bill suggested to Swartz that the Department's water tender could be available to refill the engines. His two engines were getting low on water, and expected the other engines would soon be in similar status. Swartz mentioned his concern to Bill that he didn't want to drain all of Prairie Fire's resources by requesting their water tender, which would be the closet available tender. Bill said they had one more attack engine on standby, plus they still had two structure engines to handle any structure fire. He suggested to the IC that they could provide the tender, and could extend the use as long as needed, but he would need to release at least engine 2 as soon as he felt comfortable in doing so. Swartz told Bill to make it happen, and he radioed Interagency Dispatch regarding the additional request, and that the water tender is being supplied by Prairie Fire. In the meantime, Bill asked his Dispatch to tone out Prairie Fire and announce the need for the water tender, with two volunteers on board. In less than three minutes, the water tender was headed out the station door, on its way to the fire.

Engine 1 had found the entrance to the old logging road that the pilot of Alpha Tango 49 Romeo thought might lead to whatever was giving off that very dark smoke. Having found a safe place to park, Bill and the volunteer took off walking the old road while Sue stayed with the engine. After about a ten minute hike along the crude road following tire tracks left in the dust, and clearing burning debris from the road, the two came upon something still putting out black smoke. As they approached, they could make out the outline of a pickup truck. It was still hot, so they could not get close enough to look inside. The tires were still burning, the rubber burning away from the metal wheels. It was hard to determine the type of pickup, and the license plates had either been removed or melted. Having radioed the IC with the find, Bill radioed Sue to bring the engine.

The water tender arrived to top off the engines, and the type 2 hand crew had just reached the incident. Engine 1 arrived to the location of the burnt pickup, and Bill explained to Sue and the nozzleman what they were tasked to do. Sue switched the attack engine to foam and the nozzleman foamed the little bit of the pickup still burning, such as the tires and some of the interior. As Bill looked in, he saw a strange lump on what used to be the front seat, but was now just a bunch of metal coils. Remembering the body from the house fire a few days ago, he said to himself 'this better not be another one'. Using a pike pole from off the engine, Bill carefully poked around the lump. "Damn it, it looks like another burn victim. What the hell is going on?"

Bill radioed the IC, telling him the fire in the pickup was out but there was a code black. Swartz asked Bill to go ahead and take care of doing what was necessary, figuring Bill was more trained to handle this sort of thing. Bill radioed Dispatch and asked for a Deputy to respond to his location, that there was a code black. Bill asked Sue and the nozzleman if they were okay with the situation, if they needed to leave the gruesome scene. If that charred body had been someone they knew, they may have needed to leave before being overcome by the tragedy. Not recognizing the burnt pickup, and not knowing who it was that was burned beyond recognition in the pickup, helped a little. So both agreed to stay and guard the area while Bill walked out to catch up with Swartz. By the time Bill caught up to Swartz to briefly explain the situation with the pickup and the body found, the Deputy arrived. The Deputy was driving a four wheel drive pickup, so Bill caught a ride with the Deputy to the scene of the pickup truck fire.

The Deputy started taking pictures and jotting down notes as soon as they arrived alongside engine 1, and near the burned out pickup. Careful to leave as few tracks as possible, the Deputy followed the same narrow path to the pickup as had Bill. Thanks to the fire, there probably wasn't much evidence to find, but it was best to leave the area intact with the least amount of disturbance as possible. Swartz radioed Bill that the Forest Service investigator arrived, and that she will work her way over to join Bill at the pickup location. Both Bill and the Deputy felt this situation was not an accident, and wanted someone with better training then they have to look over this scene. Bill had a hunch regarding the pickup and victim. He talked with IC Swartz about his theory, and then called Dispatch and asked the Dispatcher if she could contact Amrit, the fire investigator, and send him to the scene. Sounds like this incident will be investigated to death, but Bill recognized that each investigator had an expertise that hopefully, when put together, will shed some light as to the four w's: who, what, why, when.

Beth, the Forest Service investigator, arrived to the pickup location after getting directions from Bill on the radio. Bill was impressed by Beth's immediate professionalism, and by her stature as she stood next to him and the Deputy. Beth was a tall, well developed woman of African American decent. Bill guessed she was in her forties, and from her cute southern drawl, she must have been from the southeast, like maybe Georgia or South Carolina. They had made their introductions and Bill led Beth to the pickup, warning her first that it was not a pretty sight. Beth mentioned she had been on a couple of fatality fires, so she expected she would be seeing nothing new or shocking. Bill mentioned to Beth that he asked that Amrit, a fire investigator, come to the scene and assist. "Beth, I have a suspicion that this may be related to an incident that happened a few days ago. Amrit came in to start that investigation, and if my feelings are correct, this may tie into that incident. I hope that is not going to be a problem for you."

Beth said she welcomed Amrit's expertise. She told Bill she had meet Amrit at an arson investigators conference a couple of years ago, and she thought they could work together. She took some pictures and notes, then walked around the perimeter, carefully watching for signs of fire direction and intensity. Her main interest was to determine where the fire started, and then hopefully how. That information could then be tied into the investigation of the death of whoever was in the pickup. Did the fire originate from the pickup or did the forest fire burn the pickup? When Amrit arrives, they will hopefully be able to find out how the pickup caught fire. As to the identity of the body, that will be left up to the medical examiner.

Chapter 15

Bill was remembering that just yesterday they had finally heard from the medical examiner handling the identification of the remains removed from the deadly house fire a few days ago. It turned out that the body was confirmed as that of an older female, but there was a strange block on the records when trying to determine identity. When the request was made for dental record comparison, the request came back from the FBI as inconclusive. The few pieces of good evidence gathered at the house were leading to a big fat zero. The pressure was on the law enforcement people to get a positive id. The fire investigator and medical examiner had come up with arson and murder, with lots of supportive documentation. Everyone wanted to get the person responsible. However, with what seemed to be a block on the records, the task was going to be near impossible. No one yet knew for sure who the victim was from the house fire. If the general consensus was correct, that the victim was the female half of the older couple, then where was the male? What they knew about the older couple wouldn't fill the head of a pin. No one knew the why of this whole mess, and at this rate no one would.

Over a cup of coffee just yesterday morning with Bev, Bill heard Bev's frustration regarding the problems both hers and Liz's Departments had in trying to learn what they could about the older couple. To Bev, it seemed the more this event was dug into, the more they were losing ground instead of gaining. Neither could believe the idea they both came up with, but it almost seemed that someone high up was hiding something.

Chapter 16

The humans were gaining on this wildfire, so Swartz contacted Bill and told him he could release engine 2. Swartz would prefer to keep the water tender working on supplying the engines with water. He also would like to keep Bill and engine 1 on scene at the pickup truck, guarding and working with the investigators.

"Swartz, 672 copies that engine 2 is released, water tender is to continue, and myself and engine 1 will stay at this location." With that acknowledgement out of the way, Bill checked to make sure both volunteers were able to stay, that they didn't have commitments they needed to keep. Both said they were fine, nothing that can't be dealt with later on. Bill had the crew of engine 1 catch up with the water tender and refill. Once the tank was full, engine 1 returned to the burned out pickup and settled in to wait with the Deputy, Beth, and Bill for Amrit and the State Police investigator.

Dusk turned to dark, and the ever artful Supreme Being splattered the black sky with billions of white blinking dots that could be seen peeking through the swirling smoke. Moving his eyes from the heavens to the ground, Bill thought it looked like a city of red flickering lights. There were thousands of small pockets of flame of all different sizes scattered around him. In the fire's rush to grow, it whipped through the flashy fuels, leaving the bigger materials for later. The fire's rush had been stopped by a combination of a rise in humidity and the work of the firefighters, both on the ground and in the air. So now it was time for the fire to hunker down and continue to survive by feasting on the slower burning bigger fuels it had left in its rush to grow.

Bill radioed Swartz and asked if there were extra MREs (meals ready to eat) for himself, his two volunteers, and the deputy. Beth kept an extra MRE in her gear bag, which was with her wherever she went. Swartz said there were extra MREs on engine 5467. Bill had Sue and the other volunteer take engine 1 over to meet up with 5467 and grab four boxed MREs. Getting back to the burnt pickup, Sue distributed the MRE boxes to the deputy and Bill, while the volunteer had his opened and already attacking the individually packaged parts of the meal. It wasn't fancy cuisine, but the entrees warmed up tasted not bad.

Both Amrit and the State Police investigator showed up just as everyone was finishing their MREs. It was fortunate Amrit was working a case only a couple of hours away. Amrit and Liz had met up at the Prairie City Police station, then drove out together to the fire's location. They met with Swartz first, who gave them a brief overview of the fire, then gave them directions to Bill and the burnt pickup truck. With the arrival of Amrit and Liz, Bill had Sue fire up the generator that powers the scene lighting system on engine 1. Since the investigators were arriving in the dark, Beth's photos helped the team get a better idea of the area as it looked in daylight. With the powerful lighting system from engine 1, the area was workable. "Liz, Amrit, welcome back, although I apologize for the reason you are here," Bill said. "Looks like we have another fire fatality on our hands. We have tried to protect the area as best as possible, and at least we have been the only ones in this area. So hopefully the fire hasn't eliminated all of the clues."

Amrit said he would start a walk around with Liz and Beth, doing his preliminary before getting into a more detailed investigation. Liz said, "Damn, Bill, what's going on in your community-two fire deaths in a few days."

Bill replied back that he sure didn't know, but was hoping she, Amrit and Beth could figure it out, and damn soon. The Deputy had been hanging around to gather information to take to the Sheriff, but a call came in needing his assistance. Bill agreed to send anything the investigators gave to him, and with that promise the Deputy took off to the new call.

Once Beth, Amrit and Liz finished their walk around, they quickly compared notes regarding what they had seen and documented. As soon as the coroner arrived, it took nearly everyone on scene to help in getting the body carefully removed and loaded into the coroner's vehicle for transport to the morgue. After finishing the sample gathering and preliminary investigation, everyone left to go to their appropriate stations, leaving the Forest Service to finish mopping up the fire.

Chapter 17

Once again the stress management team was put on call for the Prairie City firefighters to provide counseling to anyone needing help coping with yet another tragic situation. Francis was there to help as well. Since fewer volunteers were involved in the pickup truck fire, the need for the stress management team was not as great. Both Frank and Bill wanted the team available, though, just in case one or more volunteers had trouble trying to work around not just one, but now two horrific incidents.

It had been only yesterday since the pickup truck/forest fire incident, and Bill had been told by Bev that they were running into the same problems trying to identify the body found in the pickup as they did in trying to identify the female from the house. They did confirm the victim in the pickup was an older male, but once again it seemed like brick walls were in place regarding any help from the FBI. Evidence from the house fire was still being analyzed, and what little evidence taken from the scene of the pickup truck fire was in the waiting line at the lab.

Amrit, the Police, and the State Police met to discuss this latest incident, to review what's known and try to shed some light on what to do to eliminate some of the unknowns. The only positive piece of information, if it could be called that, was the pickup had been identified as that belonging to the missing couple. Well, at least the State DMV was forthcoming with their records. Amrit had a sense that something was not right, that some of the evidence so far pointing to a murder and suicide situation just didn't feel right to him. He couldn't put his fingers on the reason yet, but there was just something nagging his thinking. And of course there were the blocks on their attempts to identify the victims, like someone was purposely hiding some of the puzzle pieces. This aspect of the investigation was not something he had run into before.

The team discussed the few facts that they had to work with so far. The badly burnt body from the house fire was a female, and it was determined that she had been stabbed. The medical examiner had also found a skull fracture, but couldn't be sure that it had not been done by falling debris. An accelerant had been poured over her and part of the room and in places in the house, then set on fire. The time of death estimate correlates with when the neighbors were woken by strange noises. The body in the pickup truck was a male, and a drug screen proved positive. Time of death was undetermined, with the drug and other tests results providing some very strange readings. The pickup truck did belong to the couple that owned the house that had burned. And evidence of an accelerant, although slight, was found in and around the pickup.

Frank remembered his wife Dora had mentioned that on the morning of the wildfire, she had waited on one person fairly early in the morning and not part of the normal early morning crowd. A couple things she remembered about the customer were the accent, like the person was from New Jersey or the New York area. And that there was a bit of a fuel type odor, like something spilled on the person's clothes. It didn't smell like diesel or gasoline, but something in between. Probably was nothing, but for lack of more enlightening facts, this tidbit was added to the notes. And Dora said the other thing she remembered was waiting on the same person the morning after the house fire a few days ago. Dora had a good memory, what with having to take meal orders for years without a notepad.

The team was frustrated because requests put through to the national crime data base for further information on the couple had so far been unanswered. Yes, they all agreed it was kind of early for results, especially from overworked government labs. In the meantime, while awaiting any response from the Feds, it was agreed that each member of the team would send a copy of their findings to Amrit, who would keep all the data together, and attempt to make sense out of a troublesome lack of data. In looking over the limited amount of data so far, one thing was evident: the only inquiries and lab tests returned to the investigators were those handled by the State. Any requests for information and lab work sent to the FBI had not been answered as of yet. To Amrit and Liz, who have worked with the FBI numerous times, this was not typical. After finishing their meeting, Beth, Liz and Amrit grabbed their collected evidence and each left for their offices.

A typical early morning at the Grainery Café, where Dora waitressed, would find a group of old farmers and ranchers sitting around the table drinking coffee while the sun was waking up. On this particular morning, with the discussion about world and national events exhausted, one of the guys mentioned the recent tragic fires, a topic that had been hashed about daily for the past few days with no resolve. The local news had not provided any information yet as to who the victims were in the two fires, but rumors traveled fast in the small town. The guys were throwing out various scenarios, one of which was the old man killed his wife and then himself. One of the old codgers, during the discussion of why someone would kill his wife, boldly said, "Well, if she were anything like my wife, I'd have gotten rid of her."

Without their wives present, this group was full of bravado. But the truth be known, most of these guys had been married for over 40 years, while a couple of the men were widowers, having lost their wives to cancer. While bringing more coffee, Dora had overheard the comments, and with a stern face and a pointing finger said, "Joe, you big bag of wind, you know you love Helen dearly, so don't give us none of that crap about getting rid of her."

Joe grumbled his apologies, a few of the old guys laughed, and the conversation moved on. As the old men calmed down after Joe's dressing down by Dora, they continued discussing some of the weird happenings lately. The old man running the butcher shop and cold storage business mentioned he had some person call a few weeks ago and rent a cold storage locker. One of the guys asked, "So, what's so strange about that?"

"Well, people usually don't rent until hunting season, or they are butchering one of their animals. And this person didn't come on to me like a rancher."

"Where was he from?"

"Hell if I know. Paid cash, and spoke with a kind of weird accent, the few words I heard on the phone. Sounded like maybe New York or someplace like that. Never did come into my office. Spoke on the phone and dropped off the money in an envelope in my mail slot."

"Did you tell Bev or Walt about that?"

"Shit no, I just now thought of it. I guess I had better say something to Walt."

One of the guys piped up, saying, "Probably some damn government agent from the department of agriculture sent out to check on you."

"Oh hell, Charlie, everything is government conspiracies to you."

"Well shit, look at the country. We can't say the Pledge unless we leave God out of it. We can't say them damn murdering towel heads are terrorists because that might upset them. Kids are learning a whole different version of US history than we did. Don't even know what marriage is anymore, and our guns are being taken away from us. Millions of illegal aliens have more benefits and rights then me and hell I fought for this country. And look at the Blacks versus Whites racial thing..."

"Oh crap, who wound Charlie up anyway? Let's change the subject, quick!"

Chapter 18

Francis was in a serious dilemma. After hearing that confession in which someone admitted to be being a part of the killing of an older couple, Francis' thoughts have been a mixed up mess. As a priest, he was bound by certain Church laws that were extremely hard on a human being. One of these laws, the sanctity of the confessional, was right now especially tough on Francis. Being a volunteer firefighter and having been on the tragic house fire in which the woman was found, Francis was wanting the culprit or culprits caught and justice delivered, just like everyone else. And here was perhaps one of the persons responsible for that tragedy, and he, Francis, could do nothing but pray for that individual. He loved his life's calling, but there were times when he questioned his choice. It was terribly hard to sit in on a meeting of the volunteers, to hear the talk regarding the latest on the fire deaths, and not be able to pass along the important information from the confessional. Of course he didn't know who it was and couldn't identify the penitent, but he still might be able to recognize the voice. He desperately needed to speak with a fellow priest, to discuss this and get some counseling before this problem ate away at his sanity. He had a congregation to work for, so he needed to be strong and ready to help others. It was time he prayed for even more strength and guidance.

Liz had been assigned to work with Amrit on this arson/murder/suicide case, and had been digging into information about Jill and Roger, the older couple seemingly at the heart of this tragic mess. Going over Amrit and

Bev's interview notes regarding the house fire, she put together an initial profile of a couple that stayed fairly alone, didn't socialize other than a little bit with a few neighbors, and had lived in the town only about three years. Certainly there had to be more information on this couple then the little bit she has so far. She had placed an inquiry with the FBI, a standard request for background on the couple, but strangely hadn't heard a single peep, not even a "we're working on it." Something about this couple was fishy, and her stink alarm was beeping. Putting a few puzzle pieces together, she arrived at one conclusion that seemed to make sense. So she made an appointment to visit with Bev at the Prairie City police office, and tell her theory as well as review the scant information, and see if the two of them could glean more information from the locals. Hopefully in the meantime, the FBI will come through with more information. It was really bugging her that the records on Roger and Jill where unavailable, it was like the couple had just appeared out of nowhere. It was strange that the FBI had not even acknowledged receiving the inquiries from Liz. Yep, her stink alarm was beeping.

Bev had Liz follow her to the meeting room where they could talk and lay out the case paperwork on the table. Liz had mentioned her frustration, and it was shared by Bev. Even though the house fire was a week ago, there was a serious lack of information. It was like these people, Jill and Roger, just appeared out of the blue, with no history to be found. The only positive thing out of the digging they have done was to confirm that the burnt pickup did belong to Roger. However, that piece of information just added more mud to the already muddy waters. "Bev, this whole thing has been bugging me. I can think of one thing that would make sense: the Symsins were in a witness protection program."

Bev, initially shocked by the idea, soon found it did make some sense. "But we should have been notified by the U.S. Marshalls office that there was a witness protection effort going on. That was standard procedure, right?"

Liz agreed that standard policy was to notify the local authorities about a witness protection, but Liz just shrugged her shoulders, wishing there was an answer as to what was going on.

While reviewing the scant details they had managed to acquire, the door to their meeting room was wrenched open and in walked a couple of suited, tough looking individuals. Wearing sunglasses and no expressions, they looked like Federal agents that had jumped out of a gangster movie. The lead suit reached into his shirt pocket and brandished his credentials, introducing himself and his partner. "I am US Marshall Doriano Zurosky, and this is FBI Special Agent In Charge Ricardo O'Shaunsy. We are here regarding your recent fires, and we request all of your files regarding both fire incidents. FBI Special Agent In Charge Ricardo will take over the cases, and will be your contact person."

Ricardo, the lead FBI agent, didn't bother with a handshake or a pleasant greeting. "Which one is Bev?" As Bev identified herself, Ricardo handed her a document he had been carrying inside his suit coat. Ricardo said, "We want all of your files regarding the two recent arson fires, and we want them now."

Ricardo grew up in the Bronx of New York, the product of a Puerto Rican maid and a hot tempered Irish construction worker. Ricardo's life was not an easy one, with his parents gone a lot working, and when his Dad was home, there was a lot of yelling and fighting. Finishing high school, Ricardo leaped at the chance to join the Army to get away from his parents and the Bronx. He became a MP, Military Police, and learned to enjoy his chosen job. While in the MPs he saw a chance to join up with the FBI for better hours and money. When his second tour of duty ended, he joined the FBI. With his tenacity, learned by hard knocks, he moved up the ladder, but he did not have the necessary 'smoothness' to move very far in the system. Political correctness and Ricardo were not simpatico. At forty nine, he wanted to be further up the ladder, and strove to do so, not worried about who he sideswiped on the way.

Liz's phone rang, breaking the momentarily angry quiet. "Liz, what the hell is going on. The FBI are here wanting to take all your files from the Prairie City arson case."

"Boss, the FBI are here at the Prairie City Police Station also, and they are grabbing all of Bev's files too. Some idiot agent by the name of Ricardo is here raising a big stink. And some US Marshall seems to be the ring leader."

Hearing part of the conversation, Ricardo said, "Oh, and you must be Liz. Sounds like my team is doing it's job at your office as well. Anything you two have on both the house fire and the pickup truck fire, we want and we will have."

Glaring at Ricardo, Liz asked, "What the hell is going on?" Liz, never having been treated like this before, was angry and her voice did not hold back the anger.

Ricardo, having fun being the bully, said, "I understand you were asking for information regarding the alleged victims, but from this moment on neither of you are cleared to know about this case. You both should know what the penalty for noncompliance is, so I suggest you move your cute little asses, now."

Liz, not liking this situation one bit, knew she was outgunned by Ricardo and his FBI thugs. She looked over at the U.S. Marshall, but he was too busy on his cell phone to care about what was going on. Since there was nothing she could do, Liz told her boss she would leave shortly, then stormed out of the Station and headed to her car.

Bev had no choice but open her office to the FBI agents, letting them rifle through her files, trying to find anything regarding the arson cases. Walt had been out on a call, and had just arrived to the station and into the middle of this serious interruption of the daily Police operations. Having gotten a very brief overview of the situation from the on duty officer, who had been bulldozed by the FBI agents earlier, Walt stormed into Bev's office and yelled, "What the hell is this all about? And who in the hell are you?"

Without a word, Ricardo pulled out his credentials, flashing them at Walt. "FBI, huh, so why did you not give us notice you were showing up to get the files? You could have simply asked for the files instead of being such an ass."

"Ah, but then we wouldn't be having this much fun now would we. We issued a search warrant for some files your officer has, and that is all you need to know. Now get out of the way or I will have you arrested for obstruction."

Walt was fuming, and couldn't believe this was happening. Pointing a finger at Ricardo, Walt told him that this was not over with, then headed to his office to make some calls. No one bothered to introduce him to the U.S. Marshall, also standing in the room.

Liz had reached her car only to find a FBI agent rifling through the car. Pulling her gun she yelled at the agent and told him to get away from her car now. The agent yelled back that she had better put the gun away before she got into serious trouble. He explained briefly that he was with special agent in charge Ricardo, and was working under the search warrant. Liz called her boss and told him about the car search. Her boss blew his stack and placed a call to his boss, the Colonel of the State Police.

Walt called the City attorney, hoping to catch him. The attorney, having only a five minute recess during a trial, heard the quick rendition of the FBI intrusion. His only comment was to get a receipt for the stuff they are taking, but other than that they were stuck big time. So Walt walked back to Bev's office and approached Ricardo. After a brief growling match, like two male wolves getting ready to fight over a carcass, Walt demanded a receipt for everything the Feds were taking out of the office. Ricardo just laughed and gave him his business card with his boss's name and phone number on the back. "Here, give him a call and demand the receipt. Ha, ha, see how far you get with that."

Ricardo and his henchmen finally left the Police Station, satisfied they had gotten everything relative to the arson cases. On his way out he said over his shoulder to anyone listening, "this never happened, and if you know what's good for you, you will forget everything about these cases."

His FBI bizjet was waiting at the small airport. He was to meet his fellow lead agent at the airport at the State Capitol, once the other team had finished up with Liz's office at the State Police headquarters. While waiting for the other team to arrive, Ricardo and US Marshall Doriano discussed the recent events surrounding the warrants that had been issued and how it went. The team that hit the State Police office had a lot tougher time than did Ricardo. Legal council was on site, which made the agent a little more careful in handling the warrant. Ricardo laughed and said he felt like John Wayne, going in with guns a blazing. He said, "Man, what a rush, especially to issue a warrant to a cop. We should do that again."

Doriano was pleased with the raid on the files, and said so to Ricardo. "I like your style, Ricardo. You don't mess around but go right for the jugular."

After a little longer making sure all was moving correctly, Doriano said his goodbyes and hopped on his own plane to fly back to his office. Ricardo settled in for the two hour flight, and was anxious to get into the files and see what kind of damage the investigation of the arson incidents had done. Ricardo figured they would have easy pickin's in grabbing Amrit's investigative reports and then this situation would just go away for good.

While Bev's office was being ransacked, a boiling mad Liz had calmed down enough to think of calling Amrit. Pulling off to the side of the road, Liz called Amrit. "Amrit, did you get hit with an FBI warrant yet?"

"No, what are you talking about?"

Liz gave him a very brief synopsis of the issuing of the warrants, both her office and Bev's office being ransacked for the information. "Okay, Amrit, then grab as much stuff as you can and get out of town now. Get someplace where you can copy everything and then store it someplace safe. I have a feeling you will be next on their warrant list. Something is very wrong here and I think we want copies of as much as we can get regarding these two latest incidents. I don't like it and I am not about to take this lying down. Your files are all we have left."

"I am grabbing my stuff as we speak. I'll call you when I get situated and have these copies made."

Liz then called Bev, and making sure she was in a secure area, told her what she and Amrit talked about. Bev was also still madder than heck, and wanted to use Ricardo for her weekly self defense training. She felt better just thinking about what she would do to that smug face of his. She mentioned to Liz that, with Walt's permission, she will try to gather up some more evidence and see if she can rebuild some of the information they had gathered. Both Bev and Liz felt there was something very rotten going on.

Chapter 19

Walt was also still madder than hell over this invasion by the FBI. He contacted his local County Sheriff and gave him a quick update on the situation. Walt, having just spoken with Bev, mentioned the concern that Liz brought up, thinking that Amrit's investigative notes were next to be appropriated by the feds. The Sheriff, one of many in the State that took a dim view of how the feds handle some of their tasks, said he'd contact the Sheriff of the County Amrit's office was in and see what could be done. The Sheriff was way too eager to put a wrench in the feds machinery.

The Sheriff of the County where Amrit's office was located was given a quick and abridged story of the recent events surrounding the arson/deaths cases in Prairie City. "Damn, I don't have a lot of time but let me see what I can do. This could be fun!"

With that, the Sheriff, looking at the clock, ran to the Dispatcher's desk and told her to call all the off duty officers in, radio the on duty officers in the area and have them immediately respond to the airport. "Tell them to meet me at the visiting pilots lounge, and have the off duty officers do the same as they check in. Time is critical. Thanks."

The Sheriff then ran out to her patrol car, and while heading to the airport, phoned the police chief and quickly explained the situation. The Sheriff knew the local police chief was also no fan of the feds' heavy handedness, but she also knew that the police could not legally challenge the feds, whereas she, as the Sheriff, could, to a degree. Therefore, the

Sheriff asked the police chief if he could have a couple of officers hurry over to Amrit's office and help him to protect his files in whatever way they could.

"I'll see what we can do, and if you need some assistance in slowing down the feds, let me know. We could put up some detours or road blocks or something."

"Thanks Chief, I'll keep you informed. We may well need those diversions."

Arriving at the airport, the Sheriff was happy to see no new planes on the tarmac yet, so she was ahead of the arriving feds. She spoke with the office and maintenance people at the lounge, who offered to assist in whatever way they could. It was agreed that the two maintenance guys would take a couple of pieces of equipment out onto the runway. One of the office clerks knew the rancher adjacent to the airport, and asked if he could push a few of his grazing cows unto the runway right away. The rancher was not eager to do this strange request, until the clerk quickly told him that the Sheriff needed to delay a plane load of FBI agents. Having had numerous battles with the EPA, BLM and other alphabet soup government agencies, he was only too eager to join in this little skirmish.

The Sheriff had four of her deputies at the airport with her, and another two arriving within ten minutes. She received word from the police chief that two of his officers were assisting Amrit in photocopying the files. The officers were running stacks of papers to the police station where they could use all the photocopiers in the station. Even the clerks and off duty officers were there to help. The rancher had herded about twenty of his cows unto the runway, and was going to get a few more when the Sheriff heard the FBI pilot radio the airport that he was twenty miles out, nearing final.

When the pilot radioed he was on final, the airport manager radioed back telling the pilot to abort, that he had a crew working on a section of runway. The pilot yelled for Ricardo to come to the cockpit and explained the situation. Ricardo, angry with this delay, grabbed the copilot's headset and promptly reamed the manager. "Listen asshole, this is Special Agent in charge Ricardo of the FBI. Clear the runway NOW."

"Well, sir, I do not have radio contact with the crew, but I sent out my clerk to tell them to finish immediately. I expect them to be clear of the runway in about ten minutes."

"Hell no, tell them to move their asses. We need to land now."

"Sorry, sir, but the runway is not clear. If you need to land right away, might I suggest diverting to the next airport, about fifteen minutes away."

"You listen and listen damn good. I am the FBI and you had better get the runway cleared now, damnit."

"Sir, we are trying our best. I will head out there myself."

With that the manager set down his microphone, started to giggle, and meandered to his four wheeler parked out front of the lounge. He drove slowly, got about halfway to his crew, when he turned around and headed back to the lounge. Grabbing the microphone, the manager called the FBI pilot and warned him that there is a herd of cattle on the runway, and he will work on getting them off while his crew is readying the runway. "You damn fool. What the hell kind of operation you running here anyway? How much longer before we can land?"

"Sorry sir, it will take about ten minutes to clear the animals off the runway. By then the crew should be done as well. We are working on a shoestring here, since the FAA cut our funding to near nothing. Used to be we had a bigger crew and better equipment."

"You just wait until I finish with you and your idiotic airport. You'll be cleaning snow off Adak airport in the Aleutians with a toothbrush."

Everyone in the lounge was laughing. "Hells bells, we haven't had this much fun since last year's greased pig catching contest!"

The Sheriff, after sharing a laugh, called the police chief to get a status report. The police chief said he will need another thirty minutes to finish the copying. "I think I can hold the FBI here for another twenty minutes, then if you can have a couple of road blocks and detours set up, I can send a couple of my people to assist you," said the Sheriff.

"Sounds good, I'll get on it and let you know where the detours will be," replied the police chief.

After another seven minutes, and more haranguing from Ricardo circling overhead, the manager finally radioed the pilot the all clear to land. The Sheriff and her deputies waited in their vehicles until the FBI jet landed. As the jet taxied to the lounge, the Sheriff vehicles surrounded the jet. As the jet stopped, so did the Sheriff vehicles, with the Sheriff herself parked near the airplane door that had not opened yet. While the deputies got out of their vehicles and assumed the gun battle stance using their vehicles as shields, the door to the airplane opened. Once the stairs unfolded, a fuming Ricardo stepped out.

The Sheriff, nearing the base of the stairs into the airplane, told Ricardo to keep his hands where she can see them, and to tell the rest of his agents to remain in the plane. Ricardo was incensed and cussing the Sheriff. The Sheriff calmly told him that it was proper protocol to contact the local law enforcement agencies before carrying out an operation in that jurisdiction. And to remind him that she was the head law enforcement officer for this jurisdiction, period. "Now, Special Agent Ricardo, what is it that brings you to my jurisdiction?"

"First of all, get your people to stand down and let me bring my agents out of the plane."

"Not going to happen, Special Agent Ricardo. You and I will have a chat about why you are here, then maybe we will let your agents out of the plane. Now, you can do it my way, or turn around and take your plane back to Washington DC. It's your choice."

"Lady, you have no idea what you are dealing with. I can make your life miserable."

"Special Agent Ricardo, are you threatening me? I must warn you, I am wearing a video cam as are my deputies. It's SOP for our Department. Do you wish to continue with this approach or would you like to do as I suggested?"

"Ok Sheriff, you win this round, but I warn you."

"Follow me and we will talk in my patrol car, then we can see what needs to happen."

While Ricardo was walking toward the Sheriff, the Sheriff was on the radio warning her deputies to keep a close eye on both Ricardo and the plane. She wanted to make sure Ricardo heard the radio transmission.

Once situated in the patrol car, Ricardo carefully reached into his coat pocket to retrieve a search warrant. It was a warrant to search Amrit's office, to take anything related to the recent arson and murder investigation going on in Prairie City. Fortunately the Sheriff had been quickly briefed by the Sheriff of Twin Rivers County as to the cases and what the FBI did in Prairie City. Playing like this was the first she heard of it, the Sheriff asked a few pertinent questions. After getting assurances that Amrit wasn't to be arrested, only his paperwork was to be taken, the Sheriff reluctantly agreed the search warrant was in order, and told Ricardo he could gather his agents and head to Amrit's office to serve the warrant. But that he was to leave immediately when his search of Amrit's office was finished. And that two of her Deputies would accompany his task force to the site and a couple of city police officers would be there to assist on site.

"Special Agent Ricardo, I still do not understand why you people are doing this?"

"Sheriff, I just do my job and I suggest you do yours."

"Oh, but I am doing my job. The next time you want to visit our community on business, you call me first, Special Agent Ricardo. You can get out now, and have a nice day."

Before a chastised but fuming Ricardo opened the door, he asked the Sheriff for the use of a couple of her Department cruisers. "Special Agent Ricardo, if you had only called ahead I could have seen to it. But you arriving like this gave me no chance to arrange for vehicles for you and your team. I suggest you call one of our car dealers. Here is the phone book. You can keep it as a memento of your visit to our beautiful County. Have a good day."

The Sheriff then left Ricardo, gathered her deputies and assigned two to ride herd on Ricardo and his agents, one to stay near the plane, and two to catch up with the police officers on detour duty.

Ricardo, chastised but incensed, was expecting the local law enforcement agencies to bow, scrape and provide transportation for him and his agents. With that plan burnt to a crisp, Ricardo had to arrange for transportation, getting a local car dealer to bow before the FBI and cough up two vehicles. In the meantime, the efforts of copying Amrit's investigative files had been progressing nicely. The delaying tactics of the Sheriff had taken more time than anticipated, and the transportation snafu was an added bonus. Therefore, the police chief decided to work just one detour and not worry about any road blocks. The detour would add eight minutes travel time to the FBI caravan, which would be enough time to finish Amrit's files. The chief called the Sheriff and explained the plan and the status of the operation. The plan changes sounded good to her, so she moved a couple of her deputies in closer to Amrit's office to assist the police if needed. Besides, she thought a show of force and union between deputies and officers would send a message to the FBI.

After arranging for transportation and following the detour, Ricardo and crew finally arrived at Amrit's office. Looking around, he could see a few officers and deputies standing behind their vehicles, watching. Well, this isn't going down with the fun that the other two search warrants had, thought Ricardo.

Marching in to Amrit's office, Ricardo handed the warrant to Amrit, who asked to see Ricardo's credentials. Pretending to be there on another pretense, the police chief asked Amrit if there was something wrong. Amrit handed the warrant to the chief and asked him if this was enforceable. Ricardo just about screamed, "Of course it is enforceable. It's from the FBI and signed by a Federal judge, you moron."

Amrit still wanted the chief's opinion, not feeling threatened by Ricardo's attitude. The chief handed the warrant back to Amrit, telling him that it looked official and that he should comply. Amrit shrugged, said he was extremely irate, but he stepped aside and told Ricardo, "Do your damn job, then get the hell out of my office."

Two hours later, Ricardo and his agents figured that had everything they could find on the case. Without a word, they left Amrit's office and drove back to the airport. A line of law enforcement vehicles followed the two rental cars, like a procession. The Sheriff and her deputies pulled off from the procession and raced to the airport to meet with her deputy, who had been watching the plane. The deputy said no one came or left, that all had been secure. So the Sheriff once again positioned her deputies to surround the plane and await the arrival of the agents. Ricardo's entourage stopped alongside the airplane, and the agents carried the boxes of seized materials into the airplane. With the rented vehicles empty, Ricardo left them for the car dealer to worry about. Ricardo had noticed the going away party outside the airplane, hosted by the Sheriff. He hadn't remembered being this angered and humiliated in a long time. He'll have to figure out a way to teach these damn back country hicks some proper manners. He yelled to the pilot to get this damn plane out of here and get going to Washington DC. He then yelled for the cabin attendant, telling her to bring a bottle of Highland Park 30 Whiskey and a glass of ice. He figured he had earned this luxury, paid for by the generous tax payers, and it was going to be a long flight back to headquarters. Damn hicks anyway.

Chapter 20

W hile Ricardo's plane was heading east, the arsonist was busy working on the next assignment. An old house, still occupied, was standing in the way of progress. The 'family' was involved in a high rise complex being built, and the site the old house was standing on was to be the parking garage. But the owners were being extremely stubborn, not listening to reason. The best offer had been made and refused, so it was time to take matters to a higher level and deal with the problem in a quick and decisive manner. This was the Burner's specialty, and the pyromaniac jumped into the task with enthusiasm.

The Burner was not completely void of emotions. A rough childhood, a rough family life, and a tough pathway to the level of respect the Burner now holds left the arsonist scarred. Emotions lead to weakness, as the Burner came to believe. Ever since the Prairie City job, the Burner was having a hard time sticking to the mantra of no emotions. Something buried deep inside was trying to wake up, and it was threatening to affect the Burner's stoic exterior. Strangely, the Burner was slowly losing control over the lid that buried memories of circumstances years ago best left forgotten.

Unbidden memories invaded the Burner's conscious. Bits and pieces of childhood memories started to pop up, and the Burner was struggling, trying to suppress these long forgotten times. The Burner's grandfather was a very hard man, and had not been a real loving grandfather to the Burner. The Burner's mother had disappeared while the Burner was just a toddler, and the arsonist never knew a father. The care of the child was provided by a nanny, and they all lived in the grandfather's heavily guarded mansion. The Burner did not remember feeling any love amongst the family and staff living in the mansion. Whenever the young Burner asked about a mother and a father, the subject was immediately changed. It was no wonder the Burner wanted to keep the memories deeply buried.

It took an extreme effort, but the Burner managed to shut down the old memories and get on with the task. The arson job did not require a killing, which was just as well. Any job requiring a killing mixed in with the burn down would bring in one of the 'family' hit men, usually Elmo. The Burner had issues with Elmo, who had been with the 'family' for quite a few years. Elmo was crude, vulgar and enjoyed his work way too much. There was another reason for the Burner's despise of Elmo, one that could not be explained, but was a strong feeling of hatred for something hidden in the back of the Burner's memories. For being usually emotionless, the Burner felt hatred and fear whenever doing a job with Elmo. Fortunately this job did not require Elmo, so the arsonist could enjoy the work in solitude.

The arson job went as planned, and the 'family' was pleased with the results. The work was able to move forward with the impediment removed. The Burner had free time, and once again started to replay memories unbidden. Years ago, when just a child trying to cope with parochial school and bullies, the young child became increasingly interested in fire, setting small fires in trash cans and getting bolder, to putting fire in dumpsters. The Burner's friends realized quickly that it didn't take much convincing to get the young arsonist to go out and set a fire.

When the arsonist went so far as to set fire to some pallets alongside a warehouse, the young arsonist ended up spending a short stay in juvi. After the short stay in juvenile hall, in which the grandfather had exerted pressure in the right places, the young arsonist was sent away to a strict Catholic boarding school. The young arsonist did not lose the interest, some may call obsession, in fire; just merely learned how to be more careful and sneaky. Completing the boarding school, and having no where to go, the Burner reluctantly returned to the grandfather's mansion. After a few days it was evident the arsonist was unwanted there, so the Burner repacked and walked out the door vowing never to return. Before leaving town, the arsonist spoke with a long time family friend who had practically raised the Burner. Giorgino, an old time hit man with the 'family', had tried to treat the Burner as his own. When Giorgino heard that the Burner was leaving, he arranged for one of the Chicago 'families' to give the Burner a job and a place to stay. So the Burner headed to Chicago and a new life.

After settling in and not having lost interest in fire, the arsonist applied to the Chicago Fire Department as soon as the announcement of job openings was made. Unfortunately for the Burner, a zealous fire officer tasked with eliminating candidates from the huge list of applicants, found a reference to the stint the Burner spent in juvi for fire starts. Normally that stint in juvi would not have been an issue, especially since the incident had happened in New Jersey, but with the Chicago Fire Department having thousands of candidates for a couple of hundred positions, a simple thing like time spent in juvi was enough to remove the Burner from the list of candidates. That did not sit well with the arsonist, who immediately set out to get even.

The young arsonist methodically studied articles on the internet regarding fires, especially the arson end of the subject. Having gathered books on the subject, the pyromaniac started to practice what was being studied, trying to enhance an already practiced skill. After a few successful small fires, the arsonist graduated into larger fires and varied the tactics in an effort to hone in on something that worked the best. The arsonist was getting a reputation for quality work, and was soon nicknamed the Burner. While enhancing the skills of an arsonist, the pyromaniac developed a somewhat unique way of starting a fire. The fuel mix used by the Burner became a signature, a forte, a calling card, part of a game of "catch me if you can". In the meantime, the Chicago Fire Department investigators, overworked and under paid as the excuse goes, were stymied trying to find the arsonist. Since no one had been killed or injured in the rash of arson fires, the investigations into these minor arsons cases were low priority. So the arsonist continued experimenting and getting better with practice. The Chicago 'family' was impressed and as time went by the Burner was able to work into more demanding, more complex jobs.

By this time the arsonist was starting to make some pretty good money for the Chicago 'family'. The 'family' in turn passed along a better salary and the Burner's reputation was growing. After about five years in

Chicago, the Burner wanted to go back to New Jersey. Even as bad as the New Jersey 'family' was, the Burner was a little home sick. Also, the Burner felt the need to get away from Chicago before the investigators put the puzzle together. A call to Giorgino, and the Burner was set up with a job and a place to live. The capo in charge of the arsonist was a good friend of Giorgino, so the arrangements for a job for the Burner worked out well. The capo had called the Chicago 'family' just as a check, and was more than pleased with the report on the Burner's skills. So the Burner started work for the 'family' without the grandfather knowing about it.

One day a special favor was asked for by the capo's boss. The boss needed to exterminate a competitor, but it would have to look like an accident. The arsonist was given the job, as kind of a test to see if the Burner could be promoted beyond being just a special soldier. Unknown to the pyromaniac at the time, the 'family' was looking at the Burner to become a capo, which meant better pay and more responsibility. Being a capo was like being a lieutenant in the military.

Having been given the task, the arsonist set out to put together a plan to fulfill the boss's desire. Monitoring the victim's habits, the Burner developed a plan to catch the victim off guard when he was alone. The plan worked, and the arsonist finished the task with a well executed vehicle crash and burn, with the evidence pointing to it being just another terrible accident. The victim was immolated in what the newspapers reported as an "unfortunate fiery car crash". This was the first arson fire in which the Burner had to use a 'family' hit man. Elmo, the hit man, killed the victim and did it in such a fashion that the evidence would easily be destroyed by the fire set by the Burner. Up to this point the Burner's victims were left unharmed, physically unharmed that is. The Burner did have a conscience, tempered by the years of parochial school. "Thou shalt not kill." The fifth commandment. Some argue that a truer translation from the Hebrew would be "Thou shalt not murder," which would lead to an argument over the difference between murder and killing. As with a majority of people, the Burner selected which commandments to strongly adhere to and which might be adhered to depending on the conditions of the moment. The Burner felt strongly that any killing associated with an arson job needed doing was to be done by someone else, and that going to confession to express guilt and sorrow for the killing would be acceptable, and a release of culpability.

The administration running the 'family' was quite pleased with the arson work the Burner was accomplishing, so they made the Burner a capo and was assigned a small crew of soldiers. Going to confession eased the Burner's conscience, and the loss of life at the hands of violent Elmo took a back seat to the joy of advancement. Things were looking up for the arsonist. That was a couple of years ago, but things were still good. The pay was great, benefits were fabulous, the jobs were for the most part enjoyably challenging, and the grandfather had still not known the Burner was his grandchild. And it was exciting, trying to stay ahead of the investigators in this cat and mouse game of arson. But the Burner didn't realize there was more than just a psychological need to start fires. Lurking under the Burner's subconscious was a hidden piece of memory stimulating this need to create fire and play the game of catch me if you can.

The arsonist was contemplating the most recent job, and how the old house had burned to the ground so quickly the local Fire Department couldn't save a thing. And the owners of the house disappeared, so the 'family' was happy and able to move forward with the high rise job since the last obstacle had been taken care of. Satisfied with the job, the arsonist was thinking, "I wish I had stayed near Prairie City to watch the wildfire I started." Putting fire into buildings was getting to be old hat and boring, but wildfire could be a refreshing uptick, a new challenge. "I need to ask the boss if there are any jobs out west, where I could practice and work on some arson tactics for the wildlands."

The arsonist was getting excited just thinking about it, and hoped there was an opportunity coming up very soon. In the meantime the Burner would continue to study and practice, trying to improve the arson game.

While the Burner was working on the high rise job, Ricardo and his fellow agents had arrived back to FBI headquarters, hauling in the boxes of materials they legally stole from the Prairie City arson investigation. After dumping the boxes in the meeting room, Ricardo headed to check in with his supervisor, Bennie. As soon as Ricardo was let into the supervisor's office, the yelling started. "What the hell kind of mess did you leave in Prairie City? I got this phone call from the big man upstairs. He told me he had received a call from the head of the State Police there as well as a call from a Senator from that part of the State. They complained vehemently about your actions. So now I am in hot water thanks to you. Damn, Ricardo, can't you do a job without creating a hell of a mess?"

"Hey boss, I get the job done. If you wanted someone to traipse through the tulips with people, find someone else. I do what I am told and my record speaks for itself."

"Yes, you are my best agent, but I need to send you to a people skills school, again. Maybe one of these days you'll actually pass the class and we won't have to spend so much time trying to clean up after you. Now fill me in as to the Prairie City case."

Chapter 21

Back in Prairie City, a clandestine meeting was going on between the key players in the arson investigation. Walt, Bev, Liz, Amrit, Frank, Bill and George were all together in the meeting/training room at the fire station. This was their first meeting since the FBI debacle, and there was a sense of anger, frustration and determination. The emphasis of this first meeting was to line out the future strategy, to answer questions such as where do we go from here, how shall we proceed, should we proceed, and who's to do what if we decide to move forward. And how do we continue and not wake up the ire of the FBI? Bill said it best when he stated, "Our community has been traumatized by whoever is responsible for these tragedies. People don't feel safe. We need to find the culprit and put him away. Then our citizens can feel safe again."

With everyone in agreement to move forward, Liz asked if everyone was okay with working behind the backs of the FBI. "You realize that we could be in serious trouble if we continue. The FBI is bound to find out, and the repercussions will probably be very bad for each of us."

Everyone agreed they needed to continue with some sort of investigative work. With the way the FBI has handled the situation already could they trust the FBI to proceed with the investigation. Frank suggested they contact the Sheriff and bring him into the group. Bill added his suggestion that they carefully bring in Nick, if he would promise to keep quiet on this investigation until the group gives him the go ahead to make it public. Bill's idea was if the FBI jumps all over the group, the group can threaten back with the power of the press, even if it is just a small local paper. Everyone in the group liked both suggestions, and it was decided that Liz would talk to the Sheriff, and Frank and Walt would corner Nick. They set a next meeting date, to include the Sheriff and Nick, and to have everyone bring whatever they have as information pertaining to the arson fires. Until a better location is found, they will continue to meet at the fire station.

It had been about three months ago when all hell broke loose in Prairie City, and things had finally settled down to just about normal for the small community. Autumn was nearly over and, other than the arson investigation, the police and fire departments were back in the routine, dealing with the typically mundane activities. Bill, all alone as usual, decided to have breakfast at the restaurant for a change. As he entered the busy place, he heard a, "Bill, over here, there's an extra seat."

Looking around he found the voice, belonging to one of the old timers in the daily coffee group. He walked to the old timers' table, greeting some of the numerous town's folks on the way. Bill said his greetings to all the old timers, guys he has known for as long as he could remember. After seating himself, Dora came over, kissed him on the cheek, poured him some welcomed coffee and after a few minutes of chit chat, took his order.

One of the old timers teased Bill, "How come you get a kiss and I don't?"

Bill teased back, "Because I am so much better looking than you are Ralph!"

After a few minutes of loud guffaws and back slapping, one of the old timers broke the merriment by asking Bill what's the latest on the arson investigations. Bill told them he hadn't heard, not wanting to tell them the whole truth, since these guys could be worse than old ladies at gossiping. One of the old guys popped out with, "I still think it's a government job."

"Oh pipe down with your conspiracy stuff," said another. One of the old farmers remembered a previous conversation at this same table and asked the butcher if he had told the police about the strange person that rented the cold storage about the same time as the arson fires. Bill perked up and asked the butcher to fill him in.

"Well, you know my memory ain't so good no more, but like I was telling these guys, I rented a cold storage unit to somebody around the same time as the arson fires. Guy paid in cash, and rented it for just a month. Never saw him, just talked on the phone. Had a funny accent, a nasal thing, like maybe he was from around New York or New Jersey. I remember in 'Nam, we had a couple New York-New Jersey boys in our platoon and he sounded kind of like they did. I checked the cold storage unit at the end of the month he had paid for, and it was empty, all cleaned out."

Bill asked if anyone else had been inside the cold storage unit, and the butcher said not yet, but hunting season was about to start and he would probably have it rented out shortly.

"You don't happen to have surveillance cameras at your shop do you?" Bill asked. Unfortunately, the butcher did not. He didn't even own a computer, didn't trust modern technology. The conversation moved along, changing from the arson fires to the price of wheat and barley, and on to world affairs. Bill finished his breakfast, said his good byes to the morning coffee gang, paid for his tasty breakfast, and kissed Dora's cheek as he was leaving. He had a little bit of time before he had to be to the golf course for work, so he stopped by Walt's office at the police station. Walt listened to Bills' recital of the butcher's story, and some flash bulbs went off in his mind.

Having thanked Bill and walked him to the door, Walt called in Bev and filled her in. Walt asked Bev to call Liz while he called Amrit, and it was suggested they meet with the team and review this latest piece of information. Both the Sheriff and Nick were invited, but Amrit was unable to attend this meeting. That evening, when all were gathered in the fire station meeting room, Walt asked Bill to reiterate what he had heard that morning. All agreed after hearing the brief statement that it was pretty slim to go on. The Sheriff suggested he could have his Deputies ask around at various businesses in the County to see if somebody with a strange accent had been around during the time of the arson fires. Amrit, by telephone, suggested Bill and Frank start looking into reports of arson activity around the United States. Amrit knew that Bill looked over some of the bi weekly reports through a couple of on line fire news web sites. Amrit also knew that certain areas are more prone to arson fires than others, and since these recent fires in the Prairie City area looked like professional work, it could be that the arsonist came from one of the news worthy areas. It would be a long shot at best, but shake the can enough and something is bound to fall out. The Sheriff would have his detective head out to the cold storage facility and get some finger prints before the unit was rented, hopefully. With no further business to add, the meeting was adjourned and everyone went either home or back to work.

Chapter 22

Enjoying being back in familiar haunts, the arsonist had been handed a couple of easy jobs to do. As usual, the Burner completed the jobs in spectacular fashion. The Burner, however, was still left unsatisfied. Something was tickling the Burner's fancy, hinting there was something else out there to do. The Burner was an avid reader, reading books and news regarding fire research and activity in between reading a good mystery or western, or not wanting to admit it, but even a heart throb once in awhile. One day while doing some fire research using the internet, the Burner stumbled upon mention of a thesis paper done by a college student back in the early 70's. It was a rare find, because not many thesis papers were published to the internet from the days of before internet. What brought this particular paper up in the internet search was the fact it was on the use of remotely piloted vehicles, called rpvs, in fire fighting. Nothing had come of this topic for nearly forty years, but recent leaps in technology had made the rpv, now called a drone, smaller, more capable and more affordable. After finishing the story, the arsonist's brain started working on a plan. The Burner felt excitement, a rejuvenation as it were, but thoughts of a time long ago came creeping into the Burner's conscience, tempering the excitement.

The Burner was mother and fatherless, raised by a nanny, living in the grandfather's house. The grandfather was too busy and the grandmother did not want anything to do with the child. When the Burner turned six years old, it was decided to send the child to a private parochial school and get some social interaction started. The grandmother was more than happy to have the young child boarded, which meant she would only have to put up with the troublesome child during holidays and school breaks. Wishing and wanting love and attention from the family, the young child just got into trouble. But the young child barely received attention, and certainly no love. The young Burner got into numerous scrapes with other children, and the school officials threatened to remove the troublesome child from their high quality educational institution. The young child was hoping to be sent home, but a large monetary gift to the school from grandfather destroyed the child's plan.

By the time the young Burner was in sixth grade, a group of like-minded children had gotten together and started raising havoc. The Burner became part of this group. The group leaders were well versed in causing trouble, yet never getting caught, and the techniques rubbed off onto the Burner. A few of the group members liked to set fire to nearby dumpsters, and soon this sport became the most favorite thing the Burner liked to do. When set afire, the dumpster spewed out plenty of dark and stinky smoke, but it was so much fun to watch. It was hard to figure out whether the young Burner got the most kicks from the flames or from watching the fire department when they showed up. There was an obvious attraction to fire, but was it just a childhood kick or was it something deep down inside? It was not until much later that an answer could be found.

One of the young members of the troublesome group had invited the gang over for a party, and the young Burner admired the collection of airplane models hanging from the boy's ceiling. The boy having the party was definitely into model airplanes, and saw the look of wonder in the Burner's eyes. "You think this is neat, follow me," said the young boy to the Burner. Out in the garage was a work bench, and on the work bench were three objects that made the Burner's heart race. The objects were obviously model airplanes but these were not like the ones hanging from the boy's ceiling.

"What the heck are these?", asked the young pyromaniac.

The young boy proudly announced to the young arsonist that these were the new radio control models. "I have been flying these for just a short time, still trying to get used to the controls. The guy that runs the hobby store in the East Mall has been giving me lessons."

The young arsonist just gazed at the radio control planes, and finally asked the friend if they could take one out to fly. The boy was glad there was someone he knew that seemed to share the interest in flying, and suggested they meet at the hobby store Saturday morning and go out with the hobby store owner. The Burner was trying to hide the disappointment, and was going to go bonkers waiting two whole days before flying the planes. Patience was not a well used commodity in the Burner's world.

That was over 20 years ago, and the memories of that time were mostly painful. Once the grandfather heard about his grandchild's radio control interest, he put his foot down saying that was an expensive and stupid hobby, and that was the end of the Burner's dream of flying the planes. Now having read about the wild idea of using radio controlled aircraft in fire management work written by a college student nearly forty years ago, the Burner's suppressed passion for flying radio control planes crept to the surface of consciousness. Having seen a few ads for the new radio control aircraft called drones, the Burner started researching drones, from the micros that fit in the palm of your hand up to the larger commercial types costing thousands of dollars. These newer drones have the much quieter electric motors instead of the noisy gas engines that could be heard for blocks on a quiet day. A notion started to form, and the arsonist worked over an idea that as far as the research went, no one had either tried it or had been caught trying it. At least nothing was found on the internet searches.

With a plan in mind, the Burner ordered a quadcopter drone on line for less than one hundred bucks. This quadcopter was a flying platform with four engines, each driving a six inch horizontal blade similar to a helicopter. When it arrived a few days later, the excited arsonist unpacked it like it were a cherished Christmas present. Once the battery was charged up, the Burner headed out to a large, grassy park ready to fly the drone. This time the grandfather could not say no.

The quadcopter transmitter box consisted of two joy sticks and six buttons, plus the power on/off switch and an antenna. The left hand joy stick controlled both the throttle and the yaw, or rotation; and the right hand joy stick controlled the pitch, the tilting forward or backward, and the roll, which was the tilting to the left or right. The buttons were for trimming the movement of the joysticks, for flipping the quadcopter 360 degrees, and for controlling the tiny camera. The Burner had glanced at the almost non existent instructions, but was able to figure out how to bind the control box to the quadcopter. Bind and fly is the process in which you turn on the quadcopter, and once the running lights are blinking, you turn on the power to the control box. Then you run the throttle stick all the way up and then all the way down. When the running lights on the quadcopter turn solid and a brief audible tone is heard, the quadcopter and the control box are communicating, called bound, and you are ready to fly.

The Burner bound the quadcopter to the transmitter, and slowly applied throttle by moving the left stick up. As the electric motors started turning faster, the quadcopter started rising off the ground. At first, the controls were way too sensitive, or the Burner's fingers were too generous in their movements. The drone was buzzing around like a bee high on fermented honey. After numerous crashes in a short seven minutes, the battery was used up, ending the fun for awhile. This short span of flying definitely whetted the appetite for more, so the Burner ordered more batteries and chargers to extend the flight time.

Weeks passed by while the arsonist spent available free time flying the quadcopter, getting more and more familiar with the controls and putting the little drone into tighter and tighter situations. The biggest problem the arsonist had was in remembering to switch the controls when the quadcopter was heading to the Burner. When the quadcopter was going away from you, you simply moved the joysticks in the direction you wanted the drone to go. But when the quadcopter was coming toward you, you had to remember to move the joysticks opposite of where you wanted the drone to go. Luckily for the arsonist the little quadcopter was fairly robust, and even after numerous crashes, it still flew.

Chapter 23

After taking a break to do a couple more jobs for the 'family', the Burner spent as much time as possible flying the quadcopter. Feeling confident, the Burner decided to move up into the next level of drones, the FPV. The FPV drone, the FPV stood for first person view, consists of a real time video camera capable of sending instant video back to a smart phone, a special screen or laptop device. Moving into this type of quadcopter meant a lot more money, but so much more capability. Such as automatic return of the drone if the signal is lost, programming of a route the drone is to travel using a GPS, plus the instantaneous view from the drone itself. Almost like being in the cockpit! The arsonist was making good money working for the 'family', and being single, the expenses that were not reimbursed by the 'family' were minimal. So after a few months of practicing on the initial quadcopter, the decision was made to move up and a FPV quadcopter was ordered. While waiting for the new upgraded quadcopter, and while still flying the initial quadcopter, the Burner started to formulate a plan to use this new technology in the field the arsonist was most familiar and good at.

As soon as the new FPV quadcopter arrived, the arsonist charged up the batteries, and started researching on line for any mods that others have successfully accomplished on this model of quadcopter. These modifications included such notions as lengthening the antenna for better signal strength, or fixing the drone to run on a longer lasting battery, or mounting a different camera to the drone. While doing the research, there were a lot of sites referencing the need to get a license from the FAA to avoid a very heavy fine. The Burner was in a catch 22 situation, and thought long and hard about this licensing issue. Deciding to get the license, the Burner used one of the fake ids and credit cards that the 'family' provided, and after spending an easy six minutes on line to fill out the form, the Burner received the two year license. In learning about the license, the arsonist saw the list of does and don'ts, including flying below 400 feet, do not fly near people, and do not fly around emergency activities such as fires. Well, that last one is going to have to be ignored, and the Burner figured on being extra vigilant when the time comes to put the developing plan to work.

A day later, with batteries fully charged and time available, the Burner took out both quadcopters to the grassy field. Once the transmitter and quadcopter were bound, where the radio and drone are talking to each other, the Burner launched the new quadcopter and started checking out the controls. The electric motors were more powerful, and the sound up close was more like a high speed drill rather than a group of buzzing bees. Being larger, the drone was easier to see and was a little more stable in the air than the smaller quadcopter. "I'm going to enjoy this", thought the Burner.

With weeks of practice, the controls became more familiar, and the flights moved further and further away and higher into the sky. It was time to hook into a smart phone and start learning how to use the FPV feature. Having replaced the quadcopter battery and bound the drone with the transmitter/smartphone combination, the quadcopter took off under the control of the arsonist. Once the drone reached a comfortable height above the ground, the Burner started to use the Smartphone for controlling the quadcopter's camera. The arsonist had found an app for controlling the quadcopter and downloaded it to the smartphone earlier, so the arsonist only had to swipe or tap a spot on the smartphone screen to control the drone.

Flying the quadcopter with the GPS and smartphone turned out to be just what the arsonist needed. It was fairly easy to program how the quadcopter will fly and to where. After bringing up the software, you simply brought up something like Google Map or Google Earth, pinpointed the location, followed the prompts and built the program.

Once the program is synched to the quadcopter, pushing a start button tells the quadcopter to proceed. If the quadcopter loses its signal with the smartphone, the quadcopter automatically heads back to where it started from. The arsonist spent weeks with this new quadcopter, getting better and improving upon the precision that will be required in the tasks the arsonist had in mind. The next hurdle for the arsonist was to develop an incendiary device to carry on the quadcopter.

The Burner had been different ever since coming back from the Prairie City job. It was like something there triggered some strange, deeply buried emotions. And like a siren of Greek mythology, it was calling the arsonist back, back to Prairie City. It was like an emotion that had been purposely buried and was now trying to come forth. The Burner remembered that weird sensation while watching the firefighters attack the Symsin's house fire. It was unexplained, but seemed to be tied with the feeling of a need to return to Prairie City. There was yet another change the Burner noticed. Being able to burn a building took talent, but it was a contained thing. Having whetted an appetite for the bigger challenge, the Burner wanted to do more with wildfire. The thought of starting a fire under controlled conditions but in an uncontained setting kept gnawing at the Burner's pysch. Unfortunately the Burner had not been able to watch the wildfire outside Prairie City. "I need to go back to Prairie City, to find out what's calling me and to practice some more wildfire starts," thought the Burner.

So plans were started for a vacation the following summer, and this time the Burner decided to bring a pickup, camper, and four wheeler for better mobility. The Burner had a couple of soldiers to assist with various jobs, so part of the plan was to give these soldiers more experience which would free up the Burner to work on heading west. Sitting down with Giorgino, the Burner explained the interest in drones, and the plan to use drones to assist in the arson work. The Burner also explained the need to work out west and gain confidence in the drone arson experience. Giorgino, having known and liked the arsonist since the arsonist was a young parentless child, could see benefits in the proposal, and after some thought, even suggested the Burner take on a job as a cover. "Let me make some calls, and get back to you," he told the Burner.

A few days later Giorgino called the Burner in for a meal and talk at the family's main restaurant, a favorite meeting spot. "First, your grandfather likes the idea of using the drone in his operations, so he was in favor of you getting more training. Your vacation has been approved as well. And I found just the job for you. You need to call this number and speak with Sergi. Sergi said he can quickly train you and send you out as an agricultural chemicals rep. Oh, by the way, your grandfather still does not know who you are," said Giorgino. The Burner realized this would be a perfect cover, and profusely thanked Giorgino. Things were looking good.

Chapter 24

Ricardo's boss, Bennie, had a nagging feeling in the back of his mind, and it kept bugging him. It had been months since Ricardo had taken care of the Prairie City incident, but something about that situation kept him awake some nights. Bennie had received the agreed bonus payment from the 'family' for his part in the Prairie City operation, but something was worrying him. Like a sixth sense telling him something wasn't finished. And if something wasn't finished in this job, the 'family' would see that his sojourn on this earth be cut very short. So he called in Ricardo to his office one morning with a plan he had been working on for some time. "Ricardo, I need you to pick one of your best young agents and send him to Prairie City."

"What for boss, I thought that was done and over with."

"Ricardo, I have this bad feeling that something is still not right, that quite possibly someone there is still working on your case."

"Hey wait a minute, that was not my case. I just followed your orders."

"What ever, I think you may have missed something when you gathered all the files."

"I don't see how, we scoured the offices of everyone involved and took everything that even remotely looked like it had something to do with the old couple."

"Well, something is nagging me, so I want you to send an agent to Prairie City, have him become embedded in the community and listen to the area gossip. See if you can pressure one of the businesses into hiring your agent so he has a job, and that would help him get started with the community. It will take awhile, but if someone is working behind our back, I want to know about it and be ready to quash it."

Ricardo didn't fully agree with the boss's assessment, but Bennie was the boss. So Ricardo sat at his desk and started working through his agents and finally picked the person he figured to be the best choice. Ricardo called Mac into his office. Mac was a young agent, in his early thirties, with blue eyes and blond hair, a babe magnet according to the gossip. Unlike Ricardo, Mac was a personable and friendly young man. After graduating from high school, valedictorian of his class of 23 seniors, Mac attended college majoring in business. During his senior year at college, he attended a job fair and happened to visit with a FBI representative. Graduating with honors and a Bachelors in Business Economics, Mac went back home for the summer to work on his parents' farm. One evening while perusing the internet, Mac read the FBI was opening a two week recruitment period. The visit with the FBI representative stuck in his mind, and figuring on nothing to lose, he followed the internet link and applied on line for a Special Agent job. Mac pushed the Send button on the last page of his on line application, and waited.

Most of the summer had gone by when Mac received a call from the FBI's local office, wanting him to come to the office for a job interview. Mac had read on the FBI's web site the requirements for a job with the FBI Special Agent division, and made sure he met or exceeded the requirements. After working through the grueling interview, Mac went back to the farm and considered looking for other work. A few weeks after the interview, Mac was called by the FBI office and asked to come in. Mac was pleasantly surprised to find out he had been one of 164 applicants selected for the Honors Internship program, out of 10,000 people that had applied. This meant that Mac was soon to start training, and getting paid while working to become an agent. That was eight years ago. The past four years he spent working under Ricardo, as part of Ricardo's team of Special Agents.

Ricardo invited Mac to a chair in his office and promptly presented Mac with the plan for a special operation. Mac was to work his way into the Prairie City community and find out if there was anything going on regarding a couple of deadly arson fires last year. "We confiscated all of the files we could find regarding the incidents, but there may be some illegal work on the cases going on." Mac listened intently to the details of what Ricardo wanted, and tried to put together a picture in his mind. He asked Ricardo why the concern, and why did the FBI confiscate the investigation. "This is a need to know situation, and you need to know only what I tell you, nothing more. Just trust me and do what you are told."

Since Mac was not in on the confiscation of the Prairie City arson investigation paraphernalia, he would not be recognized as part of the FBI. But that meant he also did not know anything about that incident. Prairie City sounded a lot like where he was from, Mac decided, and felt he should be able to fit in with a bit of care. Mac knew from experience that the smaller communities are much more suspicious of new comers, or at least word spreads of a new comer in the area. So it would be wise to put together a fake background and find someone in the area they could pressure to bring Mac in as a relative and get a job on a farm. With Mac's background in farming, that would be a benefit.

Mac, having come from a small community, suggested one way to get into the heart of the community fairly quickly was to become a volunteer firefighter or EMT. Ricardo, liking the sound of 'quickly,' was in favor of Mac's idea. With Mac's background in farming, they just needed to work on firefighting skills. Living and working on a farm, Mac had fought a few field fires while growing up, so he wasn't completely unfamiliar with fire. Therefore Ricardo sent Mac to the Washington DC Fire Department headquarters and had the Chief set Mac up with a couple weeks of concentrated training. At least Mac's muscular physique would help him with the grueling training that Mac needed to complete quickly. With the training, Mac would be able to show an aptitude regarding some aspects of fire fighting that would hopefully impress the locals into letting him into the group of volunteers. Mac knew enough to recognize the danger in knowing or perceived to know too much. He had been in Washington DC long enough to know that this same sentiment held true for not just the rural communities.

While Mac was spending time with the Fire Department, learning the Essentials of Fire Fighting and studying to become a Fire Fighter 1, Ricardo was studying the people of Prairie City. He was looking for someone with a weakness that could be exploited. A couple members of Ricardo's team drove to Fort Meade in Maryland and spoke with the FBI liaison to the NSA, the National Security Agency. Even though NSA had been formed back in the early 1950s to gather intelligence on foreign sources, it was not until a NSA employee blew the whistle a few years ago that it was learned NSA was also gathering intelligence on United States sources. Ricardo's FBI team explained the need to glean data records from the Prairie City area, which would include phone and internet usage by various residents. A phone call by the liaison to Bennie at FBI headquarters confirmed the authentication, and from that point NSA stepped in to assist. With billions of pieces of intelligence collected, trying to find a needle in the haystack would be a monumental task, however there were plenty of employees to put to work on the task. NSA was one of the largest intelligence organizations in the United States, with a budget and employee base to match. Therefore a few of the NSA employees were directed to work on the segmented data files, sorting the stuff dealing with Prairie City residents and businesses.

It took nearly a week but the NSA data provided some interesting reading for Ricardo and his team of agents. Sorting through the mundane everyday traffic, such as on line purchases of everything from deodorants to sex toys, the team zeroed in on an internet user of child porn, and a lawyer emailing about a serious interest in politics. After some more help from NSA, the team was able to come up with a name and address for the politically motivated lawyer. Ricardo sent a couple of his agents to visit with the lawyer. The lawyer agreed to cooperate, after receiving a promise of a hefty campaign cache. With visions of living life large as the governor, the lawyer agreed to help as long as the money and election were in the bag. The lawyer was given the necessary documents and background to be able to bring Mac into the community, and promised to assist in anything else regarding this particular operation. If this was all he had to do for the money and governor's job, what a small price to pay!

Looking over his list of clients, the lawyer narrowed his search to those running a farming operation close to town. Having found a likely candidate, the lawyer called the farmer in and made him a deal. The farmer would hire the lawyer's 'nephew' in exchange for free legal services for a year, and possibly longer if required. Plus, the wages for his 'nephew' would be paid by the lawyer. Sounded like a win -win situation for the farmer, so he agreed. "Just send him to me and I'll put him to work," said the farmer as he walked out of the office. The lawyer's phone call to Ricardo's office set the operation in motion. Operation Goose was going to be Ricardo's partial pay back for his mistreatment by that damn woman sheriff. Even though the town of his embarrassment was different, it was in the same State, which he figured was close enough for retribution. Retribution: how he loved that word.

Chapter 25

During the remaining part of the winter, Prairie City had settled down and was more of its normal self. With winter, the golf course was shut down. So Bill was into maintenance mode on a part time basis, and doing odd jobs around town to help with the winter income. The Fire Department had a few chimney fire calls, a couple of wrecks, two dumpster fires and a garage fire, so it was just about normal. The arson and murders last year had just about played out in people's minds, but Bill and Bev were still pushing the group to continue looking at any and all reports and rumors. "We owe this to the dead couple, and we owe it to ourselves. Someone needs to pay for the deaths caused and the trauma dropped into our laps," Bill said to the investigative group at one of their winter meetings. Everyone agreed, but most were getting frustrated with nothing new coming in for months now.

Fortunately, the FBI had not got wind of this little mutiny yet, or they would be back as before, throwing badges and weight around, trying to impress with arrogance. The group had no idea whether the FBI was in fact doing anything regarding the arson and murders. No one expected to hear from the FBI regarding the cases, with the attitude that was demonstrated to all of them last year by that damn Ricardo. But the group wanted closure, for a variety of reasons. Everyone in the group felt that the end result was to find the person or persons responsible. But how to make sure that was being done? The only sure way was to continue digging by themselves. It was doubly difficult, since they were trying to avoid using any of the standard resources that might make its way back to the FBI. No sense in kicking a sleeping pit bull.

Both Bev and Liz had checked with all the businesses in the County, asking if any of the employees remembered someone out of the ordinary in their store around the time of the big house fire last year. Did they remember anyone with a kind of east coast accent, or someone purchasing strange items? Other than a manager at one of the agricultural firms thinking he remembered a sales person with what he thought to be an eastern US accent, there hadn't been anyone else admitting to having remembered such a person. If nothing else, the team was convinced the arson fires and murders were definitely professionally done. It was like trying to solve a puzzle, with multiple pieces left out of the box. And it seemed like the FBI and US Marshall's office probably had those pieces. Liz, frustrated like the rest of the team, spouted out with, "Does anyone besides me feel this mess is fishy?"

Bill returned with, "Fishy and damn twisted." Unfortunately he had no idea how twisted this situation would get.

During the winter months, the Prairie City Fire Department trained in doors while the weather was lousy, watching videos and running chalk board scenarios. Video clips from various bystanders and from the reporter, Nick, were used to discuss the arson structure fire, in an effort to learn about things to look for that might shout out 'arson'. Everyone had seen the video clips numerous times, but it was good to rehash since this type of fire had never occurred in this community before. While watching the videos, Francis couldn't help but think back on the confession he had heard shortly after the arson fires. A hell of a burden to be carrying, Francis was under an oath to not divulge that confession. His fellow firefighters felt something was wrong, because Francis was not his normal outgoing self. But no one could get an answer out of Francis, and just attributed his change in attitude with the specter of the arson murders. They were only partially correct.

After a brief winter in Prairie City, the weather turned surprisingly mild. The old timers sitting at the morning coffee table at the café would remind each other of the good ole days when at least one of them had to walk to school in the ass deep snow five miles uphill both ways. Of course that talk was mostly for the benefit of any youngster seated near by. Undeniably, the weather was mild, and the usual snow depth was less than normal. Every once in a while, when the topics of the day got stale, someone in the group invariably would start up on global warming. One of the farmers would then rant and rave over his cows' farts being blamed for the warming. That was always good for a thirty minute discussion, until the waitress, usually it had been Dora, would wander over to the table and tell the guys to quiet down. The old timers did agree that it hadn't been this dry for quite sometime. They all missed getting told off by Frank's wife Dora. Each admitted it was a shame that Frank's wife was undergoing cancer treatments. Just wasn't the same without her at the café to give them a hard time in jest. Just wasn't fair.

Once spring hit the region, the affects of the low moisture winter started to show. Bill and the rest of the volunteers were busy responding to more grass fires than they could remember having in the past. People would be outside doing their normal spring cleanup work and burn the raked debris piles, just like they always did. And just like they always did, assumed the grass was still wet enough to not worry about. Unfortunately, some learned the hard way that they should have been better prepared, because the green grass was not wet and hid a lot of dry, dead grass. A number of fence posts, a couple of power poles, a garage, a barn and quite a bit of hay ended up consumed by the 'controlled' burns that got away. There were also a few fires along the highways in the District, caused by passersby throwing their smoking cigarettes out onto what they normally assumed was wet, green grass. In meetings between the Fire Department, Forest Service, and State Department of Lands, all in attendance were hoping for a wet late spring to slow down the already busy fire season that officially hadn't even started yet.

One day during the dry spring weather, Bill was chatting with a friend working for the fire division of a large logging company. In the discussion of what this fire season was shaping to be, the friend commented he was involved with a drone program for his company. The company had purchased a drone to monitor forest health and wildfires, and he was to be one of two pilots for this drone. While listening to the information on the drone program, Bill remembered back to earlier days when he was about twelve years old and had been introduced to airplane models and radio control airplanes by a couple of uncles. Bill was visiting with an uncle, and after looking up at the home office ceiling, he vowed to do the same thing. Hanging from the ceiling were meticulously finished model aircraft, put together by the uncle from kits made by well known kit manufacturers Monogram and Revell. From that moment on Bill would save money from his paper route earnings, less what went into his savings account, and go buy a model to build. He concentrated on the planes of World War 2. He even found models of the planes being used as aerial retardant planes that he watched fly out of the local airfield during the summer. Those he painted to match, making them as realistic as he could.

Another uncle got Bill interested in flying line control airplanes, and then radio control aircraft. Building and customizing airplane models to hang from his bedroom ceiling was great fun, but actually flying a model was even better. Flying the line control planes was alright, but flying in a circle, going around and around, was not a lot of fun. Flying the radio control was so much better, but definitely a bigger challenge. Bill finally saved up enough money to purchase a complete radio control airplane kit for beginners. Called an ARF, which meant almost ready to fly, there was little work to do to get the plane ready for flight. And being a beginner's plane, the construction of the airplane was designed to take a few light crashes. Bill had a blast flying, but the busy life of a working and schooling teenager took over his time, and Bill slipped away from the radio control hobby.

A question brought Bill out of his reminiscence, and he heard his friend asking if Bill wanted to see the drone in a couple of weeks. "You bet I would. I was just thinking back a number of years when I just barely got started into the radio control hobby, but couldn't keep the hobby going."

"Bill, you should check out the new stuff available in radio control products. Fun stuff, and the prices are very reasonable. Heck, you can get started with a small quadcopter for under fifty bucks."

After they were finished, Bill made it a point to go online that evening and start searching the internet for radio control deals and information. His long buried interest was coming alive. Shoot, maybe it was time he got a hobby.

Chapter 26

Mac had finished a fast two weeks of concentrated fire training, and had his travel bags packed and ready. Ricardo's Operation Goose was still a go, so Mac hopped a flight out of the Washington DC area headed west. With the arrangements made, Mac flew to an airport a long day's drive to Prairie City, rented a pickup truck, and headed to Prairie City with his fake documents. Mac arrived in Prairie City, and stopped along the road to find his map. Bev, on patrol, stopped alongside the pickup and asked through her open passenger window if he needed assistance. Mac, caught off guard by the woman officer's green eyes and red hair, stammered and finally got out that he was looking for his uncle's office. Once Bev heard who the uncle was, she gave Mac directions, than decided to just have him follow her.

Parked in front of a large two story well cared for Victorian style house, Bev got out of her patrol car and walked up to Mac's driver side window. "Well, sir, here is your uncle's office. Hope you have a nice stay here in Prairie City." Mac, still a little tongue tied, said, "Thank you very much mam. By the way, my name is Mac. I didn't catch your name."

Bev said as she was turning away, "You are welcome. My name is Bev and I hope you will be staying for awhile."

Mac watched Bev walk to her patrol car, and thought, "Wow, I think I am going to like it here."

Mac went into the lawyer's office to start the process of community assimilation. His real thoughts were on hoping to see Bev again and get something started. After the introductions, the lawyer drove Mac out to the farm at which Mac was to work, and introduced him to the farmer. The farmer had few words to say, there being no small talk in his vocabulary. But he did tell Mac what was expected, and when he should start in the morning. That was fine by Mac, so they said their goodbyes and the lawyer drove Mac back to town, dropping him off at his pickup. The lawyer had arranged a place for Mac to rent, and gave Mac directions on getting there.

After a brief visit with the landlord, Mac unpacked his stuff into the rented little house, and took a walk. Not much different than the town he grew up in, he walked the town's main east-west, then north-south streets. He saw the time was near 7pm, so he headed to one of the bars to grab a bite, a drink and listen to the gossip. There were five bars in town, so he chose the one with the most vehicles and liveliest sounds wafting from the open door. This bar just happened to be near the firehouse. As he stepped into the noise filled saloon, he waited briefly for his eyes to adjust to the darker atmosphere. He looked around, spied an unoccupied table and went to it and sat down. Being in no hurry, he waited for the bar maid and looked around the room, picking out bits of conversations amongst the noise of the television set to an ESPN station. Eventually the bar maid made her way over and took Mac's order for a bourbon and seven. Mac placed his food order with the bar maid when she delivered his drink, then he sat back to once again try to pick up on any conversations.

Aware there were a few patrons openly staring at him, Mac figured he was being scoped. He knew how it worked—a stranger in town and standing out like a sore thumb. Many town folk were nosy and wanted to know something about the stranger, while others could care less as long as they were not impacted by the situation. But no one wanted to jump up and join the stranger in conversation. Not yet anyway. So Mac ate and drank alone, expecting nothing different for this first night in town. When he had finished, the bar maid wandered over and asked Mac if he needed anything else. Mac mentioned the food and drink were quite good. The bar maid asked him if he was just passing through, and Mac provided a bit of his cover story. He knew this was the best advertisement. The bar maid was a bit surprised, and welcomed him to town and said she hoped to see him again. He assured her he would be back, and after leaving a generous tip he sauntered out the door. Heading back to his rented house, which was more like a converted garage, Mac was pleased with the progress of the plan. Now he needed a good night's sleep to get ready for the early morning job start.

As ordered, Mac was at the farm early, and promptly found he was being quizzed by the old farmer. Pleasantly surprised that Mac knew the answers, the farmer started Mac on the typical morning chores involved in a farming operation. Spring had barely started, yet the ground was drying up. The farmer needed to get his spring wheat crop in soon to take advantage of any moisture left in the ground. Prayers for rain would accompany the planting. Mac, remembering the years he drove tractor on his family's farm, stepped up to the John Deere 8530 dually tractor and started checking the fluid levels. After the fluid levels were verified, Mac walked around the tractor and checked the tires, and checked the hitches. Already hooked up was the planting train, so Mac just had to check the cables, hitch, and chains for each member of the train. Satisfied that the equipment was in good shape and properly connected, Mac climbed into the cab. Closing the door to the air conditioned and sound reducing cab, Mac fired up the 330 horse engine, engaged the transmission and towed the planting train out to the field. The old farmer had watched Mac's walk around and was impressed, thinking to himself he wasn't going to have to babysit this one.

The planting train consisted of the drill and the fertilizer trailer, hooked together and cabled to the tractor. Inside the cab Mac watched the monitor, which allowed him to adjust the drill depth for the type of crop to plant, and adjust the fertilizer rate. The monitor was also set to show the operator if there was a problem in one of the pieces of equipment, such as an air hose plugged. An on board GPS (global positioning system) was tied into the monitor and farm software. Through the expensive farm software, the fields had been mapped out, type of seed input, and recommended fertilizer application selected. The computerized system then took over and controlled the drill and anhydrous ammonia application. There was hardly a need for the operator any more. Many farmers accepted the technology only grudgingly, and preferred to maintain some control of the planting even if it was just sitting in the cab listening to music while the tractor drove itself. This luxurious cab was a far cry from the days Mac drove his father's open cab tractors, where you listened to the sounds of the tractor and inhaled plenty of dust.

The seed Mac was planting, spring hard white wheat, would hopefully mature into a good harvest destined for the Asian markets, if all went well. The hard white wheat was a favorite for use in noodle making, and usually had the recommended nutrient level the Asian market preferred. So Mac lined up the tractor with the first row to drill, set the computer to start the drill process, and listened to the local country music station. He actually was enjoying this, especially after four years in the Washington DC rat race working for Ricardo. The music filled cab, the sun beating in through the windows, and the slow 6 miles per hour travel speed of the tractor nearly lulled Mac to sleep. Day dreaming of Bev, Mac forgot for the moment why he was in Prairie City.

Chapter 27

Two days of the drilling and seeding, and Mac was finishing up the first field when he spied smoke in the distance coming from the west, between him and the edge of the timber. Mac keyed the microphone on the CB radio in the cab of the tractor and called the farmer. The farmer said he had just heard about the fire, which was threatening Henry's house and barn, quickly spreading through the winter dried weeds that Henry was trying to burn off. The farmer was in his pickup and heading to the fire to help. Mac said he had had some fire training and would love to help, so the farmer changed direction and Mac was able to see the rooster tail of road dust thrown up behind the farmer's pickup as he approached. Mac shut down the equipment, grabbed his water bottle, and jumped down from the cab and waited alongside the road for the fast moving pickup. The farmer slammed on the brakes, and once Mac was inside and even before Mac had the door shut, the farmer popped the clutch and the pickup surged ahead in the direction of Henry's place and the fire.

Mac and the farmer arrived to the fire in a cloud of road dust just as another prairie farmer arrived with his son to help. A neighboring farmer was bringing his tractor towing a plow, slowly traveling the road toward the fire. The Prairie City Fire Department attack engine, having been dispatched about ten minutes ago, was just a couple of minutes away. Resources were arriving and on the way, but it was going to be close whether they can stop the fire before the fire hits the barn and house. The fire had the head start.

With hardly a word, the arriving farmers grabbed their shovels and headed to the house and barn, hoping to keep the flames and sparks from setting the buildings on fire. Each farmer could feel the tragic consequences if it were their own buildings being threatened. A couple of the farmers went to the house and started shoveling a scratch line, breaking the continuity between the dry grass and the wood siding. The other two farmers went to the barn and started doing the same. Henry was helping his wife gather their precious memories in case the house caught fire.

Bill and his two volunteers in engine 1 arrived just ahead of the tractor plow, and in doing a quick size up, Bill saw that the barn was in more of an immediate threat than the house. Bill radioed the incoming rural engine 2 to take the house, while the attack engine would help initially with the barn. The tractor plow arrived and started plowing between the house and barn and along the backside of both structures since it was too hot and close to get between the barn and fire. Bill radioed the fire station personnel standing by to send the water tender out, and then he asked the Dispatcher if she could phone one of the agricultural companies to see if they could send a tank truck full of water to assist. The water aboard both engines would hardly touch the fire if it got into either of the structures, so Bill wanted a fair amount of water backing up the attack.

With the tractor plow working the sides and back, the farmers and the volunteers could concentrate on the front, the fire side. A couple more farmers arrived to help, and Bill had them be lookouts, one for each building. Afraid of sparks getting into the wood siding, Bill wanted the newly arrived farmers to pay close attention and yell if they thought they had seen a puff of smoke coming from anywhere on or in the buildings. With the water tender on its way and engine 2 just arrived, Bill went ahead and had the volunteers frugally spray water on the fire side of the barn, while the engine 2 crew were setting up to do the same at the house. The lookout for the barn spotted a small smoke coming from inside the barn, so Bill grabbed his nozzleman and carefully headed into the barn. Mac was working the shovel and saw the volunteers head into the barn, so he worked his way over to the large barn door and started into the barn, following the volunteers and the hose they were moving forward.

Mac caught up with Bill and asked if he could help, and Bill figured with another set of eyes they could better find the source of the smoke and get it before it spreads beyond control. With the old boards and layers of straw dust and dried manure, the inside of the barn was a torch waiting for a light. As the three people in the barn were searching, they stumbled upon a total of nine spots that were smoldering, waiting for the right time to flame up. Mac helped with his shovel, stirring the dried and smoldering detritus while the volunteer nozzleman applied water. Bill noticed the team work, and thought he had better have a chat with this young farmer when things settled down.

Outside, the flames starved for lack of fuel, thanks to the efforts of the farmers with their shovels, the tractors, and the volunteers with their water. Both the Fire Department water tender and a tank truck from one of the agricultural supply companies had arrived and started to refill the engines. Fortunately, dusk was drawing near, and that meant the moisture in the air would rise while the temperature would start to edge downward. The small hot spots in the grass would have a hard time keeping alive. Only the glowing coals found in the fence posts, the larger stems of the few scattered bushes, and the scattered manure piles would continue to burn. So a couple of the farmers worked over the hot coals with their shovels while the volunteers sprayed the coals with water to put them out. Mac, Bill and the volunteer working the fire hose finished with a sweep of the inside of the barn. A couple of the neighboring farmer's wives brought over drinks and dinner for everyone, a perfect time to take a breather and sit down to enjoy a well earned rest.

While the ladies were dishing up the wonderfully aromatic dinner, the soot covered and tired farmers and firefighters started telling stories, just like if they were at the diner in town nearly every morning for coffee. Bill, with his filled plate in hand, had thanked the ladies, then walked over to where Mac was sitting. After finding a seat, Bill started up a conversation with Mac. After introductions, Bill said, "Mac, I was impressed with how you helped with this fire. Looked like you have done this before. What kind of experience do you have?"

Mac, finishing a mouthful of fried chicken, told Bill that he had been raised on a farm, and had a little volunteer fire fighter experience as well.

"Mac, the Prairie City Fire Department sure could use another volunteer, especially someone of your abilities and age. Are you interested?"

"Well, if it is okay with my boss, if he would let me leave the job to respond to a fire, then sure." Mac's boss was within ear shot and heard part of the dialogue, so Mac and Bill filled in the old farmer. The old farmer, feeling a kinship with many of his fellow farmers, and seeing the results of such kinship just today, said it would be fine with him.

"Mac, would appreciate it if you would call me either on the CB or cell phone to let me know you have to take off so I can step in to finish your job."

Bill was pleased and told Mac when the next training session was and that paperwork would be waiting for him to get him officially signed on.

While the farmers and fire fighters were finishing up their welcomed meal, they were introduced to Mac. Mac answered the series of questions thrown at him by the farmers and volunteers as best he could without giving away his true reason for being there. After seeing how well Mac worked the fire with the fellow farmers and volunteers, the old farmers invited him into their morning coffee ritual, only if his boss would let him and he didn't have to be at the farm early. Mac was pleased with himself and surprised that with this fire, his acceptance in the community grew much faster than he could have anticipated. Now if only he could pick up on some scuttlebutt that would make Ricardo happy.

That evening when Mac drove into town to get showered and grab a bite of dinner, he spied a patrol car parked in an empty parking lot watching traffic go by. It looked like Bev's, so he drove up alongside and was relieved it was Bev in the car. He said hello, and she returned his greetings. "I hear that you got your first taste of Prairie fire fighting today. Looks like you are still wearing part of the prairie!"

Mac grinned and said he was heading home to shower and grab some dinner. "Where is a good place for dinner?" asked Mac. Bev suggested the Planter's Grill, and told him how to get there. "If you are free, come join me for dinner. I'll probably be there around 7pm."

Bev said she was on the night shift, but could probably take a break for dinner if there were no calls. Mac said he would hope to see her soon, and drove to his rented living space.

After a refreshing and cleansing shower, Mac dressed up and headed to the Planter's Grill in hopes of seeing Bev. Not surprising, Bev wasn't there but Mac waited for 30 minutes than went ahead and ordered. As he was digging into a very scrumptious meal, Bev walked in and seeing Mac at the table, walked over and sat down. "Sorry, I had paperwork to finish up before I could take a break. Looks good."

The waitress came over with a cup of coffee for Bev and asked if she wanted her usual. Bev, not wanting too heavy a meal for sitting around all night in the patrol car, opted for her usual small salad and one piece of toast. Mac asked Bev where she lived, and then told her where his little rental was. Mac asked Bev if she was originally from here. She told Mac that she had been from a large city in California. After graduating from college, she took police training at the prestigious Los Angeles County Sheriff Department. She spent a few years with the Sheriff's Department, than realized she had seen more serious crime in one year than most people would see in ten years of TV crime shows. A job on the Prairie City Police Department came open and she was hired. When Bev was asking Mac about his background, Mac had to be careful. He so wanted to be truthful, but that would ruin the operation, and he just barely got started. So he had to stick with the made up story, wishing he could have been honest with this beautiful police woman. It seemed like only minutes had gone by, but Bev noticed the time and had to get back out on patrol. They both wanted to get together again so they exchanged cell phone numbers and said goodnight.

Chapter 28

After Bill's visit with his friend in the logging company about the company's new drone, Bill used some of his little bit of free time looking up drones on the internet, and finally ordered a small inexpensive quadcopter to play around with. When it arrived, Bill took his time in going through the pieces, reviewing the bare bones instructions, and charging up the battery. Bill patiently waited for the battery to fully charge. In the meantime he watched a few drone videos on the internet. With the battery fully charged and remembering a few tips from the internet videos, Bill went out to the golf course while no one was around and fired up the quadcopter.

On the transmitter were two joy sticks, along with a few sliding switches and a couple of buttons. Each joystick controlled two functions, depending on whether you moved the stick vertically or horizontally. Bill found it easy to remember that moving the left stick forward provided more speed and more height. It was a little more difficult to remember the yaw, which was the left to right movement of the left stick. Yaw produced a right or left rotation of the quadcopter. Bill realized this was an important feature to get proficient with since it was a major adjustment to using a camera on the drone. It took a bit to remember that the joystick on the right controls the drone's nose attitude: forward, backward, left, or right. Then there were the trim buttons, used to adjust the amount of stick movement, and the video button for taking either pictures or videos.

Within the seven minutes of flight time allowed by the battery charge,

Bill crashed the quadcopter five times. But each crash was a little less intense, and Bill was feeling the exhilaration of flying the little drone. Damn, I should have done this a few years ago, he thought to himself. He quickly realized that he needed more batteries in order to extend the flight time, so an order was placed for six more batteries. He didn't have time for any more flying until the next week, but by then he had received the extra batteries. He spent a couple of batteries getting reacquainted with the controls, than tried out the attached camera. It was not the FPV type camera, so he had to wait and plug the memory stick into his computer to see how the pictures and videos turned out. He could see where the more expensive drone with a FPV system would be the better way to go. But he also was savvy enough to realize that crashing this cheap drone was far better for training than crashing a more expensive one. The more expensive drone will be the reward for learning to fly the cheaper one without crashing.

While the wildlands around Prairie City were dry and burning early, the wildlands near the Burner's home were still green and lush, with a light layer of dried leaves from last fall. The Burner had been working during the winter on developing a crude fire delivery system for mounting to the quadcopter, but the theory had not yet converted to the reality. In reviewing the material regarding aerial ignition, the Burner zeroed in on a couple of techniques. One type of aerial ignition used ping pong balls with a special potassium powder stored inside the ball. Injecting a milliliter of antifreeze caused a thermal reaction that would lead to flame generation in 20 to 40 seconds. Another type of ignition, but usually applied by ground instead of by air, requires a mixture of gasoline and a thickener, which creates a flammable gel. The problem with this was the need to have something to ignite this flammable gel. The Burner had used this type of ignition numerous times, and played around with adjusting the amounts and looking for alternatives to the gasoline and thickener. The engineering problem was how to develop a device that would either inject the ping pong ball or ignite the gelled gasoline, then release the ball or container.

The ping pong ball ignition scenario was going to require a much larger drone to carry the equipment. So that technique was ruled out. It looked like the choice was to be the gel scenario, which fit in with the Burner's preferred choice of M4 as the thickener agent for the flammable solution. So the Burner had to then decide on whether the drone needs to return for future duty or can the drone be sacrificed as part of the ignition source. Determining that answer would than answer the question of what type of drone would be needed. To use an expendable drone, it needed to be inexpensive and leave as little a foot print as possible when destroyed. The ignition device could utilize the drone as part of the ignition source. With a reusable drone, the ignition device would have to be safe in order to keep the drone undamaged so it could return and be reused. Current devices being used for aerial ignition were bulky and carried in helicopters, so the scale of the device would need to be shrunk way down. Fortunately the scale of the operation could be kept to a minimum. The Burner only needed one ignition source, but it was still a struggle to try and find a happy place between delivering enough material to start a fire and starting enough fire to quickly grow into a destructive force.

Thanks to the various connections the 'family' had throughout its operations, the Burner was able to get the use of a laboratory and materials to play around with. After explaining to the immediate boss what the Burner had in mind, the 'family' reviewed the notion and figured there was merit and potential profit in the successful development and application of this scheme. So with albeit limited support from the 'family', the Burner was able to spend some time in between 'family' commitments to work on the aerial ignition problem. After some laboratory work, the Burner decided to try one of two ideas regarding the ignition delivery. In order to carry enough material to get a fire going, the Burner ordered a hexcopter, which thanks to its six powerful motors, could easily carry a two liter bottle.

The plan would be to use the hexcopter to carry an amount of flammable gel in a plastic container. The container had an igniter specially designed by the Burner, and was activated by a tiny watch battery. To keep the igniter inactive until needed, the Burner used a measured length of string tied one end to a piece of plastic and the other end to the hexcopter. The idea was to push a button on the controller, which would release the bottle of flammable fuel and igniter. Tethered to the string, when the bottle reached the end of the string, the jerk would pull the plastic away from the switch contacts. In the lab, the resulting spark caused the flammable gases in the bottle to flash and set the fuel on fire. The Burner needed to see if the crude process would work in the field, so after searching for a good testing spot, the Burner decided the best spot to test the idea would be in the famed Pine Barrens of New Jersey. It was close, and it was burnable.

Chapter 29

It was almost a year ago that ordinary, sleepy Prairie City was violently awakened by two grisly and deadly fires. The investigation team members were frustrated, knowing the trail was cold and too much time had elapsed since any new information had come in. The FBI, after forcefully taking all of the work the team had gathered regarding the deadly fires, had not spoken to any member of the team. Bill seriously thought the FBI had locked the gathered data away in a drawer and threw away the key. The rest of the team members felt equally frustrated. Bill was not the only one who felt there was some hanky panky going on with the FBI, but what could they do about it? Someone needed to pay for taking away Prairie City's innocence.

When not doing odd jobs and working at the golf course or flying the drone, Bill would be reading various fire journal publications that the Fire Department received regularly. A particular article sparked his interest, coming out of the New Jersey Pine Barrens area. Upon first glance, he thought the article titled "Jersey Devil is Back?" should not be in the fire journal he was paging through. However, curious as to why the article was in the journal, Bill read through the short report. Brief mention of a couple of wild fires in the Pine Barrens, which was a fire prone area anyway, was not the important part of the article. How the fires started was what the article hinted at, with a link to an article in the Pine Barrens Tribune, the local newspaper covering the Pine Barrens area of southern New Jersey.

Bill typed in the link address in the search window of the browser he had opened in his computer. Finding the full newspaper article, he read it and came to the paragraph describing what a hiker in the woods claimed to have seen. This hiker was a local individual, a 'piney', and was quite familiar with the forest since he was born and raised along the fringe of the large forested reserve called the Pine Barrens. He said he was hiking along and minding his own business when out of the corner of his eyes he saw something coming down from the sky. Just before it hit the ground, the thing caught fire. It was probably a good couple of hundred feet away in a sparsely forested area along the edge of the meadow. The 'piney' hurried over to the smoke and found numerous small fires just getting started in the pine needles and grass. He said he stomped out the fires before they grew together, then called 911. He remembered hearing what sounded like a busy hive of bees just before he saw something falling out of the sky. But after getting the fires stomped down he looked and did not see any bee hives close by.

The 'piney' said for some unknown reason he remembered one of the stories told to him by his grandma when he was a young boy. The 'piney' explained the story to the reporter. According to the old tale, back in the mid 18th century, a woman living in the Pine Barrens gave birth to a thirteenth child on an extremely hot day. When the child was finally delivered, after a very difficult time for the mother, the attending nurses especially thought the child to be a monster, even calling it a devil. This child devil attacked the mother and nurses, then flew out the chimney to hide in the Barrens. The name for this child monster became the Jersey Devil, and every once in a while someone claims to have seen this fiery beast. Could it be the 'Jersey Devil' was back?

It seemed like just a local superstition, and Bill was wondering why the article was in the journal. Doing a little bit of digging in the internet, Bill found mention of a couple more fires in the Pine Barrens that after investigation were found to have undetermined starts. It was not uncommon to have fires that, even after investigation, did not yield the method of their start. Bill thought back and remembered numerous fires where the exact how the fire started had not been figured out. A best guess was left with some of the fire reports, while others were left with an undetermined in the box for what caused the fire. So it wasn't the undetermined cause that intrigued Bill, but the sighting of something that had fallen and caught fire, and the hearing of bees but none could be seen. If it had been something like a meteorite, the media would have been all over it. Statements from scientists galore would have filled up the papers and web sites. And some 'end of the world' fanatics would be pushing the gullible to give everything away, preferably to them of course, in order to be ready for the soon to come end of the world. But everything was quiet, so the couple of similar fires that happened in the Pine Barrens were still a mystery, and got Bill's curiosity started.

Chapter 30

The month of May had quickly exhausted twenty five of its thirty one days, when late in the afternoon the Sheriff's Dispatcher received a call from the Forest Service asking for assistance. A fire had been spotted a few miles out of Prairie City on Forest Service managed lands, but no Forest Service units were able to initially respond. The seasonal employees making up the bulk of the Federal and State fire crews were not scheduled to start for another week or two. And the few employees able to fight fire were all out committed on a couple of small fires, and wouldn't be able to respond in a timely fashion. The Dispatcher activated the tone for the Prairie City Fire Department from her computer/radio console, and within twenty seconds all the operating radios and pagers in the Fire Department started beeping their alerts. Bill was finishing setting a zone of sprinklers at the golf course when his radio beeped, causing him to jump while the adrenaline juices started producing. It didn't matter how many years Bill had been doing this firefighting as a volunteer, the beeping of the radio always made him jump and his adrenaline pump fired up.

Frank was tied up at the hospital with his ailing wife, so Bill had been acting chief for the past three weeks. Making sure George was available to cover the town, Bill headed out with the attack engine, with Sue driving and Mac riding in the middle. While heading out of town, Bill radioed Stan, the assistant chief trainee, and asked if he would jump on rural engine 2. Bill was thinking of putting Stan in charge of this fire, to help him gain experience. As soon as Stan had two more volunteers jump on board, he took off with rural engine 2, a few minutes behind Bill.

This fire was outside the District boundary, but thanks to the mutual aid agreement with the Forest Service and State Department of Lands, Prairie City Fire Department could assist until the responsible agency takes over, and visa versa. The important issue was to make sure enough volunteers and equipment were left in town to cover not just a town fire but also a District fire outside of town. Therefore Bill had George hold all resources after rural engine 2 left the station. After making sure of the Prairie City Fire Department response status, Bill radioed the Interagency Dispatch. "Dispatch, this is Prairie 672."

"Prairie 672, go ahead with your traffic for Dispatch."

"Dispatch, Prairie 672 is responding to a wildfire. I am with rural engine 1 and have rural engine 2 responding as well. Can you provide further information regarding this fire?"

"Prairie 672, this is Dispatch. Understand you and engines 1 and 2 are responding. Latest fire information is this fire is burning in a lightly forested section, about 2000 feet off the 643 road. Estimated size is 1 to 5 acres, slope according to the map looks to be less than 10%. ETA of nearest agency engine is one and a half hours. Based on the resource availability, we will try to have smokejumpers overhead, but the ETA is approximately 60 minutes out. Helicopter and aerial retardant resources are unavailable at this time."

"Dispatch, this is Prairie 672. Copied the fire and resource status. I will report when on scene. Should be there in about fifteen minutes."

"Prairie 672, Dispatch copies you will be on scene in about fifteen. Will advise any further and await your report. KOC743."

Bill suggested to Mac to keep a lookout for any vehicles traveling in the opposite direction. There had been no lightning yet this season, so it was a strong chance the fire was man caused. And if they saw a vehicle traveling in the opposite direction, someone needed to write down the license number and/or vehicle description. Bill radioed the same recommendation to rural engine 2. Never hurts to be reminded to be vigilant. If it were an arson fire, it would be nice to catch the culprit quickly before the situation escalated.

Rural engine 1 arrived on scene, and after radioing both Dispatch offices of being on scene, Bill had Sue stick with the engine to wait for rural engine 2. Bill grabbed a shovel and Mac was given a Pulaski. Each had dressed into their wildland gear and made sure they had a couple of canteens of water. Both Bill and Mac took off hiking to the fire. Because the fire was a ways from the road, Bill had grabbed a roll of plastic flagging tape from the engine, and tied pieces of flagging at various places along the trail they followed to get to the fire. With the flagging tape marking the path, additional firefighters would be able to follow the flagging to the fire as well as firefighters on the fire could find their way back to the road easily enough.

Hearing the crackling of the hungry flames, Bill knew they were just about to the fire's edge. Another forty feet of walking through the trees and the two firefighters caught up with the edge of the fire. At the same time, rural engine 2 arrived on scene with Stan and two more volunteers. Bill radioed Stan to lock up the engines, have everyone tool up and head to the fire, following the yellow flagging tape to the fire.

Bill started a quick assessment of the fire, looking for such things as the direction of the fire, what was burning and what was going to burn if the fire remained unchecked. As soon as Stan arrived at the fire, Bill turned the fire over to Stan. Bill would be there to help Stan, guiding Stan in doing the initial assessment. He needed to know how large of an area the fire had burnt, and where is the worst area of the fire. In checking the perimeter, Stan would also get an idea of how easy or difficult the fire line construction could be. He would have to walk the perimeter in order to get the best picture of this fire, but first Stan needed to get his volunteers started on an attack plan. Stan wanted the four volunteers, two with shovels and two, including Mac, with Pulaskis, to start building fire line from a rock outcrop near the spot where the yellow flagging tape met the fire's edge. But first, they needed a safety zone, a place where the firefighters could jump into to safely ride out a fire that turns rogue. Bill agreed with Stan that the rock outcrop was big enough, and with a little brush clearing, would serve nicely if needed.

Mac felt the adrenalin flowing, the excitement of working a type of fire he had not worked with before. He was used to field fires, and through the short training in Washington DC, he was a little familiar with working in structure fires. But a wildland fire, in the timber, was a new experience for him. Bill gave Mac a quick lesson on the Pulaski, and how they were to build a fireline. "Mac, whatever you do, pay attention to your fellow fire fighters. Safety is number one, and takes priority over all things. We don't want injuries. We want everyone to go home when done with this fire, so heads up and watch and listen. Keep ten feet from the nearest fire fighter, drink plenty of water, and watch for spot fires as you are working the fireline." Bill continued with a few more fire fighting commandments, and made sure Mac's questions were answered. So, while Stan and Bill took off to reconnoiter, the four volunteers worked on the safety zone.

It took the two assistant chiefs awhile to walk the perimeter, but when they finished and sat down on a rock for a break, Stan radioed the report to the Interagency Dispatch. It was estimated they had a five acre fire, burning in ground fuels, with a slight wind out of the southwest. The slope is less than twenty percent, and the aspect is facing southwest. The Interagency Dispatch center confirmed the message from Stan, and updated the etas for the response to the fire. Aerial retardant was on its way and should be over the fire in about twenty minutes, while the first engine was to arrive in forty five minutes. Stan radioed back to Dispatch, telling the Dispatcher he had copied the etas. Finished with the radio traffic, Bill and Stan caught up with the volunteers, who had finished cleaning up the safety zone and were working on building a fire line.

The plan was to build fire line from the rock outcrop, following the edge of the fire, toward the head of the fire. This flanking operation would be safer than trying to put the volunteers at the much more dangerous head in an attempt to stop the forward progress of the fire. Bill and Stan figured on leaving that situation to the Agency resources yet to arrive. These resources are better trained on wildland fire fighting and are more physically fit than the volunteers. Running into a few fallen trees that were slowing down the line building, Bill offered to go get the chain saw from rural engine one.

While Bill was hoofing it back to the engine parking area, Stan was on the radio with the first aerial retardant plane, just arriving to the area. Stan, talking with the pilot, suggested he take a look at the head of the fire where it was eating into the thicker timber. Once the pilot overflew the fire, he radioed back to Stan and suggested a couple of loads of retardant be dropped on the head to slow it down. He said right now the flanks look ok, until the wind changes direction, which would normally happen in the early evening. Stan agreed with the pilot's observation and suggestion, and told the pilot he would walk to the head and check the area out after the retardant drop was made. The pilot rogered the radio communication and lined his plane up for the first drop.

The pilot armed the fire retardant control system in the cockpit, dialed in the airspeed, and the number of gallons to dump. The computer system would take over controlling the dump gates when engaged, freeing up the pilot to keep the plane in control. He watched the elevation, lowering the plane to between 150 and 200 feet above the trees. As he got closer to the drop spot along the head of the fire, turbulence became more pronounced. But this pilot was used to it, having over 6000 hours of flight experience, much of it in fire situations. The pilot lowered his speed to 125 knots, and as he flew over the drop spot, he hit a switch on the control lever which told the computer to go with the program. The dump gates opened, the retardant pumped out, and when finished, the dump gates were closed. The pilot was able to concentrate on the plane controls, getting the speed up and climbing out. He radioed Stan that he had completed the drop, then he headed back to Prairie City airfield where the temporary retardant base was setup.

Stan watched the drop, and finally made it to the head of the fire to see what effect the retardant had. Even though the drop was only 800 gallons, the SEAT's loaded capacity, under the control of an experienced pilot this amount of retardant can be quite effective. With the dry, thicker timber in the path of the fire, the intensity of the fire was going to be building up, which was not a good thing. Stan radioed the pilot and told him the drop was in a good spot, but it looks like a couple more drops at least would be needed. Especially since there were no boots on the ground yet to enhance the retardant line with a fire line. Retardant lines are a great tool in fire fighting, but it was a well known fact that unless you have firefighters punching in a fire line alongside the retardant, the retardant is just what the name implies, it retards the spread of the fire, not stop it. So this first load of retardant was just one part of the expanding fire fighting effort against this 'dragon'.

With the temporary retardant plant set up at the Prairie City airfield, the Air Tractor 802 aircraft was able to refill its 800 gallon specialized tank and bring a second load of retardant to the fire in just ten minutes. As the pilot was bringing the plane around to line up with his previous drop, he checked the fire to give Stan a current status from an aerial view. It looked like the fire had grown a couple of acres, but the good news was the fire still was on the ground. If the burning conditions were just right, the fire would move up into the crowns and this fire could become a gobbler. With the fire just starting into heavier fuels, the possibility of a crown fire became greater. So ignoring the flanks for the time, the pilot dropped the second load of retardant across the head, and immediately turned for the airfield and another load of retardant, after a fuel fill up.

Bill had brought the chain saw to the crew, fired up the saw and started in on cutting the trees that were in the way of the line construction. One of the Pulaski operators took a break from chopping and changed over to swamping for Bill. As a swamper, the volunteer was responsible for clearing out the cut branches, brush, and logs, keeping a clear path for the saw to work in. With the chain saw working the heavier stuff, the volunteers were able to build about 150 feet of fire line in that first hour. Didn't seem like much when you consider that there were probably over 4000 feet yet to go to contain this fire, estimating that it was eight acres by now. If they had a type 1 hot shot crew, or a load of smokejumpers working this fire, the fire line would be built much more quickly. But that wasn't happening. So the volunteers did the best they could and chopped and scrapped until they ached, painfully sucked in air, and kept going against their protesting muscles.

A third load of retardant was brought in and dropped along the slowing head of the fire. Stan and the pilot agreed that the next load should be spread around the corner of the head and hit the flank of the fire where the volunteers were working toward. Then another drop would be needed around the corner of the head and along the opposite flank from the volunteers. Bill suggested to Stan that the volunteers take a break for about ten minutes, which Stan added to his list of things to monitor as a leader.

Chapter 31

During the break, Bill mentioned to the volunteers to be mindful of anything that looks out of place. Things didn't make sense, in terms of what caused this fire, and Bill was stressing the need to watch out and not accidentally destroy any evidence that could help determine what caused this fire. The likely hood this fire was started by lightning was out since there had been no lightning yet this season. An arson fire would have been closer to the road. Perhaps it could be a hold over fire from last year. Bill remembered a fire years ago that was started as a control burn of a slash pile of logs in the fall. The Fire Department had to respond to that same area the following July to extinguish a wildfire. For eight months the burning logs, covered by a layer of dry dirt, had smoldered. Than on a hot, dry, windy July afternoon, the conditions were just right for the smoldering fire to reach some drying cheat grass and brush. Enough smoke was given off so the fire could be seen and reported. So it was possible a hold over fire could be the cause for this current fire they were working on, but Bill had his doubts. Even though this fire was not his jurisdiction, Bill was curious and wanted an answer.

During their short break, both a State engine and a Forest Service engine arrived on scene. While the volunteers got up and started back to line building, Stan hiked out to meet with the just arrived engine crews. Catching up with the engine crews, Stan filled in the engine bosses with the current situation regarding the fire and the retardant. The senior engine boss, qualified as a type 3 incident commander, took over the fire operations, after Stan gladly agreed to relinquish the job of incident commander. Once the proper radio protocol had transpired, effectively documenting the transfer of command, Stan hiked back to the volunteers, leading the newly arrived wildland firefighters to the fireline. Upon joining up with the line building volunteers, the incident commander (IC) took Bill and Stan for a hike around the fire, getting a feel for what Stan had presented in his earlier report. While the bosses were scouting, the engine crews jumped in with the volunteers to extend the fire line.

Walking around the fire, Bill had a second chance to look over the area, and his eyes focused in on something out of the ordinary. Bill was watching the burn patterns on the trees and the general direction of the bent branches and charred grass stems, to get a quick feel for where the fire may have come from. Following the signs left by the moving fire, Bill noticed the signs seemed to be pointing to an object that caught Bill's attention. Having pointed this anomaly out to the IC and Stan, and after a quick look and an attempt to not disturb anything more than the fire had already accomplished, the IC flagged the area and contacted Interagency Dispatch requesting an investigator. Once back to the line building crew, the IC told the firefighters about the location of the potential ignition point for this fire, making sure everyone knew so they could protect the evidence.

The IC suggested Stan have the volunteers take a break from the line building and assist one of his engineers with laying a fire hose from the road to the fire while the rest of the wildland firefighters continue building fireline. It was going to be a long hose lay, but the Forest Service was equipped to handle long lays, and the State engine was equipped with plenty of inch and a half and inch hoses as well. Therefore the volunteers did not have to pull any hose off the two rural engines, keeping them both ready to respond to another incident. The volunteers laid the inch and a half hose along the traveled path to the fire, then started laying hose along the freshly constructed fireline. At strategic points, they set up laterals, placing a gated wye and a couple of rolls of inch hose with a nozzle at each lateral. They were building a hose system that would give the firefighters water to assist in the suppression and mop up of this fire. Once they ran out of inch and a half, they hooked in some inch hose to finish the line. The next job was to bring to the fire some mop up equipment. During mop up, the firefighter tries to conserve water, and would use a garden hose instead of the bigger supply hoses. So the hardware necessary to adapt from the one inch to garden hose size was placed along with lengths of garden hose at the strategic points.

Now all that was needed were more firefighters to make the job of corralling this fire easier and quicker. The IC asked if Bill and Stan could keep their volunteers on scene until the next engine crew arrived. The IC wanted his State and USFS wildland firefighters to continue line building while the volunteers operated the hose lines. Making sure George was available to continue covering the City, Bill said it was okay to stay. Bill suggested to Stan that he line out two volunteers per hose line to continue attacking the fire, and cooling down the edge of the fireline. Bill and Sue were teamed together, Mac was teamed with one of the volunteers, and Stan teamed up with the remaining volunteer. The Prairie City firefighters took turns switching between running the hoses and shoveling, knocking down the fire as it tried to cross the quickly built fireline.

The IC had determined that after the fifth load of retardant, and the progress being made, no further aerial retardant drops were warranted. After about a half hour of progressing with the attack lines, another Forest Service engine arrived and was tasked with taking over from the volunteers. While the volunteers were handing off the hoses to the newly arrived engine crew, Bill and the IC walked back to the location of the possible starting point of this fire to look at the object that caught Bill's curiosity. Not wanting to get too close and cause a problem with the investigation, Bill took some photos in hopes he could blow them up and see what the object was. From their view point, the object was badly melted and may never be determined, but sometimes the investigators can do wonders with stuff. After getting what he could in terms of notes and photos, Bill shook hands with the IC and told him if they needed more help to call. With all of his volunteers accounted for, the tired Prairie City volunteers left the fire scene as Bill radioed Dispatch that they had been released from this fire and were returning to the station.

Bill felt tired, but the tiredness felt good. The volunteers helped in the efforts to stop a fire from getting bigger, straining muscles they didn't know they had. But Bill was thinking about the object they had discovered near the potential fire start. It could be just debris from a hunter, like a plastic water bottle dropped instead of carried out. Even though the area was some distance off the road, one would be amazed at where people have walked, leaving signs of their passage by the trash on the ground. However, Bill had this little nagging voice in his head telling him this object was not someone's dropped garbage and the fire was not accidental. Maybe he had been reading too many mysteries, he thought. Whatever, Bill was anxious to find out from the Forest Service investigators what they came up with regarding the cause of this fire, and what the object was.

"Chief, do you see that pickup camper parked in the logging road over there to your right?" Sue's utterance woke Bill from his thoughts, and he quickly scanned in the direction Sue had pointed. Sue slowed down so that Bill could take notice of the pickup, but he could not read the license number, nor could Mac. Switching his radio frequency to the Interagency Dispatch, Bill told the Dispatcher about the pickup and rough location. The way the pickup was parked on the old logging road, you couldn't see it heading toward the fire, and just barely see it when leaving the fire and heading back to town. Bill figured it was probably just mushroom hunters, or someone out for a stroll along the old road running through the woods. But he thought it wouldn't hurt to mention it so the investigators have this piece of information to work with.

Both engines arrived to the station just as dark was settling in. Bill went to fill out the paperwork while the volunteers worked on refurbishing the engines so all would be ready for the next call. When all the paperwork and refurbishing was completed, Mac asked if anyone wanted to go get a drink at the bar. Bill thought it was a good idea, and so did Sue and a couple of the volunteers. The rest of the volunteers had to get home, so they took a rain check.

At the bar, as the fire fighters sauntered in, Bill exclaimed, "I don't know why bars have to be so dark inside but I guess it is a good thing for us since we are pretty grungy."

Mac and Sue laughed and said they hoped their odors were masked as well by all the booze smells lingering in the air. Finding a table, the five tired, dirty and smelly fire fighters sat and the waitress took their drink order. Bill was glad that the light was poor in the bar as it was hard for anyone to see from a distance the soot and dirt caked on the faces of the five volunteers. In the good old days the cigarette smoke would have been heavy enough to cover up the stench of the wildland smoke and perspiration that all five emitted. Oh well, the smell of stale beer and spilled alcohol partially masked the odors. The waitress placed the drinks on the table and the five volunteers toasted to a good fire job, and tossed back the first gulp. They talked over the tactics used on the fire, and enjoyed each other's company while slowly consuming their drinks.

Finished with the one drink, each of the five slowly stood up, plopped money on the table for the drinks and waitress, and painfully walked to the door. They had sat too long and the efforts of the afternoon worked over some muscles each didn't know they had until the pain hit. As Bill was walking toward the door he had a chill shake him, but he wasn't cold. He quickly looked around to see if anyone saw him shake, but it seemed everyone was engrossed in their drinks and conversations. All except one lone person sitting in a dark corner. He could see the person staring at him briefly, then the eyes moved off his. For a brief moment he thought those eyes had triggered a memory from a long time ago, but then again he could be just so tired that he was imagining things. "I am too tired to worry or even think about anything but a shower and bed," he said to himself. He vaguely remembered the same type of weird feeling happened before, but he couldn't remember when. Shrugging it off, he opened up the door and walked out into the night. Getting into his pickup, he drove home to his quiet, lonely house.

Chapter 32

The arsonist craved another fire. Those ignition tests in the Pine Barrens had whetted the Burner's appetite for more wildland fires, for expanding the 'catch me if you can' game. Trying to find out why the Prairie City area seemed to be calling the Burner, the arsonist had packed up and headed west to Prairie City.

Having arrived in Prairie City, the Burner spent a little time searching the forest for a potential site in which to start a wildfire. After finding a good looking location, the Burner set up the hexcopter and flew it to the location of where the fire was to start. Adjusting the gimball mounted camera on the hexcopter, the Burner released the self designed incendiary device and watch the released bottle of flammable gel burst into flame just before hitting the ground and dispersing burning fuel. The number of fire starts from the scattered burning fuel helped get a fire started quickly. Depending on the amount of flashy fuels present at the location of the drop, the resultant fire could potentially move quickly.

Having the hexcopter overhead while the fire took off, the Burner got to watch the slow progress of the fire. Though it was boring for awhile, once the flames started in on the tree branches and started to candle a tree, the Burner's excitement grew with the fire. The flight time of the hexcopter was getting short, so the Burner decided to bring the drone back and replace the battery. The Burner wanted to watch the fire a little longer, so after replacing the battery, the drone was guided back to the fire. By now the fire had grown, and the camera on board the drone was showing a few firefighters getting out of their engines. The Burner perked up when the drone's camera caught the arrival of the small aerial retardant plane. After the second retardant drop, the drone's 30 minute battery was getting low, and it was time to replace it. After a quick battery replacement, the Burner sent the drone back to the fire area to watch the action. The fire fighters were making quick progress, and the fire was being slowly corralled, so there was not much more to see that was exciting. It was time to button up this job and leave the area.

The Burner decided to run a quick search of the road out from the pickup to see if anyone was on the road that could be a problem when the Burner drove away from the parking spot. The road looked clear, so the arsonist loaded the hexcopter into the pickup, and was ready to move out of the area before being caught. As soon as the Burner stepped into the pickup, a red fire engine drove by heading toward Prairie City, sending a slight shiver through the arsonist. Knowing there was another red engine on the fire, the arsonist decided to wait a bit to see if the second engine drove by as well. Sure enough, a few minutes later the second red fire engine drove by heading to town. Waiting a bit more, the Burner decided it was time to leave, and slowly followed the fire engines to town.

The arsonist stopped at what looked like the most popular bar, wanting a cold drink, and to listen to any conversations regarding the fire. The waitress saw the Burner walk over to a small table in a dark area of the bar and sit. After the waitress took the drink order, the Burner's eyes kept searching and ears were opened to voices. One conversation the Burner picked up on was something about the authorities were looking for a pickup seen parked near the fire area. Damn, that was probably me, thought the arsonist. The Burner made plans to immediately trade in the pickup for a different one, and to be more careful next time.

While thinking about trading vehicles, the Burner saw five people come into the bar and sit down at an empty table. In the poor light the Burner couldn't see the streaked faces, but the Burner's nose was sensitive to smoke odors, and caught the scent of wildland smoke and perspiration. Concentrating on listening to the table of five, the Burner picked out some pieces of the discussion regarding today's fire. From a few things heard, the Burner figured these five to be part of the volunteer fire department. What could be picked out of the conversations amidst the noise did not raise an issue with the Burner. The Burner was slowly nurturing a second drink when the five volunteers finished their drinks, stood up, and headed to the door. While looking each one over briefly, the Burner was surprised by the last one, the oldest of the five. When the Burner's eyes starred into the eyes of the older man, a strange feeling hit the Burner, kind of like déjà vu mixed with an electrical charge, quickly surging through the body. The Burner immediately turned away to break the eye contact, but the eerie feeling and a chill was slow to evaporate.

The Burner left the bar shortly after the five fire fighters, and headed out of town. The arsonist planned to return the rented pickup, and find a different vehicle to rent from another town. No sense in attracting more attention. The arsonist could not understand that eerie sensation, and realized that it had brought back the notion that something in this town was calling. It felt like something from a time long ago, something long suppressed, was trying to wake up. But what was it?

A couple of days later the incognito arson investigation team met after many months. Amrit had called to say he had finally received the results of some laboratory testing he had done. Amrit drove down from his office, which was a four hour drive north of Prairie City, catching up with the rest of the team at the fire station. Everyone looked to Amrit for an optimistic piece of new information, some reason why they could continue on with what was looking more and more like a lost cause.

Amrit presented the results of his 'behind the back of the FBI' lab work on the carpet samples from the house fire and pickup fire samples that he had carefully hidden from the FBI search months ago. Amrit said the testing lab found traces of M4 fuel thickener mixed with gasoline in some of the carpet samples, and in one of the plastic containers found at the rear of the house, as well as some samples from the pickup fire. The ratio of M4 to gasoline was the same in the samples from both the house and pickup.

Before anyone else could ask, Nick spoke up asking what this M4 was all about. Amrit explained that M4 was a fine powder that when mixed with a flammable liquid, such as gasoline, makes an almost paste like substance that burns hot and is hard to extinguish. It was one of the primary thickeners used to make napalm for war use. Some farmers use a little when they burn off their stubble fields. A few mining companies use the M4 to enhance their blasting. Quickly digesting the information,

Nick thought out loud that, "since M4 was not a household word in these parts, might we assume someone from out of the area was responsible for the fires?"

Beth jumped in and told Nick that they had pretty much agreed someone from outside the area was the arsonist, but these lab results might give them a direction to start looking into.

Walt volunteered a couple of his officers to start checking the local hardware businesses and fuel companies to see if any of them handles M4 fuel thickeners. The usual packaging for the M4 is either in 2.5 lb cans or 55 gallon drums, so storage wasn't an issue. The County Sheriff said he would have his Deputies check the same type of businesses throughout the rest of the County. It was agreed that if either Department personnel stumbled upon a business handling the M4, they needed to get a look at the records to see if there are any data that could help identify the person or persons purchasing the M4.

Nick was busy jotting down notes on this latest piece of information, glad that something has happened in this stalemate. Walt however threw cold water on Nick's dream of getting this latest information out to his reader public. "Sorry Nick, but this stuff is still in the 'what you hear and see here stays here' category. If the FBI got wind of this we'd all be wearing orange jumpsuits." Against Nick's journalistic nose for the story, Nick agreed to hold off printing anything. He didn't think he would look good in orange either.

The meeting was about to break up, no further information to discuss, when Bill remembered to mention the pickup truck seen near the wildland fire a couple of days ago. Neither law enforcement authority had yet been notified of this incident, so Bill provided a brief on the fire, and that he and Sue had seen a pickup parked off the main road not far from the fire. Bill said, "I haven't heard from the Forest Service inspector yet, and don't expect to for some time. The pickup could have simply been parked there for legitimate recreational reasons. If the fire is determined to be arson, then law enforcement will want to look into this pickup. If we spread the word quietly, then we might help the investigation."

Walt and the Sheriff agreed to quietly look into the pickup, and give the scant information on the pickup out to the patrolling officers and Deputies. Bill remembered the strange object they found at the fire, and filled in the team members. "That object is probably in the hands of a Forest Service investigator by now, but if it were me, I would be highly suspicious of arson, and that object may well be the starter of the fire," said Bill.

Again, Nick was cautioned to not let this discussion go public. No sense in stirring up a hornet's nest without an escape plan. The clandestine meeting broke up with a little hint of optimism in the air. After months of nothing, perhaps there is a little hope. Like a single firefly in a dark tunnel.

Bill arrived to his typically empty and uninviting home. Pouring himself a drink, he settled into his easy chair and got comfortable. His thoughts drifted from the meeting and recent fire to his ex wife. He was remembering back nearly thirty years ago, when Armida left while Bill was typically out fighting a nasty wildfire. They had been arguing often, especially about Bill being gone on fires so much during the spring through the fall. Bill still remembered how shocked he was to find Armida gone. Sure, they had argued but they had always made up. Even after many years Bill still felt there was something odd about Armida's sudden leaving. He had done all that he could possibly do to contact her, to find out where she went and how she was, and to apologize and beg that she come back. Maybe that was why he would every so often fall into this "if only" depression, wondering if there was more he could have done to find her, or what it would have been like if he had been around more often. His friends chastised him over these moods, telling him to let it go, but it was not easy. It had been quite awhile since he had been hit with the memories of the past, so it was strange he would have them now. He thought, "What the heck brought this memory on?" After thirty years the emptiness and hurt were still there.

Chapter 33

It had been a week since the last wild fire. The arsonist decided it was time to try another one. Having picked out another likely spot in the forest, the arsonist parked the different rented vehicle quite a distance from the fire area, and a ways off the road. This time the Burner spent a little time walking around the area where the pickup was parked, then off loaded the trailered four wheeler. After driving the four wheeler closer to the area picked out for the fire, the Burner launched the drone to see the area from an aerial perspective. Feeling good with the results, the Burner landed the drone and carefully fueled the bottle and primed the string ignition system. The arsonist had been notified of another job for the 'family', so this fire needed to go well so the Burner could return to the east coast with a smile.

Remembering having read in a fire behavior textbook about certain requirements for a wildfire to progress, the Burner picked an area fairly open, with heavy brown grass. The low hanging pine branches surrounding the sparse trees on the west facing slope of the forested hillside would help fuel the growing fire. After replacing the battery in the hexcopter, nicknamed Prometheus, the Burner flew the drone toward the hillside location so carefully picked. The Burner had chosen the name Prometheus because Prometheus, from Greek legend, was the Titan who gave man fire. Prometheus also happened to be the supreme trickster of the Titans, a fact not lost on the Burner's sense of tease.

Once over the spot on the ground where the arsonist hoped to start a significant fire, the Burner pushed a button on the radio control transmitter. This button was a modification that the Burner had developed. Pushing this extra button activated a servo in the drone, causing a release of the latch holding the fuel bottle, sending it falling to earth. With the gimbaled FPV camera, the Burner could watch the bottle hit the end of the tether and burst into flame.

The drone had been hovering over a spot of thick, dried grass bunched up against a dying pine branch that had broken off the adjacent tree. The branch, which was covered with desiccant needles instead of lush green ones, was set just right, leaning against a pine tree leaking sap. Enough natural fuel was piled up to feed a small fire, and get it to carry over to the mature pine tree, which was suffering from a pine borer. The pine borer was causing multiple trails of sap, the life blood of the tree, to weep down the bark of the dying tree. This sap was flammable, and along with the stressed pine needles, made for a potential torch that when ignited, would shot off thousands of fire brands into the air. With these fire brands scattering over the hillside, the fire could spread quickly.

Using the smart phone, The Burner could see in the view screen what Prometheus was seeing; that smoke was starting to rise up amongst the scattered trees on the slope. Circling the drone over the location of the crashed fuel bottle, the Burner noted the created fire was growing, and moving toward the dying pine tree. So far the plan was working, even a bit better. Wanting to conserve battery life in the hexcopter, the arsonist brought the drone back and replaced the battery. While waiting for the fire to grow a bit more, the Burner broke out a snack and a pop, and listened to the scanner radio for any radio traffic regarding this fire. Now it was a waiting game.

The fire's smoke became noticeable, and was reported by a pilot flying his own little Cessna 182 a few miles away from the fire. Not wanting to vary from his planned flight path, the pilot radioed the airport with the estimated coordinates of where he thought he saw the smoke. The Multi Agency Dispatch Center received the pilot's transmission from the airport. After consulting a map in the computer, the Dispatcher handling the radio transmissions for that zone radioed the air center to notify them of the smoke report and possible location. The air center helicopter was out on another fire, but was available, so the Dispatcher sent the helicopter to investigate the smoke report.

In twenty minutes time, the little fire started by Prometheus had grown to about two acres, and was threatening a couple more pine trees. The fire was starting to move more quickly, finding the steepness of the slope an asset in trying to satisfy its appetite. The helicopter arrived over the area, and the pilot could see the fire was growing quickly. The fire was moving up the slope toward the thicker Douglas fir stands. Once in the Doug fir, the fire would have even more dense fuel to build upon. Providing a report to the Dispatcher, the helicopter pilot searched for a landing spot near the fire. After landing to off load the three person helitack crew, the pilot rushed back to the air center to load up a water bucket, and head back to the fire. With the report from the helicopter, Dispatch notified the air center to get a retardant plane headed to the fire. Two engines from the State were available, and started heading to the fire. By the time the helicopter arrived back over the fire with the bucket slung under the belly of the helicopter, the fire had already grown to about five acres. The crew foreman for the helitack crew was busy looking over the fire, and told the helicopter pilot to start cooling down the head of the fire once he found water. The plan was to start an anchor and pinch operation, with help from incoming resources.

Meanwhile, the Burner had heard the helicopter circling the fire, and knew from the radio traffic that the little fire was growing nicely. Not being able to stand it any longer, the arsonist just had to launch the drone to see first hand what was happening. Being careful to not get the drone near the helicopter, the Burner guided the drone toward the fire using the tree tops as a reference. As Prometheus was getting close to the fire, the Burner could see in the viewer screen hungry flames licking up the hillside and eating up a few trees. A retardant plane was coming into the area to drop the first load, and the Burner desperately wanted to see that action too. Controlling the drone so it would hover, the Burner worked the other hand on the camera control. With its gimball feature, the remote controlled camera could be moved around separately from Prometheus. The Burner positioned the drone and camera to get a view of the retardant plane working its way toward the head of the fire. In the effort to get a good view of the retardant drop on the voracious flames, the Burner accidentally let the drone get closer to the aircraft then originally planned.

"Oh hell," the Burner exclaimed as soon as the pilot of the retardant plane radioed that there was some object in the area flying around. She was unable to get a good look at it, since she was busy flying the plane, getting ready to drop the load of retardant. The arsonist had quickly brought the drone down low against the tops of the trees, and then headed it back to where the Burner was standing. "Damn it," the Burner said in frustration. The arsonist could not afford to be caught. Not only was there a twenty five thousand dollar fine for flying a drone near a fire, but the trail of arson fires that painted the Burner's notoriety would certainly be discovered after being arrested. The Burner could not imagine the rest of life behind bars.

Not wanting to be caught, the Burner decided to call it a day, and pack stuff up and get out of the area. In listening to the radio traffic, the Burner had not heard anymore mention of anyone seeing a flying object, so maybe all will be okay. Still, the Burner did not want to chance it and just left the area as quickly as possible. Besides, it was time to head back to the east and get a newly assigned job done, and hopefully return to this area for some more fun. "Damn it, I just wish I could watch the entire fire operation."

Heading back to Prairie City, the Burner stopped at the bar, taking a seat at a table in the darker part of the bar. Bummed at not being able to watch anymore of the fire fight, the Burner downed the first drink quickly. While working more slowly on a second drink, the Burner watched a group of three men take a table and order drinks. The Burner was starting to look over their faces, and recognized the first one as one of the volunteers. At the second face the Burner was startled. It was the same man from the other night that set off something in the Burner that couldn't be explained or put aside. And now that weird sensation was back even stronger. The Burner had a reputation for being cool under fire, pardon the pun, but there was something here that was getting to the Burner. And the Burner needed an answer.

Bill, Mac and George had decided to visit the bar after they had been on standby at the fire station for the past two hours. It turned out the Forest Service did not need the volunteers, so Mac and the two assistant chiefs went to get a drink before going home. The three sat at a table and took their drinks. All of a sudden, Bill had this strange felling once again, a chill walking up and down his body.

The three volunteers talked a little about the radio traffic they had heard regarding the wild fire going on. George asked if Bill had heard the radio traffic about one of the pilots thinking she saw something flying close to her retardant ship. Mac mentioned that with the experience these retardant aircraft pilots have, they would know if they were looking at a bird. Radio controlled drones were becoming very popular, and in some of the more populated places throughout the country, there were complaints of drones interfering with fire fighting activities. Mac was wondering if this could be a similar situation. Bill mentioned he was getting back into the hobby of rc flying and was having fun flying a small quadcopter. He was even considering flying the drone near a fire so he could get a visual from above. His attraction to the idea came from a different need, a need for more information about the fire. He was not aware of anyone else in the vicinity that was into flying drones, but that did not mean there was no one else. After all, the drone market was extremely popular right now. Bill said if anyone happened to know of someone else flying the drones to let him know. It would be nice to start a club.

The Burner heard parts of that conversation, and was becoming a little worried. The Burner figured out that the person that seemed to be causing the strange feeling, the chills, was named Bill. That name jarred a memory, but as much as the Burner tried to access that memory, it was too faint to mean anything. In addition, the Burner was a little worried that this Bill guy sounded like he was into flying quadcopters. The chances of running into a fellow quad pilot are getting better as more pick up the hobby. But the coincidences in this situation were cause to walk very carefully, thought the Burner. As the Burner studied the man named Bill, Bill turned toward the staring arsonist. That damn strange sensation shuddered through the Burner's body, just as a similar sensation hit Bill's. Fortunately no one was watching or paying attention, so no one saw the both of them shuddering at the same time.

Bill finished his drink and after giving up on trying to explain the weird sensations, decided to call it a night and left the bar. Mac decided he wanted one more drink, so George said his good night and headed home. Mac headed to the bar stool with his drink, not wanting to sit at the table all alone. Someone sat down alongside Mac in an empty bar stool, and when Mac turned his head to take a quick look, he saw a young, very pretty woman with a drink in hand, smiling at him. Instead of turning back to his drink like he had planned, he held his stare on the young woman, not being able to utter a word. The young woman he was starring at had light brown hair, a slight olive tinge skin color, green eyes, and lips he wanted to kiss. Trying not to be too gawking, he couldn't help but notice that she had noticeable curves in the right places. The woman chuckled and said "Hi, I am Diana. Cat got your tongue?"

Mac thought to himself, "Damn, I am liking this place even more. Two gorgeous women, in a short time. And neither seemed very shy." Laughing, Mac finally found his voice, introduced himself, and a conversation started up between he and the beautiful Diana. Eventually they both finished their drinks, and Mac said, "Damn, I do not want this night to end, but I am about ready to fall asleep right here, and I have to get up early to farm. Are you going to be here tomorrow, because I would like to see you again?"

Diana said unfortunately she had to leave in the morning and head back east to her office. They exchanged cell phone numbers, and as Mac started to get up off the bar stool, Diana placed her hand over his. Mac looked into Diana's eyes, saw the lust, and decided sleep can wait.

Diana followed Mac to his rented room, where they quickly shed their clothes and concentrated on feeding their hunger for sex. As blissful exhaustion took over, Mac thought to himself that maybe he won't miss the big city night life after all. Here were two gorgeous women that could easily put the big city gals to shame. Mac said to himself, "Yep, I think I like this job," and fell asleep too tired to even dream.

Chapter 34

It had been fairly quiet, fire wise, for the past couple of weeks when one afternoon, Bill received a call from the MultiAgency Dispatch Center asking if the Fire Department could supply a water tender to help with a wildfire. Bill had seen a little smoke and heard the helicopter and air tanker, but that was the extent of his knowledge regarding this latest fire. Once he had the location of where the fire was and where the water tender needed to be, Bill said he would send a two man crew with the tender, with an ETA (estimated time of arrival) in about thirty five minutes. Next, Bill had to place a few phone calls to find the two volunteers that could break away from their jobs to work on the water tender. Stan was able to take off work, which was good because Bill wanted an officer with the tender when the tender is being loaned out. After four more phone calls Bill finally found one of the volunteers able to leave work and family to help with the water tender. It had been a busy spring with more fire calls than normal, and some of the volunteers had been off work too much. Bill gave them both fifteen minutes to be at the station where he would meet them. Bill called George, the other assistant fire chief, and filled him in as to the fire and the request for the tender. George said he would stick around town while Bill headed out to the fire.

After meeting Stan and the other volunteer at the station to provide them with what information he had regarding the wildfire, Bill drove out to the fire ahead of the tender. He wanted to talk with the IC, the incident commander, and get a better picture of what was happening and what the estimated need for the tender was. Bill arrived at the fire and located the IC, who was one of the engine crew bosses from the State Department of Lands. The IC was able to bring Bill up to date, and that the fire was growing and already at fourteen acres. The IC commented that this fire was in a strange area to be an arson fire, yet there had not been a lightning storm pass through the area. Bill's senses were tingling, and he asked the IC if there had been an estimated point of origin found yet. The IC said there had not been the time nor manpower to look for the ignition point, but an investigator was on the way. Bill asked if he could be notified when the investigator was here and if he could tag along with the investigator. The IC didn't have a problem with that as long as the investigator was okay with the idea. After giving the IC his cell phone number, Bill went over to the just arrived water tender and introduced Stan to the IC, who then proceeded to line out Stan with what was to be done.

The IC suggested there could be a water source for refilling the tender about two miles up the road, but the dry weather may have dried up the water source. Bill said he and Stan would go look over the place and see what they could find, leaving the volunteer with the tender in case one of the engines needed a refill. Finding the location, the water source was not the best, but there was some water flowing. Bill and Stan worked on building a dam to hold back the little bit of flowing water in hopes to gather enough for the tender to use. The two volunteers than headed up the road further to see if another water source could be found. It was about another three miles before they came across another similar water situation, and built a dam there as well. Hopefully between the two places they would have enough water to squeak by.

Bill dropped Stan off at the staging area where the water tender was parked, and Stan went to find the IC. While Stan took care of telling the IC about the water situation, Bill headed back into town. He caught up with George at the fire station and told him about the fire situation. Bill mentioned that he was going to go back out to the fire as soon as the investigator arrived. He had a nagging sense this fire might be just like the one a couple of weeks ago. Bill also mentioned to George that with the fire activity, the volunteers needed to be on extra alert, and be ready to spend days away from work and family. This season was shaping up to be a bad one. And if they did have an arson taking advantage of the dry situation, it could be much worse.

Carefully controlling Prometheus, the Burner managed to keep the drone close to the tree tops. Listening in on the radio frequencies of both the fire department and the U.S. Forest Service, the arsonist did not hear radio traffic mentioning the drone sighting nor the sighting of the Burner's camper. So far so good, thought the arsonist. The fire video coming in from the hexcopter's FPV was not spectacular, but the watching of the hungry flames from above presented a different stimulus to the Burner. Monitoring the clock, the Burner noticed the drone's flight time was getting close to the return time. Not wanting to lose control of the hexcopter and have it come down somewhere in the trees, the arsonist brought the hexcopter back to where the Burner was standing. Replacing the drone's battery, the Burner bound the hexcopter and transmitter and headed the drone back to the fire area for another twenty minute observation.

Wanting a view of the flames from a different area, the Burner moved Prometheus to the other flank, where there was more fire activity. The Burner had to be careful with controlling Prometheus, since not only was there a chance of being seen by aerial resources as well as ground troops, but also getting too close to the fire could cause the drone to become very unstable. The heat and wind generated by the fire could greatly affect the hexcopter. The Burner was getting anxious, wanting to feel the thrill of watching the gobbling flames. Of course the hide and seek game was an additional thrill.

The Burner's lustful stare at the flames in the video window was shattered by the radio. An engine boss working with her crew on the fireline happened to glance up and caught a quick view of something hovering just above the trees. She thought it was a bird at first, but after a second glance at the still hovering object, she was pretty sure it was no bird. This engine boss was vigilant, like she was supposed to be, and concerned for the safety of her crew. The thing she saw may not be a safety hazard, but being unsure of what it was exactly, it could be a potential danger. So she radioed to the IC what she had seen, and the IC passed the sighting along to the aerial observer to see if he could see the object. After the previous fire incident in which a pilot thought she had seen a possible drone, this report could either be 'the little boy who cried wolf,' or the beginning of a serious problem.

Upon hearing this radio traffic, the Burner immediately moved the drone, and carefully worked the controls to bring the hexcopter back. Not wanting anyone to follow the drone, the Burner zigged and zagged, dropping into large openings then back up to tree top heights. With a sigh of relief, the Burner heard the aerial observer talking to the IC about not seeing the object of concern. These close calls were stimulating and part of the game, thought the Burner, but sometimes the adrenalin rush is too much. Once Prometheus was safely back in hand, the arsonist headed to the camper. After loading up and making sure the area was clean, the Burner drove away, figuring it was time to get back east, and to a couple more jobs needing to be done for the 'family'. The plan was to return later in the summer when things were normally more conducive to large fires. The Burner was too preoccupied to notice the brake lights come on the Forest Service pickup that had just driven by heading toward the fire.

Heading to the new wildland fire, Forest Service investigator Beth was in her agency pickup thinking about how busy she had been lately, and that the fire season had barely officially started. She noticed a pickup camper pass her going in the opposite direction. Out of habit Beth had a quick glance at the license plate, and stopped to write it down before forgetting. Jotting down the number from the plate, she continued heading to the fire a few miles away. Probably nothing, but Beth's woman's intuition and her 'Sherlock Holmes' ability to ferret things out led her to follow her own procedures, including checking the license plate.

The Burner decided to stop off at the bar for a drink and a little listening before heading east. There might be a little bit of gossip about the new fire that the Burner needs to hear before leaving town. The arsonist picked a different table to sit at this time, and noticed a couple of loggers stomp in, dragging in bits of chain saw chippings, and smelling of tree sap and perspiration and still wearing their hard hats. The Burner tuned ears to the loggers in hopes to hear some talk of the fire. The bar door opened once again and in walked Mac, heading to the bar.

Diana sat down on a bar stool next to Mac, who was pleasantly surprised to see her. "Nice to see you tonight" Mac said, his gaze taking in Diana's beauty. Diana replied that she was going to have to cut the evening short as she needed to leave town and get back to her job. "But you just got back," said a disappointed Mac. As the two of them slowly worked on their drinks, Mac asked Diana what kind of work she did that would bring her to this area. Diana mentioned it was a sales job related to the agricultural market, but she was purposely vague. When Mac pressed her for a little bit more information, she changed the subject and asked Mac if he had heard anything about the latest fire. Mac mentioned the only thing he knew about the fire was that the Fire Department sent a water tender to help out, and that one of the assistant chiefs went out to see what was going on.

One of the nearby loggers had overheard Diana and Mac talking, and said he had heard that one of the fire fighters saw something flying around, but it wasn't verified. Mac mentioned that was the second time recently that someone had seen something flying around a fire, but no one actually identified it. Diana agreed that was strange, and maybe just a bit like seeing ghosts after hearing a good ghost story.

Maybe it was the four years of being a Special Agent. Mac felt something was not right, something with Diana was not adding up correctly. He was caught between wanting to grow a relationship with beautiful Diana, and listening to his small voice telling him something was not quite right. He was mulling this thought over in his head when Diana said she had to get going, that she had a long drive ahead. Mac walked her to her pickup and, caught off guard, realized he was sharing a kiss goodbye. He was surprised at Diana's brazenness, and soon was wishing for more. Diana headed out of town and Mac drove to his rented abode, and cooked some dinner. He was thinking more of the kiss with Diana and wishing it was much more, instead of thinking about his assignment. With that tiny little sense of something strange about Diana, his lustful thoughts spurred on by Diana's kiss switched over to Bev, and he went to sleep still thinking of Bev and Diana.

Chapter 35

B eth had been waiting somewhat patiently for the results of the testing on the collected material found near the estimated starting point of both recent wildfires. There had been a pleasant break in the fire fighting during the last couple of weeks in June. A little moisture had fallen, slowing things down. Things had picked up during the Fourth of July celebrations, with a number of fireworks fires that had to be suppressed and then investigated. Beth was busy that week of the Fourth, investigating a few fires obviously caused by illegal fireworks. Her job was to attempt to find and charge the culprit or culprits with a misdemeanor for shooting off illegal fireworks. It had been nearly a month since the last significant wildfire, thought to be arson, and the lab had finally called Beth to come over and get a quick lecture on the findings.

The lab technician explained to Beth that the material was of such a small amount and quite degraded by the fire that it was very hard to tell with certainty what the material was, what it could have been. However, he went on to say that he was able to run an analysis on the solution distilled from the substance minus the normal forest litter. That test resulted in the material being recognized as predominately a type of polyvinyl chloride. "I also found traces of a fuel thickener agent along with gas and diesel traces. A trace amount of nickel and copper was also found. I would shrug and say this is a weird and unusual circumstance out in the forest if there were only one such occurrence. With both the samples showing similar enough numbers and chemical names, I would have to rule out coincidence."

Beth asked the technician if he thought this substance could be part of the ignition, but the tech would not stick his neck out that far without further analysis. He however did mention that if you put a few of the pieces together, one conclusion was that this sample was of a plastic bottle that held a flammable mix of fuel.

Beth said, "Ok, that makes sense, but what would have triggered the fire?"

"That I cannot answer yet. Perhaps the copper and nickel traces have something to do with that, but I would need more samples to test."

Beth told the technician that for now what she brought in was it. He told her that if anything different comes up, or if there is another fire in which she can find a similar substance near the fire starting point, feel free to call him anytime. With that he gave her his private cell phone number, since he was intrigued and hated to present such findings that were not definitive. He decided to spend some time researching documents suggesting similar findings in hopes he could learn what the substance could indicate.

Back in New Jersey, the Burner was assigned a warehouse burn job. Apparently the warehouse owner was delinquent on the 'protection tax' owed to 'the family'. It was decided to set an example that others would appreciate and pay attention to.

The warehouse was a large one, and the Burner thought this would be a good chance to utilize Prometheus in an indoor situation. Making sure the area was clear, the Burner launched Prometheus and flew above the stacked merchandise. It was expensive, but the Burner had found a thermal camera capable of mounting to Prometheus. With the go ahead from the Burner's boss, the camera was purchased. This was the first operational flight using the new camera.

The Burner liked using the thermal camera, but it would still be a lot better to work outside in the daylight. At least the arsonist could make out certain features that stand out from the darkness. After the initial flight around the inside of the warehouse, the Burner noticed a couple good starting places to put fire into. The thermal camera did not show any white silhouettes of a heat signature from a human, so the Burner attached the ignition bottle to Prometheus and flew the drone to the identified fire starting locations.

So far the Burner was pleased with the way the test run was working. With everything looking good, the first ignition bottle was dropped. The arsonist resupplied Prometheus, flew the drone to the next location and proceeded to drop the next bottle. The Burner spun the drone around to watch the first fire developing, and was pleasantly surprised at how quickly the fire was developing. Moving Prometheus to a better viewpoint, the arsonist watched both fires quickly expand. The heavy smoke was starting to work it's way down from the ceiling. The Burner was concerned that the smoke would soon obscure the view, as well as the temperature in the smoke would get so hot as to melt the drone. The Burner figured it was time to vacate, and the progress of the fire was acceptable. Looking back at the warehouse as the Burner was driving away, the arsonist felt a sense of pride in another job well done.

Beth hadn't gotten too far with the license plate number search. The license plate number from the pickup truck she saw leaving the fire area a week ago turned out to belong to an out of state car rental agency. Beth had to explain what she wanted to the local law enforcement people, who went to the rental agency to talk with the employees. The gathered information turned out to be of little help. Tracking the person's id ran into a dead end, and the copy of the photo was of so poor quality that the only thing that was determined from the study of the photo was the renter was a woman. And even that could be wrong if someone was trying to change their looks for the photo.

A week later Bill, Mac and a few of the volunteers headed over to the bar after the regular evening fire training meeting. Bill, trying to concentrate on the conversation at his table, was hearing bits and pieces of a more interesting topic a couple of tables away. One of the men sitting at the other table mentioned he had heard that a grey colored pickup truck had been seen leaving the fire area. Bill was curious as to which fire they were talking about. So he kept his ears tuned to the other table's conversation, hoping that some other spoken words will clarify what he had just heard. After a while of trying to pickup bits of the other table's conversation, Bill gave up realizing the topic of the pickup was long past being brought up again. He will just have to remember to ask Beth next time he saw her.

Bill was finished with his drink and was getting ready to head home when Mac threw out a question that stopped Bill in his tracks. Mac said

"Bill, I heard talk about a couple of possibly arson fires last year that were deadly. What's the status of the investigation?"

Bill, not having told anyone in the Department about the secret committee, just shrugged and told Mac he didn't know. "Mac, the FBI marched in here and took all of the investigative work that had been gathered by our police, State police, our investigator, and even the Forest Service investigator. An idiot by the name of Ricardo told all the involved agencies that the FBI was handling the cases now and that all of us are to forget this situation ever happened."

Trying to keep from flinching, Mac realized there was a lot he didn't know about concerning this whole situation he had been thrown into. But he couldn't help think Bill was saying a lot less than he knew. He figured he would carefully push the issue, but pick a better time, and soon. He now understood why the FBI was a dirty word around town, and he had better hope his being an agent with the dreaded FBI does not get exposed.

Chapter 36

Ricardo was impatient, as usual. He had not heard from his field agent, Mac. Ricardo had wanted this operation to be finished quickly. So he yelled at his secretary to get Mac on the line, and to do it now. Mac was working in the shop at the farm, cleaning equipment and doing the regular maintenance on the rolling stock before it was needed for harvesting. He saw the special caller id associated with Ricardo, and after checking that no one was around, Mac answered his cell. Mac waited through the normal rant, and when Ricardo was finished, Mac spoke. "Boss, this is a slow operation. I am working my way into the trust of these people, but it takes awhile. I think certain people on the Fire Department know more than they are willing to let on, so I am carefully trying to wiggle into that group's trust. There seems to be an arson on the loose, keeping the locals hopping. I am in the morning coffee social group now, but haven't heard much associated with the case yet."

Ricardo was not happy, of course. To be kind, Ricardo was likened to a medieval gaoler, only happy when he had someone painfully stretched on the rack. "Damn it Mac, move the operation forward. You've been there over three months now and nothing to show for it. I don't have time for your waltzing through the tulips. You are not there to make friends, you are there to get me information."

Not happy with Ricardo's rant, Mac said, "I am telling you Boss, I know these people. They are just like the ones I grew up with. Push too hard and you'll never get a thing. The only way to get these people to loosen their tongues is to make them believe that I am one of them. That doesn't happen over night. I did hear mention of the hatred these people have for the FBI jumping in and taking all of the work they had done on the arson cases. I heard your name mentioned, not kindly I may add."

"So what, I was just doing my job, like you are supposed to be doing. I don't like it one bit. Mac, get something for me and get it quick, or you will find yourself counting Aleutian cackling geese in Attu." With that final word, Ranting Ricardo, as he was called behind his back, slammed the phone down and yelled at his secretary for a cup of coffee.

At the next fire training meeting, Mac overheard a couple of the volunteers talking about the rumor regarding the pickup truck with camper that was seen leaving the latest wildfire. That was over a month ago, and other than a couple of fireworks fires, the last couple of weeks of June and the first couple weeks of July were fairly quiet. Frank was back in town for a short while. He had to return to the cancer treatment center his wife was staying at, but wanted to check on things and catch up on the latest happenings. For the training meeting, Frank had everyone check over their wildland gear and work over each of the rural engines, making sure they were ready to respond with all the proper hoses and nozzles, hand tools, fresh drinking water, and extra MREs, short for meals ready to eat. While the volunteers were going through everything, the chief officers met upstairs to plan out the next month's strategy, since the end of July and the month of August were typically the busiest for fires. The Fire Department had already broken the old response record, thanks to the wild spring, and with very little moisture since then, the outlook was bleak. Once the officers hashed over the preparation concerns, the officers left, leaving just Bill and Frank to talk about the arson investigation.

Mac had asked the couple of volunteers repeating the pickup truck rumor if they had heard any description of the pickup truck. The fellow volunteers said they had heard it was a late model metallic gray Chevy with a matching camper shell. The rumor had it that Beth, the USFS investigator, happened to see the pickup leaving while she was approaching the fire area. The couple of volunteers said they had heard nothing more. It was probably coincidence, since the metallic gray is a popular color, but Mac thought he remembered Diana's pickup was that color. But he was thinking he had seen another pickup or two that same color around town, although he couldn't remember if they had been carrying a camper shell or not. He had better be doing a better job of remembering things, and getting back to being a field agent in disguise. Unfortunately the volunteers had no further information to offer. Mac needed to find out more about the pickup, without exposing his being an agent with the hated FBI.

Curious about what was being talked about in the meeting upstairs in the fire station, Mac carefully worked his way over to the stairway to the meeting room, and sat down mid way where he could just make out the words coming out of the meeting room. He pretended to be re-organizing his war bag, as his backpack carrying personal hygiene items was commonly called, re-packing his changes of underwear, socks and extra clothing. Mac picked up a little bit of the conversation regarding the arson fires of last year. What sounded like Bill's voice was telling Frank about the latest meeting of the committee. Bill mentioned there was very little new information, but that Amrit did get results of the stuff he sent in to a special lab. The arson or arsons used an accelerant, M4, found at both deadly fires. It was not yet confirmed but Amrit thinks the same person or persons did both fires. Bill also brought up the string of wildland fires that they have been hit with, and some have been looking suspiciously like arson. "In particular," Bill said, "I was on two fires where we could see something strange, something not natural, on the ground near where the fire origin was determined to be." He had not heard from Beth yet regarding her investigation into those couple of wild fires.

What sounded like Frank's voice said he hoped that the continued clandestine arson investigation would soon find the key that would open the door to solving the arson fires. He reiterated everyone's dislike of the FBI, their gestapo tactics, and still wanted an explanation from the FBI for their behavior. Frank still felt they had to get these arson cases solved for their community. If the FBI couldn't or wouldn't solve the cases they stole, then it was up to them to bring closure. Bill was in full agreement.

Frank changed the subject and was apologizing for not being more involved. His wife was slowly doing better but the situation was slower than they had hoped for. So he had to return to the treatment center, but he knew the Department was in very good hands. Bill thanked Frank for trusting him, and said he was continuing to pray for Dora's recovery. Frank said he was grateful for good friends and the prayers. He hoped he could bring Dora home soon and get back to some normalcy. Unfortunately, Frank was only partially good at predicting the future.

The meeting sounded like it was finished, so Mac quickly left the stairs, and sauntered over to one of the groups of volunteers checking their equipment. After the meeting, Mac headed home instead of to the bar where a few of the volunteers were getting together for a drink. He knew Bev was on patrol and Diana was out of town, so there was no pretty girl to keep him company tonight. What Mac heard tonight at the fire station needed some clarification. Since Mac was not in on the FBI raids last year, he had only what he was told by Ricardo to go on. And if what Frank was saying is true, then what Ricardo told Mac was not the real story. So what was he doing here, and why? Mac decided to not wait until morning to phone Ricardo, so he dialed Ricardo's cell phone. In part, Mac figured he would get a little revenge by calling so late. The chewing out would be worth it.

Ricardo answered and was predictably fuming for being woken. Mac let Ricardo yell, then when Ricardo calmed down and was ready to talk, Mac asked about the arson fires of last year and the roll the FBI played. Ricardo told Mac that he doesn't need to know, and reminded him he was there to find out if people there were working on those arson cases behind the Bureau's back.

"Boss, it would be helpful to know what happened so I can determine if information I see or hear is appropriate to pass along or not."

"Mac, I will make the decision whether it is appropriate to keep or not. Just let me know any and every thing you see or hear that has anything remotely sounding like there is activity related to last year's arson fires there in Prairie City. You had better get me something and damn quickly or else you'll be doing guard duty at Amundsen-Scott South Pole Research Station in the Antarctic. So why did you wake me up?"

Something told Mac to not mention the bits and pieces of what he had heard, so he told Ricardo that all he has heard so far was complaining how the FBI took over the cases and nothing's been done since. "The people here really hate the FBI, so I was wondering what happened to cause that hatred."

"I don't give a damn what those hillbillies think about us. You got two weeks to either prove or disprove the existence of any clandestine investigation going on. Unless you got something for me now, this conversation is over."

Mac told Ricardo there was nothing yet, at which Ricardo slammed the phone down and went back to bed. Mac was wondering why all of a sudden he felt he should not tell his boss everything. The more he thought about it, the more he was questioning why he was really here. Something just seemed a bit fishy. What was the real situation that he was thrown into the middle of?

Chapter 37

Instead of going back east to do a 'family' job, the Burner was sent to Las Vegas, where the 'family' owned some of the casino action. The Burner was asked to scare someone into working with the 'family', and if done right it might not lead to a killing. It took about a week of watching and planning before the Burner and a couple of associates put a plan into operation. Making sure the victim (although the 'family' felt they were the victim) was out of his large well manicured office, the Burner used the special formula of M4 mix to get a series of fires going in the building. The Burner watched as the flames roared out of the windows, seeking more fuel and oxygen to supply its insatiable appetite. Satisfied, the Burner and associates spent the night in one of the casinos owned by the 'family' and were treated like royalty. The morning news showed a skeleton of a structure where once the grand office building had stood. The fire department spokesperson was telling the media that arson is suspected, because the building normally would not have been that heavily involved in the few minutes it took for the first engines to arrive. The investigation was just starting, but the Burner was confident that any investigation would run into a dead end, just as all of the carefully planned fires the Burner had performed. With the arson's job completed successfully, the 'family' had contacted the victim and was able to make him see the wisdom of working with the 'family'.

The Burner was finished with the job in Vegas, and headed back to Prairie City, figuring on spending some fun time and working with the drone. Changing vehicles once again, the Burner drove into Prairie City in the evening. To get the latest scuttlebutt, the Burner went into one of the bars and ordered a drink from one of the back tables. The Burner went about listening at various conversations, slowly scanning the dark barroom for one particular individual. The Burner had left a voice message earlier, and was about to call a second time when a movement at one of the tables caught the Burner's eyes.

Diana, having just arrived back in Prairie City, sat at one of the bar tables sipping her drink. She had been trying to listen to some conversations around her, while looking for Mac. She had left him a phone message that she was in town, but he had not responded. She finally spied Mac sitting at a far table with a gorgeous woman sitting across from him. Also sitting at Mac's table were two other guys, one of which she recognized as the man they called Bill. As she looked at him briefly, she felt a tremor shake her. Not understanding the strange feeling, she shrugged it off and frowned, as she was hoping to run into Mac and have a fun time. It's not like she and Mac were an item, for they have only been together a few times. But Diana felt that when she wanted something, it should be hers. Looks like competition is the game, but Diana was never one for accepting second best in any game. The fight was on. As the two men with Mac got up and said their goodbyes, Diana grabbed her drink and walked across the bar to Mac's table.

As Diana got closer to the table, Mac recognized Diana and stood up to greet her. Mac introduced the two gorgeous women to each other, then sat down and felt a cold draft, although it was warm in the bar. Oblivious to the under current of a cat fight brewing between the ladies, Mac was beaming, being in the presence of not one but two beauties. Discussions of who does what bounced around the table, and when Diana heard that Bev was a local police officer, the warning flag ran up the pole. Diana figured she should be extra careful, but could still have a little fun with this lady cop. The challenge was non verbally expressed to Bev, who felt her intuition tingling. Bev felt there was something she needed to dig into regarding Diana. Mac's FBI radar was very slow kicking in, probably because he wasn't thinking about his job at the moment, but he finally felt the friction and something else in the air around the table.

After their drinks were finished, Bev decided it was time to leave before any trouble could start. She had a sense that there was something different about Diana. Sinister wasn't the right word to describe the feeling, but it was somewhere in that area of the vocabulary. Bev felt there was something a little dark with Diana, and it wasn't because Bev was jealous or upset that another woman was cutting in between she and Mac. Bev liked Mac, but they had only just barely started dating, and Bev felt she could walk away without hesitation if it came to that. So she was confident her intuition or sixth sense was worth looking into. It wasn't a fueling of emotions. She decided to talk to her boss Walt and see if he would let her dig into this feeling and find out what Diana was all about.

Diana stayed with Mac, enjoying another drink. Mac had been trying to find out what Diana had been up to the past month but Diana was being carefully evasive. Finishing his second drink, Mac was trying to find a nice way to say good night when Diana surprised him by saying she wanted to go home with him. Somewhat tongue tied, Mac was caught in a dilemma: spend the night with a beautiful woman or spend the night alone. Of a sudden, Mac started to laugh at himself for even having to think about the offer. Diana saw the laugh and was a little angry when she asked Mac what that laugh was for. Mac, a little embarrassed, quickly said he was laughing at himself for even thinking whether he should or shouldn't. He said he must have been celibate for too long, and they both laughed and walked out of the bar, Mac's arm around Diana's waist.

In the morning, a tired Mac headed to the farm after saying goodbye to a sleepy Diana. Bev was at the police station early, waiting to talk to Walt. Bill was working on the irrigation system at the golf course. It was almost a typical day. After finally waking up, The Burner headed out to the forest, anxious to get to work on a practice run for the next wildfire.

Walt listened to what Bev had to say regarding Diana, and he knew enough to let Bev go with her instinct, to an extent. Walt gave his okay, with some ground rules. Bev sat down and started to plan out a list of to do in trying to identify this Diana character. This could be fun, she thought. The detective part, that is.

Mac, somewhat tired from a wild night with Diana, was trying to stay awake. It was harvest time for the winter wheat, so he needed to be alert while working the combine. He was remembering a few situations back home while growing up when either through negligence or accident, a fire started during the harvesting and burned up the crop and equipment. Mac did not want to be responsible for something like that. He also wanted to be alert in case the call for help came over the CB radio or his fire department pager. It was hot, dry and everything was more than ready to burn. While working the controls on the combine, Mac's thoughts faded in and out regarding Diana. Once he got past the physical and emotional, he kept going back to a feeling there was something clouding the aura around Diana. An internal fight was brewing in his head, and he finally decided to switch to his FBI role and make a few calls. It was time he learned more about this gorgeous, yet a little mysterious, woman.

Chapter 38

Beth was on her routine forest patrol. It had been nearly a month since the last fire that could be called arson. Since then, the local fire fighting agencies have been on 'routine' fires. She was hoping the arsonist was either out of the notion or moved away. However, the forest was unusually dry, and because it was the end of July, the forest was getting well used by recreationalists. With the increased threat of wildfire caused by a careless camper, a couple of Forest Service engines were out patrolling as well. Beth was hoping the increased visibility of the Forest Service might lessen the chances of an arsonist getting a destructive fire going. In the afternoon, one of the patrolling engines noticed a pickup truck parked just off the road, and no one was around. The two firefighters with the engine got out and walked around the pickup, checking for any left campfires or smoldering cigarette butts. All looked clean, so they assumed the occupants of the pickup were out hiking. Nothing wrong here, they figured, so they hoped back into the engine and drove off continuing their patrol.

The Burner wasn't too far away from the pickup truck and heard the Forest Service engine pull up. Unless the Forest Service people jotted down a license plate number, the Burner didn't think there was much to worry about. However, to be safe, the Burner figured on changing vehicles again, and also moving to a different area. Maybe this idea was not a good one, thought the Burner. Seems like these increased patrols are ruining the initial plans. But the Burner liked a challenge, and it meant more work was needed. The Burner decided to head back to the motel room and do more research. With Google Earth and the map of the Forest, the arsonist would be able to pick out more isolated areas in which to practice.

The harvesting of the winter wheat was a choreography of many parts. Mac was flicking his eyes between the view outside his cab and the control panel inside the cab of the John Deere S660. This 333 horsepower combine, with a Macdon 25 foot Draper header for cutting, could hold up to 300 bushels of wheat before it needed to be off loaded into a truck. The farmer and his wife drove the grain trucks, watching the combine closely as one at a time they drove their trucks alongside the combine to load the cut and stored grain from the hopper in the combine. Once the truck was full of grain, the driver turned the truck toward town and one of two agricultural companies that had grain silos for storing the wheat. While the trucks were weighed, unloaded, and weighed again, Mac kept the combine working until the hopper was full of grain, waiting for one of the trucks to arrive for a repeat performance.

While waiting for the trucks to return to empty the filled hopper, Mac thought of Diana and how much he did not know about her. Heck he didn't even know her last name. It was time he got FBI serious, not sex serious, and to learn more about her. He felt a nagging suspicion clouding his thoughts. Maybe guilt caused it, but thoughts of Bev invaded his suspicions, and Mac smiled at the hope that they will hook up again this evening and continue where they were interrupted last evening. This is getting to be hard work, thought Mac, trying to juggle dalliances with two gorgeous women. Ah, but the rewards are worth it, he thought. He caught himself trying to compare the two women, almost as far as assigning points to various parts of the anatomy to see which young woman came out ahead. His train of thought was interrupted by the farmer calling on the CB saying he was just a mile away. Damn, back to work.

Chapter 39

While moving some hoses around the golf course to better water areas that the irrigation system missed, Bill felt his cell phone vibrant and then ring. He saw it was Frank, and felt the call was probably a bad news call. Frank, his voice breaking and subdued, told Bill that Dora lost her fight with cancer. Bill, feeling tears well up inside, told Frank he was very sorry and asked if there was anything he could do for Frank. Frank, still in shock even though both he and Dora had talked about this happening, said there probably would be, but right now he wasn't thinking too clearly. He told Bill he needed a few days to finish making the arrangements that Dora and he had worked out earlier while she was still alive and fighting. Bill said he would tell the volunteers, and tell the people at the café Dora worked at for nearly forty years. Frank said his two adult children flew in yesterday, and they are helping each other get through this ordeal. Bill again expressed his condolences, and told Frank to not hesitate to ask for anything. After the connection was closed, Bill felt the tears that he could no longer hold back. Everyone loved Dora, the typical motherly waitress, friend, and listener.

It was very hard, but Bill had to repress his feelings of anger, and try to not ask why did this happen to such a warm and loving person. There are so many people out there that are more animal than human. Why don't they die? Realizing the danger of this kind of thinking with emotions, Bill dropped what he was doing and drove to the church to visit with Francis. Francis was thankfully not in the middle of hearing confessions, so he and

Bill sat down and talked. Francis was visibly shaken by the news as well, remembering the big heart of Dora. Bill asked if Francis would be willing to talk to the volunteers at a special meeting tonight at the station. Bill thought that Francis, being one of the volunteers, would be the best one to present the news and be there to help. Some of the guys had known Dora their whole life, so it was going to be hard. Bill found some solace in speaking with Francis, and hoped that Francis was finding solace in his closeness to God. Feeling slightly better thanks to Francis, Bill headed to the café to bring the tragic news to the people there. Damn, and the day had started out so well.

Later at the fire station, the atmosphere was very somber, after Francis announced the bad news about Frank's wife Dora. Mac had met Dora only a couple of times, but he could tell from the way the fellow volunteers took the news that she was someone special. The talk among the volunteers was about their remembrances of Dora, whether she was being a mother hen to them, or calling them honey while waiting on them at the café. They all agreed the community was suffering a terrible loss with the passing of Dora. The special meeting was concluded with Bill telling everyone that as soon as he knew he would let everyone know about the funeral arrangements. All the volunteers able to attend will wear their Department dress shirt, badge, and a black tie if they have one. "We will sit together in show of support for Frank and his family. Francis has offered to talk with anyone wanting help through this trying time, so feel free to meet with him. It will be tough, but we will have lots of fond memories of Dora to get us through and help Frank and his family."

After the meeting, quite a few of the volunteers walked to the bar where they pulled a couple of tables together and all sat down. When Bill walked in to the bar, that damn weird feeling hit him as it had a few times recently. He would have thought it had something to do with the stress of Dora's death, but since it had happened a few times earlier, it must be something else causing it. Reaching the tables, Bill saw Ellen seated, and immediately his spirits rose.

Ellen was a dark haired, blue eyed woman in her early forties, with a grace and figure that attracted many a man's eyes. She was a head nurse at the hospital, and she and Bill were good friends. Bill had a wish that their friendship could be more, but he felt something hold him back.

Ellen motioned him to an empty chair alongside hers, so he walked over to her, kissed her on the cheek, and grabbed a beer that Ellen had already poured for him. Still standing, Bill asked everyone at the tables to stand. With a drink in hand they all listened as Bill toasted Dora. After a moment of silence, they all said, "to Dora," and downed a healthy gulp of beer. As they finished their beer, each volunteer said goodnight and headed home. Soon, all who were left at the tables were Ellen, Bill and Mac.

Diana had been seated at a table waiting to see if Mac would show up. Watching the group of guys walk in, she recognized Mac and a couple of the volunteers. She watched as they sat, and then as the last guy walks in she felt that shiver that she had felt a couple of times before. She wished she knew what was causing that strange feeling, but brushed it aside as she saw the group of volunteers stand up and raise a toast to someone named Dora. She would have to ask Mac who this Dora was. After the toast and the guys were leaving, Diana noticed Mac sitting with the same man that presented the toast, the same man she had seen with Mac a few other times in the bar. A very pretty lady was seated with the older man, but Diana did not know who she was either. There was something about that man that was trying to open a door into her memory. She was almost bold enough to walk up to the table with all three people there, but something held her back, something telling her not yet. So she waited until Mac was alone.

Not having to wait long, Diana saw the man and lady get up and walk out the bar, leaving Mac alone at the tables. She walked over and sat down next to Mac. Mac briefly smiled and said hello. Diana asked if he was ok, and what was the gathering for. Mac explained to her about Dora's death, as they finished their drinks. They both felt she must have been a special person for the mourning going on. Diana said she would have to leave again, but would be back soon. She didn't have to leave until tomorrow morning, which Mac took as a hint and invited her for another night together.

In the morning, Diana left the same time as Mac, and once again was vague in answering Mac's questions about where she was headed and when she might be back. Mac was back in the John Deere S660, cutting a field of wheat, and watching the farmer's wife expertly maneuver her grain truck alongside the combine for a load. Mac's thoughts were bouncing back and forth between the controls of the combine and Diana's mysteriousness. He still didn't have her last name, and hadn't had time to run her license plate. With harvest on, the days have been full and there had not been a chance to take a break and make some calls. Maybe tonight he would have time to call his office and get the night clerk to run the plates.

Bev had noticed Diana at Mac's again during the night while she was on patrol. She needed to talk with Mac and find out what he knows of Diana. It was mid morning and Bev was going to get some sleep, but she wanted to talk with Mac first. Bev called Mac's cell phone, and was pleasantly surprised Mac answered. Mac was surprised by Bev's call, and asked her what was going on. Bev asked if he was going out with Diana tonight and Mac told her that Diana was away for a few days. Bev wanted to meet Mac at the bar this evening after he gets finished on the combine, and Mac said that would be great with him. He told her that he had been getting ready to call her and invite her out for dinner and drinks. He wanted to finish their date that had been interrupted the other night.

Chapter 40

The Burner dropped off the rented pickup, and grabbed a flight back to New Jersey. After checking in with the 'family', the Burner worked on a job that the 'family' needed completed. The job went just as planned, and the 'family' was able to easily convince the target to work with instead of against the 'family'. The Burner, as usual, had a fun time setting the convincing fire. But the Burner felt a calling to return to the forest, to return to Prairie City, and leave the buildings behind.

While working the 'family' job in the New Jersey area, the Burner had read about places in Utah, Colorado and Nevada with acres of short juniper trees that can burn hot and fast. With the relatively short height of the junipers, the Burner could have some fun flying the hexcopter closer to the fire, and below any potential aerial fire fighting activity. The Burner felt that perhaps the drone would be less exposed to aerial view and closer to the fire. However, the downside would be the drone would more easily be seen by the ground forces. Another problem would be hiding the pickup in that more open terrain. Well, the Burner figured these issues were challenges but not insurmountable. Studying various maps, literature and photographs found on the internet, the arsonist narrowed down the choices to the Tushar Mountains in the Fishlake National Forest of Utah. The area has a broad range of vegetation, from the pinyon pine/juniper to the subalpine fir. The population near the area was sparse, so it could mean less chances of being seen. The fire history showed not a lot of fires, but there had been a few large fires that had burned significant acreage in the past. It was probably safe to assume the area was not heavy on the fire fighting resources, which could mean that once the Burner got a fire started, it will burn longer and get larger while resources are responding. Sounded like a good choice to the Burner. Besides, from there it was a fairly easy drive to Prairie City.

After going to confession at the Catholic church frequented by the Burner, the arsonist packed up a suitcase of personal items, and stored the hexcopter in a specially built carrying case. The Burner flew to Cedar City, in southern Utah. After renting a pickup and a four wheeler, the anxious Burner drove north to Beaver and the Tushar Mountains.

It took a full day of driving around the area, but The Burner finally found a spot in the forest in which to try the drone and get a fire started. The taste for fire was too strong to ignore, and it had been too long since the last one. The next day the Burner headed back to the chosen location, arriving there close to three pm. The arsonist had parked the pickup a long ways from where the fire would be started. The Burner grabbed the drone case and drove the four wheeler to an area closer to where the fire was to be started. The drone was ready to go, as it had been charged up earlier in the day. The Burner went through the normal starting procedure: FPV camera on, transmitter on, hexcopter power on, run the throttle up and back down, and the blades started spinning. The picture from the FPV camera looked good, and the special accelerant was attached. The mental checklist complete, it was time the Burner sent Prometheus to its destination.

The hexcopter was functioning normally, and the Burner flew it right to the location where the fire was to start. Earlier, the Burner had reconnoitered this same area while trying to find a suitable site, and this one had looked like the better of the few choices. Southwestern aspect, junipers with branches down to the ground, plenty of dry grass, and a decent slope with thickening trees higher up the slope. Hovering close to the selected ignition point, the Burner did one last 360 degree look around then pushed the home made switch on transmitter to release the container of special fuel. After dropping about forty feet, the container came to the end of the tether, which activated the spark and set the contents on fire, spreading to the ground. The Burner was watching through the FPV camera on board the hexcopter, and was happy to see the plan working.

Operating the gimbaled camera while flying the drone was tricky, but the Burner had been practicing and was able to coordinate the operations fairly well. While still hovering over the ignition site, the Burner noticed the small fires started by the burning and scattered fuel were indeed spreading in the dry grass. The small fires were burning together and the wafting white smoke was starting to increase, turning a slightly brownish color. Good, thought the Burner, it is working. Now the Burner figured to change the strategy a little, and leave the area to come back later when the fire is bigger instead of waiting around. Having flown the hexcopter back to the four wheeler, the Burner boxed up the 'tools' and the hexcopter, then headed to the pickup and drove away.

The Burner had stopped in Beaver for some coffee and a late lunch. Anxious to get back and see what was happening with the fire, the Burner ate quickly while listening to any talk going around in the café. Not hearing anything regarding a fire in the various discussions, the arsonist paid the bill and left Beaver after gassing up the pickup and four wheeler. It was time to see what was happening with the fire. The nagging undercurrent of voices in the Burner's head kept saying 'Prairie City, get back to Prairie City.' So the Burner wanted to see how this operation went, then appease the voices. The Burner thought, "I wish I could figure out what the hell is drawing me to Prairie City."

Pleased there was no traffic on the forest road to the fire area, the Burner found the spot used earlier and unloaded the four wheeler. Grabbing the carrying case with the hexcopter, the Burner headed to the same vantage point as earlier. Not hearing or seeing any air traffic yet, the Burner flew the hexcopter to the fire. Operating the FPV camera, the Burner was able to scan the area Promethus was flying over, as well as looking ahead to where the drone was flying to. As the drone got closer to the fire area, the Burner noticed with a smile that the fire indeed was growing. A few Junipers had already been consumed, spreading burning needles around and catching more Junipers on fire. The spreading fire was creating a dark, heavy smoke which was becoming like a beacon in the sky, calling fire fighters to its location. The arsonist was moving the hexcopter around the area, staying just above the tree tops, getting good flame action video. While scanning the area the camera picked up a moving spot in the sky heading toward the origin of the dark smoke.

"Thank goodness I brought a couple extra memory cards for my smart phone," thought the Burner. The video captured by the camera on the drone was exciting. Flames were multiplying while a speck approaching was a medium size helicopter. The video captured the helicopter dropping off a three person helitack crew. The helicopter flew back the way it came, probably getting more people or a water bucket to start water drops on the fire. Coming from the opposite direction, the arsonist could hear the drum of an airplane engine. The Burner followed the sound and finally zeroed in on the approaching airplane. As it got closer, the Burner could make out the distinctive shape of the P2V Neptune aerial tanker. It has two engines, and carries two thousand gallons of retardant. The Burner had spent some time studying the aircraft that were being contracted to the U.S. Forest Service, which was how the arsonist was able to identify the aircraft. Not wanting the hexcopter to be seen, the Burner moved the drone closer to the scattered trees, trying to keep the hexcopter from standing out.

As the Neptune flew in closer to the fire, the Burner was trying to keep the camera ahead of the aircraft in hopes of getting a good aerial retardant drop video. It would be easier if the hexcopter was higher in the sky and be able to look down on the Neptune, but that was not possible. Keeping Prometheus hovering while adjusting the camera, the Burner fought against the urge to raise the drone higher. The Neptune made one pass over the fire and the Burner assumed the aircraft was lining up for a drop. "If I just raise the drone a few feet I think the video will turn out much better," thought the Burner. Carefully maintaining the camera on the approaching aircraft, the Burner maneuvered the hexcopter up and stopped it about twenty feet above the trees. The screen image of the aircraft and the fire below was better, and the Burner noted the repositioning had happened none too soon as the Neptune was spreading it's load of pink slurry ahead of the fire.

The Burner was in a self congratulatory mode when the aircraft radio traffic coming over the Burner's scanner immediately changed the mood. "Damn, they must have seen the drone," said the Burner, and immediately brought the drone down into the trees and heading back to the observation point. The Burner, with adrenaline flowing, was hoping the pilots would not take the time to fly around the area. That helicopter was going to be back soon, so the Burner figured it was time to scoot while the chances of being seen were less. "Damn, it is getting too close for comfort. Oh well, I did get some good video anyway."

The Burner loaded up the hexcopter and drove the four wheeler to the pickup. No one was around, either above or on the ground, so the Burner drove out of the area, and with a sigh of relief and frustration left the Beaver area and headed to Cedar City. The plan was to return the leased pickup and four wheeler, then fly to Portland and rent a pickup to drive the day long distance to Prairie City.

Chapter 41

Bev caught up with Mac, and she suggested they have dinner at her place instead of the bar. She figured they would not be interrupted this time. During dinner Bev started asking Mac questions regarding Diana, but the only thing Mac could provide at the moment was that Diana was gone for a few days. Based on the questions, Mac realized that Bev was digging into Diana as was he. He was trying to decide whether he could open up and tell Bev the truth, or keep quiet.

Bev, almost forgetting what a proper hostess should do since it had been ages since someone had been to her place, fixed each an after dinner drink and then sat down in the living room across from Mac. Looking at Mac, Bev said "Alright, what is your interest regarding Diana?" It took a few minutes for Mac to finally speak, but he looked into Bev's eyes and said, "To answer that you have to promise me that this goes no further than right here."

Taken aback by this change of conversation, Bev asked Mac what the heck was going on.

"Bev, I have something to tell you, and only you, but you have to promise me that you will not tell a soul. And you have to promise to hear me out."

"Mac, you are making me nervous and scared." After a few minutes of thinking, Bev told Mac that she could not promise that she will keep from telling her boss, depending on what this is all about, but she won't tell anyone else.

Mac said that was okay, and he said that even though he hardly knew Bev, he really liked her and wanted to get to know her better. "Because of my feelings for you, I need to tell you something. I am a FBI agent working undercover."

Bev jumped up with fire in her eyes, and yelled, "How dare you come here. After what you guys did to our arson investigation last year, you have the gall to show up here. And you have the nerve to want to get to know me better. Get the hell out of here."

"Wait Bev, please hear me out. I am sorry Bev, very sorry. Please believe me when I say I had no part in that fiasco last year. Ricardo is my boss, but I was working another assignment and did not know about this operation. I am now just learning about it. Please sit down and listen to what I have to say."

"Mac, I don't know whether to believe you or just send you packing. I guess give me the story and I will decide."

Mac replied "Fair enough, I do not want anymore secrets between us. I truly want us to be friends, more than friends actually, and be able to trust each other. Here goes."

After Mac spilled his guts about this operation and the little he knew of Diana, Bev had to get up and walk around, trying to think about what she was told. "Mac, what the hell just happened. We were talking about Diana and now we are talking about you being a FBI agent sent to spy on us."

Mac, as confused as Bev, said "I am thoroughly confused. Bev, please sit down. Let's take this slowly. Ok, I was sent here by my boss to find out if there was clandestine work being done regarding the deadly arson cases last year. That's why I am here. I really know nothing regarding the cases because my boss ignores my requests for more information. He said I didn't need the boring details, just needed to scope out the community to find out if there was activity related to the cases. He told me his boss was concerned there may be local investigation still going on. I was told the FBI was handling the case, and no one else should be involved. That's all I know."

"So your boss, that slime ball Ricardo, is waiting for you to find and expose the impromptu investigation on the arson fires and murders. Where does that put you?"

"I do not know. I would appreciate it if you would fill me in regarding the arson cases, since my wonderful boss has neglected to provide the background that I had been wanting. Please believe me that what you tell me will go no further than this room. I trusted you, so please trust me."

Bev thought for a few minutes, stared at Mac, and let her intuition speak to her. "Ok, I am putting my trust in you, so please don't prove me wrong. I need to contact some other people first and ask if they would allow me to bring you into their confidence. But in the meantime I can tell you what happened."

"I would appreciate that. I do not want to jeopardize your job or your standing in the community, so just give me what you safely can."

So Bev took a deep breath, looked Mac in the eyes, and relayed the events of both deadly arson cases. She left out anything having to do with the status of the cases after the FBI stepped in. She felt that was not her place to present until she spoke with the members of the incognito team.

It was past midnight before Bev finished her explanation of the events regarding the arson cases. When she came to the FBI involvement, Mac visibly winced and then understood why she felt such anger toward him initially. In the same situation he would have felt the same way, if not worse. Bev needed to be out patrolling, and she was late to relieve the officer currently on duty. So Mac took Bev's hands in his, looked Bev in the eyes and thanked her for telling him the situation and trusting him. He told her to call when she felt like meeting again, as they needed to figure out how in the heck they went from talking about Diana to talking about the deadly arson cases. They both agreed this just opened a can of worms, and they needed to move quickly on this. As Mac was leaving he said, "Bev, I would really like us to be more than friends. The thing with Diana is that I like her, but I feel there is something a little dark hiding in her. Part of me, the agent side of me, says to try and find out what that dark feeling is all about. But with you, I want to get to know you better for me, not for any job." With a kiss on Bev's cheek, Mac said good night and headed to his place for a short sleep before he has to head to the farm.

Bev had a night patrol to work, and was afraid that the boring duty would lead to way too much thinking of Mac and the situation she found herself in. She likes Mac, even though she just learned about him being with the FBI and here to spy on her and the others involved in investigating the arson fires of last year. And apparently he feels like she does regarding Diana, even though he must be sleeping with her. What a mess, and what to do about it? This is one time she was hoping for some criminal activity during the night to keep her from thinking of the mess.

Chapter 42

The day opened up as a normal August morning, warm and sunny. Bill had his coffee, mulling over the event of the day, Dora's funeral. He wasn't looking forward to today. He did not like to attend funerals. And Dora's was going to be an especially difficult one. It will probably be the biggest funeral this town has had in years, thought Bill. He had his volunteers agree to show up dressed in their nice Department dress shirts, and a pair of slacks or nice pants, and dress shoes. No jeans, or boots, or tennis shoes allowed. Bill reminded the volunteers that this group attendance at the funeral in their 'finery' was a tribute to one very special lady and her surviving husband, their chief. Yes, it was going to be a very tough day. Then after the funeral and burial, everyone was invited to the Grange hall where there would be enough food, drink and stories to satisfy three towns the size of Prairie City. Dora would be greatly missed, and Bill thought if only he could leave such a legacy when it was his turn to leave this world. Enough dwelling on the funeral, Bill needed to get to the golf course and check the water situation before changing and getting to the Church.

Mac's brain was too busy processing. He was thinking of today's funeral, and he was trying to get a grip on what he said and learned last night with Bev. He was thinking about Diana, and what a different person she was compared to Bev. Even Bev felt the mystery surrounding Diana was worth digging into. The problem was they both knew so little, but maybe with what each knew they would have a better picture to work from.

Of course that was what last night was supposed to accomplish, but what a weird turn of events. Mac was hoping to be able to meet with Bev tonight after the funeral activities were over. Perhaps they could move forward with looking into Diana. He put thoughts of a relationship with Bev aside for the moment. He needed to work on this nagging feeling about Diana.

The funeral for Dora was held in the school gymnasium, having the most seating of any building in town. Even at that, there was standing room only. The impact Dora had made was impressive. In the first few rows of chairs, Frank sat with his and Dora's families, while the uniformed volunteer firefighters sat across the aisle. Behind them were people from far and wide, those who knew Dora or who were there to show support for Frank and Dora's family. It was a moving ceremony, with Fr. Francis saying the Mass and providing a heart felt eulogy that brought tears to many. Francis reminded everyone that is was okay to shed tears now for the loss of Dora, but everyone must remember her kindness and warm heart, and follow her example. "We must keep Dora in our hearts, remembering not that she died and left us, but as she lived with us. We express our remorse now and wonder why the good Lord has taken her from us. But we should not concentrate on the loss, but on the gain Dora has left us. Just look around you and she how she has impacted our lives. She has shown us a way to live, and now it is our turn to continue to live as she lived and create our own legacies. What better way to honor someone we all loved and cherished? In a little while we will finish this ceremony by placing the body of our sister Dora in the ground. Our lives right now feel like that empty hole in the cemetery, but just like that hole will be filled, Dora's gift of her life to us will fill the hole in our hearts. We will gather after the burial to celebrate her life, a starting of the healing process to fill that hole in our hearts."

It took all the self control Francis had in him to continue with the Mass, for he too felt the loss. But he had prayed for strength to bring this service to the people, and help with the grieving and the healing. The Mass was concluded, and Frank's family greeted the throng of mourners outside the church doors. Once the casket was placed in the hearse, the procession of vehicles followed the hearse to the cemetery for the burial. If there had been a dry eye during the Mass, there was no longer one at the cemetery. After the burial service, most of the mourners went to the Grange hall where there was a luncheon set up. Food was in over abundance, for all the diners, cafes and restaurants within a hundred miles got together and laid out a feast. It was time to celebrate a life remembered, and it started with good friends and good food.

Bill and Francis were sitting at one of the tables, trying to make the best of this situation. Each felt emotionally drained, but with the change in atmosphere and the good food, the body was recharging. Many people spoke to Francis as they walked by and thanked him for such a moving service. Francis was quick to reply that he had good material to work with. The fellow volunteers, all sitting as a group with Bill and Francis, were talking among themselves about the concern over the hot, dry weather and the on going harvest. In the midst of the various discussions, Frank found his way over from the main table where he had been sitting with the rest of his family. Bill scooted out an empty chair and told Frank to have a seat. Mac was sharing a conversation with one of the volunteers and happened to look up as Frank sat down a couple of chairs from him. With the funeral emotions winding down and thoughts could turn toward other things, Mac was thinking of the conversation he and Bev had last night. He wondered if Bev had a chance to tell anyone, but he doubted there had been time with the day's events taking center stage for the whole town. He thought he better tune an ear to Frank and Bill's conversation just in case.

Chapter 43

It had been a couple of days ago that the whole town stopped and said goodbye to Dora. Mac and Bev were sitting at a table in the bar, enjoying a drink while talking. This was the first time since before Dora's funeral Mac and Bev could get together and continue the discussion regarding the clandestine investigation of the deadly arson fires, and the situation surrounding Diana. Bev had taken a little time the day before to speak with Bill about Mac. Bill's reaction was similar to Bev's, at first feeling betrayed and angry. Mac was such a likeable guy, hard working, and seemed honest. That was what really irked Bill, and it took some convincing on the part of Bev to make Bill see there was an opportunity here. Bill calmed down and thought it over, and could see that Mac could be helpful instead of a threat. He needed to have a sit down with Mac and Bev, before bringing Mac into the investigation, if that was even acceptable to the rest of the team.

Bev had just finished telling Mac about Bill's reaction, and the need to meet, when into the bar walked Diana. Mac saw Diana first, then quietly told Bev, who just as quietly cursed. Mac, while watching Diana, told Bev he will try to get some information from Diana tonight. "I want to meet up with you tomorrow so we can finish this discussion and pass along anything I can find out from Diana."

Bev said perhaps they can meet somewhere between town and the farm Mac works at. Mac told Bev he would call her, then they said their good nights and Bev left the bar.

Diana sat down beside Mac and kissed him on the cheek. After Diana's ordered drink was delivered, they both headed to a table and sat down to talk. Diana was her usual evasive self when Mac was asking her where her job had taken her. She did mention her trip took her to Utah, but that was as detailed as she would get. Diana asked how things were here, and Mac told her about the funeral for Dora. Diana did not know Dora, so it didn't mean a thing to her. "When I came in I saw that Bev with you."

"We bumped into each other and sat at the bar talking about stuff here in town. Not much going on, thank goodness."

Diana said, "Let's go to your place after we finish our drinks. I missed you."

Mac said it sounded fine by him. When Mac followed Diana outside, he noticed she headed to a pickup truck with Oregon plates. He asked about the pickup truck and Diana mentioned she had picked it up from a car rental agency in Portland. Confused, Mac said he thought Diana had been working in Utah. Diana briefly explained she was in Utah then headed to a job in Oregon. Mac figured he would check on that later. He was hoping to get Diana a little drunk so he could try and get some information out of her, and if that didn't work then hopefully she would go to sleep quickly so he could look through her purse. He wanted very much to find something he and Bev could work with.

At Mac's place it took awhile but after a number of drinks and a steamy session in bed, Diana was out like a light. There was finally a chance for Mac to search Diana's purse, looking for id and credit cards. Careful to not rearrange too much, Mac found the wallet with Diana's cards, and started taking pictures of the cards with his smart phone. Checking to make sure Diana was still sound asleep, Mac sent the photos on to his contacts with the FBI, and copied the email to Bev. With that task out of the way, Mac went to bed for a short sleep. It was going to be another long day of harvesting.

Mac woke early as usual, completed his morning rituals and headed to the farm. Along the way he stopped to use his smart phone to call his buddies at the FBI to see if they received the email he sent earlier. Yes, they had received the email, but it was still being processed. He told his buddies thanks, and to call him as soon as they had information. Matt continued on to the farm, and prepped the combine before starting work in another field of wheat. Before the slow and monotonous drive in the combine, Mac called Bev and asked if she received his email. Bev said she had received Matt's email and had passed it along to Liz at the State Police. Mac told Bev that his office was working on it also, but they had nothing to provide yet. They both wanted to meet later that day for a couple of reasons, but Mac suggested that meeting tonight may be better than this afternoon when they may still not have information. Bev mentioned her skepticism over the FBI helping out, but Mac assured her he did not go through his boss with this. Based on what Bev had said, Mac figured he had better hold off as long as possible before bringing his boss into the picture.

Chapter 44

Bill was still wondering what the Forest Service investigation of the recent fires had determined, so he contacted Beth. Beth told Bill what she had learned, which wasn't much. Bill was jotting down some of the details when he stopped at the reference to a fuel thickener agent found in some of the soil samples collected. The lab also tested the contents of the melted blob that Bill had seen at a couple of the wildfires near where the ignition point was estimated. The predominant compound was polyvinyl chloride with some fuel thickener residue. Beth added that a closer examination of the area of ignition for each fire showed multiple ignition points, not just one. But all of the ignition points seem to gather around where the blob of melted material was found. "However," Beth continued, "the really weird piece of this puzzle is the lab found some traces of metals mixed in with the blob. These metals were lithium, manganese, and some copper."

"So what did the lab conclude with all this stuff?"

Beth answered, "Right now we are only sure of one thing, and that is arson. Someone started these fires, and it looks like the same person."

Bill asked Beth if the lab could determine what type of fuel thickener was found, but Beth did not have the answer yet.

"I will ask our lab to see if they can provide what type of fuel thickener they found and get back to you as soon as possible."

Beth was able to get the lab to priority run the fuel thickener samples again, this time for the determination of the type of thickener. Each of the different thickeners had slightly varying chemical signatures, and it didn't take too long for the lead technician to find the chemical components. The technician compared the names and amounts to the industry standard list of known thickeners and their corresponding chemical signatures. Pleasantly surprised at how quickly the lab was able to determine the type of thickener, Beth immediately called Bill with the results.

Bill, having finished working at the golf course for the day, was home relaxing and wondering what to cook for dinner. Beth called and said the lab had identified the thickener as being M4.

"Beth, is it just a coincidence or are we looking at a potential link to all these arson fires, even the pickup and house fires of last year?"

"Well, we can't yet say it is the same person, but I don't believe in coincidences."

"Beth, I agree. We better call the group together and hash this over." Bill thanked Beth for the update and for keeping him up on the investigation, and they hung up after saying their goodbyes. They both took half of the list and made the calls for a meeting tomorrow evening. Each member of the team was told there was important new information to discuss, but the detail was left until the meeting.

When Bill spoke with Bev, Bev reminded him of Mac and whether this next meeting would be a good time to bring Mac in. Bill had discussed the Mac situation with Amrit and Liz, and after a little hesitation, both thought perhaps Mac could be an ally instead of an enemy. Bev said she was going to be talking to Mac this evening, and would see what was happening with his investigation.

"What investigation is that, Bev?"

"Oh, sorry about that Bill. I had forgotten to tell you, but Mac and I, and now Liz, are following up on some stuff regarding a young lady we have some suspicions about. Mac and I have spoken to her or have seen her around here a few times, and both mine and Mac's warning tones were beeping. Hopefully it is a false alarm, but we are checking into her background as best we can."

"How does that tie into what we are working on?"

"Bill, I am not sure if it has anything to do with the arson cases we are working on, but something is definitely fishy, and it could be related to the latest wildfires. I thought I would mention it to help prove that I think Mac is okay to be on the team with us."

"Okay Bev, bring him around to the meeting and we will see what happens."

Chapter 45

The Burner needed a fire. After waking up and grabbing a breakfast at the café, the arsonist decided to go for a drive. Listening to the weather broadcast on the radio scanner, the Burner heard the Prairie City area was going to be under a red flag warning that afternoon, for dry lightning and winds, thanks to a dry cold front passing through. The Burner may have been deficient in the morals department, but certainly was not in the brains department, and quickly thought of an advantage to this weather approaching. "If all goes well, I could get a fire started while lightning was starting other fires, and I could have my pick of fires to watch. Plus who would think twice about a fire being man caused in the midst of a rash of lightning caused fires. There may be additional Forest Service patrols wandering about watching for lightning fires later today, but I'll just have to be more careful. This could turn out to be a great day after all."

After spending the morning driving around and checking over likely locations for setting a fire, the Burner parked on a side road just off the main Forest road west of town. This was near a large meadow, where a steep stretch of forest climbs up Snake Peak. Getting a good ground view of the area and confirming what the Burner saw on the map, the arsonist decided this was a good area to get a fire started. There looked to be plenty of dead and dying fuels to help carry a fire along, and the terrain was conducive to spreading a fire. The weather looked good, with the afternoon being hot, the humidity low, and winds out of the west picking up in front of the coming storm. The Burner needed to find a good place to hide the pickup and offload the four wheeler. The choreography was to be different this time. Prometheus will have to wait until later. This time, to change things up, the Burner wanted to set a timer to start the fire later in the day, hopefully when other fires are keeping the firefighters busy. Besides, if the storm is going to be as bad as the prediction, the winds could make it very difficult to control Prometheus. If the weather prediction holds true, there should be numerous fires burning later today and tonight, and the Burner was getting excited just thinking about all the flames.

Mac, listening to the agricultural weather station on the combine's radio, heard the storm warning broadcast. This was not a good time for a storm, right in the middle of harvest. And if there was dry lightning associated with the storm, that could be worse. Mac called Bill to let him know about the forecast, in case Bill hadn't heard. Bill listened to Mac's report, and told Mac to be ready and be careful working in the middle of all that uncut fuel. Then Bill switched his fire department radio to the weather channel and listened to the fire weather forecast for the local zone. It didn't sound too good, so Bill called George and Stan and passed the word to them. It could well be that later today they would be inundated with fires. Or it could be a dud of a storm, with nothing happening. Between the three of them, calls were made to most of the volunteers telling them about the possible situation later today, and to be ready and available. Bill didn't want to bother Frank, but figured he had better interrupt Frank's mourning and let him know about the forecast for the afternoon. Frank did not answer the phone, so Bill just left him a message.

Chapter 46

It was about 4:15pm, and the clouds associated with the cold front were approaching from the southwest, when Bill was jarred by the boom of thunder. "It begins," thought Bill, and he decided to head to the fire station and play the waiting game. While driving to the station, Bill could see numerous flashes of lightning and hear booms; the flashes and sounds seemed closer each time. At the station, Bill opened the doors and made sure the engines were ready. George and a couple of volunteers arrived with the same idea as Bill, and they stood outside the roll up doors of the station watching the sky.

About fifteen minutes into their sky watching, Bill and the group of ready volunteers were jarred by all four pagers going off at once. "Prairie Fire, please respond to 6807 Buck Shot Road for a field fire."

Bill sent George with two volunteers in the attack engine, then fired up the water tender while waiting for a couple more volunteers. Bill also called Frank to let him know what was happening and to see if he was ready to jump back in if needed. Frank answered the phone this time and said he would stand by and help if things got bad. Bill explained his plan, and Frank said it sounded good. He would take over the station if and when Bill had to head out to a fire. Frank also thanked Bill for calling earlier. He apologized for not answering, but was thankful for a chance to think about something other than his loss of Dora. Bill said he understood, and would probably see Frank shortly.

Volunteers arrived quickly to the Station, and Bill sent two in the water tender toward the Buck Shot Road fire. Bill told the two volunteers in the water tender to be heads up and be mobile, not to get too deeply committed to one fire. He may need them to head to other fires with their load of water if things got crazy. He wanted them to be extra careful since they maybe doing a lot of driving. Bill reminded them that there were too many deadly water tender crashes in the fire service throughout the country, and he did not want them to be a part of that statistic. Stan and two of the remaining volunteers were told to standby with rural engine 2. The rest of the volunteers would stay with Bill at the station and be ready to jump on a next fire call, or help cover the current fire call. Bill was wondering how many fires would be started. Well, unfortunately, this storm was definitely not a dud.

The Interagency Dispatch office was likened to the floor of the New York Stock Exchange during a major buy/sell off. Lightning without rain and dry vegetation was a bad mix, and that was what they had. So far, the Dispatch office had handled a bunch of phone calls that had turned into nine fires. And the storm wasn't finished yet, so the Dispatchers were getting ready for a ton of personnel and equipment requests once the responding engines and smokejumpers radio in the status of the fires. The Dispatchers knew that even after the storm moved on, there could be a lot more fires popping up in the next days. The people in the Dispatch office were very sensitive to the old saying about government employees, but no one better kid them about earning their pay this time. It was going to be a long night.

Things were not quite as hectic at the Sheriff's Dispatch office, but the Dispatchers were fielding numerous calls from people seeing smoke. These calls were logged, and then called into the Multiagency Dispatch office for handling. One of the calls, however, was from an excited individual seeing smoke puffing up not far from his house and barn. In looking up the E911 information for the caller, it was shown that the property was just barely in the Prairie City rural District, bordering the forest. The Dispatcher activated the page tone for the Fire Department and provided the location. The Dispatcher then contacted the Multiagency Dispatch office to let them know about the fire and that the Fire Department has been paged out.

"Damn, there's the second one," said Bill upon hearing the page and location. Bill immediately sent Stan with rural engine 2, and called George for a status report on the field fire. George was pleased with the progress, thanks to the number of farmers showing up with equipment to help. The two tractor plows had almost lined the fire and one of the farmers brought in a thousand gallon water tank on his truck that they can refill from. The attack engine, with a couple of farmer's pickups, was working the edge of the fire from inside the burnt wheat. "At this rate, Bill, we should be buttoned up enough to get out of here in less than twenty minutes."

"Sounds good George. That second fire call is in the Tamarack Subdivision, so as soon as you can, you need to head to Tamarack. The farmers can finish up the mop up."

"Roger that. I will try to get us out of here in about ten minutes."

"10-4, George. I will turn the water tender toward the Tamarack fire to help Stan's crew. You can top off your tank from the farmers' water tanks and then head to Tamarack. Be careful."

Bill radioed the water tender and headed them to the second fire to support rural engine 2. He then radioed Stan to let him know he will have the tender to help him and that George with engine 1 will be heading his way as well. Stan told Bill he was less than five minutes from the location and would radio him upon arrival. All Bill could do now was to be patient and wait, traits not normally associated with Bill. So far they had been lucky, but if another fire happens in the District things will get ugly fast.

Chapter 47

I t was like a party to the Burner. Having picked a reasonable vantage point, the Burner could see at least five smokes, two of which were puffing up nicely. The Burner happily noted that one of the puffers was in the direction of Snake Peak. From listening to some of the chatter on the fire radio frequencies, the Burner heard that so far only one of the fires was threatening structures, and Prairie Fire Department was responding to that one. Needing to get closer to one of the fires, the Burner drove in the direction of the Tamarack subdivision, where the structures were threatened and where the Prairie City Fire Department would be working.

Stan had arrived to the fire in the Tamarack subdivision and immediately saw the flames gobbling up the understory not far from the closest structure. Looking around Stan could see another structure close by, then a couple of driveways heading into the timber. While Stan sent the two volunteers to scout around the nearest structure, looking for hoses and ladders that belonged to the home owners, he radioed Bill. From Stan's report, Bill could see there was a serious problem. He was thinking about how long it would take him to get there in his own vehicle compared to the time George would arrive. Bill radioed George for a location, and George said, "10-20 near the junction of Prairie View and Larch. I heard Stan's report and we are hurrying as best we can. Should be there in less than fifteen minutes."

"Copied. I am heading there now and will catch up with you when you get there." Then Bill called Frank and told him the situation and that he was heading to Tamarack. Frank said he would head to the Station and stand by with any volunteers there.

Stan had scouted around the one structure a little further from the approaching fire, and then caught up with his two volunteers at the threatened structure. "Stan, we checked the house. No one was home but we were able to get into the house and pulled the flammable stuff from the windows and doors. We made sure all the windows and doors were shut, and filled a couple of large pails with water. We found three water spigots outside and a couple lengths of garden hose. Found a ladder so we could get onto the roof. Fortunately the power is still on."

"Good job guys. Ok, each of you take a house and using the home owner's hoses, get a line on the roof and wet it down. Run enough of our one inch hose from the engine to the fire side of the houses and attach a nozzle to it. We don't know how much water is available in their tanks, so we will have to be careful and try not run their system dry. But we will use their water until the power goes out. Use their garden hose to wet down the side of the house facing the fire as best you can, as well as keep the roof wet. We will save using our hoses and water until the very last. I will go back and line out a hose at the next place. Bill is coming to help, and engine 1 is on the way. The water tender is also heading this way."

As Stan's volunteers were finishing up the hose lays, a pickup with a four wheeler on a towed trailer drove up to where engine 2 was parked. A young, beautiful woman got out of the pickup and saw the two firefighters getting a drink of water from their canteens and walked up to them. One of the volunteers asked the young woman what he could do for her. She asked if he was in charge, to which he replied no but he could contact Stan who is in charge and working a couple of houses away. The volunteer contacted Stan by radio, mentioning he was needed at the staging area where their engine was parked.

Stan, upon briskly walking to the crew, saw a woman speaking with his crew. Wondering what this lady was doing here, Stan asked "Mam, do you live here?"

"No, I was just in the area and saw the smoke. I thought maybe I could help. I have this four wheeler, if you need it, and I have a small drone with me. Could you use some aerial camera work?"

Stan was caught between a rock and a hard place, thinking the aerial views would be nice, but concerned for the lady's safety. And the four wheeler would be handy to use for checking on the other buildings. Just then George in engine 1 arrived with Bill right behind him in a cloud of dust.

As Bill stepped out of his vehicle, he looked around and felt a weird sensation as his eyes came across a woman talking with Stan. Bill and George came over to meet with Stan and the woman while George's crew joined up with Stan's crew hanging around the young woman. "Hi Stan, what ya got?"

Stan filled in what he and his crew have done so far, and mentioned he has not checked other residences yet. Bill said he could do that, and told Stan he was doing a good job of getting things ready. "Who's the young lady?"

"She showed up just a few minutes before you got here, and was asking if we wanted some help. She said she has a drone with her and she would be willing to get us some aerial shots. And she has a four wheeler she has offered for our use as well. You showed up before I could give her an answer. I didn't get her name yet."

Bill was trying to ignore the weird sensation he was feeling, one that he had felt just a few times recently. He had a serious situation to worry about, not some damn strange shaking. He agreed with Stan, wanting to have the recon from the drone and the use of the four wheeler, but worried about the woman's safety. "Damn, I would like to have an aerial view. Mam, I am Bill, this is George, and you have been talking with Stan. I understand you are offering your four wheeler and drone?"

While Bill was speaking to the woman, George finally noticed the volunteers hanging around. She was a beautiful young woman, so it was no wonder that his volunteers were gathered around her. He motioned for the volunteers to follow him, and told Stan's crew to get back to their structure protection. George told his crew to grab engine 1 and drive to the next driveway, and check out the structures for what needs to be done to protect them from the advancing fire.

Bill's memory kicked in and he thought he had seen her a few times in the bar recently. As they shook hands, both Bill and the woman felt a jolt, like a charge of electricity shooting through their hands and into their arms. After a longer than normal holding of the hands and gazing into the eyes, the woman finally broke the connection.

"Pleased to meet you Bill. I am Diana. You can use my four wheeler, and I was hoping I could be of some help with my drone."

Bill told Diana he was very pleased to meet her as well, and told her he could use the help. Bill told Stan to get a place ready to set up the porta tank when the water tender gets here shortly. "George, I want you to grab her four wheeler and scout up ahead. Check on your crew, then see what kind of structures are further up the road." Both Stan and George said the plan sounded good to them, and both went to their assigned tasks.

Diana led Bill to her pickup and showed him the drone, a hexcopter with a gimball camera and a FPV view screen mounted to the controller. Bill was impressed, and said "Wow, nice drone. A lot nicer than my cheapy little quadcopter. Think you can handle this drone flying with the turbulence caused by the fire?"

"I don't think there will be a problem. I've done this before. So you fly too?"

Bill caught her words about doing this before, triggering a thought about looking into this comment later. At the moment, however, there was a much more pressing matter. "I just barely got started flying, so I am not that good. At least I am not crashing my quadcopter like I used too!"

Diana laughed and told him she knew exactly what he meant. She felt more comfortable chatting with Bill than she could remember ever feeling.

"Are you sure you want to stay here and help us? If the fire hits us, and it looks like it will, it will be very scary."

Diana said she would be fine, she has dealt with close calls with fire before. Bill raised an eyebrow at that additional comment, but figured now was not the time to ask about it.

"Ok, as long as you agree to follow either George's, Stan's or my commands without question or hesitation, you can stay and get us some aerials."

Bill had Diana leave her pickup keys in the ignition in case the vehicle needed moving, and then told Diana what he needed first. "We need to know where the other structures are in relation to us and the fire. So if you could fly the area and find the other structures, that would be a big help. Once we get to look at the aerials then we can plan our defense a little better. Hopefully by then the Forest Service will have air attack on this and we can get you out of here."

Bill gave Diana safety instructions, including telling her to stay in the meadow they were parked in. He told her that if the fire drove at them, the safety zone was this meadow. They will have a portable tank and an engine and plenty of space to protect everyone from the heat and flames that the wall of fire would bring. Bill then had George, who was real good with four wheelers, offload Diana's four wheeler and told him to drive to the farthest threatened structure and check out each structure on the way back.

As Diana was getting her drone ready, she was remembering when she shook hands with Bill, and that weird sensation that had shook her clear down to her boots. And it had nothing to do with the fact that she was giddy about the coming wildfire, about getting up close and personal with a wildfire. She wished she could figure out what was up with this strange sensation. Whatever it was, it seemed strongest around Bill, and yet she felt so at ease near him at the same time. Well, she had work to do so she let the excitement of working the drone over this fire push other thoughts out of the way. Diana thought this was quite the change, from having to worry about being caught watching a fire to be actually helping with the fire attack. It really kind of felt good.

Watching Diana controlling the hexcopter, Bill was impressed. Standing alongside Diana looking at the view screen on the controller, Bill noticed a button on the controller that was not part of the original controller, but didn't want to interfere with Diana's concentration to ask her about that add on. The FPV view from the hexcopter was fairly good, and as Diana was flying, Bill was able to see a couple of the structures nearby. Looking at the real time video, Bill was able to get a feel for how good or bad the access was to the nearby structures. There was a brief moment in which Bill desperately wanted to take over flying the hexcopter, but Diana was handling the drone better than he could. Bill had a feeling something was familiar about Diana, and had remembered how he felt that strange sensation when they shook hands. For some reason he felt very comfortable with Diana at his side. Something was nagging him about this situation, but right now the fire had to take the forefront.

Chapter 48

Thanks to the drone real time videos, Bill was able to let George and Stan know where the fire was and where the other structures were and their condition. The water tender arrived, and after the portable water tank was set up, dumped its load of three thousand gallons of water into the portable tank. With a portable pump and plenty of hoses, the tank of water could act like a stationary fire engine and provide some protection to the two structures in the immediate area. After refilling engines 1 and 2 with the remaining water, the water tender took off for another load of water. Stan was doing a good job having his crew jumping around amongst the structures near the meadow. George's crew on engine 2 had caught up with George and were stretched thin between three structures to the east of the meadow that could easily be threatened should the fire change direction.

Bill, working with Diana, heard the page tone for yet another field fire. Frank was on the radio immediately, telling Dispatch that he and city engine 3 would be responding. Then Frank radioed Bill, telling him that he was taking Mac and one other volunteer and heading to the fire. They both knew that the city engine couldn't get into the field and hit the fire directly, but at least they could go and support the farmers and protect any structure in the way of the fire. Bill told Frank that they were stretched thin, but hopefully he could free up engine 1 if any State or Forest Service engines would show up.

When Frank mentioned Mac's name, Bill happened to see Diana

look over at him briefly, then back to concentrating on the drone. Bill remembered seeing Diana and Mac together in the bar, but he didn't think anything of it at the time. He also remembered Bev talking about both she and Mac were interested in a woman they had a few suspicions about. As he was trying to remember the conversation, he felt another strange sensation as the name Diana crept into the memory. If he remembered correctly, Diana was the woman Bev and Mac were watching. Unfortunately it was just a suspicion, Bev had told him, and they did not have any concrete evidence to point to Diana. But that Bev was suspicious of Diana was note worthy. As he was trying to push any non-fire thoughts out of the way, Bill was jarred from his thoughts by radio traffic coming from a Forest Service crew working on a fire near Snake Peak.

"May day, may day. Engine 3452 has been over run by the Snake Peak fire. I need air attack and I need an engine. I lost communication with 3452 and the fire is blocking me from getting to 3452."

"Unit with traffic, this is Dispatch. Copied your may day. What is your identifier?"

"Dispatch, this is State engine 4556."

"4556, what is your location and what is the location of 3452?"

"Dispatch, I am with my engine on the main road trying to get to the junction of the meadow access road. Engine 3452 was working on the access road protecting the line cabin. The fire blew up and we lost visual and radio communications with 3452 shortly after the blow up. And the fire has us blocked."

"4556, copied your transmission. We are trying to get air resources retasked to you and will dispatch an engine to you as soon as we can."

"Dispatch, this is 4556. Copied."

Bill felt a lump in his throat when he heard the may day radio traffic. Fellow fire fighters were possibly injured or dead. He knew the Snake Peak area from previous hunting trips, and knew that it was not far from his location. Bill told Diana that he had to leave, and that she was to listen to Stan for instructions. He told her to be careful, and stay in the meadow unless Stan tells her otherwise.

Bill grabbed Sue from Stan's crew and both he and Sue took off in engine 1 for the Snake Peak incident. He radioed George and told him what he was doing, that he had Sue and engine 1, and was going to see about assisting in the search for engine 3452. Bill mentioned that George was in charge, and that due to the Snake Peak incident, further resources may be even slower in coming. After telling George to be careful, Bill radioed Frank to fill him in. Frank said that as soon as they could, he would send engine 3 with three volunteers to help George. Frank still had two volunteers with him if they had another fire.

Then Bill contacted Multiagency Dispatch and told them he was responding with engine 1 to assist engine 4556 with the search. He also radioed the Sheriff's Dispatch and told them the same. Once the communications were finished, Bill could better concentrate on what was up ahead and was hoping it was not as bad as he was thinking.

In the cab of engine 1 both Bill and Sue were thinking of what they could run into at Snake Peak. Bill had been trying to get engine 4556 on the radio, but there had been no answer yet. "Dispatch, this is 672 with engine 1."

"672, this is Dispatch, go ahead."

"Dispatch, are you in communication with engine 4556?"

"Negative 672. The last transmission from 4556 said they had to move due to the fire. That was about eight minutes ago."

"Copy that Dispatch. We are five minutes out and will report."

"Copy that 672. Air attack will be overhead your area in three minutes. Call sign air74. An air tanker will be there in ten minutes."

"Dispatch, 672 copies air attack and air tanker. Thanks."

The Multiagency Dispatch office was looking calm and collect on the outside but internally everyone's nerves were taunt and on edge. The priority had changed as soon as the call from engine 4556 came in. Dispatch was busy trying to find resources that could quickly break off their current efforts and head to Snake Peak. Three of the many fires that had been started by the dry thunderstorm were in locations that could be considered low priority, as compared to others. By vacating these fires temporarily, five engines and two helicopters were released to head to Snake Peak. The vacated fires will be dealt with by new incoming crews, still a few hours away. The couple of fires threatening structures were barely being staffed, and they would get priority of incoming forces once the emergency at Snake Peak was taken care. A game of Russian roulette, but the stakes were very high. It was one thing to deal with trees, but quite a torment to deal with lives. This was definitely not a game to the Dispatchers and the fire management teams.

Fortunately Bill and Sue knew the Snake Peak area. Otherwise they would have been lost due to the flames and dense smoke. Bill was finally able to talk with engine 4556 by radio, who was still trying to get back to the spur road to the cabin area. Bill decided to carefully head to the cabin road, coming in from a different direction than engine 4556. Both he and Sue had separately spent a few nights in that cabin while hunting, so they had the advantage of knowing the location. When engine 1 finally arrived to the junction of the line cabin access road, Bill had to confirm with the Sue that this was the right road. The area was covered in smoke, and the thick stand of trees that had marked the driveway was replaced by smoking, blackened toothpicks.

Bill had Sue stop before going onto the cabin road. Seeing the group of trees turned to toothpicks at the junction made Bill think of what they could encounter trying to drive the road to the cabin. Bill decided to grab the chain saw and walk ahead of the engine, clearing any downed trees and watching for any trees ready to crash across the road. Visibility was almost zero, so it was slow going. It was eerie, with the sounds of the diesel motor of engine 1 mixed with the sounds of the fire, and once in a while a tree crashing. Bill had to stop and chain saw out a couple of fallen trees, but he finally worked his way to the small meadow where the cabin was supposed to be at one end in a stand of trees.

In between swirling masses of thick, acrid smoke, Bill saw an object out of place in the forest/meadow environment. With what seemed to be feet weighted down with lead, Bill worked his way to the object while engine 1 carefully followed. Damn, damn, damn, Bill said, as he recognized the object to be a skeleton of a Forest Service engine. Paint was burned off, tires still burning and putting off black, acrid smoke. As they walked up to the still burning engine, they saw the hoses were burning and no one was around. Flames were coming from out of the cab as well as from the engine compartment. Bill quickly put out the fire in the cab of the burning engine, but a quick search did not produce any burnt bodies. Bill held out hope that the crew had found shelter, and Sue worked the siren on engine 1 to see if anyone could hear the siren and respond back. There was no response after a few minutes of waiting. Engine 4556 pulled up alongside engine 1, after a harrowing drive through flames trying to find the secondary road. Bill spoke with the engine boss, who agreed with Bill's plan for a search.

Bill wanted one of the firefighters to stay with both working engines, in case the missing engine crew members would show up. It was agreed that Sue stay with the engines, and Bill work with the crew from engine 4556. Bill told Sue if she felt safe and was comfortable doing so, that she could put out the remaining fire in engine 3452.

Bill and the engine 4556 crew stepped out into a line, with each firefighter able to just see to the next firefighter. Visibility was poor, so even with four firefighters searching, they could not cover a very large area. Air resources were overhead but complaining that they could not see the ground. Bill took the middle and headed the line toward the cabin.

The cabin should be right here, thought Bill. His remembered landmarks were either gone or obscured, but Bill figured the cabin was only about two hundred feet from the engines. Bill saw a pile of burning logs just up ahead, and soon confirmed his suspicion. The cabin was hard to see because it was no longer standing and no longer recognizable as a building. It was basically a pile of burning logs. If the missing engine crew took shelter in the cabin, it will take awhile to find the bodies. Bill was trying to remember what else was in the area, someplace the missing crew could have gone for shelter. He thought there was a stream maybe less than three hundred feet from the cabin to the left. Taking the same search arrangement, the four headed away from the cabin in hopes of finding the stream and the missing crew.

One of the engine crew members shouted as he came to the stream. Bill and the other firefighters joined up at the stream, and decided to continue the search using the stream as the guide. Bill took the furthest out post, with one firefighter keeping an eyeball on the stream. They went about eight hundred feet, then turned to the other side of the stream and went back to where they first came to the stream. Bill thought they should continue the search along the stream for about another three to four hundred feet, than turn back toward the cabin. The search progressed about seventy five feet when the engine crew member closest to the stream noticed a different lump of smoking material alongside the stream. He moved closer to the lump and soon realized that it was a body. As he realized this was not an animal, but one of the missing crew members, the firefighter promptly got sick. After he stopped vomiting and before he got sick again, he yelled to Bill that he found one of the crew members.

Bill and the other firefighters approached the body, verified the grizzly find, and made sure the firefighter who found the body was okay. Bill had some flagging tape in his vest so he marked the location, and decided to leave a flagging tape trail as they worked their way back to the cabin. On the way back toward the cabin, they found the smoking remains of the other two engine crew members. Bill, kind of hardened to the grizzly scene by the deadly fires of last year, did not join the other firefighters in being sick. He radioed both the Sheriff's Dispatch and the MultiAgency Dispatch that he had a code black for three, and that he has flagged the path and sites.

By the time the four firefighters walked back to the engines in the meadow, all were emotionally drained. One or two firefighters had tears streaming down their sooty faces. Bill gave Sue the grim news, and all five were trying to comprehend that their fellow firefighters were no longer alive. This deeply affected the camaraderie shared by nearly all firefighters. Some call it a Brotherhood, and when there is a tragedy within the Brotherhood, it seems that the differences between volunteer, wildland, and paid professional firefighters are put aside for the moment. It is then that most remember that fire is the common enemy that forms a bond between those tasked to fight the enemy. Unfortunately, the fire won this battle. The war was still being fought.

Chapter 49

Bill didn't want to do a damn thing, as he was wiped out emotionally. Sue and the crew of engine 4556 were also emotionally drained. But there were at least two fires he had people on, and he needed to get busy and think of the living. So he talked with the engine boss for 4556, who agreed that Bill staying here would accomplish nothing. Bill would be more valuable working on protecting structures, so Bill and Sue headed back to join up with George. The trip back was deathly quiet. Sue was inwardly thankful she did not have to view the charred remains, but just as sick over the loss of the brave firefighters who valiantly fought but lost their lives to the dragon.

Engine 1 arrived to join up with engine 2 working on structure protection at the Tamarack subdivision. Bill received a briefing from George, and things were looking a little better now that the sun had receded and the humidity went up a little. Bill could see that the fire had burned around the area they had parked in. The houses survived the fire, and George had Stan and engine 2 checking on a couple of structures farther away. George told Bill that they were able to get a few aerial retardant drops near some of the homes, which helped to knock down the fire before it got to the homes. Bill filled in George and Stan briefly about the tragedy at Snake Peak.

While he was looking around, Bill noticed the drone lady was gone. "George, where is the drone lady?"

"I do not know. I was talking with Diana when we heard your radio traffic regarding the Snake fire tragedy. Diana brought her drone in and told us she had to leave right now. She looked very worried, so we helped her load up the four wheeler while she loaded her drone. Then she just took off without another word. The fire had not yet burned past us, so I don't think she was scared."

"Well maybe we can get a chance to thank her and make sure she is alright once we get back into town."

George seemed to have the fire situation around the structures under control. Bill radioed Frank to check in and see how his fire was going. Frank said they were just mopping up, and would be leaving the fire within the next twenty minutes or so. Additional resources were starting to arrive to help with the fire, so Bill told Frank that he could go back to the station instead of bringing engine 3 to Tamarack. Bill decided to head back to the station and help with getting things ready for another fire call should there be another one pop up. He asked Sue if she wanted to head into town, but she said she wanted to stay and work.

Bill wanted to talk with Francis and Frank about the tragedy, and see about a stress management team visit. Although he was the only one to see the burnt bodies, he felt that all his fellow volunteers may need a little help to get past the tragedy of losing three fellow firefighters close by.

Chapter 50

The Burner was confused by the overwhelming emotions. This was not a normal response to death in a set fire, but this was not a normal situation for the Burner. In the past, the Burner's fires had not directly caused death. Any death that was required had been done by the hitman that would accompany the Burner on these types of jobs. Now, as the Burner realized, a set fire had actually killed.

On the way into Prairie City, the Burner was thinking it was time to fold up and leave the area. Something here was upsetting the stoic balance that maintained the Burner. The Burner was not known for running from adversity, but this uncertainty, this confusion of emotions was undefined. It was not only the realization that the Burner's fire had killed that was causing the confusion of emotions. In the past the Burner could determine and attack the problem. Here the problem was only partially understood, with the reason for the feelings regarding Bill and the call to the area undetermined, and hence there was no attack plan to deal with the problem. The Burner's support base was back east, so that was where to head. But the Burner needed to see a couple of people first.

Bill arrived back at the fire station and started writing up the fire reports, getting the forms ready for George, Frank, and Stan to finish filling in the necessary dialogue to complete the report for each fire. Frank, Mac, and a third volunteer arrived with City engine 3 and Bill jumped in to help get the engine ready for the next call. Bill filled in Frank as to the only fire the rural engines were still working on. The volunteer had a family to get home to, so Frank released him. Bill radioed George for an update on the Tamarack fire. The Forest Service was requesting that the water tender and engine 2 stay the night in the subdivision. Bill asked George if the crew was okay staying the night, and he said that all had been asked and all were fine with staying. So Bill asked that George send engine 1 back to the station with Stan and Sue.

Once engine 1 backed into the station, and was refitted for the next fire, Stan needed to head home to his family. There were two remaining firefighters along with Frank, Bill, Sue and Mac who all had no one to go home to so they agreed to walk over to the bar and relax over a drink.

The Burner was in deep thought, sitting at a table in the bar, staring at a barely noticed drink. Something caused a tremor in the Burner, that same damn feeling that had been felt a few times before. Looking up, the Burner noticed Mac and two other guys and a woman with them. The Burner recognized one of the other firefighters, remembering his name was Bill, but she did not know the oldest man nor the woman.

Bill followed Mac into the bar and felt that darn shaking sensation again. Shrugging it off, he sat down at a table with the rest of the volunteers. Ellen sat down alongside Bill, answering Bill's welcomed phone call. A pitcher of cold beer was ordered, but the atmosphere around the table was far from jovial. Mac led the conversation, asking Bill for an update as to what happened, both at Tamarack and at Snake Peak. When it came time to talk about the fatalities at Snake Peak, Bill left out the gory details. Sensing Bill's inner struggle, Ellen took his hand in hers as a sign of support. Both Bill and Sue had tears in their eyes, remembering the tragedy.

Glancing around, Bill's eyes found a set of eyes staring back, and felt the same sensation that had hit him when he had walked into the bar, only stronger. The light was not very good, but Bill thought the eyes belonged to the drone lady from the subdivision fire. He wished he knew what was causing this strange feeling. Watching the eyes that had been staring at him, Bill noticed the eyes get up and start toward him. The strange sensation got stronger.

The Burner decided to chance it and go over to Mac and talk with him. Perhaps a night with him before heading back east would help calm the emotions. While heading to the table, the strange sensation of something deeply buried trying to rise up was getting stronger.

Mac saw Diana walking toward him and stood up to greet her. Both Frank and Bill stood up also, and Mac introduced everyone. Bill was correct about her being the drone lady, and told Diana he was thankful for the work she did with the drone. He told her he would like to get together sometime and go flying. From the little bit he was able to watch her, it looked like she had a much better skill at flying drones than he had. Something inside Bill said he really wanted this, and wasn't just talking to talk.

Diana, emotions stirring inside and barely controllable, heard Bill wanting to go flying together, and felt like she really wanted that to happen. She didn't know why, but a sensation of wanting to be with Bill stirred in her. Not a sex thing like with Mac, but something different, something she could not explain at the moment. Mac started to ask her a question, which brought her out of her day dreaming and back to a strange reality. Mac was asking her if she wanted a drink, and since she had just finished her first one, said sure. Frank was fairly quiet, listening to the conversations but really wanting Dora to be there. He finished his second glass and decided he needed to head home where he could be miserable without dragging others down.

Bill sensed there was some chemistry between Diana and Mac, so he whispered something in Ellen's ear and finished his glass. He left money on the table and with Ellen's arm entwined with his, they said good night to Diana and Mac. Sue needed to get home, so said her good nights and went with Ellen and Bill outside. Bill asked Sue if she was going to be alright tonight, and she said she would be fine. "Do not hesitate to call me if you are having any trouble with what happened today, okay?"

Ellen said that she would also be available, to just give her a call if she wanted someone to stay with her. Sue said she appreciated the concern, and if she couldn't handle the emotions, she would call him. They said their good nights and Bill walked Ellen to her car. Ellen, with concern, asked Bill if he was going to be alright. Bill sensed that if he asked, Ellen would spend the night with him. As much as he wanted that, something was in the way. He reluctantly told Ellen that he would be fine. He hugged her, kissed her, and thanked her for being there. Making sure Ellen got into her car and started toward home, Bill shook his head and told himself that he was the world's biggest fool.

On the way home Bill was thinking about Diana and the emotions apparently she brought on. "It has to be Diana", he thought, "because that weird sensation seems to only hit me when I am near her." As he thought trying to figure out what did this all mean, he remembered her face and realized what could be triggering the emotions. Diana looked a lot like his ex wife Armida. Thinking of Armida was enough to dredge up lots of emotions. "So maybe that explains why the weird sensations. It's the memory of Armida", thought Bill. "If I remember a little of the Italian Armida taught me, Diana means heavenly, divine. I sure can't disagree, she definitely looks heavenly, a lot like beautiful Armida did. I wish I was twenty years younger. Damn, now I'll be restless all night thinking of the brief history Armida, my enchantress, and I had."

Trying to stifle the painful memories, Bill was thinking about the fire in the subdivision and how the young woman, Diana if he remembered correctly, was so comfortable flying her drone around the fire area. As he thought about the drone, and thinking about his own drone and how he sorely wanted to be better at flying the thing, a thought jumped out causing him to pause all other thoughts. Thinking about the article on the Pine Barrens of New Jersey, and remembering the strange items found at a few recent wildfires nearby, Bill's thoughts centered around the possibility of a drone delivery for the fire starts. He defended his thoughts by remembering incidents of using helicopters to deliver fire to areas where a prescribed burn was called for. Of course the equipment in those days was bulky. But if someone where smart enough, he figured a device could possibly be designed to fit in a drone smaller than the size of a helicopter. The more he thought about it, the more he wanted to tell Mac and Bev about his wild idea. They were supposed to meet, but with all of the fires, especially the tragic Snake Peak Fire, their meeting had to be postponed.

Mac texted Bev while Diana went to the Lady's room. He figured Diana wanted to spend the night at his place, which might give Bev a chance to sneak a peek at Diana's pickup. Not proper police procedure, but Mac and Bev had a theory and were desperate to prove it either valid or not. They needed something to point them to a direction before things turned so cold that even if Diana were guilty, there would be no chance of catching her. Bev texted back she would try and would see him tomorrow. Mac quickly erased the texts just as Diana sat down. Looking at Diana, Mac said it had been a long hard day and it was time to get to bed. Diana agreed and followed Mac to his place.

Chapter 51

I t was about 2 am, a time when quiet takes over and people sleep more soundly. Bill woke up from his fit full sleep to realize he had volunteers still out on the Tamarack fire. Fortunately the café was open twenty four hours, so Bill placed on order to go for sandwiches and coffee. As soon as the food and coffee were ready, Bill drove the supplies out to George and the crew. Bill arrived to the meadow where the smoke swirled around and the nearby tree stumps and a few trees gave off crackling noises and a reddish orange flickering glow. George had just pulled up with engine 2 from a recon of the homes and joined Bill and the volunteers patrolling the meadow area on foot. Bill left the food and coffee with the grateful volunteers, and after checking that George was doing fine, headed back to town and his bed for hopefully some more sleep.

Bev pulled near Diana's parked pickup, and hoped Diana forgot to lock it in her haste. Careful to not alert the neighbors, Bev tried the door knob on the pickup canopy and was rewarded with an unlocked door. Crawling inside Bev used a flashlight to very quickly look over the stuff packed inside without touching a thing. She did not have a lot of room to move around because the hexcopter, placed in it's protective carrier, sat on top of some boxes and took up a fair amount of room itself. She carefully moved the carrier to get to the boxes underneath. In an open box she saw some empty plastic containers, about one half to one litter in size. She did not see any lids. The other thing that caught her attention was an open box of quart metal cans with the prominent warning Flammable on the box and on each can. She wrote down the information and product name from the cans. Near the cans were two 5 gallon gasoline cans, which could be simply extra fuel for the four wheeler. There were a couple of closed boxes, one still being sealed. The other box Bev carefully opened, paying attention how it was closed. Shining her light into the box she saw a few strange items that she could not explain. She took out her smart phone and pulled her police jacket over her head so it would partially shield the flash of the smart phone camera. She closed the box making sure it was arranged as before, than crawled out of the canopy.

The pickup doors were locked, so Bev could not rummage around the cab. Bev looked around to make sure no one was in the area, then headed back to her police car and started back on her patrol. As soon as she could take a break, she would be back to the police station and look up the information on those cans of flammable stuff. Than later she would contact Mac and see what he found out or what he can do with the stuff she found.

Mac was tired, but he was awakened numerous times by a restless Diana. It seemed that Diana was having a bad dream, as she was talking and gesturing in her sleep. Unfortunately, for the most part Mac could not make out what she was saying. There were a couple of times Diana said a word or two that Mac could understand even if he did not know what the words meant. He filed those words away in his memory to look into later. Perhaps Bev would know. He didn't think he could trust any of his fellow FBI agents. He finally fell asleep realizing he was going to have a short night.

Bill's night was a short one also. After leaving the food with the volunteers at the Tamarack fire, he headed home, showered and went back to bed. Sleep however wouldn't come. He would nod off but something in his head would cause him to wake up. Unbidden pictures of the burnt fire fighters flashed in his tired mind. And pictures of Diana flying the drone kept popping into his conscious. Even with a quick glance, the young woman bore an uncanny resemblance to his ex wife. Then memories of Armida, and of Ellen, popped in to his awake mind. Talk about an overload, Bill was far from sleep, but so damn tired.

He had only a very brief time watching Diana, but Bill remembered how well she controlled the drone in a tough environment. George had commented on that as well, even mentioning he was impressed that Diana didn't seem bothered by the proximity of the fire. Bill, from experience, knew that flying a drone required good concentration even when you had a visual on the drone. When flying using the FPV system, you had to rely on the real time images coming from the drone camera to the video screen on the control box. The skill to fly using the FPV was something Bill hadn't mastered yet. It took a lot of time to learn, and Bill had been just too damn busy to have fun flying his drone as much as he wanted to. Obviously Diana had had a lot more time to play and practice with her drone.

In between nodding off and waking up to once again ponder on this Diana situation, Bill was startled by his own question: what was Diana doing in the area of the fire and coincidently with her drone and her four wheeler? And he was remembering Diana's comments about working her drone on fires before. Bill thought he should ask Mac about Diana since he noticed the two of them talking as he left the bar last night. Perhaps Mac knows something of Diana's background. Bill did not believe in coincidences, and obviously something about Diana was triggering something in Bill. Bill did not like not having the answers, to not having an explanation for the strange feelings of lately, for why the memories of his ex wife Armida all of a sudden surfaced, and for his interest in Diana when he doesn't even know her. Noticing it was still early in the morning, when most people are fast asleep, Bill decided to wait until a more civilized time of day to call Mac and meet with him. I need answers, thought Bill, and finally nodded off once again to a fitful sleep.

At dawn, Bill checked in with George to see if he needed a replacement crew if the Forest Service wanted the water tender and engine 2 to stay. George had just finished talking with the structure protection supervisor, and it was determined that within about two hours the fire management team will release the water tender and engine 2. During the night a number of ordered engines and water tenders had arrived and a few more were arriving during the day, so the volunteers could be relieved. Bill said he would check in with the fire management team later and see if he could run engine 1 on a daytime patrol to assist. After all, the subdivision was in their jurisdiction.

Mac had left his place and a still sleeping Diana. Farm work was still there, and Mac had to admit he liked it. He still liked the FBI work, just not the Washington DC rat race. Bev was getting ready to finish her patrol shift, and knew Mac was already working. She called Mac and told him what she had found in the pickup, and that she had been able to do a little research, and took a few pictures. Mac said Diana talked in her sleep, but there was not much else he could add. They agreed to meet that evening at Bev's place and review the information.

A couple of hours later Mac's cell phone rang and he was surprised to hear Bill on the other end of the signal. Bill wanted to meet with Mac later and discuss what he knew about Diana. Mac mentioned that it just so happens that Bev and he were meeting to discuss the same topic, and he will check with Bev regarding Bill participating. That was fine with Bill. He did not want to force his way into something that he may not be invited into, so he said he would wait to hear from Mac.

Bill was having a tough time concentrating on work, due to a combination of lack of enough sleep, thoughts of the situation involving Diana, and remembering the burned fire fighters. Curious about the wildland fire investigation status, Bill gave Beth a call and was surprised she answered. Beth was dealing with the lack of enough sleep as well, having to investigate the rash of wildfires yesterday. She was making sure the fires of yesterday were indeed caused by lightning, and if not, what did cause the fire. Bill asked her how that was going, and she told him that she still had more work to do, but most of the fires she was able to investigate looked like lightning caused. The weird one so far, however, was the tragic Snake Peak fire. She had to call in an investigative team due to the deaths, and they were expected to arrive this afternoon. Things will get really hairy then, Beth told Bill.

Bill asked Beth why she thought the Snake Peak fire was weird. Beth said she had a gut feeling, after a very preliminary look at the area thought to be the origin of the fire. She had not been able to confirm that lightning had caused the fire. "I interviewed the initial attack engine crew, who pointed me to the area they first attacked. After checking burn patterns and typical signs pointing to where the fire came from, I came up with a fairly good idea of the origin. If I am correct, the origin would rule out lightning as being the cause of the fire. Oh, and just to warn you, the investigation team coming in today will want to interview you and your crew regarding the search you did for the missing engine crew. That was a nasty job. Are you doing ok?"

Bill thanked her for asking, and responded that he was ok, and that he and Sue were going to a counseling session tomorrow evening put on by the Forest Service. Beth said she was planning on going to it, even though she was not in on the gruesome discovery. She however did know the three fire fighters, as did quite a few of her fellow workers. He almost told her about the meeting with Mac and Bev, but he felt that Mac and Bev needed to approve of the spread of information. Beth said she would try to let Bill know what she found out regarding the Snake Peak fire as soon as she could, and they both exchanged good byes.

When Bill spoke with the Tamarack fire management team, they asked if Bill could provide engine 1 to patrol the Tamarack subdivision for the day. Frank was feeling like he needed some time away from the house, so he grabbed another volunteer that had slept well and was able to take off work, and they both took engine 1 for the day of patrolling. Bill felt like this patrol might be therapeutic for Frank.

Mac was only half paying attention, sitting in the comfort of the combine. He was daydreaming of Bev, Diana, and the tragedy at Snake Peak when he was jarred out of his reverie by his cell phone. He cringed and wished he hadn't answered it when he heard Ricardo's demanding voice. Damn, I could have gone without this today, thought Mac. Ricardo was on a rampage, and angry there has been no progress in the Prairie City situation. "I didn't send you there for a vacation, damn it. If you don't have something for me in a week you'd better be packed for cold weather." Mac, cranky from lack of sleep, fought off the need to tell Ricardo to go to hell. Instead, he pleaded for a month, but Ricardo wouldn't budge. Ricardo slammed his phone down, and dialed his boss's phone. Bennie was not very pleased with the lack of progress, but thought perhaps no progress meant there was really nothing going on. He agreed to the two weeks that Ricardo had stipulated, and promptly hung up. Bennie than called his contact with the 'family' and brought him up to date on the Prairie City situation. The contact was worried, since their top arsonist was vacationing in that area. They agreed to meet at one of the family's warehouses that evening to discuss options.

Chapter 52

Diana had finally awakened after a fitful sleep. She had to decide her next step. The deaths of the three engine crewmen had affected her. As far as she knew, her fire starts had never killed before. If a killing had to be made, Elmo or another of the soldiers would take care of the problem. This situation was different. A fire she started had killed three people. That had not been her plan, but now people were dead because of her. She was sick, scared, worried, and angry. Spending the night with Mac did not help. She needed someone to talk to, someone who would listen and to help her deal with the tragedy she has caused. Someone like a mother or a father she could run to, but she had neither.

She reviewed what she had done yesterday, trying to make sure she left nothing that would point to her involvement. Of course it was stupid of her to go and help with the subdivision fire. That was like painting a target on her, but they will have a hard time putting evidence together that incriminates her. Heck, she had been flaunting her stuff in front of the investigators for years and still remained uncaught. Diana thought she had better visit at least one of the agricultural supply firms in town to legitimize her presence. Then make her way back east and try to forget about Prairie City. But first, she realized she had not been to confession, and that could be what was causing her anxiety.

Fr. Francis was in his confessional, firmly believing he needed to be available for his flock and not the other way around. He was startled from his prayers by someone entering the confessional. He slid the screened window open to hear the person's confession. "Bless me Father…"

Francis was momentarily stopped in his blessing by the sounds of the voice. That voice had haunted him for nearly a year. When the person got to the part of the confessing of sins that included the accidental deaths of three people, Francis knew it had to be the same person. Once again Francis was thrown into a pit of despair, realizing this person was responsible for even more deaths, and there may be more. Yet as the confessor, he was bound to tell no one. When the person finished with the list of sins, Francis again stated the need for the sinner to make amends to the Lord by going to the police and explaining what happened. "Only then can you be forgiven, and the burden of sin be removed from your soul. But I am not the judge. Our God is the judge, and you need to converse with Him. I can give you absolution as the mediator, but you must go to the authorities about the deaths you have asked forgiveness for." With that stated, Fr. Francis prayed and, with a reluctant heart, absolved the sinner in the hope that his words will have an effect. After providing the suggested litany of prayers, Fr. Francis told the penitent sinner to "go with God and sin no more."

As Diana walked out of the confessional, she felt some of the burden had been removed and she was more able to attend to the current situation of getting out of the area. She wished she could do something to undo the deaths she caused, but that was impossible. She still needed to do a few things to build her cover story. She visited one of the agricultural businesses, but the manager was out until later in the afternoon. Same was true with the other store. Apparently there was a push on finishing the harvest of the late season crops. Well, Diana figured she could wait another day. Besides, this way she could have one more night with Mac before leaving, probably for good.

Mac's phone rang yet again, making for a busy day. This time it was Diana, asking Mac about his plans for tonight. Diana was a little disappointed that Mac had a fire meeting, but at least that would only be about two hours of the evening. Looking at the clock, Diana figured it was time to try the agricultural businesses again to see if either manager came in from the field work. One of the managers had made it back to the office, and was able to talk with Diana regarding supplies. "We don't seem to have a need for the fuel thickener, but I can sure look over the other items in the list and call you back." Diana said that would be fine and left the number of her work desk.

Mac texted Bev, asking her to call him when she was awake. A half an hour later, Bev called and said she was up and getting ready for breakfast. Mac explained Bill's interest in a meeting, and Bev said she was fine with Bill being involved. Mac also mentioned that Diana had called and was planning on spending the night again. They agreed on a time and figured they better meet at the fire station. Mac called Bill to let him know about the okay for the meeting. He wished he could call his friends at the FBI, but things just did not smell quite right regarding the FBI involvement. So he will just have to trust the locals and hope he wasn't killing his job as a FBI agent.

Chapter 53

Bill, Bev and Mac met at the fire station instead of going to supper first, and Bev provided the pictures and research regarding what she found in Diana's pickup. Bev and Mac knew the search was illegal, and would not be admissible in court. But they needed something to steer the investigation into the right direction. Bev's finding of the plastic bottles and cans of M4 fuel thickener could be part of the agricultural operation Diana was involved with. And her being around town at least a couple of times when there was a suspicious wildfire could just be coincidence. Or it could be related to arson. They needed something stronger than just wild guesses based on gut feelings. It was frustrating, for they needed facts to support their gut feelings, but how to get the facts?

Bill felt the same way. Now that he heard what Bev and Mac had put together, albeit shaky at best, he remembered the comments Diana had made at the Tamarack Subdivision fire. Bill mentioned them to Bev and Mac, who agreed that in itself those comments meant nothing. Another concern Bill brought up was the coincidence of Diana being in the area, with her drone at that exact time. And he mentioned the button that had been added on Diana's drone controller, as well as that she quickly left the subdivision upon hearing of the firefighters' deaths. A final comment Bill had was his talk with Beth, in which she mentioned the Snake Peak fire was looking to her like arson. However he reminded Mac and Bev that Beth has not made an official ruling, and that she will be replaced by a special investigation team who will make the official determination. Bill finished his comments by mentioning his idea that the latest suspicious fires could have been set by someone flying a modified drone to deliver fire to a specific area. Bev and Mac felt that everything they had so far was all circumstantial at best, but thought the drone, the transmitter modification, the M4 thickener, and the plastic bottles must be tied together. They needed proof, something that tied Diana to the stuff in the pickup, to the suspicious fires in the wildlands. Then if they could do that, could it be their luck to tie Diana to the deadly arson fires of the year before? It was a heck of a stretch, but maybe this was what they needed to get the stalled investigation onto the right track and homeward bound.

It was like trying to put together a puzzle when someone had thrown in a few pieces from another box. Mac said he was supposed to be with Diana tonight, and maybe something will be said that could mean something, a lead to tying a few pieces together. It was agreed to bring Amrit up to speed on the current discussion, than the three broke their meeting in order that the fire training could start.

After the fire training was finished, Bill went home and called Amrit. Bill offered to drive to Amrit's, but Amrit said he would be willing to pull into Prairie City tomorrow morning first thing and get updated instead of discussing the topics over the possibly compromised phone. After hanging up, Bill fixed a quick dinner, then fired up the computer. He had an idea and was going to look at whatever information he could find regarding fires that were found to have been started with M4. If you throw enough darts at the target, one of them is bound to hit the bulls eye.

Before Bev had to start her patrols, Mac asked Bev if she was ok with this subterfuge between he and Diana. Bev said, "Honestly, I am not liking the situation. If I were in Diana's shoes I would be terribly hurt once I found out it was a lie. But I just hope we can find something out very soon and put this to an end." She didn't tell him that she wanted to be with him instead of he being with Diana. Mac told her that he wasn't happy with the subterfuge either, and felt lousy treating Diana this way. He blurted out that he would rather be with Bev. Bev was pleasantly shocked that Mac felt the same way as she did. But it still did not make the situation with Diana any more acceptable. What if Diana was innocent of their theory? Damn, sometimes police work was no fun. She hoped this was police work and the lousy feelings were worth the efforts.

Bev went to her desk at the police station and was on the phone with Liz, catching Liz at her desk just as she was leaving for home. When Liz heard the update, she wanted to see the pictures Bev took of the stuff in the back of Diana's pickup. "Bev, do you have a decent photograph of Diana? I want to carefully start inquiries regarding some of the car rental places and some of the agricultural firms around the State. Damn, trying to do this without the help of the FBI, and without word getting to the FBI, is a real pain in the butt. But I am afraid that if I see that Ricardo again, it won't be me with the pain in the ass!"

"I know you wouldn't need help, but I would love to help you on that! It makes me feel so much better just thinking of Ricardo in a body cast!" Both ladies laughed, breaking for the moment the seriousness of the situation.

Fortunately the night before, Mac was remembering to think like an investigator and while Diana was sound asleep, he found her driver's license and copied it. It was this copy he had given to Bev earlier, so Bev immediately sent the picture to Liz. Having the driver's license was a bonus, and Liz told Bev to thank Mac for getting that. Liz started thinking about how she could work on some of the neighboring State law enforcement agencies without the FBI getting a whiff of what was happening. Fat chance, but she would initially work with those she knew and trusted. It was about time for some luck to enter into the investigation, and maybe now was that time.

Bev was thinking that Diana may leave before they can get the information they need to either confirm their suspicions or clear Diana from the list of potential suspects. With Diana's brief history of coming and going this summer, it seemed likely she would be gone shortly. Bev's intuition was telling her that this time when Diana leaves she may not come back. Bev was frustrated, having no real evidence, only intuition, gut feeling, and disjointed facts. She wished something would break open, either to prove her wrong or to prove her gut feeling was right. Her gut feeling said Diana was somehow tied to the recent arson fires, but there was also a feeling that there could be more.

Mac found a note from Diana saying she would meet him at the bar for drinks and dinner. Mac showered and tried to think over the Diana situation. Were he and Bev trying to create an answer to a question that had not been asked yet?

Chapter 54

Diana was getting anxious, wondering where Mac was. He was usually here at the bar by now. Perhaps he had a fire call, although she had heard no sirens. As she was getting ready to leave her pickup truck to go into the bar to wait for Mac, she received a phone call from her capo, a most unusual situation. When she got over her initial shock that Giorgino had called her, something he has never done before while she was out on a job, she asked him what he needed. Giorgino told her there had been some talk regarding the amount of time she had been spending in the Prairie City area, and that the 'family', especially her Grandfather, was concerned some secrets may get exposed. "You are considered a liability now, and Elmo has been given the authorization to take care of the problem. You need to run away, hide. I don't want you to end up like your Mother. I did not have the heart to tell you years ago, but Elmo was ordered by your Grandfather to take care of your Mother, who had become a liability to the 'family' as well. I am so sorry Diana, your Mother was special. I was so glad when she left. But your Grandfather drug her back before you were born, and I hated to see her so distraught. After you were born, your Mother kept trying to leave with you, apparently trying to go back to your Father. When I heard what Elmo had done to your Mother, I wanted to kill your Grandfather and Elmo, but I chickened out. I do not want you killed as well. Cazzo, I had better go before someone hears me. Goodbye, and may God be with you."

"Wait Giorgino, don't hang up." But Giorgino had already hung up.

Diana was frozen in time, not knowing what to say or do. The shock of Giorgino's phone call was still coming. She was slowly replaying the phone call in her head. Her Mother killed by Elmo. She was to be killed also by Elmo. And all under orders from her Grandfather. It was slowly sinking in that she was as good as dead. Her Grandfather, how could he? She knew he was a hard man, but she had no idea that he could even consider killing his immediate family. Perhaps Giorgino was over reacting, that he heard wrong or was trying to scare her into getting back home now. Hopefully she can talk with Giorgino. Perhaps he can help her get her Grandfather to reconsider. Well, she was planning on leaving in the morning anyway, so she will stay with Mac one more night and say goodbye to Prairie City forever. She will plead her case to her Grandfather and explain the situation to him. After all she is blood relation. It should be okay she told herself. Tomorrow all will be okay. For now, she needed a drink, so she went into the bar without waiting any longer for Mac to show up.

Diana was still trying to recover from the call from Giorgino, nursing a cold glass of dark beer, when she looked up to see Mac searching for her. Mac saw her and sat down at the table. He could see that Diana had been crying, and asked her what was the problem. She said that she had just received some bad news, but she was okay now that Mac had arrived. The small talk seemed to mask their concerns. They both seemed to be good at hiding something. Diana so wanted to talk to Mac about her phone call, but didn't dare. Mac was wanting to be with Bev for the night instead of Diana. It was not that Diana was unattractive or dull in bed. Much the opposite. It was just Mac felt something with Bev that he did not feel with Diana. Diana finally mentioned she had to leave in the morning, and would like to spend the night with him. Mac said he would be delighted, than asked Diana if she was heading to another business stop. Diana told him she had to return to the main office back east, and promptly changed the subject.

After finishing their meals and a last drink, Diana and Mac left. While driving to his place, Mac called Bev to tell her Diana would be leaving in the morning. Bev said Liz had sent the license plate information out to the State Police stations and Sheriff's dispatch offices throughout the state. "Hopefully someone will see where she goes" said Bev. "If we can follow her and see where she goes, maybe that will help us fill in some more blanks. Or maybe not."

Mac said he would talk to her tomorrow and hung up as he was pulling into the driveway of his rented place. Diana parked outside, grabbed a few things, and joined Mac inside.

Diana desperately needed someone to be with, someone to unleash her newly acquired burdens upon. She was trying to keep up appearances but she was falling apart inside. With the message from Giorgino, about her Mother's murder, and who ordered it, her tough world just went upside down. Mac was great in bed, and a friend, but that was not what she needed. She needed someone to hold her, stroke her hair, listen to her agony and absorb it while telling her he will protect her. Strangely, thoughts of Bill entered her agonized mind. Even though they had met just a couple of times, she felt that special comfort she could only remember from being with her Mother for such a short time. She finally went to sleep on her tear drenched pillow, with dreams of her Mother and Bill comforting her, telling her she had nothing to fear.

Something awoke Mac from a sound sleep. He looked at the clock and saw it was not quite three in the morning. He was trying to figure out what woke him when he heard another sound, like the click of a gun safety being released. He put his hand over Diana's mouth, and whispered into her ear to be quiet and get down on the floor. Diana was wide eyed and at first combative. But she quickly realized the look in his eyes and the tone of his voice told her he was dead serious. He whispered there might be someone in the house, and that he wanted her on the floor out of the way, now. He grabbed his gun and quietly made his way to the closed bedroom door, where he listened intently. Someone was whispering, so there must be more than one outside the door. Mac backed up to the window and carefully peeked out the curtains. He saw a shadow move in the light cast by the nearby street lamp. This is not good, he thought. He turned down the volume on his cell phone and called Bev. He whispered to her what the situation was at the moment, and that she needs to call for backup and get here asap. Mac hung up and crawled over to Diana.

"Do you have a gun with you?"

Diana showed the gun in her hand, stating she had taken it out of her purse when he was on the phone. He whispered that he figured there were at least two in the house and one outside. Mac asked Diana if she had any idea who these people were. Diana said no, she had no idea, but then she stopped mid sentence and thought about her earlier phone call from Giorgino. Elmo! Oh damn, they are in big trouble if that is Elmo out there. Should she tell Mac that maybe these guys are here for her? She decided to keep it to herself for now, and wait to see what transpires. If these guys were from her Grandfather, she and Mac were as good as dead. Oh god, where was Mother, where was Bill.

Diana was soul searching while waiting for the door to the bedroom to come crashing down. Why would the 'family' want her eliminated? What has she done? Diana was not able to figure out why this hit team was after her, but it seems obvious that she must be the target. What did her Mother do that got her killed? Her thoughts were interrupted by the crash and splintering of the door while two men rushed into the room following the door wrecker. All three had their guns firing, bullets holing the walls and the bed. Mac raised his gun and started shooting at the gun flashes while trying not to give his position away. He was rewarded with a couple of grunts and groans.

Mac heard Diana shoot and heard a welcoming grunt from the door way. Gun fire was still raking the room, though a little less in volume. As Mac was waiting to get off another shot, the window broke and he heard Diana cry out in pain. Damn, he thought, I hope she is ok. Got to get her away from the window, Mac said to himself. Mac crawled over to where Diana was collapsed, and felt for a pulse. He felt her hand on his, so he knew she was alive and conscious. He whispered, asking her where she was hit and how bad. She told him she felt something go through her shoulder and she has no feeling in that shoulder or hand. He wished he could turn on a light to see what kind of damage, but right now the dark was keeping them alive for the moment.

He dragged Diana away from where she had been laying before another shot from the window could find her. Apparently the shooters were busy reloading, so Mac took advantage and moved as quickly as he dared, towing a bleeding Diana. He was worried that they would not make it out alive, with the odds not in their favor. The shooters started up again, and as luck would have it, a bullet found Mac's right leg. He grit his teeth and did not cry out even though the pain wanted to express itself. More bullets were whizzing by when he heard Diana cry out in pain. He soon saw flashing red and blue lights against the bedroom wall, at first wondering if he was hallucinating due to the pain. He heard car doors slam and shortly a megaphone voice announced the police had the building surrounded and to give it up right now. A shot was heard, and then the megaphone once again announced the ultimatum. There were two shooters left, one in the house and one outside. They both were smart enough to realize the 'family' attorney would get them out of jail within hours. So they surrendered. After securing the two shooters, Bev led a couple of officers into the house and headed to find Mac.

Fortunately the place was small so the search for more shooters was quick. Bev found the doorway to the bedroom and before entering, yelled to see if Mac was there and could hear her. Mac returned the hail, and said they were clear of shooters but they both were hit. Bev told her fellow officers to check the two bodies lying at the doorway while she carefully entered the room. Flashing the powerful light around the room Bev made sure there were no uninvited guests lurking about. Once she felt confident no one was lurking in the shadows, she yelled for the EMTs. She quickly looked over Diana and realized Diana had been hit more than once, and that she was losing a lot of blood. Mac saw the same thing once Bev's light had illuminated Diana's wounds. He quickly reached over ignoring his single wound and put pressure on one of Diana's bleeding wounds, trying to stop the flow of blood. Bev selected another wound and put pressure on it, waiting for the EMTs to move in and take over. While waiting, Bev looked at Mac and asked him what the hell happened? "Your guess is as good as mine. I heard a strange noise, like a gun safety click off. Then all hell broke loose. Sure glad you got here when you did." They were both busy attending Diana's serious wounds as best they could, or they would be in each other's arms by now.

The EMTs arrived and started to work on Diana, so Bev helped Mac stand up and they walked out to the ambulance, where other EMTs could work on Mac's gun shot wound. On the way Mac told Bev to call the investigation team immediately. "Bev, this little party activity is going to get back to the FBI quickly. The team members need to hide and protect their work before my boss stomps in again and takes the files like before. Oh and Bev, you may want to ask the chief to place a 24 hour guard on

Diana's hospital room. I think someone was out to get Diana and may still try." Bev asked Mac if he was sure that he wasn't the target, but Mac said he didn't think so. He couldn't think of any reason why someone would be after him. Never the less, Bev was going to ask her boss if Mac could also have a 24 hour protection team. She kissed him on the cheek, handed him over to an EMT, and told him she would catch up to him after she makes the calls.

Chapter 55

Bill worked his way over to Mac, having been with one of the fire engines standing by a safe distance from the battle. Dispatch had called for an engine to be on standby near the scene in case a fire broke out in the little house. This type of operation had been talked about in preplanning, but had never been used before. Things like this just didn't happen in Prairie City. Well, they hadn't but ever since the deadly arson fires last year, Prairie City's innocence was lost.

"Are you okay Mac?"

Mac told Bill about the gun battle, that Diana was wounded multiple times, and he got one in the leg. "I don't think these guys were after me, so they must have been after Diana. I told Bev to get hold of your investigation team and warn them. I am betting this little incident will bring the FBI back."

"What the hell is this all about, Mac?"

"Bill, I don't know. The guys that hit us seemed professional, but thank goodness they were not the best or we wouldn't be talking. If these guys were after Diana, they were pretty bold to walk right in with a small army and shoot the place up. That worries me, and makes me wonder who Diana ticked off."

"Ok, if we assume she ticked someone off, it looks like whoever she ticked off is playing serious hard ball," interjected Bill. Bill saw the grimace on Mac's face as the EMT was trying to finish cleaning the wound and getting Mac ready for the trip to the hospital.

Since Mac was in the ambulance and being cared for, Bill went over to talk with Bev. Bev was talking with Walt, who when he saw Bill motioned him over. Walt explained the plan he and Bev had put together quickly, to protect Diana and Mac. Walt had asked Bev to contact Liz with the State Police, especially since she was on the investigation team. Bill said he would call Amrit, who was planning on meeting with Bill later that morning. It was still early in the morning so hopefully he could catch Amrit before he started his drive to meet with Bill. Then Walt asked Bill if he could recommend a couple of firefighters to act as guards for Diana and Mac. "Until I can get some help from the State or the County, I need a couple of your people that can handle a gun and are willing to help me out. I would only need them until I can get re-enforcements."

Bill said he would help, and he knew a couple of others who had concealed carry permits and were fairly good shots.

"Thanks Bill. Looks like the ambulances are ready to head to the hospital, so let's put our plan into motion. Bev, you and Bill work on the protection team and I will get hold of finding help. I will meet you at the hospital later. I need to get these perps, dead and alive, taken care of. Be careful and keep a sharp lookout. We don't know what we are dealing with here. Obviously it is serious, so they may try to take out Diana and Mac in the hospital."

On the way to the hospital both Bev and Bill made their phone calls to Liz and Amrit respectively. Once at the hospital, Bill contacted the couple of volunteers he had in mind to help, and asked them to meet him at the hospital as soon as possible, and bring their guns.

Bev told Bill she wanted to meet with the volunteers as soon as everyone was here. While waiting, Bev caught up with her fellow officer, who was sent to the hospital ahead of the patients to check things out. He told Bev that he was able to quickly search the rooms set up for both patients, but didn't have time to check out the rest of the hospital. Bev said as soon as she talks with the arriving volunteers, they will search the hospital. Bev told the officer to continue to watch the rooms, and then she went to talk with the head nurse.

Ellen, the head nurse, was anxious to find out what was going on, concerned for her staff and patients' safety. Bev and Ellen knew each other, not only through emergencies at the hospital but they had done a few things together around the town. Bev told Ellen that she would like her to join in a meeting to be held shortly, and wanted to know if a meeting room was available to use. "As soon as a couple volunteers show up, we will start the meeting and get us all dialed in to what is happening and what we need to do. Hopefully we will be able to answer your questions, and you ours." Bev and Ellen made sure each had current cell phone numbers, and Bev said she would call shortly once the rest of the team arrived.

Bev checked on Diana in ER1 and then went to check on Mac in ER2. One of the nurses told Bev that Mac would be out and wheeled to his room shortly. The doctor wanted to keep Mac in the hospital for a few days and then get him into a rehab program. Fortunately the bullet did only slight damage, but Mac wouldn't be running any marathons for awhile. Diana was a much more serious situation. She was going to be in surgery for awhile yet. One of the bullets went into her abdomen, bounced off a rib, and damaged a lung. Bev radioed her officer on duty guarding the rooms and warned him that Mac would be coming out of the ER very soon. Then she caught up with Bill, who was waiting with a couple of his volunteers and another police officer.

Bev phoned Ellen that everyone was here and they could start the meeting. Ellen appointed one of the nurses to take over the patient care, caught up with Bev and took the group to the meeting room. Bev started by telling what they knew as to what happened, and why they felt a need for protecting Diana and Mac. "It seems the people after either Diana or Mac or both are serious and may even try to take out the two of them here in the hospital. They might even use a disguise and pretend to be staff, gaining access to the rooms that way. I want the head nurse to issue photographs of each member of her staff and you will use the photographs as a guide to who you can allow access to the rooms. If you don't recognize the person, immediately call for help and deny access as best you can. No heroics though. We do not need anymore of you laid up in a hospital bed."

Bev continued, telling the members of the protection team that her boss was calling for reinforcements, but in the meantime this team was it. She broke the team into two groups, one for each room, and then set a schedule so that each group would have a four hour shift. She was hoping that in less than eight hours the reinforcements would be here to take over. But if not, the rotation would have to continue. She and Bill would be roaming the hospital, and would be available for backup. There being no questions from the group, Bev dismissed everyone and motioned Bill over to join her and the head nurse.

Bill greeted Ellen, and was surprised when Ellen hugged Bill. They had dated a few times, and they seemed to have a good time when they got together, but the spark never seemed to become a flame. Bill really liked Ellen but something just seemed to get in the way of a serious relationship. Bev made sure Bill and Ellen had each other's cell phone numbers, and Ellen told Bev she would get the photographs of the staff to her as soon as possible. Bev suggested the staff be cut back to just the bare minimum required to handle what they have. The fewer people in the middle of what could be a war the better.

Noticing Ellen's nervousness, Bev said "We are all nervous as hell. Just have your people be on the lookout for anything out of the ordinary and report it immediately. Hopefully Walt can get a Deputy or two here shortly to help. But to be blunt, the next eight hours will not be fun. Do you want me to order you anything from the deli? I noticed you have a nice kitchenette, and I can have someone bring in some food and beverages. Why don't you talk to your staff and find out what they would like and I will get an order placed." Bev was thinking on her feet, and figured Ellen would be tied up with her staff for awhile getting the list of food items. Ellen left to check on her staff and get the staff pictures. Bill was impressed with the way Bev was handling the situation, and said so. Bev appreciated the compliment, and asked Bill if he would be willing to concentrate on Diana's protection while she on Mac's. Bill said he had no problem, but teasingly warned Bev to not associate with the patient, sensing that Bev's concern for Mac was a lot more than ordinary. Bev playfully slapped Bill on the arm, than left the room to start running errands.

Chapter 56

Beth was awakened by the phone ringing next to her bed. Couldn't be a good phone call at this hour of the early morning, she figured to herself. "Beth, it's Bev. Hate to bother you but we have an incident and need your help. Walt asked that I give you a call. Come asap to the hospital loaded for bear. Mac and Diana have been shot. It looks like a professional type operation, and we think they may hit the hospital. I'll fill you in when you get here. Be careful and watch for activity near the hospital."

Beth, jarred awake by what Bev briefly stated, told Bev she would be there shortly. While she was dressing and making sure she had her gun and extra loads, Beth was thinking about the situation and how it got to this huge mess. She thought she remembered meeting Mac, one of the new volunteers. But she didn't remember a Diana. Well, even though she was a Forest Service law enforcement officer, she did have authorization to assist other law enforcement agencies. And it sounded like she was definitely needed. She radioed the Sheriff Dispatch office and the Multi Agency Dispatch office that she was in route to assist at the hospital, and sped to who knows what.

For about another thirty minutes or so things were fairly quiet at the hospital. It was still dark out, with daylight maybe an hour away. Bill and Bev had dialed Beth into the situation, and she assisted in the watch over Diana's room. Bill had made his rounds a couple of times and had just settled down for a sit in Diana's room. With a somewhat relaxing

231

quiet, just the beeping of the monitors watching over Diana, Bill was thinking of the weird feeling he had while being in the room. Similar to the few times he had felt a weird sensation while in the bar recently, just stronger. He remembered the same strong feeling when he shook hands with Diana at the Tamarack Subdivision fire a couple of days ago. He kind of remembered the first time he felt that strange sensation. It was during that house arson fire last year. He had never felt like that before, at least not that he could remember anyway.

While Bill was spending time in Diana's room, he finally was able to take a good hard look at Diana. Even though she was white as a sheet, with a breathing tube obscuring part of her face, Bill saw an uncanny resemblance to his ex wife Armida. He thought to himself how many years ago was it she left? Must have been about the same age as Diana when she left, he thought. Was it that she looked similar to Armida that caused his strange sensations?

Bill was sitting in the chair near Diana's bed day dreaming about Armida when he was awakened from his thoughts by a woman's voice saying, "A penny for your thoughts, Bill."

Bill stood up and greeted Helen with a quick, friendly hug and a kiss. "Hi Ellen. How are you doing? You are looking good."

"Thanks Bill. I am doing ok, and you must be doing okay since you look pretty good yourself." Ellen walked over to check on Diana, and after looking at her chart, the monitors, and Diana's coloring, Ellen looked over at Bill. "Bill, you never told me you had a daughter."

Completely caught off guard, Bill replied, "What? Ellen, what the heck are you talking about? I don't. Armida and I wanted children but it just did not happen. But it is funny you mentioned that because I was just noticing how Diana looks like my ex wife Armida."

"Well, I thought I could see a resemblance of you in her. Bill, what blood type are you?"

"I am type AB positive. Does Diana need more blood?"

"Yes, she is still losing blood, and I checked earlier on our stock of AB positive and we are almost out. Looks like we could use you in a little while to start building up a blood supply for her."

"Great, whatever I can do just say the word."

Ellen noticed the look in Bill's eyes and the concern in his voice. It wouldn't take much more to convince her that Bill has a daughter he did not know about.

Ellen left to do her hospital rounds, so Bill got up to do his check on the volunteers doing guard duty. He found one of the volunteers available to fill in on the watch in Diana's room while Bill did his rounds. He found Beth, and asked her if she could take his place with Diana when he had to go give blood. She said sure, but then asked Bill who Diana was and what was this all about. Bill said he wasn't quite sure, but filled her in as to what happened, explaining they did not know the why. While talking, something clicked in Bill's mind, and asked Beth if she could remember the dates of the latest wildfires, especially ones she thought were suspicious. Beth, surprised by the question at this time and situation, told Bill to give her a minute. She mentioned it was funny he asked about the recent fires because she was working on some reports just last night before falling asleep.

After a few minutes, Beth mentioned to Bill a couple of dates in which there had been wildfires she considered suspicious. Bill thought about the dates, then thanked Beth and said he needed to get back to Diana's room to do some thinking. He would let her know when he needed to give blood, and if he comes up with anything regarding the dates she just gave him.

While walking the halls and checking with the staff, he kept thinking about what Ellen had said about Diana. Armida and he had been trying to have a child, but Armida had not gotten pregnant. It was probably a good thing as it turned out, because a child in a divorce is traumatized, sometimes permanently so. It seemed like only yesterday, that night he and Armida spent together after he got home from a two week stint on a wildfire in Alaska. When Bill arrived home from the Alaska incident, Armida was angry and glad at the same time. While Bill was showering, Armida was telling him she wanted him home more, so they could raise a family. Bill, having heard this before, was selectively listening. Things will settle down and settle out he figured. Well that was certainly some bad advice back then, he thought to himself. After a dinner in which they brought each other up to date, Bill helped Armida with the dishes. With the kitchen cleaned up, Bill led Armida to the bedroom, and they both fulfilled their urgent needs. Bill could remember how good it was with Armida, and always felt a little guilty wondering if the sex was the only thing he wanted from Armida. No, that was not true. He wanted more than just the sex, and even now years later he painfully knew he had had more with Armida, but let her get away.

Chapter 57

Bennie was in his office and had just hung up from a disturbing phone call. Yelling to his secretary, he told her to call Ricardo into his office asap. The 'family' wanted a favor, and Bennie was obligated to deliver, if he valued his life that is. Apparently the 'family' wanted a young woman handed over to them, but there was a complication that Bennie was being asked to take care of. The woman was being held in a hospital in, of all places, good ole Prairie City. Ricardo had had experience with Prairie City, so it seemed only logical to send Ricardo to grab the woman and bring her back. Bennie had a little trouble trying to convince Ricardo that this next task was super critical. He told Ricardo, "She has critical information, and I want her here where we can watch over her and protect her."

"But boss, if she is that important, shouldn't we send multiple teams instead of just mine?"

Bennie said, "The fewer the people involved the better, and the more secure this situation will be. You need to get your team headed to Prairie City immediately and take care of this problem, before something happens to her and we lose the information she is carrying. Standard protocol, you talk to me and me only about the operation. And I know it will be extremely hard for you, but try to keep it low key and not raise a big stink, again."

Bennie had his own reasons for wanting Diana brought back asap, and he wasn't about to share them with Ricardo. Ricardo hadn't known the truth about the Prairie City situation since Bennie threw him into it last year. So Bennie wasn't about to tell Ricardo the truth now. He wanted Diana to be a gift to the 'family', in hopes they would leave him alone. Of course the extra income for the job would be nice for his retirement when the time came.

As Ricardo left Bennie's office, he muttered to himself, "Very funny, everyone's a damn comedian. I can't wait until he retires and I can move into his office. Damn comedian." And now he had to rush back to that damn town full of podunk Neanderthals. He had tried calling Mac, but he wasn't answering his phone. He said to no one in particular as he slammed his phone down, "The damn kid must be bedding some pig snouted farmer's daughter out in the barn. Just wait til I catch up with you, Mac. See how you like living in Antarctica."

After he yelled at his secretary to contact his agents and tell them to be at the airport asap, Ricardo took a minute to assess this latest task he was thrown into. He set aside his anger for a minute and realized something just didn't feel right. This thing with the woman just smelled a little fishy, but he had nothing to go on but a sense. Well, he had his orders, damn it all.

Once on board the FBI jet, Ricardo yelled for a glass of Highland Park 30 Whiskey. "Keep the bottle handy," he told the attendant, and proceeded to try and enjoy the smooth warmth of his favorite whiskey. He smiled as he remembered the fun he had slamming those idiots in Prairie City last year. With the whiskey settling, he thought maybe this might be okay after all.

Chapter 58

Heading toward Diana's room from checking on his volunteers, Bill noticed a hospital staff member heading toward Diana's room also. Bill knew that Beth had taken a potty break, and one of the volunteers had taken the inside watch in Diana's room, and Bev had taken a break and was in Mac's room. Something about this orderly bothered Bill, and even though they were still a fair distance apart, Bill didn't recognize the orderly from the staff introductions earlier. The orderly was pushing a heavy laundry cart, but something in the way the orderly was acting caught Bill's attention.

Bill called Bev on her cell phone and quickly told her it may be nothing, but there was an orderly with a laundry cart heading to the rooms and acting a little strange. Bev said she would be there shortly. Bill was behind the orderly, who was working his way toward Diana's room pushing a laundry cart. Bev, with Bill's warning still fresh, moved into the hall and spoke to the guard of Mac's room, passing the warning. She asked the guard to be extra vigilant while she quickly told the police officer in Mac's room. Bill called the volunteer firefighter in Diana's room and told him to be extra alert, something may be going down. Bill thought about calling the resting team in the break room to get here, but he didn't have time.

While Bev was closing the door to Mac's room, she heard a crash, like glass breaking, and then a shot. It sounded like it had come from Diana's room. She had been trained well, and immediately got on the radio while heading to Diana's room. Her radio call for help went to the Dispatcher, who immediately put a call out to all units to converge on the hospital, possible armed intruders trying to assault the hospital. Walt, still trying to get more help lined up, ran out of his office and hot rodded his chief's car toward the hospital. A couple of officers and close by Deputies who had been left to run the normal patrols also broke the speed limit racing to the hospital.

Bev had her gun out and was carefully walking toward Diana's room door when she heard a noise and saw an orderly approaching with a laundry cart from the opposite direction. Half her thoughts were working on the other side of the door, so she missed the signs and too late realized the orderly was the one Bill warned her about. He had a gun pointed at her and the bullet was already coming. Fortunately when Bev turned toward the sound, her position had changed just enough that when the bullet hit, it slammed into her shoulder instead of the chest. The impact sent Bev to the floor. Bill had his gun out as he peaked around the corner, and saw the shot and Bev go down.

No, no, no, Bill said out loud and ran toward the orderly. Taken by surprise, the orderly spun but not quick enough to get a clear shot off at Bill. Bill's hurried shot smacked into the intruder, putting the intruder out of the game. As he was hurrying to Bev, Bill saw a second intruder, rising out of the laundry cart and trying to get a bead on Bill. Bill was moving so quickly the second gunman had a difficult time lining up the shot. Bill's adrenalin was pumping full bore and gave him the courage and strength to quickly change direction and run smack into the laundry cart. The momentum careened the cart, with the second gunman still in it, into the wall. The gunman's head slammed into the wall, and he fell into a heap with the crashed cart. Bill, slightly dazed by the crash, told one of the approaching volunteers to get the guns and secure the perps. He then got up off the floor and finished his dash to Bev. Bev had a pulse, thank goodness. He found the bleeding wound and took a towel from the overturned cart, wrapping the wound tightly to staunch the blood flow.

Bill needed to get to Diana's room, but he did not want to leave Bev unattended. One of the volunteer firefighters ran to Bill, who had the volunteer hold the towel on Bev's wound. A nurse was on the way from down the hall, so Bill told her to work on Bev's wound while he checks out Diana's room. During his gun battle, Bill wasn't sure if he had heard other shots being fired from the rooms, but assumed something bad was going on. He opened Diana's room door with gun at the ready. He was scanning the room when he saw his fellow volunteer firefighter slumped in the chair. As Bill started toward the volunteer, one of his other volunteers called him on the radio and wondered what he and the officer with him should do. Bill told him to have the officer check Mac's room. Bill told the volunteer, "Find a nurse and bring her with you, and hurry. Joe is bleeding from a head wound." Bill glanced over at Diana, who seemed no different than a little while ago. Bill than went back to helping Joe. Joe, the volunteer, was bleeding from a head wound, but thankfully he was awake. Bill found a clean towel and held it to the wound on Joe's head. Joe told Bill that he only saw one intruder, and he was pretty sure he shot the intruder as he tried to enter through the broken window.

Ellen ran into the room, and was relieved to find Bill hadn't been shot. Thankfully Joe's wound was mostly superficial, so Ellen carefully cleaned and bandaged the wound. Freed from holding the towel over Joe's wound, Bill worked his way to the broken window and saw a body sprawled on the ground outside the window. Joe must have got off a great shot, proof that his numerous marksmanship trophies were earned. Fortunately Joe's wound was more a bullet graze to the head, leaving Joe with a bloody mess and one hell of a headache, but nothing more serious.

Walt arrived with a couple of reinforcements and started gathering up the intruders, two alive and one dead. Bev and Joe were rushed to the ER where their wounds were taken care of. Fortunately the bullets did not hit any vitals, and the doctor was able to safely remove the bullet from Bev's arm. Bev was wheeled into the new room Diana was placed into, and Joe was wheeled into the room Mac was resting in. Now that a couple more reinforcements were on scene, the original protection team members could relax a little and take a well deserved break. Walt warned everyone that this thing may not be over yet. Whoever is involved in this attempt may try again to finish what they have failed to accomplish. He asked that more food and beverages be brought in, and that the members of the original protection team get some rest, but to stick around for support should another effort be made against the hospital. Perhaps, with the sun just starting to peak over the eastern horizon, they may get a break. Or it could be one hell of a long day, thought Walt.

Chapter 59

Bill headed to check on Mac, saw that he was still sleeping, then went to check on Bev and Diana. Both ladies were sleeping, and the guard was a fresh State Police officer. Bill went to the lounge to lie down and get some sleep, if sleep would come. He lay down, thinking of what Ellen had said regarding Diana, than fell asleep. It seemed he had barely fallen asleep when he was awakened by Ellen telling him it was time to draw blood. A reclining chair had been brought in for Bill, and after he sat down, Ellen rolled up his sleeve out of the way and prodded to find a vein to tap into. Once the needle had been inserted and the blood started flowing, Bill relaxed a little and closed his eyes. Ellen woke Bill up, explaining that he needed to stay awake for the blood flow to work quickly, making the blood transfusion go faster. Ellen tried to engage Bill in a conversation to keep his blood pumping.

Time passed by quickly, and Ellen told Bill the plasma bag was full and she would disconnect him. After the needle was pulled out, Bill was given a cotton ball to press against the slight leak of the vein. Ellen then led Bill to the kitchenette and gave him some protein and drink to help him recover his strength and make more blood. While sitting in the kitchenette, Ellen noticed Bill looking at a stack of puzzle magazines lying on the table. "I love to work on puzzles, all types of puzzles. It keeps my brain thinking on how to see a pile of things as going together. Maybe that's why when I saw how much Diana resembles you I had to say something. Are you sure Diana is not a relation of yours, a daughter of a brother or sister?"

Bill was tired, but the question got him thinking. "No, I only have one other brother and he has two sons, no daughters." Thinking of Diana and trying to provide answers to the nurse's question, Bill was reminded again that he thought Diana looked a lot like his ex wife Armida.

"Bill, you said your wife had left you in August, twenty nine years ago. If you don't mind telling me about it, I would like to hear what happened." So Bill, feeling a little more awake now that he was reminded of the past, told Ellen what happened years ago. How he was devastated to find Armida gone one day after he got home from a long stint on a fire. It took a long while but he had come to the conclusion he was to blame. His job kept him away during the summer, and the ranger station where they lived was out in the boonies, so Armida was left with the few wives at the station as friends. He loved Armida very much, but he took her for granted. He tried to find out where she went and if she was doing ok, but all he heard from was the attorney. And once the papers were signed, he never heard from even the attorney. Ellen kissed him on the cheek and said she had better get back to her rounds as well and would look forward to talking to him some more.

Bill checked in on Mac, who was awake but a little drowsy from the medications. "How are you feeling?" Mac said he was okay, but kept falling asleep. He said he remembered a little of why he was in the hospital, but his memory was still fuzzy. He asked how Diana was, so Bill brought him up to date including the recent attack in the hospital.

"Is Bev okay?"

Bill noticed the concern in Mac's question, and told Mac that Bev was ok, the bullet was removed successfully and she was recovering in Diana's room. Mac wanted to get out of bed and go see Bev immediately, but Bill told him he needed to stay in bed until a nurse could help him. Mac was too tired to argue, and ended up going back to sleep. Joe, the wounded volunteer, was propped up in the other hospital bed with his head bandaged. Bill asked him how he was doing, and Joe told him luckily the bullet grazed his head, so he was doing fairly well considering. After teasing Joe about being hard headed, and that fortunately the bullet went for the head which was his least important body part, Bill padded Joe on the shoulder, told him he did a damn good job, and headed to see Diana and Bev.

It was quiet in Diana's room, except for the beeps and clicks coming from the patient monitors that were hooked up to both Diana and Bev. Looking at Diana, Bill was again reminded how much she looked like Armida. He was very tired, but the weird sensation when he walked in the room had jolted him. Damn, he thought, I wish I knew what was causing this strange feeling. He went over to speak with the deputy guarding the room from inside. The deputy told him everything had been quiet. Bill asked him if he needed a break, but the deputy said he was good for another hour or two. So Bill walked back to the lounge area. He was thinking of getting some sleep, but Beth was sitting at the table drinking coffee, so Bill sat down with her and grabbed a cup.

Beth asked Bill how he was feeling, to which Bill replied that he was sore but glad that Bev and Joe were not hurt badly. Bill asked Beth if she had heard anything about the funeral plans for celebrating the lives of the three wildland fire fighters killed by the Snake Peak fire. Beth said the arrangements team had been working with the families, and she had not heard a schedule developed yet. She would definitely keep Bill in the loop, knowing he wanted to be there and lend support. Beth could see Bill's eyes trying to close, so she said she needed to check to see who needs to be relieved and left Bill to get some rest, hopefully.

Ellen, efficiently handling the situation, had called in a couple more of her nurses and placed the injured perps in a guarded hospital room. Outside she exuded confidence, but inside she was shaking with fear and anxiety, not just for herself but for her staff as well. Even though the nurse's curriculum included training in handling gunman situations, it was always different when you bumped into reality. And here she was in the thick of reality. The book learning didn't help much now.

After listening to Bill explain his relationship with Armida years ago, Ellen realized that Bill had been holding a candle for all this time. She had felt there was a shadow between she and Bill, and now she knew what it was. It gave her hope that she and Bill could move ahead, if only Bill could get past his self imposed punishment. Hopefully Ellen could bring Bill around to see he was needlessly punishing both of them.

Chapter 60

A couple of hours later, Walt woke Bill up and told him the FBI team would be arriving in fifteen minutes. Damn it, what the heck is the FBI doing here? Looking at his watch, Bill figured this whole mess was only five maybe six hours old, but it felt like a lifetime. Just the thought of the FBI raised hackles, and Bill said he needed a cup of coffee to help clear the cobwebs of sleep. Walt laughed and said he needed something much stronger than coffee to deal with the FBI. Bill asked Walt, as they were finishing their quick cup of coffee, "What do you plan on doing if the FBI takes this over?"

"I am sure they want to take it over, and probably will. I have the Sheriff on his way to help me, and I have his permission to keep his deputies in the room. We may well lose control of this situation to the feds, but I damn well won't just hand it to them."

Bill asked Walt if he knew where Bev's work was on the arson fire investigations, and Walt said she had hidden the files at the café where Dora had worked for so many years. "Bev figured that would be one of the least likely spots the FBI would look."

Walt's radio chirped and one of the outside police officers told Walt that the FBI had just pulled into the parking lot. "Well Bill, the fun is just beginning. Care to join me?" The two men headed to meet the FBI, feeling like walking to the wall to face a firing squad.

While walking to meet the FBI, Walt suggested to Bill they don't let on that they know Mac is an FBI plant. That was fine with Bill, as he didn't want to see Mac in trouble. Mac may have been a FBI plant, but the town adopted him. Walt had called the City attorney as soon as he had heard the FBI was soon to arrive, and Bill had called Amrit and Liz to let them know. After the sting of the FBI tactics last year, they were not going to be as unprepared this time. Liz was on her way to assist, having gathered three fellow State Police officers. But they were two hours away yet so she radioed the one State Police officer already helping at the hospital and asked him to catch up with Walt and the Sheriff as they meet the FBI. It wouldn't hurt to show solidarity.

The group of locals meeting the FBI team had grown by the time the FBI team reached the hospital lobby. The group included the City attorney, the Sheriff, Walt and Bill, and the State Police officer. They faced an angry Ricardo, whom they let simmer while not a word was spoken. "Ok, I need to see the woman patient now."

Trying very hard to not go ballistic, Walt said, "I am sorry but we need to see some identification."

Ricardo, thoroughly angry for being sent here by his boss Bennie, said, "You know who the hell we are. Get on with it."

Walt, standing his ground, once again asked politely for the identification. Finally realizing he was getting no where, Ricardo flashed his FBI credentials and told Walt he would vouch for the rest of his team. "Sir, we will need to see everyone's identification before anyone proceeds. A short while ago we were attacked here at the hospital and we will not take chances."

The Sheriff spoke for the first time, and told Ricardo that he should have called ahead and explained what he wanted, and how many he was bringing. "That is proper procedure, and we do not take kindly to fellow law enforcement people wanting to obfuscate the common decency between agencies. As the police chief said, we need to see everyone's credentials, or you can leave."

The atmosphere was tense as a violin string. Bill was shaking with nerves on edge, hoping that Ricardo would see the light and abide by the simple request. Finally, a confused Ricardo relented, and told his team to show their badges. With the team members all confirmed, Walt's team led the FBI toward the lounge where they could better explain the situation. Ricardo wanted to get the woman and get the hell away from Prairie City, but Walt stood his ground and told Ricardo that they will first fill in the

FBI with what happened. "By the way Ricardo, you didn't mention which patient you were here to see." Noticing the dumb look on Ricardo's face, Walt told Ricardo, "Let's get you caught up on what kind of a day we've had here, and then ask the doctor or head nurse if the patients can be disturbed."

While walking to the lounge Ricardo, noticed the number of armed volunteers, deputies and police. He decided he had better go along with the piss ant police chief for now. "I hated this place before, and hate it even more," said Ricardo to himself as he reluctantly followed Walt and his team. Besides, he desperately wanted to know what the hell he just walked into.

While the FBI agents were being briefed in the lounge by Walt, Bill escaped and went to check on Diana, Bev, Joe and Mac. Damn, he thought, in less than eight hours six hospital beds became occupied. Four were from the good guys' team. If it is Diana someone is after, that someone wants her awfully bad. He informed the interior guards that the FBI team was here and being briefed as they spoke. He relieved the guard in Bev and Diana's room, and walked around the room checking everything. He noticed Bev waking, and pulled a chair alongside her bed. He let her wake gradually, not wanting to scare her. Opening her eyes slowly, she started to look around the room and she stopped at Bill. Bill grinned and said hi. Bev, trying to speak with a cotton dry mouth, finally got out the word hi. There was a glass of water on the hospital cart by the bed, so Bill placed the straw in Bev's mouth so she could get some refreshing water.

With the drink, Beth felt the cotton mouth disappear and asked Bill where she was. Bill told her she was in the hospital and asked her if she remembered what happened. "Was I shot? I think I remember being shot." Bill told her what had happened, and then she remembered what had been just a fog. Bill then told her that the FBI showed up, lead by their favorite person. It took a moment, but Bill knew Bev was going to be fine when she cursed and said, "Not Ricardo. Please tell me it is not Ricardo."

Bill let out a laugh, than told her it was indeed the idiot Ricardo, "and he is apparently here to take Diana." She looked over at Diana and asked how Diana was doing. Bill told her she seemed to be holding on, according to the nurse. "The nurse said she hasn't degraded. Apparently after that last bag of blood she stabilized and is not going through the blood like she was."

Ricardo had reluctantly listened to Walt fill him in on what happened at Mac's apartment, and what has been happening at the hospital. Unbelievable, thought Ricardo. As he heard Walt explaining the situation, his investigative part of his brain was working and spitting out a warning that this mess he found himself in was damn fishy. He also, albeit grudgingly, had to admit some small amount of respect for these Neanderthals, and how they have dealt with this weird mess. Perhaps he may have misjudged them. Well, so much for his quick grab and run scenario. Now he had to find Mac and the other injured people and spend time interviewing them. Shaking his head in frustration, Ricardo uttered to himself, "Bennie, what the hell did you get me into?"

When the guard came back from his quick break, Bill told Bev he would be back with news regarding Mac, who he was going to go see now. Bill, walking into Mac's room, noticed Mac was sitting up and talking with his guard and Joe. Mac saw Bill enter the room, and said, "Maybe you can catch me up with what the heck is going on and tell me how Bev and Diana are doing."

Bill told the guard he could take a break if he needed to, to which the guard responded, "thanks, I need one."

Bill then sat down in the chair vacated by the guard and told Mac that Bev was awake, and he had spoke with her briefly. "She seems to be okay and was asking about you. Diana is still out, but the nurse said she hasn't gotten worse." Mac asked what the commotion was outside a little while ago. "Your boss Ricardo has shown up with a team of FBI agents. Walt and the Sheriff have them held up in the lounge for a briefing. But Ricardo is insisting he remove Diana from this hospital asap."

Joe overheard the conversation and asked Mac, "Are you a FBI agent?"

Bill apologized and told Mac he was sorry he let the cat out of the bag. Mac told Bill that it was alright, and told Joe that he was a FBI agent working on a case involving the arson fires of last year. "Sorry we couldn't let everyone know, Joe. The FBI is not well liked here and I needed to be part of the community and pick up information for my boss." Seeing Joe's expression, Mac decided to continue. "I am really sorry to have deceived everyone. I was supposed to have gathered information quickly and gotten out of here without a problem. However I made a bunch of good friends and learned some stuff not complementary to my employer. I hope you understand. I don't know what will happen next, but when I have to go back I will take a lot of this place with me, especially friendships."

Bill spoke up and told Joe that he, Beth and a few others trusted Mac and they were all working together on the immediate situation as well as the arson fires of last year. Joe, thinking about what was said, told Mac that if Bill trusted him, he would also. Bill and Mac thanked Joe for his honesty and for continuing to look on Mac as a friend.

Mac was not looking forward to having to deal with Ricardo. Ricardo's bedside manner was non existent. Bill felt the doctor would not allow Ricardo to take Diana. Mac said, "Good, maybe Ricardo will leave. And then we could get to interview Diana instead."

"Right now we need to deal with the nightmare of Ricardo" exclaimed Bill. "How were you able to work for that man? I've been around him what, maybe fifteen minutes and I already believe that the term obnoxious is sugar coating his description."

Mac started to laugh, and explained to Bill that he loved the job and looked forward to moving up the ladder or moving to a different office where Ricardo was not his boss.

The guard came back to take over the watch, freeing Bill up to get back to Diana's room. Bill asked Mac, "You like Bev don't you. What about Diana? The word around town is you have been sleeping with Diana."

"I guess I should have expected that, having grown up in a small town where everybody knows everything. Yes, I find myself liking Bev and wanting to be with her more. I did like Diana when we first met, and I kind of still like her. But there is a cloud over Diana, a cloud of mystery that may or may not be true. But that cloud is there, and both Bev and I felt we needed to do something to find out what the mystery is and if it relates to our arson fires. Bev said she understood that I am playing a part to try to get information from Diana. I sure hope she is not just saying that because I would rather be with her than anyone else."

"Mac, look at it this way. Even though I wouldn't do what you did to Diana, you feel guilty about sleeping with her to get information. And by being with Diana, you saved her life. And until we can find evidence to prove our suspicions, we can't turn our backs on her and feed her to the likes of Ricardo." With that, Bill left Mac's room and went to Diana's room.

Chapter 61

Bill pulled up a chair alongside Diana, instinctively taking her hand, and talked to Bev about his conversation with Mac. Bev was pleased that Mac was doing better, and that he was thinking about her. Ellen came in to check on both patients. After checking Bev, Ellen went to Diana and noticed Bill holding Diana's hand. Ellen smiled at Bill, and after checking Diana, she motioned for Bill to go with her outside. Bill asked the guard to radio him the minute the FBI showed up, than he walked with Ellen. They ended up outside in a small gazebo setup for patients and guests wanting to be outside when the weather was nice.

Ellen took one of Bill's hands into hers and said, "I hope you don't mind me dragging you out here, but I needed to talk with you about Diana. Actually, it is about my idea concerning Diana. If you don't want to hear it, you can tell me so and I will not bother you again. But I have something on my mind and hope you want to hear what it is about."

"Ellen, of course I want to hear what you have to say."

"Bill, I think Diana could be your daughter."

Ellen's statement caught Bill completely off guard. Ellen could see the deer-in-the-headlights look in Bill's eyes, so she continued with her reasoning. "I like to work all sorts of challenging puzzles. I guess it keeps my brain active, especially during quiet times here in the hospital. Something got me to look a little closer to you and Diana. With the little bit of information I have, it felt like a puzzle, a challenging puzzle that needs solving. Would you mind if we did a DNA test? I don't believe in coincidences."

Bill looked into Ellen's eyes and saw the genuine concern. "Um, okay. When would we know the results," asked Bill after he finally recovered from Ellen's surprise.

Ellen, still holding Bill's hand in hers, said, "We just need to take a swab of the inside of your cheek. We already have samples from Diana. They will be sent to a lab we use, and we should have the results back late tomorrow, or the next day at the latest."

Bill asked if the test was conclusive. Ellen told him, "I dapple in genealogy. I guess it goes along with my enjoyment of puzzles. I have seen the DNA test used to find a range of relatives, or to disprove a relation. It is easier to disprove then to prove a biological parent through DNA testing. Legally, the DNA test could be evidence of a biological parent when the results come out to 99.99%. There could still be an argument in court, but it seems that the law favors that high of a likely hood of being a biological parent."

Ellen looked at her watch and told Bill she just had a few more minutes before she needed to start her rounds again. She asked Bill to follow her to the lab where she did a quick swab of the inside of Bill's cheek, and placed the swab in a sealed tube and packaged it for the special medical delivery service. Bill thanked her, and asked if she would join him at her next break. Ellen smiled and said she would like that, and she walked to the nurse's station to grab the patient charts.

Bill walked the hallway back to Mac's room, his mind in a swirl of thoughts and emotions. He felt he could not confide in anyone other than Ellen. Not yet anyway, especially as he had no idea whether he was Diana's father or not. Ellen's the only one that mentioned the possibility, so her notion may be just a shot in the dark. "But if I am Diana's father, maybe that explains the weird sensations I get when I seem to be near Diana", thought Bill. "What a damn mess. What do I do?"

As Bill approached Mac's room, he could clearly hear the voice of Ricardo. The thought of Ricardo knocked Bill back to the reality of the situation in the hospital. From the voice and words coming from Ricardo, Bill could tell that Mac was getting slammed. Bill felt sorry for Mac, having to endure that type of verbal abuse. The anger drumming up inside of Bill gave him a renewed sense of mission, as he walked to Bev's room, ready to protect the girls, if necessary, from a verbal attack by Ricardo.

Bev was looking comfortable, with her eyes closed. As Bill walked over to see Diana, he heard Bev call his name. Bill asked how Bev was feeling, and she told him tired but ok. Bill told her Mac was being grilled by Ricardo. Bev was concerned for Mac, but with a little of her sedatives kicking in, she promptly fell back to a light sleep. Bill brushed a few strands of hair from Bev's face, then sat down by Diana. He took her hand in his and talked to her about things, about what life was like when he and Armida were an item. It just seemed the right thing to do.

Ricardo wanted desperately to finish the interviews, load Diana up and get the hell out of Prairie City. His instructions from Bennie were to find Diana and bring her back. And here he was within shouting distance of the girl, and he was being stymied by a bunch of Neanderthals. "I said it before and I say it again, I hate this place", Ricardo said to himself. He was seething after his interview with Mac. And now he was marching to Bev and Diana's room to do more interviewing. Oh joy.

While Bill was talking to an unconscious Diana, Ricardo came marching in with his entourage, expecting to grill Diana and Bev. Finding both unresponsive, Ricardo jumped on Bill, asking him who he was and what was he doing here.

"I am the assistant fire chief of this community, and I am here because three of my friends and this young lady are here lying injured. I have no idea why this is happening, and on top of this mess we get you showing up to even make a bigger mess. As if your presence last year to steal our hard work was not enough of an insult, you come here now treating us like dirt and once again trying to steal from us. You make me sick."

Pointing to Diana, Ricardo asked, "Is she Diana?" Bill simply said yes to the question. "So, she must be more than just a friend?"

To which a shaking Bill replied, "No, I really don't know Diana, but I feel sorry for her all alone and with the worst injuries."

"Well it looks like you may be more than just a helpful soul that took pity on her."

Bill, releasing Diana's hand, stood up and glared at Ricardo. Trying to reign in his anger, and wanting to kick Ricardo's pompous ass, Bill told Ricardo, "We will continue this discussion outside." Bill promptly walked to the door and held it opened while motioning Ricardo to get out of the room.

Out in the hallway, Ricardo continued, "Apparently then you must be friends with Bev and Mac. Tell me what you know about them, what they were doing, if they mentioned anything about any cases they were working on together or individually."

Bill told Ricardo that he had known Bev for a number of years, and respected her for the serious way she took on her job as police officer. He had no idea what she was working on, he said. Bill told Ricardo that he has only known Mac a few months, having met Mac during a fire incident and came to be friends through the fire department. "Mac works for one of the local ranches and is a volunteer. That's all I know. I do not know anything about the two of them working on some case." Bill was hoping Ricardo would buy the story. He wanted Ricardo to leave, since he felt sure that Ricardo's aura was enough to set back the healing process Bev and Diana were going through. Bill told Ricardo, "Unless you have anything else of import, I suggest you take your people back to the break room and take a rest. I am sure that with the doctor's or head nurse's permission, you can grill the women later when they are awake and responsive. But I warn you, I will be here, and if you verbally abuse either of these young ladies I will rearrange your smug face."

Ricardo walked away, leaving a very shaky Bill trying to calm down after the adrenaline rush. It took awhile for Bill to realize that he had probably made a serious enemy of Ricardo, but then he figured with a person like Ricardo, so be it. Calming down, Bill walked back into the room, checked on both Bev and Diana, and then sat down.

Meanwhile, Ricardo was both fuming and thinking, walking with his entourage to the break room. That last bout with Bill left him somewhat stunned. His shell was cracking, seeing and hearing these people of Prairie City working in the midst of a crisis. Damn it, Bill's words stung, but instead of fighting because his feelings were hurt, Ricardo felt like he needed a rest to do some introspection. This mess had much more to it than he was led to believe, and that needed his attention. He needed to be thinking about what kind of mess this thing was turning into, and why.

Chapter 62

Things were quiet for a few hours. Bill had nodded off to sleep in the chair, waking up often to listen for anything peculiar or threatening. The door opened, and Bill slowly looked to see who it was coming into the room. He recognized Ellen, and said hi as he got out of his chair to stretch. Ellen smiled and asked him how he was. "I am tired, hungry, and thirsty! How about you?"

Ellen replied as she was looking over Bev, "Me too! Diana is my last check and then I can take a break. You want to join me?"

Bill replied with renewed vigor, "You bet. I would like that."

"Looks like Bev is doing good, getting a nice rest. Diana seems a little better as well. I don't know, but maybe both your presence in the room and your blood flowing into her veins are helping her. I will have the doctor check her but I think she has turned the corner and the worst is over. Let's go across the street to the café and get something to eat and drink." Bill said that suited him just fine. He was realizing that even though he enjoyed being around Ellen the times they had been together in the recent past, there was something more this time. He hadn't felt this way in a long time. Perhaps it was just the stress and tiredness making him feel this way. Or maybe it was the beginning of something else.

Bill was enjoying his time with Ellen at the café when his phone rang. "Bill, they are trying to take Diana away. You better get here quick."

"I'll be right there. See what you can do to stall them."

Ellen saw the look on Bill's face and asked "What is it, Bill?"

"We've got to go now. That ass Ricardo is trying to take Diana out of the hospital."

"Are they nuts? She can't be moved yet. I am calling the doctor."

As they both were running to the hospital, Bill called Walt to tell him what was going on. "That idiot Ricardo. I'll be there in a couple of minutes."

Walt hung up and immediately called the Sheriff, who when he heard what the FBI was trying to do, said he would be there within ten minutes and send a couple of his deputies that were on rotation from the hospital duty to help. Walt said he didn't like the idea, but he wanted to call Nick and get the news media involved. The Sheriff felt the same, but agreed that might be the best temporary strategy they had.

Nick couldn't believe the phone call from Walt. He had been trying to get a story on the shooting. All he had was rumors that people were killed and injured, one badly, in a gun battle. But none of the officials were talking, and he wasn't allowed in the hospital wing where the victims were supposed to have been kept. Then he heard rumors the hospital had been attacked, and then the FBI showed up. Damn, possibly his biggest story ever and he had zippo, nada, not a damn thing to write a story with. Then Walt calls and offers him the whole enchilada, well a big piece of it anyway. Nick was on his way to the hospital in a flash with dreams of a Pulitzer prize playing in his mind. He was not really paying attention to the warning Walt had mentioned.

Bill and Ellen ran to Diana's room, in time to see a gurney trying to get through the door, which was being blocked by a couple of his volunteers. Ellen had been able to get hold of the doctor handling the patients, and he was as incensed about this FBI tactic as everyone else. He was getting a police escort, and should be there shortly. He told Ellen that he didn't authorize the move, and would block such a threat to the patient's welfare. So when Bill and Ellen ran into the room and saw Ricardo on the phone, they both stood on either side of Diana's bed in an attempt to block anyone from getting to Diana.

Ricardo saw the maneuver and nearly growled his displeasure as he hung up on whoever he was speaking with. Bill was on the radio to the dispatcher and asked her to dispatch the fire department to the hospital to assist with manpower, while Ellen was asking Ricardo what the hell he was doing. "This is out of your hands little lady. My orders are to take Diana regardless of condition, and that is what I intend to do. So get out of my way."

"Don't you little lady me you, you ignorant inconsiderate egotistical piece of garbage. She cannot be moved for fear of killing her. The doctor is on his way to tell you that. So you back off and leave her alone."

Bill was impressed with Ellen's verbal attack. Ricardo was incensed, and using his radio called his team to the room for backup.

Bill had just finished talking to the dispatcher, and knew a few of his volunteers still helping in the hospital would be there quickly. Bill, angered by the way Ricardo was treating Ellen and trying to take Diana, wanted to reach out and 'touch someone', preferably with a knock out punch to Ricardo's smug face. Bill walked right into Ricardo's space, and angrily said, "Ricardo, I warned you earlier. Get the hell out of this room, now. Better still, get out of this hospital. In a minute or two you and your team will be vastly outnumbered. None of us give a damn if you are FBI. To us you are just what Ellen said you are, a piece of garbage. If you want Diana you will have to go through me first, so you had better reconsider your strategy."

Before anyone could say another word, Ellen quickly said, "And that goes for me too," as she stepped up to Bill's side and grabbed his hand. Bill finished his verbal attack by saying, "Ricardo, we thought you might be on our side, the side of justice, but you know what? You are just as bad as the guys attacking us, injuring Diana, Mac, Joe, and Bev. We are not taking this crap, so you had better quickly make up your pea brain. Join us, or be prepared for one hell of a fight."

Nick had rushed into the doorway just as Bill was ending his little speech to Ricardo. He was writing and taking photos when Ricardo's team ran up and grabbed Nick. Nick was yelling, saying he was here as a member of the press and with permission from the police chief. Just then Walt arrived, and told the FBI to unhand Nick and let him alone. When Ricardo heard Nick was a reporter, he came unglued. He told his people to get Nick out of the room, at which Bill told everyone to get out of the room. Ricardo was incensed that Walt had the audacity to ask Nick to be there. Just as Ricardo was going to spew a tirade, a dozen volunteer firefighters arrived, some carrying axes. Bill had stepped out into the hallway to greet his fellow firefighters, and told them to stand by for further instructions. Right now they were a show of force, and depending on what Ricardo did next would determine what the crew would have to do.

Ricardo's face was turning a bright crimson. He was angry, but that guy Bill's retort had hit a nerve. And when he saw the Sheriff walk into the crowded hallway with a couple of deputies, he had to quietly admit that these people were a lot smarter and tougher than he had thought.

Bill was watching Ricardo, thinking to himself, "Surely Ricardo is not that stupid to want to press on with trying to take Diana. Hell, he is outnumbered three to one."

While Bill was looking around at the number of his friends and neighbors standing against the FBI, he happened to see a nurse walking into Bev and Diana's room. In the huge commotion, he had forgotten about guarding the room. Something about the nurse didn't seem quite right, so he ran to the door of the Diana and Bev's room. He saw the nurse jump back from Diana's hanging fluid bag as Bill opened the door and stepped into the room. The nurse was holding a syringe in one hand and the other hand was in a pocket of her smock. Before Bill could move any closer the nurse had a gun pointed at him and told him to keep quiet.

After Bill was made to hand over his gun and radio, he was told to lie down in the corner by Diana's bed, where the nurse could keep an eye on him and finish the job she came to do. Bill was not happy at all, getting put into this position and not being able to keep the nurse from doing whatever it was she was going to do to Diana. He was watching the nurse, when all of a sudden one of those refillable plastic drinking jugs with a straw sticking out crashed into the back of the nurse's head. Thanks to Bev's quick thinking and good arm, that plastic water jug smacked the nurse in the head. As the nurse turned and was pointing her gun at Bev, Bill moved like he hadn't in years. He jumped onto the chair by Diana's bed. Gauging the distance like a cat, Bill leaped over Diana's bed, arms extended out in front to try and grab the nurse. Bill knew his landing was going to hurt. He only hoped he would land on top of the nurse. His foot caught on the bed railing, bringing him down shorter than he expected. So much for gauging the distance like a cat. However his outstretched hands were able to just reach the back of the nurse's smock as he was crashing down. Fortunately the smock held and the nurse was pulled backward.

Bev was afraid she might get a bullet for her efforts, when the nurse's head was jerked backward. Bev saw Bill heading to the floor head first with the bad nurse's back coming down with him. The gun went off toward the ceiling, she heard a crack, Bill's cry of pain, and then the smack on the floor. Then nothing. She screamed.

Ricardo, running his hands through his dark black hair, was beside himself. His instructions had been simple: pick up the girl and bring her back. Bennie had provided very poor reasons, but Ricardo had his orders. So, what started as a simple job has turned into a complete nightmare, and Ricardo was wondering what could go wrong next. Upon hearing the shot and the screaming from Diana's room, Ricardo yelled at his team to secure the hallway and asked the Sheriff to take control of the hospital. The remaining volunteers and deputies fanned out to work with the FBI agents. Walt joined Ricardo as they followed the police officers into Diana's room.

Bill was unconscious. It was probably a good thing for the immediate time. When Bill's foot caught on the bed railing it had snapped, causing Bill to let out a scream of pain before he face planted to the floor, still holding the nurse's smock. The face plant would have been worthy of an Oscar award for the best stuntman, but alas there was no pillow to land on and no movie to earn money from.

After screaming for help, Bev frantically pushed the nurse call button, hoping a nurse, a real nurse, would get here quickly to check on Bill. She ripped out the iv's and was trying to get to Bill when her fellow officers charged in and took over the situation. One of the officers had ripped the gun out of the fake nurse's hand while the other officer dragged the criminal away from Bill. While both officers were busy securing the bad nurse, Bev had succeeded in painfully sliding down to the floor alongside Bill. She checked Bill for a pulse, found it, and decided not to move him for fear of causing more damage. She sat there with her hand on Bill's hand waiting for help, the iv holes in her arm bleeding.

Chapter 63

Ricardo and Walt ran in behind a couple of volunteer firefighters and police officers rushing into the hospital room. Both took a quick view of the room, and saw that the police officers had the nurse incapacitated. They saw Bev on the floor with blood leaking out from where she pulled the iv tubes out. They saw Bill, not moving, a foot caught in the bed and his head on the floor alongside Bev. Walt went to check on Bev while Ricardo was trying to make sense of what he was seeing. Ellen came rushing in with another nurse, took in the scene quickly, then asked the nurse to check on Diana. Ellen quickly checked Bev, who told her Bill had a pulse, and then asked Ricardo and Walt to help her get Bev back in her bed. Next, Ellen asked a couple of fire department volunteers to help her with Bill. Bill's foot was at an awkward angle, so Ellen assumed it was broken and had the volunteers carefully dislodge the foot from the bed railing where it had caught. Once Bill was laid out on the floor, Ellen took his vitals and checked for any major bruising or strange lumps on the head and face. She made arrangements to get Bill loaded onto a gurney and to the emergency room where the doctor could go over Bill in more detail.

While Ellen was seeing to Bill, the other nurse, who had finished checking Diana, was working on getting Bev's ivs repaired and fix the damage caused when Bev had pulled the ivs out. Walt was talking with Bev when Ricardo told the nurse to stop. Bev and Walt were surprised, and figured Ricardo was up to his intimidation tactics again. But Ricardo, having seen a syringe on the floor by Diana's iv bag stand, carefully picked up the syringe lying on the floor where it had fallen during Bill's attempt at being superman. He handed it over to Ellen and suggested she change the iv bag immediately, but not in his usual bullying voice. Ricardo then asked Bev if she was okay. Both Walt and Bev were completely unprepared for the concern in Ricardo's voice. With a strange look, Bev said she would be fine, and then Ricardo asked if she felt like telling he and Walt what happened. Still kind of in shock, from both the attempt on Diana's life, and Ricardo's new attitude, Bev told Ricardo and Walt all that she could remember happening.

Mac came into Diana's room, wheeling his wheel chair as quickly as he could to check on Bev, and saw Walt and Ricardo at her bedside. Immediately thinking the worst, Mac was going to jump all over Ricardo even if it meant losing his job. However, before Mac could jump all over Ricardo, he noticed that Ricardo was unusually quiet and looked like he was actually listening to Bev. Ricardo saw Mac and said, "Ah, there you are Mac. Bev was just filling us in as to this latest incident. I think I am through with questioning Bev for now. Walt and I are heading to his office to see what we can get out of the fake nurse."

Then turning to Bev, Ricardo said, "Thanks Bev for helping out. You did a fine job and helped save Diana's life."

Bev was amazed at Ricardo's change in demeanor, and commented about it. "Gee Ricardo, you can be human when you want to be!"

Mac cringed and expected Bev to be verbally assaulted, but with what almost looked like a grin, Ricardo said, "Don't expect it to last, Bev. I'll be back later."

Mac looked at Bev and asked her if that was really Ricardo, and Bev laughed as best she could without hurting too much. "Weird isn't. But that was really Ricardo. I don't know what happened, but Ricardo is not quite the same."

Mac agreed and said, "I've known him longer than you have and I have never seen him like this. It scares me!"

Bev went on to tell Mac what happened to Bill, and that he was taken to the ER. Mac was torn between staying with Bev, or staying with the rest of the volunteers waiting for Bill's recovery. He decided to stay with Bev, arguing that there were too many people already waiting for Bill. Besides, he wanted to be around Bev, in case another attempt on Diana would happen. Mac figured he needed to be useful instead of stuck in a bed worrying. Even though there was a police officer in the room and one outside, Mac felt better if he were helping, although how much he could help with was a question.

While Bill was being checked over and repaired in the ER, Walt was talking with the Sheriff regarding what to do with the prisoner. Ricardo joined in and rather than throw his weight into the conversation, he listened. He finally asked if he could go with them to the jail, where they planned on doing some interrogation before putting the prisoner behind bars to join the other recently acquired prisoners. Ricardo asked Walt and the Sheriff what he could do about housing the prisoners since he figured the County jail was getting crowded. Walt and the Sheriff were taken aback by Ricardo's change in attitude. Ricardo made some phone calls while in route to the jail, and told Walt that the State Police will send a special bus to take the new prisoners to the State Prison where there is room, if Walt said it was okay. Both Walt and the Sheriff agreed it was a good idea and Walt told Ricardo to make it happen. The Sheriff decided he should stay and get ready for the State Police bus, and made arrangements for a lady deputy to assist at the jail.

After making the prisoner arrangements, Ricardo called his boss to bring him up to date. When Bennie heard what had happened, he blew his stack. "I sent you to do a simple job, to just bring back the girl. Not only don't you have the girl in custody, but you've got the whole damn world protecting her. I can't believe you failed me. I guess I need to take care of it myself."

After slamming the phone down, Bennie called his contact with the 'family' and told him they needed to meet now. The contact suggested a familiar location, in twenty minutes. Bennie realized that was the best he was going to get, but he was impatient. He told his secretary he was leaving for a meeting, and that he wasn't sure when he would be back. He was both nervous and angry at the turn of events, and worried that the 'family' will decide he failed them and put him on the wrong side of the grass.

Ricardo was adding things up in his mind, and not liking the way the numbers looked. He was impressed with the way the locals had jumped in and had taken the bull by the horns. Realizing that three of the locals ended up injured trying to protect Diana, a person they really didn't know, made Ricardo relook at the people he had considered not much better than dirt. And that last stunt by the local guy, Bill if he remembered the name correctly, was something Ricardo didn't know if he could do in the same circumstances. Ricardo had admitted to himself that these people garnered a lot of respect, something he had not given them, and decided to try and become a team member and work with these locals.

After his phone conversation with an angry Bennie, Ricardo's review of the whole situation here in Prairie City was beginning to stink badly. Things were adding up and pointing in a direction Ricardo did not want to go to or want to believe possible. If he really wanted to be on the team and work with these locals instead of berating them, he had better talk with the police chief and explain the situation, something he has never really done before. Ricardo was hoping that if he talked with Walt, something would fall into place and prove his fear was unwarranted and that the FBI was not complacent in this operation. But Ricardo was not holding his breath, and was re-evaluating his role in the situation. If the situation is as bad as he is starting to believe it is, was he an unknowing accomplice? Accomplice to what, though?

Chapter 64

The emergency work on Bill was done quickly. Fortunately the hospital had its own MRI, so the doctor was able to get a scan of Bill's head. After reviewing the scan results, the doctor was fairly certain there was no brain damage, but a stay in the hospital for observation would be a necessity. Ellen was both relieved that Bill did not have serious head injuries and happy that he will be spending time in the hospital. His foot was broken, but the doctor was able to set and cast it without much trouble. The doctor told Ellen that Bill will feel a heck of a headache when he wakes up, but that will only be temporary. Luckily Bill was in fairly good shape, so the broken foot would heal quickly as long as he took care of himself. Even though Ellen was a nurse, the doctor could sense that Ellen was being more than a nurse regarding Bill, so he spent a little extra time giving Ellen the instructions for caring for Bill.

Ricardo had asked Ellen to have the hospital lab analyze the contents of the syringe found on the floor in Diana's room. The hospital lab found it to have a high concentration of sodium bicarbonate. The lab technician explained that this injection into the iv tube of a patient would have lead to a heart attack. When word got to Ellen, sitting alongside Bill's bed in Mac's hospital room, she squeezed Bill's hand that she was holding and told him he had saved Diana's life. Of course Bill was still out of it, but Ellen wanted to sit with Bill as often as she could until her shift was completed. Then she planned on going home, checking on things, cleaning up, and returning to be with Bill during her off hours. It was just something she felt was right.

Francis, having been on a retreat for the past few days, had just listened to his phone messages in his apartment at the Church rectory. The hospital had called letting him know that they have new patients and could use his presence as a Chaplain to attend to any religious needs of the new patients. Francis was wondering what he had missed while in retreat. He looked over and happened to see his fire department pager blinking. What had he missed?

Francis pushed the play back button on the pager, and was astounded by the page for volunteers to help at the hospital. Not wasting any more time, he quickly drove to the hospital, anxious to find out what happened. Arriving to the hospital, Francis was surprised to see one of his fellow volunteers holding a rifle in the hallway. A further look down the hallway showed a deputy and another volunteer standing near room doors, each holding a rifle as well. Stopping alongside the first volunteer, Francis asked, "What the heck is going on, Jim?"

"Hey, Francis, glad you could finally make it! Been a weird situation, and the hospital is getting crowded. Let's see, Mac and some girl he was with got shot. Then Bev got shot. Joe got shot while guarding the room Bev and the girl are in. Bill is in the ER, after stopping some fake nurse from killing the girl. Plus we got a couple bad guys in the hospital, about three or so in the jail, and numerous bad guys are dead. About sums it up."

Shock was an understatement. Francis could not believe what he was just told. It took a bit for him to get his thoughts back in line as to why he was here. "Thanks for the condensed version, Jim. Where's the head nurse? Who is the worst injured?"

"Well, last I saw the head nurse, she was making rounds, but Ellen is with Bill, waiting for him to get out of the ER and into a room. I don't know about the bad guys, but I think the girl is in the worst shape. Mac got shot in the leg, but he is doing okay. Joe got shot in the head, but fortunately it was just a graze, so he is doing okay. Bev got shot in the arm, and she seems to be mostly okay. I heard Bill may have broken his foot and smacked his head."

"Do you know what caused all this?"

"Well, what I heard was some bad people are after the girl. Apparently they want her real bad or real dead, 'cause they have even tried attacking the hospital twice."

"Wow, this is just unbelievable. What kind of manpower do we have here?"

"Well, there's about a dozen of us, volunteers, cops, and deputies. Even a couple State cops. Then a little while ago the damn FBI showed up with about five. We almost got into a gun battle with them damn feds, but after Bill's attempt at being superman and stopping the fake nurse from killing the girl, the FBI have seemed not so arrogant now. They are even talking of helping us, maybe."

Francis just shook his head, thanked Jim again, and asked him which room the girl was in. He thought he had better start with her and see what kind of spiritual assistance he could bring. He started praying as he headed to Bev and Diana's room, praying for the injured, the dead, and all those caught in this mess. And he prayed for guidance and strength he could pass on to the injured.

In the interrogation room at the County jail, Ricardo and Walt were getting nothing from the woman prisoner. They decided to leave her alone for a bit, and stepped into another room to interrogate one of the two prisoners taken during the first attack on the hospital. Walt and Ricardo attempted to grill the prisoner, but once again they hit a brick wall. The prisoner acted like he had been through this numerous times before, telling the two law men that he wanted to call his lawyer now and he wouldn't say a thing until his lawyer was present. The jailor took the prisoner back to a cell, and brought the second male prisoner into the interrogation room. This prisoner did not speak very good English, whether intentionally or not, and both Walt and Ricardo were frustrated. "Say nothing. I know rights. Bring lawyer," was the extent of the verbiage from the prisoner. Leaving the interrogation room, Walt and Ricardo sat at a table and reviewed the situation. What they came up with pointed to a fairly professional type hit on the hospital, but they still had no idea of why and who was behind this.

While Walt and Ricardo were discussing the lack of cooperation from the prisoners, Ricardo told Walt about his worry concerning possible dirty FBI involvement. Walt was dumbfounded for awhile, and asked Ricardo to repeat why he arrived at this notion. Once Walt heard the details a second time and was ready for them, the conclusion reached was the same as Ricardo's. Walt looked at Ricardo and said "Shit, what do we do now?"

"Hell if I know, chief, but you and I had better come up with something and quickly."

"This is a personal question, Ricardo, but I noticed you seem to be completely different than when you first showed up. I don't understand, what happened to change you?"

Walt was wincing, afraid of a Ricardo tirade coming at him. Instead, after a minute or two of dreadful silence, Ricardo answered. "I don't know how to answer that. Maybe it was the way you people stood together against me, and especially against the attackers. Even putting your lives at risk for a person you really don't even know. For all you know she may be guilty of terrible crimes. You and your people seem to have a strong sense of community, something I have not experienced before. I will probably go back to being an asshole when I get back to the office, but while I am here I will try to work with you instead of against you."

Walt, dumbfounded, stared at Ricardo, then went up to him and shook his hand. "Thanks Ricardo. I think maybe we can do this together." Walt was a little concerned though, and not sure how much he could trust Ricardo.

It had been a wild twenty one hours, thought Bev after looking at the clock. Bev was settled back into the hospital bed with the damaged ivs going again. She and Mac were holding hands and talking. Bev and Mac were trying to make sense out of this mess. Seven people in the hospital, an attack on the hospital, three antagonists in jail, and from what Bev had learned, there were at least six attackers killed. It seems obvious now that someone was seriously after Diana, but what for? And the immediate question, will there be another attack?

Bev was surprised to see Fr. Francis walk into the room. Francis greeted Bev, then Mac. Taking turns, Bev and Mac provided a little more detail to the current situation, filling in the gaps left by Jim's synopsis. After making sure Bev and Mac did not need anything from him, Francis recited a couple of prayers for healing.

While Francis was finishing the prayers for Bev and Mac, Diana started groaning and moving. Bev looked over at Diana and decided she had better call for a nurse. Francis turned his attention to the girl they called Diana, starting a prayer for her healing.

As the nurse rushed in to Bev's room, Diana's eyes started flickering, trying to open. Bev told the nurse that she may want to check on Diana. As the nurse was checking Diana's vitals on the monitoring machine, Diana's eyes finally opened and stayed opened. It took a little bit for Diana to focus, but once she had her eyesight in focus she started to take in her surroundings. She at first scanned past Mac and Beth, but then came back to them with a slow dawning of who they were. Diana then saw a man wearing the collar of a priest, and a nurse standing by a beeping machine. The nurse was pleased with the readout, and asked Diana if she needed anything. After a tiny sip of water, Diana turned again toward Mac and Bev and noticed they were holding hands. Diana turned away for another sip of water, then looked back to Mac and asked in a weak voice, "What happened?"

Mac moved his wheel chair over to Diana and asked her what she remembered. She remembered getting shot, but than nothing more. Mac proceeded to fill her in with the events at the house, and up to getting to the hospital. Bev than filled her in with the events inside the hospital, including Bill's saving her life. Diana could hardly believe what she was hearing. It was too much to take in all at once, to realize that she was the cause of all this mess and tragedy. When she had heard of the sacrifice Bill had made to save her from that fake nurse, Diana started to sob, and asked how Bill was. Mac said Bill was recovering in his room next door, but was probably still sleeping.

Then Diana looked to the priest, who introduced himself as Fr. Francis. "Although the circumstances could be better, I am pleased to meet you, Diana. If there is anything you need, please let me know and I can see what I can do. Of course, I am here for any spiritual needs as well."

"Thank you Father, I appreciate that. I would like to take you up on the offer of spiritual help. Will you be sticking around the hospital for awhile?"

"I will be here whenever you want to pray with me or even just talk. I will be checking in with you every so often, or you can buzz the nurse and she can get hold of me anytime. I will go check on some of the other patients, and will be back later."

After Francis left, Mac asked Diana if she would mind looking at a photo of the fake nurse that tried to kill her. Diana said she felt up to it, so Bev grabbed her radio and called Walt. Diana was confused about Mac. It sounded like he was a cop. "Mac, what's going on; are you a cop?"

Chapter 65

Walt told Ricardo about Bev's radio transmission stating that Diana was awake and coherent and willing to look at photos of the prisoners captured during the attempts on her life. Ricardo, just from habit, had already snapped a few photos of the prisoners with his smart phone. He had not had a chance to send them on to his office for identification. He told Walt about the photos, and he was just about to send them on to his office when Walt suggested he wait. "Ricardo, I agree with what you said earlier, something stinks with this whole affair. I don't want to get young Mac in trouble, even he had reservations about your office. So maybe let's sit on the information for a bit and see what we can learn ourselves."

Normally Ricardo would let fly a stream of verbiage that could strip the paint off a car, but his brain had kicked in and realized Walt was making sense. "Thanks for reminding me Walt. I need to look at my previous office dealings a little more critically. I'll just keep these photos here for the time being."

Leaving the County jail, Walt and Ricardo headed back to the hospital to speak with Diana. On the way, Ricardo decided to call his boss again and see what he had to say. Walt and Ricardo both agreed this could be the test of their theory. Bennie's secretary told Ricardo that Bennie left in a hurry after Ricardo's last call and said he would be at a meeting. She had no idea where, and that Bennie had said he may not be back in today. Ricardo told her there was no message, thanked her for the information,

266

and hung up. "That is strange. Bennie usually tells his secretary where he is going and keeps a fairly tight rein on the clock," Ricardo told Walt. Ricardo was thinking perhaps his fears were real, and that Bennie has some explaining to do.

Francis was in the hallway heading to visit the couple of hospitalized bad guys. He was trying to remember why Diana's voice seemed familiar to him. It was there in the back of his mind, the little piece of memory that just wouldn't come out of hiding. Oh well, thought Francis, it will come to me sooner or later. As he stepped into the room where the injured bad guys were laying in their hospital beds, he remembered where he had heard that voice before. Francis said to himself, "In the confessional. I remember hearing her voice in the confessional. It must have been just before I took off for my retreat. And that has been haunting me ever since that first confession."

Francis needed to concentrate on prayers for the injured bad guys, so he tried to put thoughts about Diana aside. It was tough, for he kept thinking of her confessions, of the admissions of her part in the deaths of people. And now this mess, with so many people affected. "Lord, give me strength to help here in this situation, to provide the spiritual and moral support these people need. And especially give me the strength and knowledge to help Diana. I think she is going to need all the support she can get."

Chapter 66

Ellen had stepped out of Bill's room for awhile to check on her other patients. Once she had finished her rounds and was satisfied all was running back to normal, she went back to sit with Bill. As she was sitting down in the chair close to Bill, Bill started moving and his eyes were trying to open. Ellen took a quick look at the monitor, noticed the readings were fine, and went back to holding Bill's hand. Bill finally felt the smooth hand in his, and turned to Ellen as his eyes were making an effort to stay open. He heard what sounded like a deep voice coming from a tunnel, as he saw Ellen's mouth move. As he was trying to concentrate on Ellen, he realized his whole face hurt like heck. Ellen could see the pain grip hold, and as she was talking to Bill, he started to hear her normally and started recognizing some of the words. Ellen grabbed the drinking water mug, and holding the filled straw to Bill's lips, let the water in the straw drip slowly onto Bill's lips and into his parched mouth. Bill lightly squeezed Ellen's hand, then fell back to sleep.

"I am sorry, Diana. Yes, I am a FBI agent." Mac was still in the room with Bev, trying to get some information out of Diana. With Mac's admission, Diana was even less cooperative, partly because she was going in and out of consciousness, partly she was afraid of saying anything, and partly because she was furious over Mac's duplicity. Mac and Bev were losing patience, trying to get Diana to realize that not only was she the target but people had been injured trying to protect her. The least she could do was tell them what this mess was about. "Diana, I don't care what you think of me, but you have to realize your life is in danger. Someone is out to shut you up permanently. Bev and I do not want that to happen to you. You have got to tell us what you know, who might be after you."

Walt and Ricardo arrived at the hospital and bumped into Francis in the hallway. Walt introduced Ricardo to Fr. Francis, then Walt and Ricardo headed to Diana's room. Francis decided he had better find Bill, a good excuse to stay out of the room while the FBI was busy.

Ricardo went to work while Walt stood by Mac and listened. When Ricardo showed the photo of the fake nurse to Diana, there was a visible hiccup from Diana. Before Ricardo could respond, Mac had jumped in and said, "Looks like you know this person, Diana?"

Ricardo, noticing a hesitation, told Diana that the person in the photograph was trying to kill her, and perhaps she hadn't yet realized the seriousness of whoever wanted her dead. Before Diana could say anything, Ricardo brought up a photo of one of the men prisoners. "Diana, this guy was one of the ones we captured here in the hospital. Recognize him?"

Diana, confusion on her face, finally realized the truth. Her employer, her Grandfather, was taking care of loose ends, and she was a loose end.

Diana was getting tired, and it was showing. She told Ricardo that she needed some promises before she presented her story. Mac, concerned for Diana, suggested that Diana get some sleep and they would continue when Diana woke up and felt better. Ricardo, Walt, Mac and Bev were all impatient to hear how Diana ties in with this mess, but they all agreed to wait and hope a little rest will get Diana to tell them what they needed to know.

Walt, Ricardo and the Sheriff had a meeting at the hospital and came to an agreement regarding the continued protection detail. No one was convinced that the attack on Diana had been aborted. But they recognized that some of the volunteers, police and deputies had been on duty for nearly twenty four hours. The Sheriff had a Posse he could call up, and Frank, who had arrived shortly after hearing of Bill's crash and burn trying to play superman, could replace his volunteers with a few others more rested up. The State Police were attempting to replace a couple of their officers as well. A more rested protection detail would soon be in place, but Mac and Bev were going to keep their weapons close by, and Bev was keeping her hand held radio close as well.

Ellen had finished her shift, a long and exciting shift unlike any she had worked before. She checked once more on Bill, than rushed home. She showered, packed an overnight bag with extra clothes, checked over the house once more and locked it up. She started to feel the let down tired of an extremely dramatic day, and the shower only caused her to want to go to sleep. The drive to the hospital was short, and once she checked on Bill she went to Bev's room to check on Mac, Bev and Diana. She suggested Mac get some sleep in his bed where he would be more comfortable, but Mac wanted to stay awhile with Bev. Ellen went back to be with Bill, got herself settled in the recliner near Bill and was soon sleeping, a rest well deserved.

Bill woke up in a daze before the pain brought him back to reality. As he looked around his room, he saw Ellen sleeping in the chair and felt a brief moment of tenderness. The pain from his head and foot took over, reminding him of his current situation. He did not want to wake Ellen, and figured he needed to handle the pain anyway. Looking around the rest of the room he noticed Francis sitting in a chair reading a thick book. Francis looked up and saw Bill looking at him, so he smiled and walked over to talk with Bill. "How are you feeling, Bill?"

"Hi Francis, I hurt but it could be a lot worse. Glad you are here. There are a few of us needing your spiritual help. Have you been told about this situation?"

"Yes, Bill. Bev and Mac filled me in. I have made the rounds of all the injured people. I briefly met Diana, before the FBI agent started to ask her questions. This is all so unbelievable."

"Yep, tell me about it." Looking at the clock on the wall, Bill realized it had been about thirty hours ago when Mac and Diana had been attacked, starting this whole mess.

"Bill, I will come back in a little while. I am going to grab a bite and then check in with Diana." Francis made the sign of the cross over Bill, squeezed Bill's shoulder, then went out into the hallway. Bill was about to doze off again when he heard commotion out in the hallway. "Now what," he thought. Ellen awoke with a start, also wondering what the commotion was all about. Ellen smiled at Bill when she realized he was awake and looking at her. She asked how he was feeling, and told him he was a poor liar when he said he was fine. Ellen kissed him on the forehead and said she would be right back after checking on what the commotion was all about.

Bill was frustrated, stuck in bed, feeling lousy and wanting to know what was going on, and helpless to do anything about it. Ellen came back in to Bill's room and told him what she had learned from the events going on outside his room. "Some high level FBI guy, apparently Ricardo's boss, showed up with a team of agents and demanded they take Diana." At Diana's name, Bill jumped a little out of concern for her. "Right now the Sheriff is blocking the FBI guy from entering Diana's room. Mac and Bev are still in the room, and both have their guns ready. I heard Ricardo chastise his boss, suggesting he go talk to the prisoners while they wait for permission to move Diana. The day time head nurse and I stood our ground as well, and reminded the FBI guy that the doctor had the final say and he was on his way back to the hospital to review the situation. The FBI guy didn't like it, but he apparently backed off. I finished checking on Bev, Diana and Mac, and here I am. I will check on Joe, then I can settle down here with you." Bill's frustration at not being in the middle of the situation outside his door was just about balanced by the feeling of warmth having Ellen nearby.

All of a sudden a shot was fired, then some loud words. Both Bill and Ellen were wide awake, as was Joe who had been catnapping in the hospital bed. Bill wanted desperately to go see what the heck was going on, but by the time he was helped out of bed and helped into a wheel chair the incident would be long gone. Joe was having a hard time moving his sore head, and Ellen told him stay in bed. Ellen ventured to the door into the hallway, but Bill told her to stay away from the door until they knew if it was safe. There was a second shot fired, and Ellen moved over to be closer to Bill. A few minutes later the door opened and one of the volunteer firefighters came in to check on Bill and Joe. Bill immediately asked the fellow volunteer what the shots were all about, and what was going on. There was a second chair in the room, so the volunteer grabbed it and sat down next to Ellen's chair, between Joe and Bill, and proceeded to fill them in.

"Well, you probably heard that the big muckity muck from the FBI showed up with a few of his people and tried to take Diana. Walt and the Sheriff were having none of that, and told the FBI idiot the doctor would say whether Diana could be moved or not. That FBI guy told his team to disarm everyone and take over the hospital. There were only a few of us right there, the rest were either patrolling or resting in various locations. Well the FBI idiot used his radio and called in a half dozen people that didn't look at all like FBI people. One of the Deputies, on a rest period, happened to walk around the corner when this was taking place and quickly realized it looked bad and dirty. He quickly backed up out of sight before anyone saw him, and ran back to the lounge for help. The lounge had a mix of law enforcement and us volunteers, and after being filled in by the Deputy, a quick plan was formed.

"So there are six of us in the hall against eleven bad people. All of a sudden we hear 'Police, you are surrounded. Drop your weapons and raise your hands high. Do it now.' One of the bad people decided to raise his gun instead of dropping it, and that was the first shot you heard. One of the State Police officers shot the guy in the knee cap, knocking the guy down and giving him such pain he forgot to be a tough guy. 'The rest of you drop your weapons or you will end up like your buddy there withering on the ground, or worse. Your choice, but make it now.' Fortunately most of the bad guys followed orders, and we quickly grabbed our dropped weapons and assisted the officers and deputies in immobilizing the bad guys.

"I guess in the melee the FBI big shot snuck away from the party and went into Diana's room. Fortunately both Mac and Bev had their guns out. So when the big shot FBI guy walks into Diana's room, with gun out stretched, he is surprised to see two guns pointed at him. As the FBI idiot was trying to do a quick aim on Diana, Mac fired off a quick shot that ripped into the guy's gun arm. Ricardo and a couple Deputies rushed in and they secured the room and had the FBI guy in cuffs. That's when I came to check on you and Joe." Bill told Ellen he needed out of bed now, and after winning the argument, he was helped into a nearby wheelchair by Ellen and the volunteer. Barely managing the pain of the move, Bill suggested the volunteer check out the hallway before he and Ellen head over to Diana's room.

Diana was floating in and out of consciousness. When the first shot was fired, her conscious was trying to sort through the stimuli and come up with a response. Diana saw Bev was sitting up, holding her gun pointing to the door, and Mac was in his wheel chair also aiming his gun toward the door. Bev was trying to use the radio, but there was too much excited radio traffic. Somebody rushed into the room holding a gun, but he was wearing a FBI jacket. Diana could see in slow motion the gun arm moving toward her, then a shot was fired. Diana winced, but she realized she had not felt a bullet. Mac's gun was smoking, and a quick glance back at the intruder showed he had dropped his gun and was holding a bleeding arm. A couple of Deputies rushed into the room trailing the other FBI guy, Ricardo she thought the name was. They handcuffed the intruder, and a nurse that had followed everyone onto the room started working on the injured shoulder. Diana was worried. She did not know what the heck was going on, but it seemed very clear now that she was the target. People had been telling her that, but only now did she start believing. She needed to make a phone call and find out for sure.

Adrenalin, flowing profusely a short time ago, was now phasing down. Volunteers and law enforcement people at the hospital started winding down from the adrenalin high caused by the brief gun battle. Walt met with the Sheriff, Frank, and Ricardo to work up a plan to continue to deal with the situation. Ricardo was stunned over what happened with his boss Bennie. He was trying to process the turn of events, what was Bennie doing, what was he involved with, and who else could be involved in this mess. He needed to report this situation, but who could he trust in his organization? After talking it over with Walt and the Sheriff, Ricardo felt he had better call Bennie's boss. Walt and the Sheriff, in the meantime, had to deal with an overflowing jail. Fortunately the State Police prisoner bus was due to arrive any minute, which would be perfect timing to get the newly rounded up prisoners headed to a bigger jail. The Sheriff got on the phone with the State Police and made arrangements for more assistance if needed. It made the situation worse in not knowing if there were more bad guys coming at them. These attackers were damn bold, and from an initial view, had even a high ranking FBI in their pocket. Definitely not a time to relax and think the worst is over.

Diana was pretending to be dozing, waiting for Bev to go to sleep, and the guard to leave for a potty break. Diana needed to make a phone call and find out what the heck was happening. But she did not want to make the call while people were listening. She caught a glimpse of the guard getting up and walking out of the room. Diana quietly called Bev's name, and when there was no answer, she grabbed the phone and dialed the special, memorized number.

"Si."

"Giorgino, it's Diana. What the hell is going on?"

"Diana, where are you?"

"Giorgino, is the family after me?"

"Yes, Diana. Your Grandfather put the word out. He said you failed the omerta. And you know that failing the code of honor means death. I don't know what you did but you are now expendable."

Diana was at a loss for words as the tears started flowing. "But I am his granddaughter and I've done nothing wrong!"

"That doesn't matter, your Grandfather ordered the hit, just like he ordered your Mother's hit years ago. He considers you a threat, no longer a contributing member of the fare, the family. Elmo is the one heading up the kill team. I had overheard he was your Mother's killer. I am truly sorry but it does not look good for you now. I wish I could help you, to make this go away, but I dare not cross your Grandfather. God bless you."

Diana was devastated and tears were flowing hard as she hung up the phone.

Something woke Bev up, and as she took in her surroundings she noticed what woke her up: Diana crying. The guard walked into the room and noticed also that Diana was crying. Bev asked Diana what was the matter, but Diana refused to talk. Diana felt so alone. She was trying to think of someone she could turn to for help. It was too much, finding out she was targeted by her Grandfather, and that he had had her Mother killed. While she was sobbing and thinking of what her life has been, recent memories of the special feelings of excitement and calm tried to invade her dread. She was briefly thinking of the few times she enjoyed being with Mac, but then she remembered Mac was FBI and using her. Her thoughts moved onto Bill. Yes, she thought, he seemed to bring something to her, a strange feeling of excitement yet calm. Maybe he can help her.

Chapter 67

Diana told Bev that she had some serious information to tell, but she needed Bill to be with her before she would talk. So Bev asked the room guard if he would tell Bill he was needed asap. Mac was still tied up with a meeting between Ricardo, the Sheriff, and Walt. When the guard gave Bill Bev's message, Bill asked Ellen to help him into a wheel chair so he could get to Diana. Ellen helped Bill into the wheel chair and wheeled him as close to Diana as he could get. Bill grabbed one of Diana's hands and cradled it in his hands. She was sobbing and he felt sorry for her. He was wishing he could hold her, but that was not possible in their injured conditions. So his holding Diana's hand was all he could do for the moment.

Ellen used a wet wash cloth and wiped Diana's tear stained face every so often, and the two of them just let Diana cry out until she finished. As Diana's crying was lessening, she glanced over to Bill and Ellen, seeing them through her teary eyes, and seeing their concern. Having Bill holding her hand had sent chills through Diana's body, which were having an effect on her crying. Diana finally stopped crying and fell asleep with Bill still holding her hand. Bill was trying to figure out this feeling he was having; having Ellen's hand in one hand and Diana's hand in the other felt like it was just supposed to be. Ellen had to start her rounds, relieving the other head nurse. So she squeezed Bill's hand, and kissed him on the cheek. Bill fell asleep in the quiet of the room. The room was quiet, and Bev fell asleep caught between her worry for Diana and her concern that Diana may be a criminal.

Diana tossed and turned, a fitful sleep. Bill was awoken by a thrashing Diana who must be having a nightmare. If Bill could carefully stretch just far enough, he could touch Diana's face, so he did. He tried speaking soothing words while running his hand along Diana's face. He spied the wash cloth Ellen had used earlier, freshened it and wiped Diana's sweaty face. Diana finally came out of the nightmare, and focused on Bill. "Bad dream?" Bill asked.

Diana, still looking at Bill, said, "I wish it were just a bad dream."

"Can you tell me about it?"

Diana thought for a moment, then changed the subject. "Are you and Ellen married?"

"No, we are just good friends."

"Were you ever married?"

"Yes, for a couple of years."

"Any children?"

"No."

"What happened to your marriage?"

"Let's just say I blew it big time and let her get away." Bill continued, "What's with the questions? Now it's my turn. What happened that made you cry so hard a little while ago?"

"I had some intense pain that finally got to me."

"Diana, I want to help, so please be honest with me. What happened that set you to crying?"

After a long wait, Ellen walked in to be with Bill for a short break. She checked Diana's vitals, and asked her if she needed anything. "Ellen, Diana was just about to tell us why she was crying so hard earlier, right Diana?"

Diana, unused to the feeling, felt like these two people with her could be trusted and befriended. Diana seriously needed friends right now, and these people were begging.

"My life is over," blurted out Diana.

Ellen and Bill looked at each other, than back to Diana. "Tell us about it, Diana. Perhaps we can do something about that."

"You can't do anything to help me. I am as good as dead. And look at all the trouble I have caused already. And if you continue to stay here with me, you'll end up dead too."

"Talk to us Diana. If anything, you'll feel better to get it out. And we want to help, we don't want you to be alone." Bev woke up to the sounds of talking and joined in, telling Diana she was there for her also. Diana started crying again, but this time when Bill and Ellen took her hands in theirs, Diana felt a slight surge of something flow through and energize her. She stopped crying, looked at both Ellen and Bill, then started to tell her story.

It was some time into Diana's story that Ellen had to make her rounds again. That gave a chance for Bill to use the facilities and check on his fellow volunteers while Diana had help from one of the nurses. Diana felt like eating a little, so Ellen had a light dinner brought for all of them. After the trays were taken away, Ellen had a chance to sit with Bill. A little refreshed, Diana continued with her story.

Neither Ellen, Bev or Bill wanted to stop the story to ask questions, so they were trying to remember what to ask Diana later, after her story was told and things needed clarification. Ellen and Bill eyed each other when Diana had gone quickly over the early period of her life, the memory of her Mother and when she moved in with her Grandfather after her Mother disappeared. Bill had some questions he needed to ask, but he knew to bite his tongue and patiently wait, not one of his strengths.

Diana unburdened herself, and it almost was like going to confession. Other than a few breaks when Ellen had to check on her patients, Diana was left to tell her story. Ellen and Bill winced only a couple of times when a few of the details were gory. Bev felt the same, and recognized that she also should let Diana finish her story before posing any questions. She also knew that the FBI should be in the room taking notes, but she had an inkling that Diana may well clam up in front of the FBI. Bev might get into trouble over this, but she felt right about the situation. Blame could come later.

Diana talked about the house and pickup fire she had a hand in last year. She talked about the interest in flying drones and the work on the ignition system. When it came time to talk about the Snake Peak fire, Diana broke down. She had not planned on the tragic deaths of the firefighters, and expressed serious remorse. She had made the distinction between job related deaths and the Snake Peak deaths which were caused by her, not her job.

Francis slowly opened the door into Diana's room and asked he could have a few moments with Diana, if she was okay with that. This was a good time to take a break, to let Francis and Diana have a quiet talk. Bill knew that Francis had a way with calming people, and felt Diana would benefit from Francis' talking with her after her lengthy confession to Bill, Bev, and Ellen.

Bill, head pounding and foot hurting, made sure there was a Deputy inside the room protecting Diana and Bev. There was a police officer outside the door to Diana's room as well. With Bev armed and awake in the room, and volunteers taking turns patrolling outside the hospital, augmenting the State Police manning road blocks around the hospital, the protection level looked pretty good.

Bill wheeled himself down the hallway to the lounge where he figured Walt, the Sheriff, and Ricardo would be. Bill saw Walt talking with one of the State Police officers, while Ricardo, Mac and the Sheriff were each trying to get a power nap. Walt finished with his meeting, saw Bill waiting at the doorway, and stepped into the hall to talk with Bill. Bill explained the story Diana was telling them about. Walt was not happy for numerous reasons. "Bill, you need us to take care of the interrogation."

"I know, Walt. But Diana started talking and it didn't seem right to stop her just so I could bring you guys in. Besides, Bev is in the room and was listening to the conversation."

Walt was really bothered by the mention of the crime family that Diana was a part of, and that they wanted her eliminated. "Bill, this stuff about Diana has now opened up an even bigger can of worms. I think I will ask the governor for National Guard assistance."

Bill chuckled, but Walt scowled and told Bill this was serious. "Bill, do you know anything about this family Diana is part of?"

"Sorry Walt, I thought you were joking. No, I haven't heard about this family before."

"This crime family makes the Mafia that we are familiar with look like school children. They are ruthless, and they are so tight that there is no way someone can infiltrate. This is bad, and we are in big trouble if they decide to continue trying to take out Diana while we have her."

Bill realized that it was no wonder Diana was so upset. Bill told Walt, "I will check with Diana to see if she is alright with an audience, or if she wants just you to do the interrogation. There are a few questions of a personal nature that I need to talk to Diana about, then I will see what she wants to do about retelling her story to you."

"Ok, Bill. But I really need to talk to Diana. I will tell Ricardo and the Sheriff what you told me, and then I expect to be talking with Diana shortly."

Bill signaled he understood and wheeled himself back to Diana's room.

On the way to Diana's room, Bill remembered Armida telling him of her family situation. He remembered how upset she was in telling him how tragic her family life had been. What the heck, was he just mixing up histories or was there some kind of connection here?

While Bill went back to be with Ellen, Diana and Bev, Walt woke up Ricardo, Mac and the Sheriff. Walt filled in the three law enforcement men with what Bill had told him. The Sheriff agreed with Walt that more bad stuff was probably headed their way. It was suggested they talk with the Colonel in charge of the State Police and let him know what was happening. Ricardo was waiting to hear back from Bennie's boss, but he was inclined to agree with getting some help from the Guard. Mobilizing the National Guard would take less than two hours, whereas the FBI would need about six hours to get more agents on site. So it was agreed that a contingent of close by State National Guard soldiers move in to relieve the tired volunteers and officers that have been on guard duty for many hours. The State Police Colonel also agreed, not able to relocate more of his scattered resources quickly enough to help. Walt placed the call to the Governor's office, briefly explained the emergency to the Governor's aide, then waited for the Governor to return his call.

Bill wheeled himself into Diana's room and saw Diana sleeping, while Bev was awake and working on her smart phone. Ellen had to make the rounds again, and Fr Francis had left to allow Diana some rest, Bev told Bill. Bill asked Bev what she was doing. Bev said she was researching information on the crime family Diana had been a part of. "Looks like we are dealing with a seriously nasty group," said Bev.

Bill told Bev, "Kind of proves what we already know. If the leaders of this 'family' are willing to kill their own flesh and blood, yes we are in deep trouble." Bill proceeded to tell Bev about the plan to bring in the National Guard to assist with guarding the hospital. Bill finished his update to Bev with, "I am not as worried about the protection here at the hospital. But I am worried about what happens after we all leave the hospital. I hope that somebody besides us realizes Diana is in very serious trouble."

Bev could sense the deeper than normal concern in Bill's tone of voice. She decided to tease Bill and said, "What's this Bill, you thinking of trying to get a date with Diana? Damn, you are old enough to be her father!"

Ellen had stepped back into the room and had heard Bev's teasing. "Bev, you might be more right than you think!" Bev turned to Ellen with a 'you lost me' look. Ellen told Bev her theory that Diana could be Bill's daughter. "I love doing puzzles. Sometimes there would be shifts here in the hospital that were very quiet, so I would work on puzzles to make the quiet time not so boring. I just had an intuition when I saw Bill and Diana and how they reacted to each other. So I had Bill agree to a DNA test, and hopefully in a few hours we will have some results on both Diana's and Bill's tests. But I have a feeling I am right and that Diana is Bill's daughter."

Chapter 68

Bill was lost in thought, thinking about what Ellen was insinuating. If Diana really was his daughter, then that would mean Armida had been apparently killed by her own Father. The more he thought about it, the worse he felt. He was blaming himself, and he was angry. If only he had spent more time with Armida instead of spending so much time on fires. He was overcome by emotions, wanting to flail away at the people who took Armida's life, and at the people wanting to take away Diana's life too. But he didn't know if all this was true. He was also still trying to accept the fact that if Ellen was right, he had a daughter. A daughter whose life may be ended before he had a chance to know her. Why does life have to be so damn complicated, he said to himself. Ellen looked over to Bill and felt his emotions. She walked over to Bill's wheel chair and said, "Bill, let's go for a walk."

Bill looked up to Ellen with his emotionally charged face and said, "Okay." Ellen wheeled him to the outside gazebo where they could be alone and hopefully enjoy each other's companionship.

Ricardo had been on the phone with Bennie's boss. The FBI was in an uproar over the realization that Bennie apparently was tied in with the 'family'. The immediate concern was how many more FBI agents were corrupted. Bennie's boss was worried that Ricardo may be corrupted as well, so he had a trusted team of agents flying to Prairie City in one of the FBI Learjets to take over the situation. Ricardo was not happy but understood the predicament. He should have been more critical in his dealings with his boss, although he realized it was a fine line between questioning commands and critically assessing commands. This whole mess gave Ricardo the opportunity to look into his own situation and how he had been handling various tasks and commands. He found a nagging awareness that he was too engrossed in power to stop and assess the why and the how of a given command. Perhaps if he had been not so enamored with the power of the badge, he may have felt there was something not right about Bennie. Well, he could remember the ancient adage 'hind sight is 20/20.' Ricardo figured he had better let Mac and Walt know about the FBI team flying in.

Ellen was holding Bill's hand, enjoying the two of them sitting in the hospital gazebo, taking a break from the past couple of days of over stimulated nerves and emotions. Even though Bill was hurting from his injuries, he was enjoying being with Ellen, who just seemed to exude a positively charged aura. As he was drifting off in a day dream enjoying frolicking with Ellen on a sunny white sandy beach, a sound of a vehicle coming to a screeching halt brought him back to reality. Immediately Bill caught in his peripheral vision something that brought his attention away from the enchanted solitude of being with Ellen. A van had slammed on its brakes on the road paralleling the hospital, and two people jumped out. Each person was carrying something large, but Bill could just barely make out some kind of tube shaped item. His memory kicked in, and from his time in the military, he thought he recognized the objects as being similar to a hand held rocket launcher.

Cussing a blue streak, Bill grabbed his radio and keyed the mike. "May day, May day, emergency traffic. Evacuate Bev and Diana NOW. Two possible rocket launchers outside hospital. Repeat, evacuate Bev and Diana NOW." Bill told Ellen to get to safety while he tried to draw the attention of the two launchers. Ellen desperately wanted to stay with Bill, knowing he needed help. But Bill was insistent and she knew she had to help with patients, so she kissed Bill and told him to be careful. Bill told Ellen the same, then as soon as Ellen was out of sight he wheeled himself out of the gazebo and toward the launchers. He had his pistol, with all that had happened he had not wanted to be without some kind of protection, but a lot of good that will do. He couldn't fire and work the wheel chair at the same time, and the range was too far for an effective shot. However, he was hoping if he could get a little closer and start firing his pistol he could disrupt the launchers. Damn it where was the patrol that should have been out here?

Walt, upon hearing the may day, told Mac and a few of the officers and volunteers close by to make sure Bev and Diana got out now. Walt asked the Sheriff to get the patrol over to the launchers. Asking Ricardo to come with him, Walt ran outside to where Bill was supposed to be. They heard pistol shots, and ran faster to the sounds. As they past the gazebo, Walt saw Bill in his wheel chair shooting at the launchers. Ricardo was only carrying a pistol, so he could do no better than Bill. But Walt was carrying his rifle, so he stopped, steadied himself, and took aim at one of the launchers. Walt's bullet hit the launcher in his leg just as his finger depressed the firing switch. The leg shot caused the enemy to fall to one side just as the small rocket was escaping the tube. The small but deadly rocket fired out of the tipping tube and flew into a parked car, exploding it into an inferno. The second launcher hurried and got off his shot. Walt fired again and took down the second launcher as the small rocket crashed into the base of the outside wall of the room Bev and Diana were in.

Ricardo, who hadn't stopped running, caught up with Bill to see if he was alright. Bill's head was pounding and his foot was hurting like heck, but he knew they both needed to get back inside the hospital quickly to see if everyone were okay. Seeing Bill was in pain, Ricardo pushed Bill's wheel chair ahead of him as fast as he could, while Walt carefully headed to the launchers he had shot, making sure they were out of the game.

The small hospital was a busy mess. Nurses and volunteers were pushing patients in beds and wheel chairs. Smoke and dust was swirling in the hallways. A few volunteers were dragging a charged fire hose toward the damaged room. The hospital room that had been Bev and Diana's was a shambles. Actually shambles was too weak of a word. The outside wall and window were gone, replaced by a pile of burning debris. Dust and smoke filled the room, while flames crackled eating up bedding and other combustibles. Expensive monitoring machines were laying on the ground sparking. A couple of the volunteers were bravely trying to get water onto the fire and keep the fire away from the oxygen connections. They knew if the fire reached the oxygen connections there was a good chance the whole hospital would go up in flames.

Ricardo, out of breath from pushing Bill's wheel chair as fast as he safely could, arrived to find Mac in the hallway. Relieved to see Mac, Bill yelled out, "Where are the girls?"

Mac yelled back "Everyone is safe. The girls are in the ER with a beefed up guard."

Both Bill and Ricardo emitted sighs of relief. Looking over the damage, Ricardo commented, "It looks like the rocket hit the base of the wall instead of the window. If that rocket had come in through the window, there would have been a hell of a lot more damage than just this room."

Bill's fellow volunteers had subdued the fire with the hospital fire hose, and finished the job as soon as the fire engines showed up. Fortunately no one was injured seriously, although one nurse, two volunteers and one of the deputies on guard were treated for smoke inhalation. Those not tasked with searching and guarding the outside of the hospital were helping the nurses evacuate the patients. With the smoky conditions and the damage, it was quickly decided to move the patients to a different hospital. Additional ambulances were called in and some deputies from the neighboring counties arrived to help guard the ambulances. It was like a war had engulfed the small town of Prairie City, and no one in Prairie City really knew why.

Chapter 69

Bill caught up with Ellen, and both hugged each other and were relieved each was safe. They both went to check on Diana, hoping she was ok. Ricardo caught up with Walt as he was making sure both attackers were incapable of moving. Walt's shots counted and both had died from their serious wounds. Ricardo, seeing Walt had the outside situation handled, went over to the ambulance loading area to check on that operation of moving the hospital patients to another facility.

Ricardo noticed Ellen was efficiently controlling the task of the patient move. Ricardo finally recognized how serious the situation was surrounding Diana, and contacted Bennie's boss. The boss, still in transit with his group of agents, agreed to move Diana to a special government supported hospital where the FBI could provide better protection. Mac was still recovering from his wound, and he being a FBI agent, it was decided to send him along with Diana to the special hospital. Ellen suggested to Ricardo that Bill should go and be with Diana. Ricardo asked her why, and Ellen explained her notion that the DNA testing results she is waiting for will show a high probability that Bill is Diana's father. She told Ricardo that the blood tests already show a possibility, and that there are certain features that are very similar between Diana and Bill. She also threw in the bit about her looking at the similarities from a professional and from a woman's intuition angle. Ricardo was swayed and after discussing the arguments with his current boss, it was agreed that Bill could go with

Diana. Ellen was asked to make sure all three patients were ready for transport.

Bill and Diana had been transferred into one of the ambulances that could handle two gurneys. Ellen had climbed into the secured ambulance, sat between Diana and Bill, and mentioned to Bill what the plan was for he, Diana and Mac. Ellen restated her belief that Diana was his daughter, and she felt he needed to spend time with her. As they were talking, Ellen sitting alongside the gurney holding Bill's hand, Bev came in. Diana was sleeping, apparently tired from the emotions and stress. Bev sat next to Ellen. Bill asked how things were going, and Bev mentioned right now they were quiet. She told Bill that she and a deputy had just finished searching Mac's rented room, trying to find anything belonging to Diana that she might need. Bev had a sack, which she told Ellen that some of Diana's personal items were in there. "Also, I found this locket that I am sure is not Mac's. I opened it and there was a picture of a young, very attractive woman who looks a little like Diana."

She handed it to Ellen, and Ellen opened it to view the photograph. Ellen turned the locket so Bill could see the photograph, and Bill let out a gasp. "Where did you find this?" asked Bill.

Bev explained she found it on the floor near the bed stand in Mac's bedroom. "What is it Bill, what is the matter?" asked Ellen.

Bill reached out and took the locket from Ellen's hands to have a closer look. Both ladies looked at Bill with concern. Finally Bill said, "Uh, sorry Ellen, sorry Bev. This woman in the photograph looks identical to my ex wife Armida."

Ellen took back the locket when Bill was finished staring at the photograph. Ellen and Bev stared intently at the photograph and compared it to Diana's facial features. While studying Diana's face, Diana woke and once her eyes cleared and she could focus, she saw Ellen and Bev staring at her and holding a locket. Looking at the locket, Diana realized it was hers. "Hey, what are you doing with my locket?", she asked the ladies.

Before either could answer, Bill asked Diana who the lady was in the photograph. "That's my mother" said Diana.

Bill asked Diana for her mother's name. "Her name was Armida," Diana stated.

"You said 'was'?"

Diana looked at Bill and said, "She disappeared when I was only about three. I just found out recently that she was killed by my Father's right hand man."

Ellen took Diana's hand in hers as she started tearing up. "When were you born?" asked Bill. Diana told Bill her birth date, and Bill did some head calculations. Bill looked over at Ellen and told her she may be right after all. He then turned back to Diana and told her he had been happily married to Armida, who had left him after two years of marriage, and he had never been able to talk to her or know where she went ever since. "If my calculations are right, you were born about eight and a half months after the time my Armida left me. What is the name of your Father?"

"I never knew my father. No one ever mentioned his name and there were no photographs of my father."

"Who is your Grandfather, Diana?"

"We always called him Grandfather, but one time I heard Elmo, father's right hand man, call Grandfather Adamo."

"Did you have an uncle named Marino?" asked Bill.

"No one ever told me" said Diana.

Ellen handed the locket to Diana and looked back to Bill, noticing the emotions taking over. With Ellen providing moral support, Bill said, "Diana, I think you and I may be related. You may well be my daughter." All four broke down and let the tears come.

Chapter 70

The special hospital the FBI wanted to use for housing and protecting Diana would be a two hour flight. Ricardo, assisted by his boss's secretary, arranged for a State Police helicopter escort and a National Guard medivac helicopter for the three patients; Diana, Mac, and Bill. The doctor had checked Joe's head wound and decided that he could stay home in the care of his wife.

After discussing the locket, and realizing that Ellen's intuition seemed to be right on target, Bill told Diana about the plans for their evacuation to a special hospital. Diana was glad that Bill was going with her, but she also wanted Ellen to stay with her. Bev was thinking ahead and saw that having Ellen with Diana and Bill would work from two angles: first, Diana seems to trust Ellen, and Bill and Ellen seem to share a concern for Diana's welfare; and second, it would be good to have Ellen with the patients as a special nurse. Bev caught up with Walt and Ricardo, mentioned her idea, and after a short argument, Walt and Ricardo agreed with Bev.

With extra protection in place, and the FBI team waiting at the special hospital, the medivac helicopter landed near the hospital to load passengers. Bill had his pistol with him, and the medivac team went nuts. Ricardo, waiting to load into the medivac helicopter, stepped in and told the crew that he vouched for Bill and it was safe and necessary that he carry his pistol. After the three patients were loaded and strapped down, Ellen, Bev and Ricardo loaded into the helicopter. As soon as the medivac helicopter was given the all clear, it flew up and was joined by the State

Police helicopter and headed in the direction of the special hospital. Ellen sat nearest Bill, holding his hand while Bill was holding Diana's hand. Bev, feeling a lot better with something to do instead of laying in bed, sat next to Mac and held his hand.

The two hour flight went by quickly, and the moving of the patients into the hospital went smoothly. Once settled in, the hospital staff was introduced to Ellen, who was going to assist for awhile in the care of the two patients. Mac was healing and getting more mobile, so he wasn't in as much need of care. Besides, he was needed back at the FBI headquarters asap to help in the review of this mess in the FBI. Bev and Ricardo had gotten a ride back to Prairie City in the State Police helicopter, both needing to finish their work on the huge mess over Diana and the failed attempts at killing her.

With Bennie's perceived involvement with the 'family", and the potential duplicity of Doriano of the U.S. Marshall's office, both the FBI and Marshalls office scoured their staff trying to clean up the mess and deal with any leaks left over from the Bennie and Doriano fiasco. A day after being ensconced in the special hospital, Ellen received preliminary DNA test results for Bill. The results provided a 99.99% probability that Bill could be Diana's father. Ricardo's temporary boss listened and reviewed what Ellen presented in support of her belief Bill is Diana's father. The FBI seemed satisfied with the blood tests, the DNA tests and the locket photo recognition and accepted Bill as Diana's father. Because of that Bill was allowed to stay with Diana in the hospital.

With granting Bill and Ellen permission to stay with Diana, the FBI was hoping to encourage Diana to agree to testify against her Grandfather's operation, in exchange for protection and a new life. Bill, Ellen and Diana talked at length about the future for Diana, what she could expect if she did or did not accept the FBI's offer. The outlook was better if Diana accepted. At least she would live for awhile longer, maybe to a nice, long, close to normal life. Certainly death waited fairly quickly for her if she refused the offer. Jail time was a guarantee, with the strong possibility she would be killed in jail. The more Diana thought about it the more she put a plan together for her future.

Bill, remembering the Snake Peak fire tragedy, asked Diana what she felt should be done to address that terrible situation. "Bill, I am torn between the joy of you and Ellen being with me, and living with the death I have caused. I remember hearing the radio traffic while I was helping at the Tamarack subdivision, and I was devastated to hear the fire I started caused death. That night I hoped Mac would be able to console me, but that did not help. Going to confession did not help. I want, I need to pay a price for those deaths I caused. I have been so busy with this other stuff that I had not had a chance to discuss this with the FBI agents helping us. I don't know what to do."

"Diana, you know we are both here for you no matter what happens. Yes, I do not like it, but you will have to face the consequences of those tragic deaths. We certainly can't belittle the tragedy, but perhaps there is some mitigation that can be agreed on due to the circumstances surrounding this whole mess."

After a lengthy silence, Diana said, "I want to accept the FBI's offer of a new life in exchange for testifying against my Grandfather. And I want to talk to the agents about what can I do about the deaths I caused. I am willing and ready to do whatever to atone for those firefighters killed in the fire. However, I want to demand an additional caveat to their offer. I needed to get your approval to my request. I have only known you both for a very short while, but I want you both to be with me. Bill, or should I call you Dad, I feel it in my heart that you are my Father. And now that we have stumbled into each other I don't want to lose you too. Ellen, I feel something special with you as well, and I sense you and dad have something that needs to grow. And I want to be part of that."

The room was still as Ellen and Bill looked at each other and held hands. After a few minutes, Bill broke the stillness. "Ellen, I know we hardly know each other, but over the past few days I find myself wanting you more and more. I find being with you is exciting, and I would like to spend the rest of my life with you. I enjoy our times together, and I do not want them to stop. Diana, for the past nearly thirty years I never knew you existed. Now that I know, I do not want to lose you. I want to be with you and be your support as you work through this situation. If Ellen is willing, I hope the three of us can enjoy a new life together for the rest of our days. Even if you have to do time in jail, I will be waiting, and I hope Ellen will be with me."

Ellen moved off the edge of Diana's bed and sat in Bill's lap, carefully turning his head with her hands and kissing him on the lips. After a few kisses, Ellen went over to Diana and kissed her as a mama would kiss her child. "If you both want me that badly how can I say no! I think there is more to look forward to with you two than what I would be leaving behind!"

Bill carefully stood up from his wheel chair, limped closer to Diana and gave her a fatherly kiss and then put his arm around Ellen. Then he got back into his wheel chair, and said, "Okay then, let's call the FBI agents in and see what we can arrange, and get started on our new lives."

Printed in the United States
by Baker & Taylor Publisher Services